2042 UNCERTAINTY

"God does not play dice!" Albert Einstein could never wrap his brilliant mind around Werner Heisenberg's Uncertainty Principle. In many cases, Heisenberg's theories are counter-intuitive and contradict what our senses tell us about the nature of reality. Einstein referred to Quantum Entanglement as "spooky action at a distance". To Einstein, Heisenberg's sub-atomic quantum reality was something akin to voodoo magic. Popular subjects of today's cutting edge physics, such as Zero Point Energy, Quantum Computing, and The Multiverse, can all be traced back to the 1932 Nobel Prize Winner's Quantum Mechanics.

During World War II, Heisenberg led German efforts to produce a "uranium device", an atomic bomb. As the fortunes of war turned against Nazi Germany, its Führer, Adolf Hitler, desperately sought a "wonder weapon" to turn the tide. Toward war's end, German scientists developed futuristic weapons, including cruise missiles, ballistic missiles, and jet aircraft, but those weapons arrived too late to make much difference. Who knows what other wonder weapons were on the Nazi drawing boards? Historians debate how the outcome of the war may have changed if Nazi Germany had more time.

Nearly 100 years later, the American Resistance is locked in an existential struggle with a radical, totalitarian regime, known as The Collective. As in most conflicts, the outcome is uncertain. The fortunes of war ebb & flow like sub-atomic particles in Herr Heisenberg's Quantum Mechanics.

The Katzenjammer Kid

"Captain, what in the hell just happened?"

Captain Bill Green was struggling to regain control of the plummeting B-17, "You tell me, Pee Wee, you've got a better view from the ball turret than I do up here in the cockpit. What just flashed through our formation?"

"I don't know. Wasn't a Messerschmitt 262, it went by way too fast."

"Faster than a 'Turbo'? Maybe it was one of those plywood rocket planes. What do the Krauts call those deathtraps?"

"No, not a Komet either."

"Don't tell me we're seeing Foo Fighters."

Pee Wee didn't respond to the Captain. The only sound crackling over the Boeing B-17's interphone was static.

"Captain, look at the compass!" Copilot Sammy Wilson was pointing at the Katzenjammer's compass needle, now spinning almost as rapidly as the Kid's four props.

"Sweet Jesus!" Captain Green couldn't believe his eyes. Lady Liberty, another Flying Fortress in the Kid's combat box formation, exploded in a massive fireball.

Green finally levelled the Flying Fortress a scant hundred feet above a Dutch windmill, "Sammy, do you see any Kraut fighters, or triple A?"

"No sir, we just left Germany. I think we're back over Holland."

"Then what just happened to Lady Lib?"

"Do you see any chutes?"

Captain Green didn't answer, but the look on his face told Sammy that Lady Lib's crew never had a chance.

Sergeant Pee Wee Dexter climbed up out of the ball turret and stuck his head into the cockpit, "Captain, what in the hell just happened to Lady Lib?"

"I was hoping you could tell me."

"I haven't a clue, but every steel surface down in the ball turret is magnetized."

Captain Green pointed at the spinning compass needle, "No wonder the compass is going nuts. Why is this shit coming down on our 25th mission and on New Year's Day, for crying out loud? I was hoping 1945 would be a good year."

Pee Wee shook his head in disbelief, "Lady Lib was not hit by enemy fire. We haven't seen any antiaircraft, nor fighters."

The port waist gunner squeezed past Pee Wee and leaned into the cockpit, "Captain, check out the Kid's wings."

St. Elmo's Fire was dancing along the leading edges of Katzenjammer's wings.

The Captain regained his composure, "You two pass the word to the rest of the crew that the Kid is OK. There's no problem with her engines, or flight control surfaces. Good thing this happened on our homeward leg. Wouldn't want to be carrying a full load of bombs with all this electrical discharge."

The Kid was returning to England after dropping her bombs on oil distribution facilities in Dollbergen, 20 miles east of Hanover.

Pee Wee was left scratching his head, "Captain, what in the hell just happened?"

Home For The Holidays

Tom Jackson's weather prognostication was accurate. December 2041 was bitterly cold. The extended Wu family were freezing their Southern Californian asses off in the Northern Nevada town of Austin. James, his wife, two daughters, mother-in-law, and father-in-law, were hiding out in that one-horse 19th Century boomtown. At an elevation of 6,000 feet, winters in Austin were a far cry from the balmy winters in sunny Southern California.

The Collective had branded James' wife and mother-in-law enemies of the state. Their crimes were imprinted upon their very DNA. James' mother-in-law, Katrina, was "Hafu", half Japanese and half Caucasian. That made James' wife, Hana, one quarter Japanese. One quarter Japanese blood was enough to earn Hana a one-way ticket to a death camp, if she were ever apprehended by The Collective, or Chinese State Security.

James was also a hot commodity. While attending Stanford University, James had been recruited by Chinese State Security. After the 2026 Peoples' Revolution, The Collective welcomed their new, closest ally, the People's Republic of China, with open arms. For the ensuing 15 years, CSS Inspector James Wu faithfully served his communist overlords.

Although James was a native born Chinese American, he tried his best to forget his American heritage. Shortly after the 2026 Revolution, Inspector Wu aided The Collective in the "reeducation" of Caucasian Californians. In 2030, James helped liquidate the Zionist threat in Southern California. Like all collaborators, James rationalized his behavior as "just doing his job".

When The Collective began rounding up Japanese Americans in early 2041, the shoe was suddenly on the other foot. Not only was Hana one quarter

Japanese, on his employment documents, James had lied about her ancestry. To make matters worse, James' two daughters attended public schools, public schools run by The Collective. To avoid diplomatic unpleasantries, CSS policy required that the Wu family "blend in" with everyday life in the Peoples' United States. The daughters Wu could not simply "opt out" of public school. That was a big problem for James and Hana. The Collective's new "Freedom of Sexual Identity & Expression Program" was designed to liberate the Young Members from their parents' antiquated, repressive sexual mores. Throughout the Peoples' United States, inside the public schools, small cubicles were under construction. Volunteer Sexual Guides were being recruited. These Sexual Guides were not required to have any specific training. The Guides were selected to represent the broadest possible cross-section of sexual preferences and orientations. Nothing was off limits. Sexual diversity and gender fluidity were The Collective's only considerations.

The Peoples' News Network incessantly chronicled the plight of many parents across the Peoples' United States, as they strived to escape the sexual shackles imposed upon them by the White supremacist, Judeo Christian, Capitalist society of their youth. Those sexually stifled parents were ill prepared to raise enlightened children. Those poor, misguided parents could not be allowed to interfere as the Young Members explored their sexuality. It was imperative that The Collective step in and guide the Young Members' sexual development.

It was catch-22 for Inspector James Wu. If his family remained in the PUS, his wife's and mother-in-law's Japanese ancestry would eventually betray them, resulting in their liquidation. The Wu family could not relocate to China. Japan was China's mortal enemy and, once in China, James' wife would be condemned as an enemy of state. To make matters worse, a great pandemic was once again sweeping China, a pandemic of China's own making. No, the Wu family could not flee to China.

James had only one way out. Earlier that year, with Captain Delvin Smith's assistance, James Wu defected. His family fled California to Mormon controlled Austin, Nevada. For the time being, James' family was safe, but James was a marked man. Chinese State Security, The Collective, and some unsavory underworld characters were all looking for him. Jimmy Wu came to the realization that he and his family would not truly be safe until The Collective was defeated and its Red Chinese masters were driven from America.

Perhaps James Wu had rediscovered his American roots. Perhaps he was only acting in self-interest. For whatever reason, James was now all-in with the American Resistance. He had no other choice.

Trick or Treat

On Halloween night 2025, a crowd of over 200 paranormal enthusiasts jammed into The Chapel at Chatham University. Nestled in Pittsburgh's Squirrel Hill neighborhood, Chatham's campus was rumored to be home to numerous spirits and haunts. Like most major American cities, the Steel City had been rocked by massive civil unrest following the humiliating aftermath of the Great Pacific War. Everyone had grown weary of politics and hungered for a bit of diversion. The Chatham faculty astutely scheduled a series of guest lectures dealing with the paranormal.

The final "Spirits of '25" lecture was appropriately scheduled for Halloween. They saved the best for last. If you asked a hundred random passersby out on Murray Avenue if they knew Brett Hoffman, they wouldn't recognize the name. If you showed them Brett's headshot, they would instantly recognize Brett as "that flying saucer guy". Brett had a face and physique perfect for television, blonde hair, blue eyes, and chiseled features. He was a regular contributor to various cable TV pseudo documentaries. While Brett's success on TV was understandable, his success on talk radio could not be attributed to his good looks. He knew his subject matter and was a relentless investigator. Hoffman's investigative skills had earned him a somewhat steady gig as a guest host on a wildly popular, late night, nationally syndicated, paranormal radio talk show.

The room erupted with applause as Brett concluded his presentation.

"I'm sure Mr. Hoffman will happily take a few questions."

"Most certainly. I didn't know a UFO lecture would be so popular on Halloween, but I guess Orson Welles knew what he was doing."

Brett pointed toward an elderly lady wildly waving her uplifted hand, "Mr. Hoffman, you mentioned many high-profile UFO cases in your lecture, but you only obliquely mentioned the 1965 Kecksburg incident. I'm surprised you didn't address that well documented local UFO encounter. Why's that?"

"Excellent question! Local interest, or lack thereof, is a major reason. Kecksburg is only 30 miles southeast of Pittsburgh. Some of you may not be aware that I am a Pittsburgh native. I just figured that, like myself, most Pittsburgh area UFO enthusiasts are all too familiar with that famous incident from 60 years ago.

"Perhaps I presumed too much. In a nutshell, witnesses reported that, in December 1965, a bell-shaped craft, known as die Glocke, landed or crashed, in Kecksburg. Supposedly, the military quickly cordoned off the site and hauled the craft away."

Brett next pointed at a young, dark-haired woman who looked to be in her late 20s, maybe 30, "Mr. Hoffman, is it true that the Kecksburg craft was inscribed with strange hieroglyphics or runes?"

"Yes, that is what witnesses reported, but there are no photos, or even contemporaneous sketches, to support those claims."

"Mr. Hoffman, excuse me, may I ask a quick follow-up?"

Brett smiled as he replied to the attractive young lady, "Please do."

"Is it true that NASA was sued under the Freedom of Information Act and, in 2007, a NASA official testified, under oath, that two boxes of Kecksburg related records were missing?"

"Yes, that is correct."

"Is it true that NASA attempted to explain away the Kecksburg incident as a meteor, or a Russian spy satellite whose orbit had decayed?"

"Yes, NASA released the typical disinformation."

Brett caught his breath, then exclaimed, "Man, I guess I made a major false assumption concerning the level of local interest in the Kecksburg case."

The moderator interjected, "Perhaps Mr. Hoffman could join us for a future lecture devoted entirely to the Kecksburg incident."

The audience burst into thunderous applause at the moderator's suggestion. For the next hour, Brett fielded questions about other UFO cases, signed autographs, and sold copies of his books and CDs. Gradually, the Halloween crowd began thinning out.

As Brett left the Chapel and stepped out into the cool, crisp Pittsburgh night, he heard footsteps approaching from behind.

Brett glanced back over his shoulder, stopped, then turned and addressed the tall, thin, elderly man following him, "May I help you?"

"The question is, may I help you, Mr. Hoffman?"

"Do I know you?"

"Not yet. Can you spare an old man a few minutes? Can you spare an old Airman a few minutes?"

"Listen, bud, I'm not letting you in my car. I don't know you from Adam."

"Fair enough. There's a diner over in Squirrel Hill, the Drive-n-Dine. Do you know it?"

"Sure, I know it."

"Meet me over there in five minutes. I guarantee you; it will be worth your while."

With that, the old man disappeared into the Halloween darkness.

As he released his BMW's parking break, Brett argued with himself, "It's late. At best, this guy is some kind of kook. I really need to get home."

Brett was, at heart, an investigator. Five minutes later, Brett parked his classic Bimmer a block down Murray Avenue from the Drive-n-Dine. He spotted his new acquaintance seated close to the front window.

"Oh, what the hell!" Brett took a deep breath, stepped into the diner, and took a seat.

"Mr. Hoffman, thank you for indulging an old man. I have a very short story you must hear."

"What kind of story?"

"A Kecksburg kind of story."

A tired Brett Hoffman spoke not a word while yawning and motioning with his right hand for the old man to continue.

"In December 1965, I was an 18 year old Airman based at Wright-Patterson Air Force Base in Dayton, Ohio."

The smirk on Brett's face disappeared. He leaned in closer as the old gentleman continued.

"On the evening of 9 December 1965, a recovery team and a security detail departed Wright-Patterson Air Force Base for Kecksburg, Pennsylvania. We hit the road at 1800 and arrived at the crash site around midnight, but it wasn't a crash site. By the time we arrived, the state police and county sheriff had cordoned off the area."

"What did you see?"

"The stories are all true. It wasn't a Russian satellite, nor meteor. I was part of the security detail manning the perimeter. I was armed and the use of deadly force was authorized."

"Would you mind if I take a few notes?"

"Please do, people need to know."

Brett extended his hand across the table, "May I have the pleasure of your acquaintance?"

The old man shook Brett's hand, "Jack Taylor."

"OK, Jack, would you mind if I record our conversation on my iPhone?"

"You can take my picture if you like. I have nothing to lose. I've got pancreatic cancer. My number is up."

"My God, Jack. I'm so sorry."

Brett had an investigator's eye for detail. The dark-haired young lady sitting at the counter, closest to him, slightly turned her head when Jack gave Brett his prognosis.

Then it clicked in Brett's brain, "That girl at the counter, that's the girl from the Chapel, the one with all the questions."

Jack chuckled, "Guess I better get on with the story fore I check out right here in this diner.

"That thing that landed in Kecksburg was shaped sorta like a Project Mercury space capsule, like a bell. One of the boys in the recovery detail struck it with a shovel. It definitely sounded metallic, but it wasn't shiny. It was flat black, like a stove pipe. I couldn't see any doors, or windows. It was still very hot. Just a few hours earlier, when it landed, it scorched the grass and charred some of the surrounding trees.

"I was minding my own business when I heard a noise up above me in an old, leaf bare, oak tree. A kid, about 10 or 11 years old, was perched up in the lower branches, watching the whole thing."

Brett listened intently as Jack recounted his close encounter with Stan the Man.

"Hey kid, what are you doing up there?"

"Shhh! Don't rat me out. It's a spaceship, ain't it?"

"Look kid, I don't know nothin'. How long you been up there?"

"My name is Stan, but my friends call me Stan the Man. I got here before anyone else, right after it landed. It was red hot at first, but it's cooled down a mite since then."

"Look Stan, you're going to get into big trouble."

Stan replied, "Those two guys in the black suits and sunglasses are running the show."

At Jack's mention of Men in Black, Brett got an incredulous look upon his face.

"Alright Brett, I know what you're thinking. No, I haven't been watching too much Will Smith. Two Men in Black were running the whole operation."

Despite Brett's skepticism, Jack continued recounting his close encounter with Stan.

"The Men in Black didn't get here for about a couple of hours. By that time, I already saw him."

"Saw who?"

"The spaceman! A hatch opened on the side of his ship, then he got out. Man, was I ever disappointed."

"How could seeing a spaceman be disappointing?"

"That's just it. He didn't look like no spaceman. He looked just like us. He was dressed in a black uniform with a black hat, looked like an officer's hat. Once he got out, he turned on something like a radio. He didn't say anything, just listened. Sounded like he was scanning up and down the radio dial. I heard a bunch of Pittsburgh AM stations and one show out of Philly. He quickly ran through the music stations, but he paused and listened whenever he came across a news broadcast. As he listened, he walked around a bit, never getting too far from the ship.

"When he saw the headlights coming up the road, he skedaddled back into his ship and buttoned up. Don't bother looking for the door. I done checked it and couldn't find nary a crack, nor seam."

"Just as Stan finished his tale, one of the Men in Black noticed I was gazing up into that tree and walked my way. I turned round and glance back at the MIB. When I spun back around and looked up the tree, Stan the Man was gone."

Brett was unimpressed, "That's a very interesting story, but not too much new information."

"Hold it! You haven't heard the interesting part. After the Air Force intel guys took soil samples and pictures, we loaded that spaceship on a flatbed truck and tarped it. The truck had a crane, but that thing was much too heavy for the crane alone. We rigged up a block and tackle and weuns all pitched in. That thing wasn't like any aircraft I've ever seen. It was way too heavy.

"Once we loaded that contraption on the flatbed, we threw three log chains over it and ratcheted it down good and tight. As we tarped the object, I noticed some markings etched around the bottom circumference. We weren't allowed to draw any sketches, or take any pictures, but a week thereafter, I stopped by the base library and did my own research."

"What were the etchings?"

"I am almost certain those etchings were Nordic runes, not hieroglyphs. I believe that gizmo was manmade."

Jack became more animated as he continued, "Here's the best part of the story. So, we were hauling that thingamajig back to Wright-Patt. When the convoy neared Zanesville, Ohio, every vehicle in the convoy simultaneously came to a dead stop."

"Every vehicle?"

"Yes. The oncoming traffic also stopped dead in its tracks. The object began whining like a turbine and glowing. You could see a bluish glow beneath the tarpaulin. After a couple of minutes, the tarp burst into flames and the object was gone. The wooden trailer deck was burnt in a perfect circle where the object had been sitting. The three chains were intact, still ratcheted down to the flatbed."

"Everyone's watch had stopped at the same time and all the steel parts of that flatbed truck were magnetized. St. Elmo's Fire danced like demons along the highway's guard rails and a nearby barbed wire fence."

Brett was incredulous, "It didn't take off? It just vanished? Gone, without a trace?"

"Yes, everything but the edelweiss."

"The edelweiss?"

Jack handed Brett a small, dried flower pressed between two sheets of waxed paper.

"Stan the Man told me that the spaceman had this flower stuck in his lapel and it dropped out when he turned up his collar to ward off the cold Pennsylvania night air. Here's your physical evidence of something. Just what, I don't know."

Move In Day

"Speer, bring me Speer!"

As the demoralized generals filed out of the undamaged wing of the Reich Chancellery, "The Good Nazi", Hitler's Architect, Albert Speer, was ushered in.

"Defeatists! What do these generals know of real war! They were never down in the trenches."

Speer saluted his Führer, Adolf Hitler, "My Führer, I know nothing of war. I am merely your architect."

"Speer, I am no fool. I see the production reports. This past year, armament production has soared under your direction. The Allies bomb us day and night. Stalin has an endless supply of untermenschen to throw into the meat grinder. Yet, you continue."

"That is my duty. We need more time mein Führer."

As he was wont to do, the Führer randomly switched gears, "Speer, do you know where I will be sleeping tonight?"

"Nein, mein Führer."

"Tonight, I will be sleeping in the lowest level of hell. Today, 16 January 1945, I moved into the lowest level of the Führerbunker, directly beneath this Reich Chancellery. I have fallen from the splendor of my beloved Berghof to a dank dungeon in Berlin.

"Our Ardennes Offensive has failed. The Western Allies will soon cross the Rhine. All hope of a separate negotiated peace with Churchill and that Jewish puppet, Roosevelt, has evaporated. The Bolsheviks are poised to invade the Fatherland.

"The wunderwaffen, Speer, what news of the wunderwaffen?"

"Mein Führer, the Messerschmidt 262 jets are smashing the British and American bombers, but the enemy seems to have an endless supply of both men and machines. Most of our aircraft production is safely underground, but we lack key raw materials. We are using conscript laborers from the camps to stretch our manpower. Our biggest problem is petrol. Since we lost the Romanian oil production, our synthetic fuel plants can't produce enough high-octane aviation gasoline. Therefore, jet production has been given top priority. The jets can burn lower grade distillates."

The Führer tapped his right index finger on his temple, "Speer, why can't my generals improvise as you have? Improvisation is a key trait of the Aryan mind."

"Mein Führer, we still do not have enough fuel and our access to other vital war materials is being strangled. The Allies maintain a combat air patrol over the Reich. The jets are vulnerable while on the ground, during take-off, and while landing."

The Führer uncharacteristically hung his head and almost whimpered, "My generals do not openly say it, but they think all is lost."

Speer had never seen his Führer like this, "Time is our enemy. We have weapons under development that make the V2 look like a firecracker, but we need time. Truthfully, my Führer, Germany cannot win at this time."

"Are you advising your Führer, as a loyal National Socialist, that all is lost?"

"Nein, mein Führer, I advise you that Germany cannot win at this time. But, I have just received word of a new development that may buy the Reich the time we need. As the Americans say, 'it's a crap shoot', a very risky proposition."

"Speer, my entire life has been a most unlikely story. I survived being gassed in the Great War, only to be stabbed in the back by that Jewish filth. Then, I was arrested for treason and imprisoned."

As the Führer spoke, his voice changed. He no longer whimpered. Defeat was replaced by determination.

"The Army, the politicians, the rich, the aristocracy, they all scorned me. They thought me a buffoon."

The Führer of the German Reich pounded his fist on the table and rose to his feet. Reichsminister Speer once again fell under his hypnotic gaze. It had been many months since Herr Speer had seen this man. This was the man who conquered all Europe and brought Soviet Russia to the brink of defeat.

"I have not come this far to die in a Berlin dungeon at the hands of the Bolsheviks!"

Speer submissively asked, "May I share with you what little I know?"

"Frau Junge, clear my afternoon schedule. No interruptions. Reichsminister Speer and I will be busy building a new Germany!"

The Summons

Thomas Jackson and Lame Wolf were spending Christmas Day 2041 in an upscale hotel near the intersection of US 360 & Main Street in downtown Roswell, New Mexico.

"Jackson, I have lived a long life, but I have never spent a night in a room as splendid as this."

The two men were sharing the hotel's Oil Barron's Penthouse Suite. Each man had his own plush bedroom and adjoining bath. They were relaxing in the Suite's large open concept living room/dining room/ kitchen area, sipping hot coffee and enjoying the view from the Suite's panoramic picture window.

Tom replied to his Navajo friend, "I didn't go to bed until late last night. I just snoozed here in this easy chair. Every-so-often, I'd gaze out to the east. I counted more oil rig flares than stars in the sky."

The Yuletide peace and quiet was interrupted by a knock on the door. Tom motioned for Lame Wolf to relax and remain lying on the sofa.

Tom cracked open the door and greeted a middle-aged White man dressed in business attire, "Merry Christmas!"

"Sergeant Thomas Jackson?"

"Yes, that be me."

"May I come in?"

Tom normally did not allow strangers to just waltz into his hotel room, but it was obvious that his guest represented "The Company".

The stranger paused beside an armchair, "Sorry to bother you on Christmas Day, may I sit?"

Tom replied, "You have me at a loss. I don't believe I caught your name."

"Jones, last name should suffice."

Tom smiled. He hadn't met one of the Joneses since he was interviewed for Operation Phoenix back in '25.

The agent noticed Lame Wolf relaxing on the sofa, "I wasn't aware you had company."

Tom answered as he sat back down, "Oh, that's just Lame Wolf. He ain't company. He's my Navajo guide."

"Sergeant Jackson, we should probably speak in private."

Tom forced out a laugh, "Aah, don't worry about him. He doesn't speak much English."

Without opening his eyes, Lame Wolf played along, replying in his native Navajo tongue.

Jones bought the deception and continued, "Sergeant, our technicians, here in Roswell, are evaluating the photographs you recently snapped at the Very Large Array. We are flying in a team of specialists to aid in our evaluation. We have scheduled a meeting for 0800 tomorrow morning, down in the Judge Roy Bean Conference Room. Our team of specialists will interview you first thing. Be prepared for a thorough debriefing."

Debriefing

The 10-man crew of the Katzenjammer Kid were going home. They had completed 25 missions and, amazingly, not a single crewman had been lost. It was now the mid-January 1945, two weeks since their weird final mission. Bomber crews were routinely debriefed after every mission, but the Kids had been advised not to discuss the unusual aspects of their final mission until they were debriefed by American OSS and British MI6 officers.

Immediately after their final routine mission debriefing, the Kids were whisked off base, into London. The airmen were pleasantly surprised by their accommodations at the plush St. Ermin's Hotel, located in Westminster, the heart of London. For two weeks, the Kids saw the sights, enjoyed the food, and chased the gorgeous British ladies.

The Kids had no inkling that the elegant St. Ermin's was spy central in wartime London. On 16 January 1945, the Kids were individually interrogated by both American OSS and British MI6. While Reichsminister Speer briefed his Führer in Berlin's dank, dark Führerbunker, Captain Green was comfortably seated in a plush St. Ermin's suite, sipping tea, sampling crumpets, and answering questions.

The American spook began the questioning, "Captain Green, what exactly did you see on your 1 January 1945 mission to Dollbergen?"

"We didn't actually see anything but a trail of smoke and radiant energy. It flashed downward through our formation in a straight line. It didn't maneuver. Whatever it was, it was descending to the southeast, toward Southern Germany, at a shallow angle."

The Britt chimed in, "Certainly old boy, you chaps must have caught a glimpse of something. Was it one of those jet aeroplanes?"

"No Sir! It wasn't a jet. It wasn't a rocket. It was moving way too fast. We couldn't see it, but we sure felt its effects."

"Captain Green, you were an engineering student before the war?"

"Yes sir. Carnegie Mellon in Pittsburgh."

"Are you familiar with the term electromagnetic pulse?"

"Familiar enough to know that something like that must have hit the Katzenjammer. Could something like that have blown up Lady Liberty?"

"The Britt engineers tell me that a strong EMP can induce a static discharge. Lady Liberty was on her return leg, so her fuel tanks were partially empty. A spark could have ignited the vapor in her tanks. That's our working theory."

"Pardon me, you are…"

"Mr. Jones."

Captain Green chuckled, "Mr. Jones, did we run into some kind of new Kraut wunderwaffen?"

The Britt dryly replied, "Jerry might just have himself a new toy."

I'll Leave the Tip

"Jack, can you jot down your contact information in my notebook? Full name, address, phone number, and email address."

"No problem. But my doctors tell me I'll be lucky to see 2026. I'll have a new address in a few months. Perhaps you can have one of your radio show guests attempt to contact me then."

Brett broke up laughing at Jack's sarcastic fatalism, "Pardon me Jack, but your humor in the face of death is quite unusual."

Jack plunked some change down on the table, "I'll leave the tip. As for you, Mr. Hoffman, grant a dying old Airman one last request. Thoroughly investigate what happened in Kecksburg that December night back in 1965."

Jack stood, shook Brett's hand, then walked out of the Drive-n-Dine.

Brett sat back down to finish his coffee and watched as Jack crossed Murray Avenue. A tall thin man, in a black leather trench coat and matching fedora, rose from his barstool and, at a discrete distance, followed Jack out of the diner. Brett grabbed his iPhone and snapped several photos, but in the dark, at that distance, the images were not very revealing.

Halloween 2025 was already one for the books, but the plot thickened as the dark-haired young lady, the one with all the questions, rose from her counter stool and briskly followed the man in the fedora out of the diner. Once again, Brett snapped a series of iPhone photos while remaining seated. As the question lady left the diner, Brett noticed that her right hand, inside her right coat pocket, was clutching something. Although Brett couldn't be certain, he suspicioned the young lady was carrying. Brett certainly did not want to take his iPhone to a gun fight.

Out of an abundance of caution, Brett remained seated at the Drive-n-Dine for another 30 minutes. Brett lived in Hampton Hall Condominiums in Oakland, just over a mile due west of Chatham University. If he could make it safely to his car, he could be home in 10 minutes. His Hampton Hall Condo had its own deeded, secure, off-street parking spot.

Brett slipped one of the Drive-n-Dine's steak knives into his right coat pocket. He clasped his keyring in his left hand, with the keys protruding between his fingers, ready to rake the face of any attacker. Without further ado, Brett was out of the diner and into his Bimmer. Yes, he remembered to check the BMW's rear seat.

Considering recent events, one thing was clear. The Kecksburg incident was much more than just another UFO story.

Brett began organizing his thoughts, "Jack has to be checked out. If Stan the Man is more than just a figment of Jack's imagination, I've gotta track him down. That entails a short drive to Kecksburg. Who was the young lady asking all the questions? Who was the man in black leather?"

Finally, Brett retrieved the pressed flower from his pocket, "Is this flower really an edelweiss?"

The Owl Mountains

In late January 1945, travel across what remained of Hitler's Third Reich was risky business. Allied fighter-bombers, mostly P-47 Thunderbolts, freely roamed the skies over Western Germany, while Soviet IL-2 Sturmovik ground attack aircraft shot up anything that moved in the East.

Reichsminister Speer had his orders and his Führer's authority. Templehof Airport was only a short distance from the Reich Chancellery. A modified Arado Ar234 Blitz jet bomber was standing by, ready to transport Speer to a secret underground facility along the present-day Czech-Polish border.

As the Arado climbed into the darkness, crammed into the tight confines of the modified jet, Speer had a ringside seat for the dismemberment of the Thousand Year Reich. To his east, the entire horizon was illuminated by the muzzle flashes from thousands of Soviet guns. During the short, 30-minute flight, Herr Speer could clearly discern the rapid-fire flashes from hundreds of Russian Katyusha multiple rocket launchers. Not only was the eastern horizon ablaze, cities throughout Germany were burning, as British Lancasters dropped thousands of tons of incendiaries. The great cities of the Reich had become the funeral pyres of the Deutsche Volk.

The Arado was flying as low as possible given the mountainous terrain. Even the Americans' vaunted P-51 Mustang could not catch the Arado, now streaking through occupied Czechoslovakia at over 450 miles per hour. The jet's sole passenger was lost in deep thought.

Speer had solved countless problems since assuming his position as Reichsminister for Armaments and Ammunition. As Germany's enemies tightened their stranglehold around the Fatherland, Speer's problems had grown exponentially. He gradually realized that all Germany's problems were mere symptoms of one root problem. The Nazi regime had run out of time. Herr Speer needed more time to relocate more factories underground. It would take more time to bring more wunderwaffen online. If Germany could hold out a bit longer and inflict more pain upon the Allies, perhaps a separate peace could be made with the United Kingdom and the United States. Then, together, they could defeat the real enemy, the Bolsheviks. At a minimum, the pleasure loving, isolationist American people might grow weary of fighting an endless European war. Certainly, Romanian oil and Swedish iron ore were important, but time was Speer's most precious commodity. Speer had one final problem to solve.

The runway lights flickered on mere minutes before the Arado touched down. Seconds after landing, the lights were extinguished. A black MercedesW31 type G4 convertible staff car was waiting on the tarmac. The driver hurriedly raised the rag top in anticipation of the cold ride to Ksiaz Castle. Two leather clad Gestapo officers provided security. As he approached the Mercedes, Speer raised his arm in the Nazi salute, then slid into the rear seat saying nothing except, "Heil Hitler!"

The Führer had warned his Architect about the Gestapo. Its leader, Reichsführer-SS Heinrich Himmler, considered Speer his most formidable rival in the Nazi inner circle. Himmler was envious of the Führer's close relationship with Speer.

At heart, assuming he had one, Hitler was a frustrated artist. He admired Speer's creativity. Speer could speak to his Führer as no one else dared speak, with perhaps the exception of the Führer's interior decorator, Gerdy Troost. On the other hand, Hitler was not at all close to Himmler. Himmler's fascination with the occult was publicly ridiculed by the Führer. As the end approached, Hitler's distrust of Himmler grew. That distrust was warranted as Himmler was hatching a scheme to save his own skin and possibly supplant Hitler as Führer.

Speer focused his eyes straight ahead as the Mercedes passed through a squalid workcamp. That camp housed hundreds of slave laborers, frantically excavating tunnels beneath the castle. The native rock around the castle was particularly hard, making excavation most difficult. On the flip side, tunnels through that rock were virtually impervious to aerial bombardment. This entire area was now honeycombed with tunnels. Here, in secure underground factories, the wunderwaffen could be mass produced.

Unlike his Führer, Speer would not be sleeping in an underground bunker. Upon arrival at Ksiaz Castle, Speer was ushered to his accommodations, a magnificent apartment in Ksiaz Castle's keep.

"Awaken me at 0500, I have little time."

At 0530, Speer's breakfast was waiting for him as he emerged from the water closet. After breakfast, his young SS chauffer knocked upon his door.

"Herr Reichsminister, it is time.

"You will not need your greatcoat. We will remain indoors."

The SS corporal guided Speer down a couple of narrow flights of stairs, across the Castle's great hall, then descended a wrought iron spiral staircase down a new, hand-hewn, vertical shaft.

"Herr Reichsminister, we are now 40 meters beneath Ksiaz Castle."

Speer tried his best not to notice two emaciated Jewish laborers pulling a cart piled full of skeletal corpses.

"There are more Jews where those came from. Don't worry Herr Reichsminister, you won't run out of workers."

Little did the Corporal know, he couldn't be more wrong. The Reich was facing a dire labor shortage.

The pair walked past dark, dusty, side tunnels still under construction. Speer could only shake his head in disbelief as he saw men being used as pack animals, pulling carts.

Speer thought to himself, "This operation is a textbook example of criminal inefficiency."

Then Speer remembered, "The SS oversees slave labor. Efficiency is the least of their goals."

As they walked on, the passageway became brighter and more refined, sporting smooth concrete walls and floors. Speer noticed a change in atmosphere, lower humidity, and no dust.

"Sieg Heil!"

The SS Corporal's hand shot up in the Nazi salute as Speer approached the first steel blast door. The Reichsminister barely raised his.

The sentry returned the salute, "Guten morgen, Herr Reichsminister!"

Speer nodded in response.

The second blast door, further down the tunnel, was more fortified. Two SS sentries armed with machine pistols and accompanied by a massive German Shepherd manned this post. The Shepherd was already sniffing Speer and his chaperone before the perfunctory salutations ended.

Speer reached down and gave the dog a pet, "The Führer would approve. Your dog reminds me of his Blondi."

The Shepherd's SS handler smiled, "Jawohl, Reichsminister. She is a good Nazi."

As Speer knelt and hugged the dog, the guard motioned the Reichsminister through the final door.

"Guten morgen Herr Reichsminister Speer!"

Upon seeing his distinguished host, Speer quickly dismissed his SS chaperon.

"Herr Doktor Heisenberg, what a pleasant surprise. I was not expecting to see you here today! I assumed you were in your Uranverein laboratory in Haigerloch. Your uranium device must be given top priority!"

"Reichsminister, the work at Haigerloch goes well. I anticipate our first uranium device will be ready within the year. Come, sit, we have much to discuss this morning."

"Herr Doktor, I hope we have other things to discuss. Germany cannot wait a year for the uranium device. We have little time."

The two men sat down at a conference table in the middle of what amounted to a modern clean room. They momentarily paused their conversation as hot tea and cakes were served by an enslaved Polish baker.

"Speer, are things really that bad at the front?"

"Herr Doktor, both fronts are collapsing. The Allies dominate the skies over the Fatherland. I personally estimate we have 90 days. We have run out of time."

White Christmas

2041's White Christmas was little consolation for its bone chilling cold. After their escape from California, the extended Wu family had found lodging in the vacant rooms above Austin's National Café. Back in the real world, before the 2026 Peoples' Revolution, the National Café was a historically themed bed & breakfast. In Austin's boomtown days, immediately following America's first Civil War, the National Café was a restaurant, saloon, and bordello. Many of the rooms upstairs still sported a racy bordello décor.

Katrina, Hana, and Hana's two daughters lent Miss Stormy a helping hand in the National Café's restaurant. Business was booming since the Mormon Cavalry liberated the town. A large squadron of Cavalry remained in Austin, protecting it from Collective forces based in Reno. Unlike its restaurant, the National Café's saloon had seen virtually zero increase in business. Needless to say, the Mormons were not heavy drinkers.

Miss Stormy's husband, Vince, was still recovering from wounds suffered months earlier in a barroom shootout with the Peoples' Militia. Vince was the National Café's owner and barkeep. James Wu and his father-in-law, Henry, helped Vince in the bar. Whenever they weren't behind the bar, they kept busy repairing the slowly deteriorating National Café building. The day after Christmas, both Chinese American men were busy redecorating a third-floor guest room.

Shortly before lunch, Jimmy heard someone softly rapping on the door jamb. The novice painter cast a quick glance back toward the open door, assuming that one of the ladies was bringing up some lunch. He was surprised to see a middle-aged White man, dressed in suit and tie, standing in the doorway.

"May I help you?"

The stranger pointed at Jimmy, "Inspector James Wu?"

"Yes…"

"May I have a word?" The stranger motioned with his right hand for James to join him out in the hallway.

James stepped to the doorway, then paused, "Pardon me, do I know you?"

"I'm Special Agent Jones."

Jimmy extended his hand, one intelligence operative to another.

As the men shook hands, Jones immediately got to the point, "Inspector Wu, it has come to our attention that, during your tenure with Chinese State Security, you spent some time at the Lawrence Livermore National Laboratories."

"Jimmy, is there some problem?" Father-in-law Henry noticed James' absence and momentarily paused from his painting.

"No problem, Hank. I'm just shooting the breeze with an old business acquaintance."

Henry Huang knew what that meant. Jimmy's acquaintances dealt in trouble with a capital T. The elderly engineer resumed rolling pink paint and minded his own business.

Jimmy nonchalantly replied to Jones, "Yeah, Livermore was one of my many assignments."

"Then you're familiar with Livermore's layout and security protocols."

James began laughing an uneasy laugh, "Yeah, but Chinese State Security protects that asset and they're hunting me. I'm wanted by the People's Republic for high treason."

"Yes, they know Inspector James Wu, but do they know Tony Lin?"

Jimmy replied, "Who in the hell is Tony Lin?"

Jones handed Jimmy a headshot of Tony.

Jimmy carefully inspected the photo, "This guy looks vaguely familiar."

"He should." Jones handed Jimmy three more headshots of Tony. One photo showed Tony sans glasses. The next shot showed Tony without glasses and with a full head of black hair. The third photo showed Tony with hair, without glasses, and about 30 lbs. lighter.

A wide-eyed James Wu stared at the third headshot, "Hey, that's me."

James was ethnically Chinese, but at heart he was pure Southern California frat boy. Wu was always immaculately groomed. Every jet-black hair on his head was perfectly coiffed. He worked out every day. For a man pushing 40, he was in great shape. His vision was perfect. The only glasses James ever wore were Ray-Bans.

James was a very quick study, "Oh no! My beautiful wife won't even want to look at me, much less touch me. You want me to become a Nerd!"

Jones pulled a pair of Coke Bottle glasses from his suitcoat pocket and tossed them to James, "Tony, try these on for size."

Jones smiled as a bespectacled Tony Lin in the making continued protesting while running both hands through his endangered hair, "You wouldn't! I won't do it!"

"There's a barber, a block down Main Street, and he's expecting you. Don't worry, it will grow back once you complete your mission."

"Can I just get a buzz cut?"

Jones shook his head, "No! We need a clean shave. Got to fool the image recognition software."

As James reluctantly headed down the stairway, like a sheep before the shearer, Jones tossed Tony a Hershey bar. "Eat hardy Tony! No jogging and whatever you do, stay out of the gym. You must put on at least 10 pounds by New Year's Day."

Sea to Sea AM

It was 1 a.m. in the East. The spooky, but peppy, *Sea-to-Sea AM* bumper music streamed out over the airwaves from Pittsburgh's 50,000-watt clear channel AM station, KDKA.

"Good morning to our listeners in the East and good evening to our listeners on the West Coast and throughout the Intermountain West. This is Brett Hoffman, your somewhat regular guest host, broadcasting from the KDKA studios in the Steel City. Tonight's topic is the 1965 Kecksburg incident. Hold on, before you turn that dial, or call Mr. Call Screener with irate complaints, please bear with me. Until yesterday evening, I was certain this 60-year-old incident had been thoroughly investigated. I was quite convinced that a Russian satellite crashed to earth that December night back in 1965. After last night, I'm not so sure."

In the subsequent segment, Brett shared a condensed version of his Halloween surprise with paranormal enthusiasts across North America, purposefully omitting strategic names and details. He specifically withheld any mention of the dried edelweiss.

Earlier that day, Brett strolled a few blocks from his Hampton Hall condo to Carnegie Mellon University's Hunt Institute for Botanical Documentation. Dr. Isaac Stern was an Adjunct Research Scientist at the Institute and a closet *Sea-to-Sea AM* groupie.

"Brett, what can I do for you today? Will I be rummaging through Bigfoot scat, attempting to ascertain Sasquatch's dietary habits?"

Brett about busted a gut laughing, "Nope! Today I'm not shitting you. Just need you to identify a flower."

Hoffman handed Dr. Stern the pressed flower that Jack gave him the previous evening.

"Oh, how beautiful."

Isaac broke into song, a Rogers & Hammerstein classic,

> *"Edelweiss, Edelweiss,*
>
> *Every morning you greet me*
>
> *Small and white*
>
> *Clean and bright*
>
> *You look happy to meet me*

Brett chimed in,

> *"Blossom of snow, may you bloom and grow*
>
> *Bloom and grow forever*
>
> *Edelweiss, Edelweiss*
>
> *Bless my homeland forever"*

"Well Herr Hoffman, your German ancestry shines through."

"As does yours Herr Stern."

"Jawohl Herr Hoffman! Unfortunately, most of my ancestry was liquidated 80 years ago."

Brett didn't quite know how to respond, so he quickly changed the subject, "OK, Stern. Where is this flower's homeland?"

"Alpine regions of Southern Germany, Austria, Switzerland, Czechoslovakia, and Poland."

"If a man in uniform wore this in his lapel, just who might he be?"

"Easy question, he'd be a German, Swiss, or Austrian soldier. The edelweiss is an emblem of purity and devotion, worn by elite troops."

"What if his uniform were jet black?"

Without answering, a suddenly grim Isaac silently walked over to his bookshelf, removed a volume, and flipped through the pages. He then turned toward Brett, holding the open book in his trembling left hand, while pointing at a glossy color illustration with his right index finger.

Brett gasped, "My God!"

Isaac slammed the book shut, "Brett, my friend, God has nothing to do with this."

That night's show was well received. Mr. Call Screener was working his ass off. His switchboard was twinkling like a Las Vegas casino marquee. About 10 minutes into the show's second hour, a persistent caller finally got through.

"Welcome to *Sea-to-Sea AM*. Briefly state your comment or question for Brett Hoffman."

"Yeah, I've lived down around Kecksburg all my life. I'm a big *Sea-to-Sea* fan. I heard Brett's story in the opening monologue. I was the kid up in that tree back in '65."

"Name please."

"I'd rather not. Just tell Brett I picked up the flower."

"OK, don't hang up. What's your phone number?" The caller had called in on a restricted line.

"Got it. Just hang on. When we get to the next break, I'll hook you up with Brett."

It was nearing the bottom of the hour, time to break for network news.

"Brett, you won't believe this. I've got the kid in the tree on the line."

"What is his name?"

"He wouldn't say, but he said he picked up the flower. Should I move him to the front of the line?"

"No. Get his address and arrange for me to meet him. Hey Teddy…"

Brett had never been this familiar with Mr. Call Screener.

"Hey what, Brett?

"Don't mention this to anyone. I'm not kidding. I don't know what we're dealing with."

Uncertainty

Herr Speer and his Nobel Laureate comrade got down to particulars.

"My Jewish colleague, Einstein, would tell you that time is just another dimension. Its flow is influenced by gravity, mass, and the relative velocity of objects moving through three-dimensional space. While Herr Einstein deals with the macro universe, composed of planets, galaxies, and stars, I specialize in the world of the very small, atoms and sub-atomic particles. My world is a world of probability and uncertainty."

"Yes, yes, Herr Doktor, but my world is armaments production. My goal is German victory!"

"That is why I invited you here today. Early last year, we stumbled onto something as we investigated unconventional propulsion mechanisms. Our initial aim was to produce an antigravity device. Such a device could transport our uranium devices at great speed over long distances. Using a combination of the two devices, Germany could obliterate America's industrial heartland, Chicago, Pittsburgh, Cleveland, and Detroit. Likewise, we could vaporize the Allies' financial and political centers, Moscow, London, New York, and Washington.

"Alas, we had only modest success in our antigravity efforts."

"Please explain what you mean by modest."

"We can partially negate gravity, thereby slowing the speed of free-falling objects to virtually nil. The mechanism is too heavy to serve as a means of propulsion. Its great weight is due to the exotic liquid rare earth metal alloy central to this technology. Even I am not privy to its exact composition."

"What powers this device? I hope it does not require petrol."

"Herr Himmler would say this device is powered by Vril energy, a mystical force that permeates the universe. On the other hand, I am a scientist. There is indeed a force, an energy, that permeates the cosmos. It appears to be a quality of spacetime itself. My colleagues have coined the term, Nullpunkt Energie.

"Trust me, my dear Speer, although you are an accomplished architect and a brilliant man, I can only give you a comic book description of our work. I, myself, only know the overall principle behind the device. I daresay that, by design, no one man knows this technology in its totality."

"That is as it should be. Herr Doktor, will this briefing adequately prepare me to brief our Führer?"

"Most certainly! Allow me to continue.

"This device channels Nullpunkt Energie through a liquid rare earth metal dynamo and uses that vast power to bend the four-dimensional fabric of spacetime. This allows the negation of gravity but does not produce antigravity. The device's movement through three-dimensional space is limited, somewhat erratic, and only partially understood."

"Herr Doktor Heisenberg, are you telling me you have a great invention that does not work?" Speer was losing his patience.

"I beg your indulgence Reichsminister. While the device has limited movement through three-dimensional space, it can move through the fourth dimension with ease."

Speer was dumbfounded, "Heisenberg, are you telling me that you have developed a time machine?"

Without waiting for Heisenberg's reply, Speer continued, "Do you understand the implications of such a device? We could send emissaries back to 1939, or earlier, with a complete history of the war. We could change history. We could continuously change history until we are victorious!"

Heisenberg solemnly and negatively shook his head, "Only in that Englander's *Time Machine* novel can one so easily move forward and backward through time. We are limited by the arrow."

"What arrow?"

"Herr Reichsminister, unlike the three spatial dimensions, time has an arrow. That arrow only points in one direction, forward, into the future. This involves the fundamental laws of causality and thermodynamics. Travel into the past opens the door to paradoxes that are irreconcilable. Nature does not allow such contradictions. We cannot travel to the past, only to the future."

Heisenberg then rose from his seat, "Follow me."

The two Nazis briskly walked 50 meters down the main passage, then hung a left turn into a dark side tunnel. Heisenberg threw the light switch. There, in the middle of the cavern, bathed in floodlights, sat a large, black, bell-shaped device.

"Herr Speer, this is die Glocke."

"Pardon my skepticism Herr Doktor. When I return to besieged Berlin, will I report to the Führer that I came here to see a bell?"

"This is one of two single-seat prototypes. The components of a larger model are even now in transit to Berlin's Tempelhof Airport."

"May I inquire as to the whereabouts of the other prototype?"

"Follow me."

The two men strolled down the main tunnel yet another 50 meters and once again turned left into a dark cavern. Heisenberg threw another light switch.

"I don't understand Herr Doktor. Is this some sort of monument?"

Another Glocke was halfway protruding from the left-hand wall of the cavern, about one meter off the floor.

"Nein, my dear Reichsminister. This is the second prototype. As the device moves further through the fourth dimension, its destination in three-dimensional space becomes increasingly more uncertain. We can use that uncertainty to move die Glocke through three-dimensional space with some degree of accuracy."

"This is analogous to your uncertainty principle for the quantum world, is it not?"

"Bravo Speer! Unlike the Neanderthals in Berlin, you have a sharp mind. This prototype was launched prior to our understanding of the spatial uncertainty. It was launched from the center of this cavern and was set to travel one hour into the future. When it rematerialized, one hour in the future, it rematerialized halfway inside the wall of this cavern."

"Once again, Herr Doktor, I am at a loss to see how this device can be of any practical use."

"We now target rematerialization at a point just outside earth's atmosphere, in the void of outer space. In space, there is virtually no chance of obstructed rematerialization. We cannot accurately target the point of reentry, but once the device reenters the atmosphere, it can be slowed by its limited gravity nullification abilities. Doktor Von Braun's V2 team has collaborated with Team Glocke on the device's heat shielding for atmospheric reentry."

"Does Von Braun's team know any of the details of this project?"

"Nein, Reichsminister.

"Recently, the remaining prototype successfully completed a one month jump into the future. The typical spatial uncertainty resulting from the one-hour jumps has been on the order of a few meters, carrying the risk of obstructed rematerialization. The recent one-month jump allowed extra-atmospheric rematerialization. On New Year's Day, die Glocke rematerialized over the Dutch frontier and touched down near München.

Longer temporal jumps, say on the order of 10 or 20 years, would allow for spatial targeting anywhere on Earth.

"Just remember, I said targeting. Due to the uncertainty of that targeting, every time the prototype makes a jump, we risk losing it. It could land in the ocean, a lake, or river and immediately sink. It could land on the White House lawn, or in Red Square, and be captured or destroyed. Although the odds are infinitesimally small, it could rematerialize on the other side of the universe. As I said, I deal in a world of probabilities.

"We recently discovered that die Glocke, operating at a power level just below the jump threshold, will distort spacetime just enough to form a dimensional basin of sorts. Another Glocke, jumping to the same four-dimensional target, will tend to fall into this spacetime trap, virtually eliminating the spatial and temporal uncertainties. Our thought is to use the prototype unit as a scout. After making a successful jump, the scout can form a spacetime trap, allowing the larger Glocke to jump into that trap."

"Sort of like shooting a billiard ball into the corner pocket?"

Heisenberg clapped his hands and almost squealed with delight, "Very cleverly put, Herr Reichsminister. Eight-ball in the corner pocket."

For a few moments, Speer silently mulled the Nobel Prize winner's fantastic tale.

"This better work or, as those crazy Americans say, we will both be behind that eight-ball.

"How many passengers can the larger device safely transport?"

"Perhaps two, plus the pilot."

"Will time pass for the passengers during the jump?"

"Nein, Herr Speer. If die Glocke jumped 1,000 years into the future, it would be an instantaneous event for the passengers. They will not age. Time will not pass for them."

"Herr Doktor, after you prepare die Glocke for its final jump, you will immediately return to Haigerloch and continue your work on the uranium device. Under penalty of death, you will never discuss die Glocke, or this technology, with anyone. Do you understand?"

"Jawohl, Herr Reichsminister! To where and when will die Glocke make its final jump?"

"I will be your sole contact for this project. We may eventually find a use for this toy, but we certainly do not want the Bolsheviks to get their nefarious hands on this technology. We will target the final jump to transport die Glocke thousands of years into the future, only to rematerialize in the center of the Earth, or perhaps on the far side of the Moon.

"Any conscript labor associated with this project must be liquidated. The SS will be advised that the project has failed and is terminated. A minimal number of German technicians will prepare die Glocke for its final jump. They must all be dedicated National Socialists and sworn to secrecy. We will order them not to allow die Glock to fall into enemy hands.

"The Bolsheviks could be here in a month, maybe less. Die Glocke must be ready to make that final jump on a moment's notice. How many Glocke pilots are available?"

"Only two. Both are SS officers with technical backgrounds. We recruited pilots fluent in English in the event we sent die Glocke on some type of espionage mission. They have no close relatives and all records of their existence have been expunged."

"Are they both here, on site?"

"Yes."

"I want to interview them both immediately. One will stay here and pilot the prototype. The other pilot will accompany me back to Berlin. I assume he can also pilot the larger version, now on its way to Tempelhof?"

"Yes, Herr Speer. The controls are virtually identical."

"Zehr gut! As flawed and useless as they are, we must keep both machines out of Soviet hands."

Stan's Yarn

At noon the following day, Brett parked his BMW in the front lot of the Cracker Barrel Old Country Store just off I-70 in New Stanton, Pennsylvania. He was glad to get out of Pittsburgh for the day. Petty street crime, now masquerading as political unrest, was a growing widespread occurrence throughout America's major cities. Things were much more tranquil in New Stanton. There sat Stan, in a rocking chair, on Cracker Barrel's front porch, wearing a *Sea-to-Sea AM* baseball cap. Stan instantly recognized Brett from his many television appearances.

Before Brett could make it up the accessibility ramp, Stan called out, "Hold it right there!"

Brett froze, thinking something was amiss. Stan pulled out his cellphone and began snapping photos.

"Got it! Now let's see if this gear jammer will take one of us shaking hands."

Stan grabbed a burly trucker and pitched him a proposition.

"He'll do it, but then I gotta use his phone and snap a photo of you two shaking hands. He loves listening to *Sea-to-Sea AM* on his all night cross-country runs."

After wrapping their impromptu photo shoot, the two men sat down in adjacent rockers. It was a blustery early November day in Pennsylvania, nobody else was crazy enough to sit outside.

"I can't believe I'm actually sitting here talking face-to-face with Brett Hoffman."

Brett was trying to size up Stan. Stan's mannerisms screamed out, "FLAKE", but his appearance was nondescript, late sixties, White, at least 6'2" and thin as a rail.

"Stan, please, just call me Brett. Try not to do anything else to draw attention."

"Brett, were you expecting a friend to join us?"

"No, why do you ask?"

"There's a dark-haired lady in a late model gray sedan parked two rows out. Don't stare! She pulled in behind you and she's been watching us ever since. Can't tell if she's using binoculars, or just wearing shades."

Brett acted quickly, "I'm going to stand up and take another photo with your cellphone. I'll position myself in line with you and that gray car. Your phone's camera has a decent zoom. I'll take a closeup of that broad, then zoom back out and get a shot of her car. Too bad Pennsylvania doesn't require front plates."

Brett snapped the photos, then handed the cellphone back to Stan.

Stan tucked his cellphone in his pocket and headed for the door, "Let's grab some lunch. My treat!"

It was business as usual at Cracker Barrel, a 10-minute wait. Stan and Brett feigned shopping around the Country Store while sporadically and discreetly monitoring the gray sedan parked in the lot. The gray car hadn't moved by the time Brett and Stan were seated in the dining room.

After ordering lunch, Brett began the interview, "Obviously, you don't know the woman in the sedan."

Stan shook his head, "Never seen her before."

"Listen Stan, you've got to tell me what happened in Kecksburg that December night back in 1965. I know that was 60 years ago, but you've got to be thorough and truthful."

"Well, from last night's show, it's obvious you talked to the soldier under the tree. You knew what I meant when I told Mr. Call Screener that I picked up the flower."

Brett removed the pressed edelweiss from his jacket pocket, "Yes, this flower. Do you know what it is?"

"Mr. Hoffman, I was only a kid of 11 when, whatever it was, landed near Kecksburg. Over the years, I have written down all the details I can recall and collected pictures that match both the pilot and the flower he dropped, the same flower you now hold in your hand. You may think I'm some kind of nut, but I'm almost certain the man in the black uniform was a Nazi SS officer."

"What about the flower?"

"I believe that flower is an edelweiss."

"OK, let's start from the beginning. Is it OK if I record this?"

"Go ahead, that's why you're here."

"When did you first see the object?"

"It was a cold, clear winter's night in Kecksburg. I grew up on a small farm just a stone's throw from the landing site. My Dad was a stargazer, so he encouraged me to follow in his footsteps. I was out back of the house, getting the telescope set up. It was not quite dark when that thing came streaking over the farm. It was heading southwest. As it neared the ground, it slowed down like someone slammed on the brakes.

"It was only a 10-minute hike through the woods to the small clearing where it landed. You know, it's funny what you remember and what you don't. As I neared the landing site, the air was hissing and sizzling. A bluish plasma was dancing along a barbed wire fence. I hadn't really remembered that until just now."

"That's good Stan, but make sure those memories are real. 60 years is a long time. As time goes by, witnesses tend to remember things they think happened, but didn't really happen. They're not lying. The human mind just works that way."

Stan twitched his nose, "Nah, it's a real memory. The smell, now I remember that electrical smell."

"Ozone?"

"I guess so. Smelled like a short circuit.

"The tall, freeze-dried grass around the object was smoldering. That ominous black bell was just sitting there. I saw no landing gear, but it hadn't crashed. I shimmied up a huge oak tree, crawled out on a long, stout branch and watched. About 15 minutes later, the hatch opened, and out he came."

"OK Stan, describe the pilot in detail, but don't guess, or imagine."

"He was human. I was so disappointed. I thought I was going to see a real spaceman. He was dressed in a black uniform, about 6 feet tall. He was Caucasian. I couldn't make out the details of his uniform in the darkness, but I could see the white flower stuck in his lapel. He must have been cold. When he turned up his collar to keep warm, the flower dropped to the ground."

Brett pressed Stan for more details, "The Airman told me the pilot held something like a radio."

"He was carrying an electronic device about the size of shoebox. He was turning a dial like he was tuning it. I heard a couple of local AM stations and thought I overheard a broadcast out of Philly. He seemed to be monitoring local radio newscasts. He just scanned through entertainment broadcasts. You know, now that I think about it, he had to understand English. He intently listened to news broadcasts. That's when the headlights approached. Two men in black suits got out of a black sedan. One guy took pictures with a flash camera. The other guy had a Geiger counter. It went nuts as he approached the craft. They took soil samples and samples of vegetation from all around the landing site."

"Stan, could you see their faces?"

"Not very well. They wore sunglasses. Can you imagine that? Give me a break! It was pitch black outside, except for the car headlights, and those dudes were wearing sunglasses?

"They were both plain vanilla wrappers. Average build, average height, Caucasian, black hat, black suit, and dark shades. Hell, they looked like the *Blues Brothers*.

"Finally, the military showed up. They cordoned off the area. That's when I briefly talked to the soldier. That conversation was cut short when one of the Men in Black approached.

"I quickly shimmied down out of that tree and hid in some brush. My view wasn't very good from the bushes, but I could see the soldiers were having trouble lifting the craft with the truck's crane. They quickly rigged up some winches and helped the crane slowly lift that thing up onto a flatbed trailer. Once it was on the truck, they threw some chains over the craft and ratcheted that thing down good and tight."

"Hang on Stan, you're telling me the UFO was chained to the flatbed?"

"Yeah, they chained it down, then they tarped it."

"You're sure about the chains?"

"Absolutely, three log chains ratcheted down tightly."

"Stan, the military hasn't got that craft."

"What do you mean? I saw them haul it away."

"On the way back to Wright-Patterson, that craft disappeared off that flatbed trailer over by Zanesville."

"No way! That thing was chained down. It couldn't have taken off."

"It didn't take off. It dematerialized."

"The hell you say!"

"Stan, I don't know what's going on, but watch yourself. Don't talk to anyone about this. Got it?"

"Brett, I'd bet my last Reichsmark that UFO's pilot was an SS officer and that lady out there in the gray sedan is following you."

"Yeah, she's following me. I think I've seen her twice before. We're going to get up, pay the check, and check out the parking lot. If she's still there, I'll leave first. You stay here. She probably doesn't know which vehicle is yours and let's keep it that way."

The two men walked out into the Country Store, lined up at the register, and Stan paid the check.

"Brett, she's gone."

"OK Stan, hang back a few minutes just to make sure. Call me if you need help. Otherwise, lay low."

"Will do, but I think we're OK."

When the mystery lady's sedan pulled out of the Cracker Barrel parking lot, the man in the black leather trench coat saw her leave. His black BMW was parked next door in a church parking lot. From there, he worked his way through the intervening small copse of trees and watched her drive away through his binoculars. He snapped several photos of Brett's vehicle and license plate, then hung around for a bit and snapped a few photos of Stan and his vehicle.

Roswell Roundtable

Tom Jackson made his way down to the second floor Judge Roy Bean Meeting room, 16 minutes ahead of schedule. Mr. Jones was already seated at a circular 10-seat conference table, sipping a cappuccino and eating a Danish. Two academic types were sitting to Jones' left, fixated upon their laptops. Tom wondered if they were prepping for this meeting, or just playing the latest computer game.

As he entered the room, Tom abruptly stopped, stood to, and saluted. Colonel Frank Cooper rose from his seat, directly across the table from Jones, and returned Tom's salute.

"At ease, Sergeant Jackson. Please be seated."

Jones dispensed with the small talk and got directly down to business, "We all know why we're here this morning."

Jones pointed at the older woman sitting on his immediate left, "Dr. Emily Bowser is a theoretical physicist. I can't even begin to tell you what she does."

Dr. Emily merely smiled and nodded.

Jones then pointed at the Japanese gentleman seated to Emily's left. "You may be familiar with Dr. Hiroshi Yasuda. Back in the real world, Dr. Yasuda was a frequent guest on various radio and television shows dealing with the paranormal and popular physics."

Hiroshi reached across the table, offering Tom his hand. Tom shook the physicist's hand and nodded, "Dr. Yasuda."

Colonel Cooper remained seated, "Sergeant Jackson, it's a pleasure finally meeting you. I don't get out this way much. I mostly hang around The Bunker. We do have at least three common acquaintances."

Tom shot Cooper a puzzled look. He had no idea what the Colonel was talking about.

Cooper cracked a broad smile, "A few months back, both Jones & I had the pleasure of meeting Lieutenant Josephine Parker, that character she calls 'The Keeper', and her canine sidekick, Ol' Max."

Tom grinned, "That must have been an interesting experience."

When Jones recalled that Max drooled all over his slippers, he had no time for further pleasantries, "Dr. Bowser please proceed."

The physicist flashed one of Dr. Leroy's VLA photos up on the large flat screen monitors strategically situated around the table.

"Sergeant Jackson has provided several detailed photos of construction activity currently underway at the Very Large Array, near Magdalena, New Mexico."

Thomas interrupted, "Excuse me, I simply brought you some photos. A dedicated patriot and astrophysicist, Dr. Leroy Summers, laid down his life obtaining this intel."

Tom's news rendered Dr. Bowser momentarily speechless.

Emily choked up with emotion as she replied, "Before the Revolution, Dr. Leroy was a respected astrophysicist. We were colleagues."

From Bowser's response, Tom suspected that Leroy may have been more than just Emily's comrade, "I just want to go on the record. The Peoples' News Network is putting out a line of crap that Leroy is a Hero of The Collective. The truth is, Leroy died in a shootout with the Peoples' Militia at Dish 9SE. He killed the Member who killed him."

Seeing that Emily needed a moment to compose herself, Hiroshi took over, "These photos show transmission towers under construction. They are nearly complete."

Tom nodded in agreement, "Yeah, they're fixin' to bring in a shit pot full of power."

Dr. Emily blushed at Tom's colorful language, but it snapped her out of her malaise.

Tom continued, "Dr. Leroy was stumped. He couldn't figure out why the Chinese needed to bring in that much juice. At first, Leroy implied they were gonna use the Array for transmission."

Hiroshi scrolled back to a photo showing a massive dish under construction inside The Barn, "What did Dr. Leroy think of the new dishes?"

"We didn't have time for much discussion. We were running for our lives and engaged in a major shootout. While we were running away from The Barn, after I knifed a sentry in the back, Leroy was muttering under his breath."

"What was he saying?"

He just kept repeating, "A portal, they may be trying to open a portal."

Colonel Cooper cleared his throat prior to asking a question, "Dr. Emily, do you have any idea what your deceased colleague was talking about?"

"I'm just guessing, but perhaps Dr. Summers was referring to some type of wormhole, a tunnel through four dimensional spacetime."

The Colonel rolled his eyes in utter disbelief and Thomas noticed it.

Hiroshi chimed in, "These photos from The Barn show the Chinese are indeed assembling new dishes with augmented capabilities."

Cooper needed to hear more, "What type of augmented capabilities? And please, no sci-fi bullshit."

Hiroshi ignored the Colonel's "sci-fi bullshit" comment, "Dr. Summer's conjecture should not be blown off as mere 'sci-fi bullshit'. The Chinese are enlarging the Array. They are assembling dishes capable of projecting various forms of powerful electromagnetic radiation."

Cooper replied, "So, are they communicating with someone, something, far, far, away?"

Hiroshi was skeptical, "Yes, they could send a signal across the universe with a larger and more powerful Array, but that would not be very practical.

Any message transmitted from Earth would travel at the light speed, 188,000 miles per second, regardless of signal strength. That may sound fast to us mortals, but we have not identified any potentially habitable planet close to Earth. Traveling at the speed of light, it would take hundreds, or perhaps thousands of years for a message to reach an inhabited alien world, and an equal length of time for any response to reach Earth.

Dr Emily followed up, "I agree. Dr. Summer's speculation may be more on target."

The Colonel shook his head in total disbelief, "You're talking about a portal? What kind of portal? A portal to where?"

Emily began explaining theoretical applications of Einstein's Theory of Relativity and Heisenberg's Quantum Mechanics, "Theoretically, four dimensional spacetime can be warped, folded, and tunneled through. Such manipulation of spacetime would require vast amounts of energy, much more than mankind can harness. This is possibly Stage 1 of a long-term Chinese program. The augmented VLA might produce a "dimple" in spacetime, like a pocket on a pool table, but I doubt it could open a full-fledged wormhole."

Cooper pressed the theoretician for more information, "When you say 'wormhole', you're talking about a tunnel through space, a shortcut?"

"Excellent description Colonel, except a wormhole burrows through spacetime. It's not only a shortcut to some place, it may also be a shortcut to some time."

Cooper was incredulous, "Let's suppose the ChiComs could open a wormhole. What could they do with it? Why would they place such an asset in New Mexico? They have plenty of desolate spaces in Outer Mongolia."

Dr. Emily answered without hesitation, "If they could open stable wormholes, imagine conventional or tactical nuclear weapons suddenly materializing amidst the chrysanthemums in the Emperor's garden in Tokyo, inside The Bunker beneath White Sulphur Springs, and on the tarmac at

Andersen Air Force Base on Guam. There would be no warning and no defense.

"Likewise, PLA troops could suddenly appear in Cowboys Stadium in Dallas, on the Atlantic City Boardwalk, or on Music Row in Nashville, Tennessee.

"The Chinese could explore and colonize the universe at will."

Cooper wanted more specifics, "All those scenarios deal with the 'where'. What of the 'when' possibilities?"

"That is a little less clear. Many theoreticians contend that the temporal dimension has an 'arrow' that points to the future. They contend that travel through the fourth dimension is a one-way trip. I tend to agree. Traveling backward in time introduces too many potential paradoxes."

"Madame, you have not yet answered the 'why' part of my question."

Hiroshi came to Emily's defense, "Colonel, the Trinity site lies approximately 100 miles due west of this hotel. On that July morning, back in 1945, when Oppenheimer prepared to detonate the 'Gadget', that plutonium device was not clearly understood. The Manhattan Project scientists more completely understood the uranium bomb, so they decided there was little need to test Little Boy. When Little Boy was dropped on Hiroshima, it performed exactly as expected. Some of the Manhattan scientists advised against the Trinity test. They feared the plutonium bomb might initiate a world-wide chain reaction, transforming the Earth into a glowing sun. Despite those fears, on 16 July 1945, the Gadget was detonated at Trinity. Less than a month later, Fat Man, another plutonium bomb, was dropped on Nagasaki.

"In order to open any sort of wormhole, the Chinese would need to develop and employ heretofore unknown physics. They would be 'making it up on the fly', winging it, much like Oppenheimer did with the Gadget. It would seem logical to open that wormhole as far away from China as possible."

Cooper continued his line of questioning, pressing Hiroshi further, "Dr. Yasuda, what type of unexpected consequences would the Chinese fear?"

"Colonel, there is always an element of risk when dealing with the unknown. Opening a wormhole could tear a rift in the very fabric of spacetime with unknown catastrophic effects. That much concentrated energy could form a singularity, a black hole. In a matter of seconds, the Earth might collapse in upon itself, forming a black hole less than one inch in diameter.

"There are other more far-fetched potential outcomes. Our Chinese friends might accidentally initiate a change of state, a phase change of the entire universe."

The Colonel was now even more confused, "You mean like changing water to ice, or steam?"

"That's a good metaphor. We have no idea what would happen if the universe suddenly changed state. After the Big Bang, as the universe expanded and cooled, step by step, the initial unified force began breaking up into the four fundamental forces of nature we know today."

Cowboy Tom chimed in, "Like gravity?"

Hiroshi replied, "Yes Sergeant Jackson, gravity is one of the four forces, along with the electromagnetic force and the strong & weak nuclear forces. These forces are ruled by what we physicists call, 'the God particle', the Higg's Boson."

The Colonel muttered, "You've got to be kidding me."

Dr. Emily wagged her finger at the Colonel in Hiroshi's defense, "No Colonel, he's not kidding. The Higg's Boson controls the four forces. It's a delicate balance. Although the universe seems stable, it's actually metastable. We may be living during a very long plateau, merely a phase. Without warning, in the blink of an eye, another fundamental force might emerge and instantaneously change all physical laws, like reshuffling a deck of cards. I doubt humankind would survive such a metamorphosis.

"For that matter, a change of state may have already occurred in some galaxy far, far away, and is even now rushing toward us at the speed of light.

"But let's suppose, for a moment, that the Chinese don't screw up. Suppose they open a stable wormhole. Maybe someone or something could use it to enter our world."

Thomas listened intently to the discussion, silently suspecting that Lame Wolf's darkest fears might be well-founded.

The Interview

Later that mid-January 1945 afternoon, after his morning meeting with Heisenberg, Reichsminister Speer interviewed two SS Lieutenants in the sitting room of his Ksiaz Castle suite. Both were trained Glocke pilots. One had commanded a Tiger tank on the Eastern Front and the other was an ace Messerschmitt Bf109 pilot. Once selected as Glocke pilots, both men had been transferred to Himmler's Liebstandarte Adolf Hitler, Hitler's Bodyguard.

The first interviewee saluted as he entered the room, "Heil Hitler!"

Speer returned the salute, "Please be seated Herr Leutnant."

Speer carefully assessed the man, blonde hair, blue eyes, in his mid-twenties, about 6'1".

"Leutnant Schneider, I see you are from München."

"Jawohl, Herr Reichsminister."

"You joined the Wehrmacht in 1939?"

"Jawohl. Later, I transferred to the Waffen SS."

"You were in University before the war?"

"Jawohl, University of Stuttgart, Mechanical Engineering."

"You were in the Hitler Youth before joining the Wehrmacht?"

"Jawohl."

"I see that in 1936, while still in the Hitler Youth, you informed the Gestapo that your neighbor had married a Jewish woman in clear violation of the Nuremberg Laws. To hide his crime, the neighbor falsified his wife's birth records."

"Jawohl, Herr Reichsminister! We cannot allow that Jewish filth to soil our Aryan blood!"

"I also see that you served in the 3rd SS Panzer Division, Totenkopf, on the Eastern Front. You commanded a Tiger tank during Operation Citadel."

"I did my duty to my Führer!"

"Yes, you most certainly did. Your record says you destroyed 20 Russian T-34s at Pokrovka! You were awarded the Knight's Cross."

"If I may be so bold, Herr Reichsminister. All that is in the past. How may I serve the Reich and mein Führer today?"

"Can you operate die Glocke?"

"Jawohl!"

"Tomorrow morning, you will accompany me to Berlin. You will not speak to anyone about this project. You will take all future orders from me or your Führer. Understood?"

Next, Herr Speer interviewed the other qualified Glocke pilot. Leutnant Heinz Schuster lacked Schneider's notoriety but was equally devoted to his Führer. Schuster would remain at Ksiaz Castle to ensure that the remaining prototype did not fall into Soviet hands.

Happy Birthday

The Bellaire, Ohio VFW hall was filled to capacity. Prentice "Pee Wee" Dexter was celebrating his 100th birthday. After completing his 25th bombing mission on 1 January 1945, Pee Wee returned home to the greater Wheeling, West Virginia area. Pee Wee was a local semi-celebrity. Around the steel mills, back when there were steel mills, Pee Wee was respectfully nicknamed "Ball Turret". Ball Turret had volunteered around town since his retirement in 1987. In addition to his volunteer work, from time-to-time, for a little spending cash, Pee Wee would pick up an odd job here, or there. He quit the odd jobs when he turned 85, but he continued to volunteer. For a centenarian, Ball Turret was in great shape.

In November 2025, WTRF was the only local TV station in the Wheeling area. The Pittsburg stations dominated the Wheeling broadcast TV market. The WTRF reporter was growing tired of reporting on spiraling crime and violent political demonstrations. This human-interest story, featuring Pee Wee's 100th birthday, was a nice change of pace, a feel-good story.

"Mr. Dexter, please tell our viewers just a little bit about your 25 bombing missions over Germany?"

"Well young fella, not all were over Germany, but most were. I was scared shitless every time we flew over the Reich."

"Can you give the folks at home a taste of what you faced during your missions?"

"I'm just a little guy. The crew called me Pee Wee. They always stuck the smallest enlisted man down in the ball turret."

"Describe the ball turret to our younger viewers who may not be familiar with a B-17."

"The B-17 was called the Flying Fortress for good reason. It was defended by thirteen .50 caliber Browning machineguns. Two of those guns were in the ball turret beneath the fuselage. Picture a glass fishbowl attached to the underbelly of an airplane with dual machineguns sticking out."

"Did you shoot down any enemy aircraft?"

"That's hard to say young feller. Our bombers flew in a 'Combat Box' formation with interlocking fields of fire. I may have shot down a half dozen Messerschmitts and maybe a couple of Focke-Wulfs. But, then again, maybe I didn't hit a damned thing. I didn't envy those Kraut fighter pilots one bit. When they dove through a formation of B-17s, we gave as good as we got."

"Pee Wee, did you ever see any of those Nazi wonder weapons?"

"In late 1944, we started seeing those Me 262 jets. We also saw a couple of Me 163 Komet rocket planes. The jets were big trouble for us. Good thing the Krauts didn't develop those jets earlier. At that late stage of the war, they couldn't mass produce those machines. Those plywood Komets were last ditch contraptions, practically suicidal."

"How about the Foo Fighters reported by some bomber crews?"

Pee Wee went speechless. He nervously glanced around the room.

"Mr. Dexter, excuse me, did you ever see a UFO?"

Pee Wee smiled a wry smile and chuckled, "Son, I'm a hundred years old. It's 2025. I've not even hinted at this for 80 years. They told me this was classified."

The correspondent snapped his fingers and motioned for his cameraman to zoom in on Pee Wee's face.

"What can they do to me now? I'm gonna give you a scoop!

"We were returning to England on our final mission, our 25th mission. Katzenjammer Kid, that's what we named our Fortress, was just leaving

Germany. It was New Year's Day 1945. The air was cold and clear. We were back over friendly territory, no flak and no bandits.

"I got a perfect view as, whatever it was, streaked by in a shallow dive."

"What was it?"

"All I could see was smoke, sparks, and a glowing object. It was descending much too fast to be an aircraft. Not even a jet or rocket could move that fast."

"Was it a meteor?"

"Don't know. It didn't maneuver. Whatever it was, it sure left its calling card."

"What do you mean?"

"One of the aircraft in our formation, Lady Liberty, just blew up. Lady Lib wasn't hit. She didn't crash. She just exploded in a huge fireball. That's when our intercom started spewing out static and the Kid's compass needle started spinning faster than her props. Every steel surface in the ball turret was magnetized and St. Elmo's Fire danced along the leading edges of both wings."

"Come on Pee Wee, what was it?"

Pee Wee just shook his head, "It was a damned UFO!"

Orders

Cooper caught his breath, "So, the ChiComs know they are playing with fire. They figure, if things go south, it's better to burn down the house on the other side of town, rather than their own."

Dr. Emily replied, "Something like that."

Colonel Cooper turned to Tom, "Sergeant Jackson, do you have anything else to add?"

"Colonel, Sir, this is hearsay, but I consider the source reliable. A Hispanic restauranteur on the west side of Magdalena told us about strange goings on out at the VLA. He called it "Unearthly". He said the Chinese scientists who patronize his café brag about bringing the stars closer."

"Is that all Sergeant?"

"No, there's more. This is gonna sound crazy, but I've learned to respect Native American mysticism."

Tom turned to Dr. Emily, "Dr. Leroy learned to respect it too."

"My Navajo guide, Lame Wolf, claims that the Chinese are disrupting the heavens."

Cooper was attempting to wrap his mind around what seemed like so much science fiction fantasy, "Sergeant Jackson, I cannot base my recommendations upon superstition and hearsay, but such evidence can support other, more concrete intelligence. I am convinced that something very big is going down at the Very Large Array.

"Doctors Bowser and Yasuda, continue your scientific investigation. We will forward further intel as it becomes available. You're dismissed."

Tom started to get up out of his chair.

"Stand fast, Sergeant!"

After the two scientists left the room, Colonel Cooper addressed the military issues, "Sergeant Jackson, at this very moment, Captain Delvin Smith's rare earth convoy is safely dispersed in Springerville, Arizona, less than 100 miles west of the Array. Lieutenant Josephine Parker is part of that convoy and has brought along her Huey Cobra gunship. That asset could take out the VLA, setting back Chinese efforts for perhaps months, most probably years.

"Before we destroy the Array, and destroy it we must, we need more intel as to what our Oriental friends are really doing at that facility.

"Before we do anything with the Array, we must ensure the safe delivery of those two containers of rare earth concentrates to Roswell. Then, and only then, we're gonna level the VLA, capture as many Chinese eggheads as possible, and neutralize the Array's security force.

"It's too bad we have insufficient force to deal with the Array and take out the hostile forces at Socorro and Truth or Consequences. Our rare earth highway would be wide open if we could clear out those two rat's nests. Well, almost wide open. We would still have one big problem, Dark Cloud."

Tom cleared his throat and replied, "Colonel, Sir, may I speak freely?"

Professional Courtesy

Brett had just returned to his Hampton Hall condo. He planned on catching a couple of hours sleep, then do a little show prep. Just one more night guest hosting *Sea-to-Sea*. After that, he wasn't scheduled to host another show for at least two weeks. That was a good thing. Brett's latest book, *Things That Go Bump in Steel City,* was ready for release and his schedule of personal appearances would keep him more than busy. As Hoffman undressed for bed, his cellphone rang.

"Hey Brett, it's Mike.

"I just wrapped a human interest shoot over here in Bellaire, Ohio. It'll air tonight at 11. I hear the CBS affiliate in Pittsburgh may pick it up."

"OK, should I tune in this evening before my *Sea-to-Sea* broadcast?"

"You could, but I thought you might like to take a sneak peek at the whole unedited piece this afternoon."

"Come on Mike, I'm very busy."

"Let's just call it professional courtesy. Look it, I'm heading over to a shoot at Pitt. How about I swing by your place? You won't be sorry."

"OK. I'm gonna try and catch a few winks. Ring the buzzer and pound on the door cause I'll probably be sound asleep."

"Should be there in about an hour and a half."

Upon arrival at Hampton Hall, Mike was out of the OB van in a flash.

The reporter turned to his driver/cameraman, "Stay here in the van with the engine running. This should only take a few minutes."

Parking was always at a premium in Oakland and Squirrel Hill. The OB van was parked in the loading zone out front of Hampton Hall. Usually, traffic cops cut TV news vans a little slack, but very little. Brett's third floor condo faced the front of the building, overlooking Dithridge Street.

Brett had set his alarm for 90 minutes. Mike was not yet banging on the door, but it was not unusual to get snarled up in traffic crossing any one of Pittsburgh's many bridges. Brett peeked out his window and saw the OB van parked in the loading zone. He also saw a gray sedan parked across the street. Hoffman couldn't tell if the sedan was occupied.

Mike's cellphone began playing one of those irritating ring tones.

"Hello, Mike. Don't react to anything I say. I'm peeking out my front window. There's a gray car parked across the street."

"Yes, there is."

"Anyone inside?"

"Yes, there is."

"Is it a young lady with long black hair?"

"Bingo! You're three for three."

"OK, come on up and don't stare at the gray car."

Mike replayed his Pee Wee's Birthday segment for Brett, "Well Brett, what did you think of Mr. Pee Wee's interview?"

"Can you get me a copy?"

"Will this CD be OK?" Mike tossed Brett a compact disk.

"That will do. And Mike, watch your back."

Mike broke out laughing, but his laughter disappeared when he saw that Brett was deadly serious.

"OK, can you come down to the van and do a little promo for tonight's interview?"

Brett agreed and followed Mike down to the van. Brett did a short promo for that evening's Pee Wee interview, right there on the sidewalk, out front of his condo. When Hoffman glanced across the street, the gray sedan was gone.

The Curve Ball

"Colonel Cooper, as I recall, you took part in the Wonsan Campaign."

"Yes Sergeant, back in '25, I was nothing but a wet behind the ears Butter Bar. That was one hairy situation. You did good over there, Cowboy."

Jones had no idea what the two Marines were talking about.

"Colonel, do you recall Captain Cloud?"

"Hell yes! He wasn't my direct superior, but most everybody knew The Apache. He just up and disappeared once we got back home and the shit hit the fan."

"I found him."

"Sergeant, where is he? We could use a good man like Cloud!"

"I found him over in Ruidoso."

Cooper was totally confused, "In Ruidoso? Is he Dark Cloud's prisoner?"

Tom turned to Jones, "Agent Jones, could the Colonel and I have a brief moment of privacy?"

Jones didn't respond.

"Jones! Get your spooky ass out of here!" The Colonel sternly pointed toward the door.

Once Cooper ran Jones out of the meeting room, Thomas replied, "There is no Dark Cloud."

"Jackson, have you lost your fucking mind? We constantly receive intel, from HUMINT assets all along the Pecos, detailing Dark Cloud's many atrocities."

Thomas paused, then asked a direct question, "Colonel, Sir, I mean no offense, nor disrespect. Are you still loyal to your Oath? Are you loyal to the Constitution?"

The mere fact that Thomas asked such a question shocked the Colonel, "Hell yes Sergeant, Sempre Fi!"

"Colonel, Sir, Dark Cloud and Captain Cloud are one in the same, but his people refer to him as 'Great Chief'. We have much to discuss."

Return to the Führerbunker

It was wheels up at dawn for the Arado. Albert Speer and his new protégé, Leutnant Wolfgang Schneider, had a mid-morning appointment in Berlin. It was broad daylight, so the Arado was flying much lower on its return trip, weaving in and out of the mountains to avoid detection. A flight of P-51 Mustangs briefly caught a glimpse of the Arado, but just couldn't catch her.

The jet landed and taxied up to the Templehof Terminal. Speer and Schneider deplaned and proceeded into the terminal. A driver and two uniformed Gestapo officers were waiting for the Reichsminister. Speer saluted with his right hand, then waved off the driver and the Gestapo with his left.

"My comrade and I will walk, thank you."

The driver and the Gestapo couldn't understand why Speer would prefer to walk through bomb shattered and burned-out Berlin, but they dared not question the Reichsminister.

"Leutnant Schneider, the Luftbrücke underground station lies less than 200 meters to the northwest."

Speer and Schneider quickly covered the 200 meters of war-ravaged Berlin streets and descended into the Luftbrücke subway station. Overhead, a large formation of American bombers began dropping their payloads.

"Herr Reichsminister, today it's the B-24s."

Speer sarcastically replied, "Ja, Ja, tonight, it will be Lancasters, and tomorrow hundreds of B-17s."

The two men quickly descended to the lower level of the station, amid an avalanche of humanity seeking refuge from the raining death above. Speer led Schneider to an obscure corner, somewhat removed from the rail platform. A small group of enslaved Polish stonemasons, under Gestapo supervision, were busy completing the entrance to a newly constructed tunnel.

"Herr Leutnant, this tunnel was originally planned to terminate at Templehof Airport, but I fear we haven't enough time to finish construction. So, the final 200 meters from Luftbrücke Station to Templehof must be traversed above ground."

A perplexed Schneider acknowledged Speer's instructions.

"Once you exit this doorway, on your way to make the jump, the masons must quickly brick it up and cover the entire wall with plaster. The plaster must exactly match the plaster throughout the station. Do you understand?"

"Jawohl! Herr Reichsminister, where exactly does this tunnel lead?"

"A little over 3 kilometers to the north, to the Reich Chancellery."

Wolfgang expressed concern, "Does the tunnel cross under the Landwehrkanal?"

Schneider was referring to a canal, built in the late 19th Century, running between the Führerbunker and Luftbrücke Station.

Speer chuckled, "Leutnant, if the Wehrmacht could so easily cross all those rivers in the East, while under constant Bolshevik bombardment, why should tunneling beneath a canal in downtown Berlin pose any problem?"

The two men quickly traversed the 3-kilometer tunnel and emerged in the Führerbunker, beneath the Reich Chancellery.

Schneider was confused, "Herr Reichsminister, this is not the Reich Chancellery."

"Nein, Herr Leutnant, we are below the Reich Chancellery. We are in the Führerbunker!"

Schneider snapped to attention as a forlorn, but familiar face greeted him, "Heil Hitler!"

Schneider's Führer, Adolf Hitler, returned the salute, "So, Speer, this is the mighty Bolshevik slayer!"

"Mein Führer, may I introduce Leutnant Wolfgang Schneider. Schneider was awarded the Knight's Cross for destroying 20 Soviet tanks at Pokrovka."

Hitler extended his right hand, while hiding his trembling left hand behind his back. Schneider's face was beaming as he shook his Führer's hand.

The Führer took a step back and rather theatrically pointed at Schneider with his outstretched right hand, "Speer, I submit to you that Leutnant Schneider is the ideal Aryan soldier!"

Schneider stood motionless as a statue while the Führer sized him up, "My boy, let's have some tea and cake. I want to hear the details of how you destroyed the untermenschen."

"Nein Speer! Not here in the Conference Room! Let's talk in my Sitting Room."

"Frau Junge, some tea and cake please. I wish not to be disturbed!"

The three men retired to the Führer's small private sitting room.

"So, Herr Leutnant, how did you defeat the Bolsheviks at Kursk?"

"Mein Führer, it was simple tactics. The Tiger's 88 mm cannon can penetrate the T-34's armor at 1,000 meters. The T-34 must get much closer to penetrate the Tiger's armor with its 76.2 mm gun. The Bolsheviks charged our Tiger like a pack of ravenous wolves. The T-34 is swifter, more maneuverable, and can rotate its turret faster than the Tiger. Some Mark VI crews charged headlong into battle to confront the onrushing T-34s. That was incorrect strategy.

"I constantly drilled my crew on firing while giving ground. We did not allow the T-34s to close range or take us in the rear. As we gave ground, we coolly marked our targets and destroyed the T-34s as fast as we could fire the 88.

"Our antitank guns were positioned to our rear. As we retreated, we drew the Bolshevik tanks into a killing field. I can assure you that our antitank guns destroyed many more Soviet machines."

The Führer slapped his right hand down on the coffee table, "There you have it, Speer! Just as I said the other day, Leutnant Schneider demonstrates the superiority of the Aryan mind.

"Herr Leutnant, I'm certain you are a most dedicated soldier of the Fatherland, but are you a dedicated National Socialist?"

"I have sworn an oath to my Führer. I am a loyal National Socialist as long as National Socialism is loyal to my Führer!"

Hitler was elated, "The perfect answer, my son."

Speer could see that the Führer was enamored with the young man.

"Mein Führer, Schneider has been loyal to the Party since his youth. I'm sure you have heard of his devotion while a mere lad in the Hitler Jugend?"

"Ah yes, now I recall. Your traitorous neighbor was consorting with that Jewish trash. Good job, my boy! We cannot allow our Aryan blood to be polluted by such filth."

Once again, the Führer abruptly switched gears, "Speer, is the device at Tempelhof?"

"Jawohl, mein Führer! It is undergoing final preparations."

"Herr Leutnant, can you pilot that machine?"

"Jawohl, mein Führer!"

Speer described the harrowing escape route from Templehof Airport to the Führerbunker, "Leutnant Schneider and I travelled from the Luftbrücke underground station to the Führerbunker via the new tunnel. I regret to report that we were forced to travel 200 meters above ground, from Templehof to the Luftbrücke Station. I fear the final section of the tunnel will not be completed in time."

A scowl came over the Führer's face, "Do you think me incapable of traversing 200 meters under gunfire? Need I remind you that, during the Great War, before the 'Stab in the Back', I was a dispatch runner. I ran from trench to trench, kilometer after kilometer, dodging artillery and machinegun fire. I survived being gassed, just as I recently survived that bomb planted by that traitorous Colonel Stauffenberg. It is Providence, Speer! I will survive once more."

On and off, for the remainder of the day, Speer and his Führer discussed details of their plan. Meanwhile, Leutnant Schneider familiarized himself with the Führerbunker's floorplan and the newly constructed escape tunnel to Luftbrücke Station.

Keystone State Bigfoot

"Brett, switch on your TV."

"Mike, I'm just walking out the door. I'm on air in two hours."

"It's about Pee Wee…"

"I've already watched your entire unedited interview. I even gave you a promo. Give me a break."

"Brett, he's dead. Someone busted into his house and double tapped him in the head."

Brett was momentarily shaken, "Mike, are you home? Are the wife and kids with you?"

"Yeah, we're all here. We're all OK."

"Listen buddy, something is going on. Lock all your doors and keep some lights on. Have you got a gun?"

"Whoa there cowboy, you've been in the tinfoil hat conspiracy business just a little too long. Pee Wee was just a victim of a home invasion gone wrong."

Brett peeked out his front window down onto Dithridge Street.

"Maybe you should tell that to the chick in the gray sedan. She's back."

"Have you ever considered she might be another *Sea-to-Sea* groupie, or even a Brett Hoffman stalker?"

"Don't think so. Do me a favor and watch your back. Call me if anything else develops."

Immediately after speaking with Mike, Brett walked over to his bedroom closet, opened the door, and retrieved a dusty, black case from the top shelf.

He opened the case and removed a 9 mm Parabellum. Although he didn't have a concealed carry permit, Brett had bigger fish to fry. He slid the loaded Luger into his right coat pocket, then stepped out the door.

As Brett pulled out of the Hampton Hall parking lot, he glanced to his left. There she was, parked just a couple of car lengths up Dithridge. Brett hung a right out of the lot. The chick in the sedan discreetly followed at a distance. Whoever she was, she knew how to tail a mark. By the time Brett crossed the Fort Pitt Bridge, he could no longer see the gray car in his rearview mirror, but it was dark, and the I-376 traffic was relatively heavy.

It was 11:35 p.m. when Brett pulled into the East Carnegie office park. He slowly circled the building.

"Nope! No gray sedan. Must have lost her."

Brett heaved a sigh of relief as he parked under a streetlamp, directly in front of the KDKA studio entrance. With Luger in hand, Brett made a beeline for the door.

Brett completed his show prep by 12:35 a.m. By that time, 6 invited guests were shivering outside the studio's front door. Brett checked their IDs through the glass. A satisfied Hoffman let them in, then gave them a thumbnail sketch of that evening's show and their order of appearance. At 1 a.m. Eastern, *Sea-to-Sea AM* was once again on the air.

"Good evening to our audience from sea to shining sea. Once again, this is your somewhat regular guest host, Brett Hoffman, coming to you from the KDKA studios in the Steel City. The subject of this morning's show is *Keystone State Bigfoot.* For all you fans unfamiliar with Pennsylvania, the northern third of the Keystone State, roughly everything north of I-80, is rugged, mountainous forest. It's perfect Sasquatch habitat.

"Joining me in-studio tonight are a half dozen Northern PA residents who claim to have encountered Bigfoot up close and personal. After the break, we'll welcome our first guest."

For the next two hours, Brett interviewed four of his guests and took numerous phone calls. Mr. Call Screener was once again working his butt off screening an avalanche of calls. Brett Hoffman was having yet another successful guest host appearance.

At the top of the third hour, during the break for network news, Brett's cell phone rang. It was Mike.

"Brett, my source with the Bellaire PD just called. Pee Wee was shot with a 9 mm."

"Mike, were the bullets sufficiently intact to determine weapon type?"

"Yes, one bullet fragmented, but the other is relatively intact. We should have detailed ballistics results tomorrow."

Brett replied, "I'll make a prediction. Pee Wee was shot with a Luger."

Farmhouse Invasion Fail

Stan the Man had not been charged but was being held for questioning at the Westmoreland County Sheriff's Department in Greensburg, Pennsylvania.

Earlier that morning, Stan plopped down in his recliner to listen to *Sea-to-Sea AM,* guest hosted by his newfound bestie, Brett Hoffman. Stan dimmed the lights in the living room of his ancestral family home near Kecksburg. A double barreled, 12-gauge, Remington Semi-Auto lay on the floor to Stan's right and Blue Dog was sleeping on the floor to his left. Every so often, Stan would nod off to sleep, only to be awakened as Brett returned from a commercial break.

At the top of *Sea-to-Sea's* third and final hour, Blue Dog began growling that low, angry, territorial growl. Australian Blue Heelers are known for their intelligence, loyalty, and protective nature. Blue Dog was true to his breed. His ears went up as he turned his head toward the front window.

Stan's eyes popped wide open. His right hand reached down for his shotgun. Stan slowly put his left index finger to his lips.

"Shhh, Blue, Shhh."

Blue Dog joined Stan, crouching behind his recliner. Both man and dog had eyes transfixed upon the front window. Stan glimpsed a shadow fleeting across the front porch. Blue Dog cocked his head and turned to his master, as if seeking further instructions.

Stan whispered, "Steady Blue. Quiet Blue Dog. When that bastard comes through that window, his ass belongs to us."

Blue Dog was now silently baring his teeth, up on his tippy toes, ready to pounce.

A knife blade slid up between the double hung front window and threw the latch. Stan could now see a black silhouette prying up the bottom window sash.

"Steady Blue, wait till he comes inside."

The stubborn window finally popped loose and slowly opened. A leg came through first. Stan could now see a head and torso poking through the window.

Once inside, the window slammed shut behind the intruder. On cue, Blue Dog sprang like a coiled cobra. Two pistol shots rang out, mortally wounding Stan's recliner. Simultaneously, Blue chomped down on the invader's right ankle while Stan unloaded both barrels of double aught buck from a range of 20 feet. The impact from the shotgun blasts blew the intruder backwards through the now closed window. Shards of glass, strips of black leather, and a mixed spray of buckshot and blood plastered the window casing and front porch.

"911 Dispatch, name and address please.

"What is the nature of your emergency?"

"There's a body on my front porch."

"Is the victim breathing?"

"Victim my ass! This guy came through my front window, into my living room, and fired his pistol twice."

"Is the intruder breathing?"

"Hell no! I unloaded two barrels of 12 gauge double aught buck from about 20 feet."

"Please secure all firearms. A deputy is en route. ETA: 10 minutes."

Stan stared down at the Luger, still smoking in the dead man's hand. This wasn't a local boy. His car had to be parked somewhere close by. Stan had only a few minutes to find it. Flashlight and Remington in hand, Stan & Blue Dog carefully crept out his lane to the county road.

Stan mumbled to himself, "Careful Stan, he could have kameraden hiding somewhere out here."

A black, late-model BMW was parked amongst a clump of trees along the county road right-of-way. It was unlocked. The interior of the import was spotless. The intruder's cellphone was in one of those holders attached to the dash and a high end Leica digital camera was sitting in the passenger's seat. Stan grabbed both in his gloved hands, taking care not to leave any trace of his presence. An apprehensive Stan the Man ran back to the house and stashed the cellphone and camera in Blue Dog's doghouse, out in the backyard kennel.

Two sets of flashing red and blue lights came racing up Stan's lane. The Sheriff's Department patrol car was in the lead, closely followed by an EMS ambulance. Stan laid his shotgun down alongside the dead man, then waved his flashlight at the Deputy. Every light in Stan's house was on.

"Coach Stan, what in the world happened out here?"

"Jesse, I have no idea." Stan was a lifelong Kecksburg resident and, many moons ago, Stan had been Deputy Jesse Franks' little league baseball coach.

The EMT confirmed what everyone already knew, "He's dead alright. Two blasts of double aught buck to the torso from close range. That'll do it every time."

"Coach let's go inside and I'll take your statement. The detectives are on their way. They'll probably want you to come down to the station for further questioning, but it looks like a textbook case of self-defense."

"Can I take a minute and lock Blue Dog in his run? He's real territorial. Wouldn't want him to bite any of you men."

Clues

At 6 a.m., Brett had just climbed into bed. It never failed. His cellphone rang.

"Brett, Stan here. I've got a little situation down here in Greensburg."

"Stan, it's 6 a.m. I'm tired. Can this wait a few hours?"

"I'm sure you're tired, old buddy, but the body is only getting colder."

Brett still suspected that Stan bordered on the flakey side, "What body?"

"The body of the guy I shot at the top of your third hour!"

Brett was now wide awake, "Stan, are you shitting me?"

"Nope. I'm down at the Westmoreland County Sheriff's Office in Greensburg. A couple of detectives are tying up the loose ends. They're not going to charge me. That bastard broke into my house and got off a couple of free shots."

"He shot at you?"

"Twice! Missed me but got my Lazy Boy. Come on down. You can crash at the house."

"What was he packing?"

"A Luger."

"I'm on my way. Be there in an hour."

Stan was walking out of the Sheriff's Office as Brett arrived in Greensburg. Stan the Man was calm, cool, and collected.

"Great show last night. Well, at least the first two hours were great. I was sorta busy during your final hour.

"Brett, you look like shit. Let's walk over to the White Rabbit Café and grab a bite. It'll be my treat again."

"Stan, this is one terrific place."

"Yeah, the coffee and tea are primo. The Danish and blueberry muffins are to die for. Oops, I didn't really mean that."

Stan proceeded to update Brett on the foiled home invasion, then gave him the big news.

"Follow me home. You can crash there. I've got the dead guy's cellphone and digital camera hidden in Blue's doghouse."

"You what?"

"I said, I've got the perp's cellphone and camera!"

"Stan, that could be construed as obstructing a police investigation."

"Nah, I'm not obstructing. You get some of your tech geek friends to download everything off the two devices, then I'll find them in the bushes around my front porch. I promise that I'll turn them over to the Sheriff just as soon as I find them. Now, answer your cellphone."

"Hoffman here! Hey Mike, what's the word from Ballistics?"

"How in the hell did you know Pee Wee was shot with a Luger?"

"That's my job. Now, have I got a scoop for you. I'm heading down to Kecksburg. About 3 a.m. this morning, a home invasion was thwarted by the homeowner, armed with a shotgun."

"Did he get the perp?"

"Blew his shit away, but only after the perp fired two shots. The Westmoreland County Sheriff has the weapon."

"Hoffman, don't tell me, it's a Luger."

"OK, I won't tell you, but I suspect Ballistics will confirm it's the same Luger used to murder Pee Wee."

Becoming Tony

Before James Wu got out of the chair, Ralph the Barber spun him around to take a peek in the mirror. James eyes were tightly shut. He was afraid to look.

"Jesus Christ Almighty, what kind of pussy are you? I thought you Chinamen were into bald in a big way."

James slowly raised his left eyelid. The sight left him nauseous.

Ralph was rather proud of his work, "You look like a regular cueball. After I shaved your noggin, I applied a depilatory wax. You should be good to go for at least a month."

Wu ran his right hand over his smooth, bald head, then glanced down at his hair, lying on the barbershop floor.

As Jimmy headed for the exit, Ralph passed along a parting message, "Oh, I almost forgot. That Jones character asked me to tell you to go directly to the Clinic…" Midsentence, Ralph tossed Jimmy a PayDay bar, "…and he said to eat this."

Jimmy stepped out of the barbershop onto slush covered Main Street. His exposed scalp was freezing. James reached into his coat pocket and retrieved a woolen toboggan. He pulled the toboggan over his bald head and on down over his ears.

The Austin Clinic was on Main Street, only a couple of blocks south of the National Café, an easy 5-minute walk. James wasn't the least bit hungry, but he stuffed down the candy bar as he walked. As he entered the Clinic, Jimmy expected to be greeted by Cindy, the receptionist. Cindy was not behind the counter. James opened the swinging door leading to the Clinic's half dozen treatment rooms. Neither the RN, Mary, nor the Nurse Practitioner, Juliet, were on duty. Two masked men in scrubs appeared from a small scrub room at the far end of the hallway.

The shorter man was preoccupied, reading a chart. The taller man saw James and paused.

"Hello, you must be Mr. Lin?"

James was caught off guard, but caught himself before saying, "No".

"Yes, I'm Tony."

"Step into Treatment Room #4 and have a seat."

Tony sat down in a chair adjacent to a stainless-steel exam table. The dermal laser, sitting on that table, appeared to be something straight out of a *007* movie.

"Mr. Lin, there is no need for general anesthetic. We'll only numb your fingertips. It's our understanding that we need to alter all your fingerprints?"

Tony thought back upon Chinese State Security's induction process. CSS was very thorough. They took a full set of prints from both hands.

"Yes, we must alter all my prints, including my thumbprints."

The taller doctor continued calling the shots, "OK Tony, we're not going to obliterate your prints. We're not going to completely change your prints. We're going to change your prints just enough that fingerprint matching AI will not link your new prints with your old prints on file. This device will scan your natural prints, then design a set of new prints. The new prints will defeat any known fingerprint matching program with a 95% degree of confidence. The new fingerprints will be designed to require the least amount of dermal laser alteration. We should be finished in a couple of hours. Then, we'll give you some gloves to wear for the next few days. Within a week, you won't need the gloves. Within three weeks, you'll be completely healed. The surgery will leave no trace."

One hour and fifty-four minutes later, Tony Lin slipped on a pair of protective gloves as he headed toward the Clinic's front door.

Just as Tony was about to step outside, the short, chubby doctor finally spoke, "Oh I almost forgot. Mr. Jones said you should eat this." A Twinkie came sailing through the air, in Tony's direction.

Halfway back to the National Café, a familiar face approached Tony.

Tony gulped down the last bite of Twinkie, then unloaded, "Damn it Jones, I don't wanna hear another thing. You've shaved my head, burnt my fingertips, and now you're fattening me up like a finishing pig."

Jones smiled and replied, "0800 tomorrow morning at the school. Report to Gilbert."

As Jones turned to disappear down a side street, he glanced back at Tony and silently pointed at the bridge of his nose.

Tony gritted his teeth as he slipped on his dorky Coke Bottle glasses.

Advice

"Speer let's discuss the larger issues. You can handle the details like switching the medical and dental records."

"Already in process, mein Führer, but there is much more to it than that. We must collect quantities of your blood and hair. I suspect we'll need the same from Fraulein Eva. We will plant that evidence on the burnt bodies and on your sofa. My scientific advisers speculate that, sometime in the future, some type of genetic fingerprinting may be developed."

"Speer, you think of everything. Come, let's talk in my sitting room. My comments are for your ears only. It is pure bedlam out here."

It was pure chaos throughout the common areas of the Führerbunker. Although deep underground, with 10-foot-thick reinforced concrete walls, the Allied bombing could still be heard and felt down in the bunker. It sounded like distant, rolling thunder and felt like an unrelenting and ever-growing earthquake. The Führerbunker's atmosphere was depressing. Demoralized staff officers and common soldiers milled about, dreading the inevitable, growing ever more frantic by the day and the hour.

The Führer was now seated in his private space with Blondi's pup, Wolf, cradled in his right arm.

Here, Hitler felt at ease and could speak bluntly with his beloved Architect, "Fatso Goering and that cowardly mystic, Himmler, are even now plotting and scheming. They plan to sellout to the Americans and British, then usurp my power."

The Führer began nervously rapping the knuckles of his right hand on an end table. His left arm and hand were uncontrollably trembling, hidden from view behind his back.

"Borman has been a loyal and capable administrator, but he lacks the backbone to endure the approaching apocalypse. He cannot be trusted. He is too weak."

"What about Reichsminister Goebbels?"

In a moment of candor, Hitler responded with true affection, "Mein Doktor is a dedicated National Socialist. He has never failed me. He will not be taken alive by the Bolsheviks. I submit that Doktor Goebbels, Frau Goebbels, and their six beautiful children are the model Aryan family.

"They will die here, one level above us, in the Vorbunker, defending the Reich. They must not be troubled with this plan. Only you and Skorzeny will know. No one else!"

"Mein Führer, forgive me for being so bold. What of Fraulein Braun?"

"Eva is an innocent child. She is my refuge from all the subterfuge that surrounds me. We will be married before the end. She will be with me at the end. If we prevail, Frau Hitler will be by my side. If we fail, she shall die with me. Make your plans accordingly.

"Speer, mark my words. The Allies will hold some form of tribunal, a Soviet style show trial. It is foolish to think that surrendering to the Americans or British will be advantageous in the long term. They will attempt to present a united front with the Bolsheviks for as long as possible. But do surrender to the Americans, if possible. You will receive better treatment from them in the near term.

"You will play the role of 'The Good Nazi'. That will be your post-war personae."

"Mein Führer, they will hang us all!"

Once again, Hitler became agitated, "Nein, Nein, Nein! Focus on the Americans. They fancy themselves morally superior. They constantly root for, what is the term? Oh yes, they constantly root for the underdog. You will be 'born again' as their evangelists say. You knew nothing of Himmler's Final Solution to the Jewish Question."

"Mein Führer, if I may ask, how do you know such things?"

"In my youth, I read many dime store novels chronicling the taming of the American frontier. Before the war, I watched many Hollywood motion pictures. I admire the way the Americans exterminated those red savages and expropriated their lands. If you watch those films carefully, you will see how Americans cling to their fairytale belief in second chances and redemption. You must play into their weakness. Portray yourself as 'The Good Nazi', endure, and wait. Gain their sympathy."

"What of Leutnant Schneider?"

"If we prevail, I have my own plans for that young man. As I said, he is the ideal Aryan soldier."

"Mein Führer, what of your so-called Nero Decree?"

"Do as you will Speer. Better yet, betray me! Countermand my scorched earth decree. You can use that to feed the Americans' naïve fantasy that you were the only Good Nazi.

"Nature demands that only the strong should survive. If the German people are not strong, they will die. They should die!

Once more, Hitler randomly shifted gears, "Why is it Speer that our conversations open my mind to infinite possibilities?"

"You are referring to our plan for a new Berlin, a new Reich's capital?"

"Ja, Germania. Germania would have been the center of the Thousand Year Reich. Only a dream, Speer, only a dream.

"The Bolsheviks stand in our way. Germany does not have the resources to defeat the entire world. Our people are too genteel, too bourgeois. They are Aryan, but they have lost their Wagnerian essence."

Completely out of character, Hitler burst out with a short laugh, "I should have recruited some Texas cowboys to lead my panzers in the East!"

TW POWELL © 2023

"Mein Führer, I have read that some of those cowboys were Negroes."

"I would hire only Aryan cowboys!"

Hitler's face froze in place. Speer momentarily feared that his Führer had suffered some sort of seizure, or stroke.

"Mein Führer, are you well?"

The Führer's face quickly reverted to its 1939 look of determination and certainty, "If the German people cannot save the Aryan race, then other Aryans must rise up and fulfill that destiny. They must have the resources to defeat the Bolsheviks and International Judaism. They must be inventive and resourceful. It would be better if they were not surrounded by their enemies. It is now becoming oh so clear to me."

Extended Engagement

The two 9 mm bullet holes in the back of Stan the Man's Lazy Boy recliner didn't prevent him from taking a good snooze. After all, he had been up all night, shooting intruders and undergoing interrogation by homicide detectives. Brett sacked out on Stan's feather bed, snoring so loudly that a pissed off Blue Dog finally gave up and ducked out his rear doggy door.

Meanwhile, back in KDKA's studio, *Sea-to-Sea's* producer had exhausted all his options. Vince, the regular host, was sick as a dog. Hoffman had never failed the *Sea-to-Sea* team. Brett's cellphone rang once more.

"Hey Brett, is this a good time?"

A half-awake Brett replied, "Yeah, Yeah, I was just taking a snooze."

"Sorry, I'll make this quick. Can you fill in tonight for Vince? He's really sick."

"Yeah, I'll cover. Given the late notice, we'll have to just go with 'open lines'. Is that, OK?"

"We're cool. Sometimes open lines end up being killer shows."

A now wide-awake Brett decided it was time to hit the road. He stuffed his loaded Luger under his car seat along with the dead assassin's cellphone and digital camera. Stan promised Brett that he would sleep in his recliner with cellphone, shotgun, and Blue Dog by his side.

A few minutes later, Brett's cellphone rang in through his BMW's Bluetooth, "Brett, Mike here. You were spot on. Ballistics matched the bullets recovered from Pee Wee's body with the ones fired at Stan."

"Nice work, Mike. I'm heading over to Carnegie Mellon. Let's just say I could have some major leads. Have your police contacts get you everything they've got on the dead man. They owe you big time. You put them onto the connection between Pee Wee's murder and the shooting at Stan's place.

"I'll be up late tonight. Unscheduled gig on *Sea-to-Sea*. Mike, are you packing?"

"Not yet. Swinging by my brother's place. He's letting me borrow his pistol."

"That dark haired chick in the gray car…"

"Yeah, what about her?"

"I'm pretty sure she's carrying. Watch yourself and tell the wife and kids to stay alert."

Carnegie Mellon is a Top 10 university. Its School of Computer Science is arguably the best in the nation, if not the world. Much like Mike had his contacts at police departments throughout the Pittsburgh area, Brett had nurtured an ensemble of academic cronies at Pitt, Carnegie Mellon, and the other smaller colleges and universities in the Greater Pittsburgh area. Brett's contact at the School of Computer Science was much more than a mere crony. Dr. Daniel Lipman was a Turing Award recipient. The Turing Award is also known as the Nobel Prize of Computing.

Doctor Dan had made several guest appearances on *Sea-to-Sea AM*. Only a couple of months earlier, Dan had joined Brett for a discussion of the dangers of artificial intelligence. A few months before that, Dan answered listener's questions about human/machine interfaces and the possibility of encountering alien AI. Brett had talked Dan into authoring a series of popular books on the sci-fi aspects of computer science. Dan had parlayed those books into a hit show on one of cable TV's science channels. Dan and Brett were tight.

That afternoon, Brett asked Dan to meet him at one of the many delis in Squirrel Hill. Hoffman requested that Doctor Dan bring along his best hacker, someone who could undetectably access most any device and knew how to keep his mouth shut.

"Good afternoon Brett, why are we meeting over here in Squirrel Hill?"

"Anonymity. Is this your hacker?"

Dan made the introductions, "Jerry Patel, this is Mr. UFO himself, Brett Hoffman.

"Brett, this is the perhaps the most capable hacker in the world and soon to be Doctor Patel."

Brett and Jerry shook hands and exchanged the customary pleasantries. Then Brett abruptly bade Dan a fond adieu.

"Dan, it's time for you to go."

"Well, aren't you one rude SOB this afternoon!"

Hoffman negatively shook his head, "No, I'm being your lawyer. Time for you to go. Jerry stays."

It suddenly hit Dan that his friend was protecting him.

"Yes, come to think of it, I am late for a faculty roundtable. I'm sure Jerry can advise you on possibly automating the call screening process."

Brett feigned agreement, "I'm sure he can figure it out."

As Doctor Dan walked out of the deli, Brett got down to the particulars, "Jerry, I have two devices I want you to access. Both are password protected. Can you hack into those devices?"

Jerry laughed just a bit, "Is that all? I thought you were going to ask me to plant a virus in the alien mothership or something."

Brett was stone cold serious as he handed Jerry a small plastic shopping bag, "If possible, I would prefer that our hacking be undetectable by forensic analysis."

Jerry quickly sobered up, "OK Mr. Hoffman, just what are we dealing with here?"

"These two devices belonged to a thug who murdered a man yesterday and attempted to murder another man last night. Both the victim and intended victim witnessed a UFO incident."

"The police now have the murderer in custody?"

"Sorta, they have his body."

"These two devices are most likely criminal evidence, are they not?"

"Yes."

"Why should I get involved?"

"The truth, Jerry. I don't know where all this will lead, but we need to know the truth."

"Yes, as a younger man, I hacked into government and industry networks to uncover the truth. I was more idealistic back then."

"You will receive your doctorate next summer?"

"June 2026, unless the whole damned country falls apart."

"Doctor Dan has told me there is an opening for you at Carnegie Mellon."

"Yes. At Carnegie Mellon, I can lead a comfortable life with enough academic freedom to explore my interests, but I'll never get rich."

"Jerry, I'm sure you realize that most all CMU faculty supplement their income by writing books, giving lectures, or consulting with government & industry?"

"Yes, but it can take years to line up those lucrative gigs."

"Yeah, unless you can make a big splash, like maybe appearing on a nationally syndicated radio talk show every-so-often."

Patel smiled a knowing smile, "Give me a couple of days."

"Not a word about this to anyone."

"Not a word about what?"

Brett only had one more thing to do that busy November 2025 afternoon.

Hoffman was a rock star around the Carnegie Mellon Physics Department. Department Chair, theoretical physicist Hiroshi Yasuda, was perhaps the #1 Brett Hoffman groupie in the department. Hiroshi had appeared on *Sea-to-Sea* more times than Doctor Dan. Hiroshi's field of expertise encompassed far out subjects such as warping space, alternate universes, the Big Bang, and perhaps his favorite, time travel.

"Step into my office Brett."

"Thanks for sticking around afterhours Hiroshi."

"No problem. I was just online catching your *Sea-to-Sea* broadcast from night before last. Man, you really set my mind racing."

"What would you say if I told you the military really did haul away the Kecksburg object."

"You have witnesses?"

"Two, but there's something else. That UFO was chained to a flatbed trailer and tarped. They were hauling it back to Wright-Patterson Air Force Base. About halfway over, every vehicle in the convoy stopped when their engines stalled. Oncoming traffic also stopped. The object began whining and glowing. Then it up and disappeared."

"It took off?"

"No. It dematerialized."

"Holy shit Brett! You have a witness?"

"Yes, but he's terminally ill. He said every steel surface on the flatbed was magnetized. The chains were still intact and attached to the flatbed after the UFO disappeared. That UFO didn't disappear by moving through space as we know it. While the UFO was dematerializing, St. Elmo's Fire danced along the highway's guardrails."

Hiroshi began speculating, "Something like an electromagnetic pulse could temporarily magnetize ferrous metals and disrupt automotive electronics. This event occurred in 1965. Back then, cars didn't contain the myriad of electronic devices like they do today. But an energetic EMP, perhaps in combination with some other type of electromagnetic disturbance, could blow fuses and screw up solenoids."

"Hiroshi, how could that object just up and disappear?"

"It would take tremendous energy. I'm not talking nuclear, or even thermonuclear. I'm talking something like antimatter, or perhaps Zero Point Energy."

"That's a new one on me. What in the hell is Zero Point Energy?"

"It's a result of Heisenberg's Uncertainty Principle. You do know Heisenberg, don't you?"

"He's the father of Quantum Mechanics, right?"

"Yes. While Einstein explained the movements of planets, stars, and galaxies, Heisenberg explained the sub-atomic world. Heisenberg's theories deal with the uncertainties inherent with the subatomic. He was awarded the 1932 Nobel Prize in Physics. One outcome of his Uncertainty Principle is Zero Point Energy.

"Subatomic particles, even at absolute zero temperature, have energy due to their intrinsic uncertainty. Some physicists contend that spacetime itself has intrinsic energy. Heisenberg was unaware of the expanding universe. We now know that the universe is expanding at an ever-increasing rate. Some say this expansion is sort of a feedback loop. As space expands, Zero Point Energy increases, which, in turn, accelerates the expansion. According to Heisenberg, the seemingly empty vacuum of space is actually a seething cauldron of energy.

"Einstein's theories predict that, given sufficient energy, spacetime can be bent, warped, and even tunneled through."

"Is that what they call a wormhole?"

"Very good, Brett! Yes! But the energy required to form a stable wormhole would be immense."

"Hiroshi, could that explain how the UFO disappeared? Did it 'burrow' its way through spacetime?"

"Possibly, I don't think it dematerialized. A good guess would be that it jumped through a tunnel to another point in spacetime. But that's only a guess. For all we know, that machine is now in Oz, and I don't mean Australia."

As the *Sea-to-Sea* bumper music faded, Brett Hoffman greeted his loyal *Sea-to-Sea AM* audience, "This is Brett Hoffman filling in for Vince Vittito. Vince is on the sick list, so it's up to yours' truly to hold down the fort. I'm here tonight on short notice, so we're going to run with open lines. I'm counting on all my fans from sea to shining sea to light this candle."

As Brett relaxed during the first commercial break, Mr. Call Screener gave him some good news, "Brett, here comes the cavalry to save your sorry ass. I've got Doc Hiroshi on the line."

After the break, a relieved Brett was back behind the mic, "I've got my friend, Professor Hiroshi Yasuda on the line. We all know that, whenever Hiroshi drops in, this show becomes as unpredictable as Heisenberg's quantum mechanics."

"Good early morning Brett."

"Hiroshi, this is an unexpected, but pleasant, surprise."

"It's my pleasure. You know, we physicists are just like everyone else. Sometimes, when we deal with the minutia of a problem every day, our vision narrows, then we fall into a rut. Every time I drop by *Sea-to-Sea*, my dogmatic ideas are challenged. Sometimes, even the seemingly craziest ideas contain at least some modicum of truth."

"OK folks, on that note, I'll just let Hiroshi run with it."

"Hiroshi, it's your microphone."

"Thanks Brett. This afternoon, a hardcore *Sea-to-Sea* fan visited me. Part of our conversation dealt with unconventional travel through spacetime…"

Brett covered his mic with his hand as he chuckled to himself.

TW POWELL © 2023

Hiroshi began talking off the top of his head about warping space, wormholes, time travel, and finally 'Time's Arrow'. The *Sea-to-Sea* switchboard was melting down.

"Here's Josh from Cedar Rapids, Iowa."

"Hi Brett! Hi Hiroshi! Some physicists say time travel may be possible, but it's a one-way trip into the future. You mentioned Time's Arrow. Can you elaborate?"

Hiroshi was in his element, "Most certainly Josh. While we talk about spacetime, the three spatial dimensions seem to differ from the temporal dimension. Some physicists think that the passage, or flow, of time is not real. It is but a construct of the human mind. Regardless of whether time is, or isn't real, it does appear that time has an arrow. That arrow points to the future. This invokes causality. Which came first, the chicken, or the egg? It also involves thermodynamics. A broken cup of tea is the result of a cup falling off a table. The cup and its contents change from a state of relative order to a sticky wet mess shattered upon the floor, a messy state of disorder. Those shards of porcelain and that puddle of sweet tea can't just levitate up off the floor and reassemble themselves upon the table. Causality and thermodynamics are big problems for would-be time travelers. The ability to travel backwards in time introduces paradoxes that the universe simply cannot abide. Suppose I travel back in time and kill my infant grandfather?"

After the news beak at bottom of the first hour, Brett took another call, "Hey there Mr. Hoffman, Charlie calling from Coeur d'Alene, Idaho. I saw something back in '85."

"Charlie, you mean back in 1985?"

"Yeah, I saw something like you was talking about night before last. I saw it come down. Then I saw it a few days later on the ground."

"You saw it take off?"

"No Mr. Hoffman, that thing up and disappeared before my very eyes."

"OK Charlie, describe what happened. If we push up against a hard break, just hang on the line."

Charlie proceeded to tell the *Sea-to-Sea* listening audience a tale that was now becoming all too familiar to Brett.

"I had stopped in at the Thompson Peak Ranger Lookout out here in Idaho. Nowadays, it's just a tourist spot, but back in those days, it was a working fire lookout. It was early in the season, mid-June, so no ranger was on duty. In my younger days, I made a living prospecting all over the Mountain West. I've racked up over 300,000 miles on my Winnebago. I've spent many a night camped out under the stars."

"OK Charlie, we only have a few minutes, please get to your points."

"Something came down. At first, I thought it was a meteor. It came in shallow from the east, leaving a trail of sparkles, smoke, and flame as it descended. It never changed course."

"How do you know it wasn't a meteor?"

"Meteors don't slow down."

Brett had to think quickly, "Stay close to your radios, we're going to take a required commercial break, then Charlie is going to tell us all about the meteor that slowed down."

Hiroshi couldn't believe a meteor decelerated, "Is this guy for real?"

"This is Brett Hoffman along with Doctor Hiroshi Yasuda and we have Charlie from Coeur d'Alene back with us. Charlie is telling us about a meteor that slowed down."

"Hang on young fella. I only thought it was a meteor."

"OK Charlie. Describe the suspected meteor."

"I was looking to the east, out over the Flathead Reservation. That thing began slowing at a few thousand feet. I figured it had deployed a parachute. Looked like it landed about 20 miles away, over in the foothills by Camas

Prairie. For the next few days, I scoured that country with a fine-toothed comb. You know there's big money in those meteorites.

"On the afternoon of the third day, my compass went haywire. It was pointing to the southwest, straight up McLaughlin Creek. Back in those days, we didn't have all these damned California refugees up here building vacation homes and bugout shelters. I just followed my compass needle up McLaughlin Creek. At the confluence of Hugo and McLaughlin Creeks, there's a clearing. That's where I saw it. It was broad daylight."

Brett couldn't decide whether this guy was for real, or just another loon, "Just what did you see?"

"It was a black bell-shaped object similar to what you described night before last. It wasn't shiny, but it had some shiny, brassy markings around the bottom. From a distance, those glyphs looked like something outta King Tutt's tomb."

"Charlie, did you get any photos?"

"I've got a roll of photos."

"Holy smokes, why haven't we seen those photos?"

"They're well hidden. We can talk about that off air, if you're interested."

Brett figured a shakedown was now in progress but played along, "Is that all?"

"Hell no! I watched that thing for several hours from behind the trees. That's when he showed up."

"That's when who showed up?"

"The guy in the black uniform."

"Charlie, hang with us, we're up against another hard break. Everyone stay tuned for the rest of Charlie's amazing story."

Brett wasn't up against a hard break. He just took a commercial timeout to get Charlie off the air before Charlie got himself killed.

For the second time in three days, Brett addressed Mr. Call Screener by his Christian name, "Teddy, get Charlie's contact information and give him my private cellphone number. Tell him I'll call him back after the show."

Disillusionment

Colonel Cooper popped his head out into the hallway, dismissed Mr. Jones, then returned to his seat, still somewhat in a state of shock.

"Sergeant, you're telling me that a decorated Marine officer has turned renegade?"

"Negative Colonel, to the best of my knowledge, Colonel Cloud has remained faithful to his Oath."

"How can that be? You just told me that he is Dark Cloud."

"Colonel, Dark Cloud is a figment. We have traitors in our midst. I'm not talking about turncoats for The Collective or Red Chinese. I'm talking about those who would betray the founding principles for personal gain and power."

Thomas could read the disillusionment and confusion scrawled across Cooper's face.

"Aye Colonel, you're feeling gut-wrenching nausea, aren't you?"

"Cooper nodded."

"I had the same feeling a couple of days back. I've always assumed that everyone fighting The Collective and their Chinese overlords share our dedication to the Constitution and rule of law. I fear I've been very naïve. I was projecting my loyalty onto others. I will never make that mistake again. There are those among us with no internal compass. They have no guiding principles. I think I prefer the crazed leftwing Members to those mercenary bastards."

"Sergeant, what of Captain Cloud?"

"Captain Cloud is known among his people as the Great Chief. Cloud thinks that is all so much bullshit, but his people do look up to him, so he indulges them."

"So, the Apache revere him. How about the Hispanics and White folks in Central New Mexico?"

"Colonel, when I say, 'his people', I mean all the people."

Cooper wasn't buying it, "So Cloud has become a petty dictator?"

"No, at first, he was the military governor, but they now hold elections. Cloud is the elected leader of the Mescalero Territory."

Cooper still wasn't buying it, "If Bill Cloud is such a magnanimous leader, how did all this Dark Cloud crap get started and why does it continue?"

"Captain Cloud makes no effort to dispel the Dark Cloud myth. If The Collective and other hostile forces believe in this Dark Cloud bogeyman, that works to Captain Cloud's advantage."

"What 'other hostile forces' are you referring to, Sergeant?"

"Colonel, did you fly in from West Virginia last night?"

"Yes, what does that have to do with this Dark Cloud business?"

"It was clear last night. As you descended into Roswell, did you see all the oilfield flares?"

"How could I miss them?"

"You couldn't see all the cattle, but you may have seen all the navigation lights atop the windfarms."

"What are you saying Jackson?"

"Colonel, I'm talking money, big money. Money buys power, lots of muscle. West Texas is a long way from Austin and half a continent away from The Bunker. Colonel, I don't know how high up the ladder this corruption goes. It could even involve our Japanese allies.

"I'm gonna cut to the chase, those 'other hostile forces' I referred to are mercenaries hiding behind a badge. Local militia and law enforcement who drive small ranchers and independent wildcatters off their lands. Those forces are owned lock, stock, and barrel by Big Energy and Big Cattle, perhaps by the Japanese. God only knows what else they're up to. Captain Cloud prevents those forces from dominating the lands west of the Pecos. Unwittingly, the Resistance may be aiding those corrupt forces."

The Colonel dropped all pretense of rank as he spoke bluntly to Jackson, "Tom, if what you say is true, we have big problems here along the Pecos."

Kameraden

Leutnant Schneider had no idea why he was being summoned to the Führerbunker. For the past several days, he had been down in Templehof's underground hangar, assisting in the final preparation of die Größe Glocke. Schneider reasoned that he might as well put this short hike to good use.

Wolfgang clicked his stopwatch as he left the hangar. He briskly walked through Tempelhof Terminal and jogged across the 200 meters of bomb cratered Berlin streets leading from the Terminal to Luftbrücke Underground Station. Schneider slowly descended three flights of stairs down to the train platform, emulating the time it would take to ascend those same stairs. The stonemasons had recently completed work on the doorway to the tunnel. Materials were neatly stacked nearby for the sealing of that doorway, once it served its purpose. Leutnant Schneider moved swiftly through the tunnel and, in under an hour, arrived at the Führerbunker. The entire trip had taken Schneider 40 minutes. Under combat conditions, he estimated the trek would take about 45 minutes.

"Leutnant Schneider, how goes your work?"

Schneider was somewhat taken aback by his Führer's informality. He snapped to attention and saluted.

"Alles in ordnung, mein Führer!"

"Zehr gut! Schneider, come join me in my sitting room. If we are to be comrades, we must know one another thoroughly. We must be of one mind."

The Führer continued talking as they made their way to his inner sanctum, "In the Great War, we fought as much for one another as we did for the

Fatherland. Amid the horror of the trenches, that bond of brotherhood kept us going."

"Jawohl, mein Führer! May I speak freely?"

"Of course, that is why you are here."

"Inside the Tiger it was much the same. Each man's life depended upon his comrades."

"Jawohl, Leutnant! These armchair generals have never tasted the bitterness of war as we have. Perhaps Rommel knew

real war, but they poisoned his mind against me.

"I understand that your mother was American. She was from the American West, from Idaho, of Norwegian descent?"

"Yes, mein Führer. Her family first immigrated to Minnesota, then continued west as the frontier was tamed."

"Do you remember anything of your young childhood in Idaho?"

"Not much, just images in my mind of vast spaces and snow-capped mountains. Much like Austria, but on a much

grander scale."

"Your father was German?"

"Jawohl, Idaho is a land of great mineral wealth. Deposits of gold, silver, copper, lead, and zinc were brought to the surface by the same forces that thrust up the mountains. My father traded those commodities world-wide and met my mother while visiting Idaho."

"Then your father was wealthy?"

"Nein, mein Führer. In 1926, when my mother and father returned to the Fatherland, he was quite prosperous. Then the Great Depression wiped out his fortune."

"Ah Schneider, you too have been stabbed in the back by the filthy Jews!

"I take it you speak English, Amerikanisher English?"

"Jawohl, mein Führer! My father spoke to me in German and my mother spoke to me in English. I have an upper Midwest accent, typical of Americans with a Scandinavian heritage.

"Mein Führer, why am I wasting your valuable time? My life's story is insignificant compared to the upcoming final battle for Berlin!"

"Nonsense, Leutnant Schneider! The best general fights his battles at the time and place of his choosing! While the Bolsheviks and Allies stumble about through the burnt-out ruins of Berlin, we will prepare the decisive battlefield."

Efficiency

Marian's fourth floor maisonette apartment had been selected with care. The two Dreyfus brothers' locksmith business and computer sales & service shop occupied the ground floor, with their flats occupying the second and third floors. Marian's rent included space in their garage, secure off-street parking for her gray VW Jetta.

Squirrel Hill was the perfect place for a young Jewish lady to hang her hat. Everything she needed was within walking distance, except her mother, which suited Marian just fine.

Being a locksmith, Maury Dreyfus was also a good auto mechanic and brother Ben was a computer geek

extraordinaire. The two old Jews flirted with Marian and teased her endlessly, but she was like a daughter to the brothers Dreyfus. From time-to-time, Marian would work in the computer store. Ben carefully tracked sales and determined that sales increased 31.6% whenever Marian was on the job.

31.6% is a huge number in retail. The Dreyfus brothers repeatedly offered Marian some sort of partnership. They

had no children, no family, no one to carry on the businesses once they were gone. They constantly fretted over poor, pretty Marian. She had no husband. She was all alone and defenseless in the big city.

That night, Marian was listening to KDKA as Charlie spun his yarn to Brett and Hiroshi. While Marian listened, she cleaned her Beretta Model 70, once Mossad's signature handgun.

Squirrel Hill was a fertile recruiting ground for American Mossad agents. Marian had been identified as a promising candidate while still a freshman at Yeshiva Girls High School, right there in Squirrel Hill. Even at that early age, Marian was a linguistics savant, fluent in Hebrew, Arabic, French, German, and her native English.

One corner of Marian's large bedroom served as her "war room". Maps and bulletin boards adorned every inch of wall above several four drawer file cabinets and her desk. Upon the backwall of her large walk-in closet hung an all too familiar flag, a white circle adorned with the black "cooked cross", centered upon a field of red. It had now been 80 years since that flag had flown with any authority. Some of that flag's disciples had been brought to justice. Others had lived out their lives in hiding and died in ignominy. Very few remained alive. Marian's life's work was to ensure that flag never again flew with authority.

Maury Dreyfus did most of the routine maintenance work on the building. He had noticed Marian's maps dotted with colored push pins. He had read the newspaper clippings and carefully examined the photographs pinned to the bulletin boards. He would have inspected the contents of the file cabinets and desk drawers, but Marian kept those cabinets and drawers locked. Knowing that Maury could undetectably crack any lock, Marian also kept her cabinets and drawers sealed.

Maury quizzed Marian about all her Nazi paraphernalia on several occasions.

"Maury, you're such a Yenta! I do volunteer work for a holocaust survivors nonprofit, for the Wiesenthal Center. Most of my work is sorta like Ancestry.com for the descendants of Holocaust victims and the few remaining Holocaust survivors."

Good thing Maury never had reason to sneak a peek behind that hideous flag. If he had, he may have discovered Marian's stash of weapons, well hidden in a void, behind the closet wall.

Although Marian was recording that evening's *Sea-to-Sea AM* broadcast, she took detailed notes as a steady stream of thoughts, questions, and suspicions flashed through her mind. Katsa Marian Metzner's tradecraft rivaled that of any CIA spook. She funneled a constant stream of intelligence back to Mossad's USA Desk in Tel Aviv.

Despite all her proficiencies, Marian was considered somewhat of an anachronism by her superiors. For example, back in the mid-1970s, Mossad had dropped the Beretta 70 "Jaguar" .22 LRS in favor of a 9 mm. Marian still packed the Jaguar. Her fixation upon some type of 21st Century Nazi resurrection project was considered pure tin foil hat conspiracy theory by her Tel Aviv superiors. Some of her pointed questions seemed to disturb her handlers. She had been ordered, in no uncertain terms, to focus on real threats such as the Islamic Republic of Iran's nuclear program, the growing Muslim extremist influence in America, and anti-Israeli US political movements, particularly this radical group known as The Collective.

Marian paid her Israeli handlers no mind. She was working on her own, without a net, as she hunted Nazis. Marian gave her project a proper Wagnerian title, "Operation Götterdämmerung", the Twilight of the Gods.

Follow Up

"Welcome back from the break. We seem to have lost Charlie from Idaho. We'll try to get him back on the line. Meanwhile, let's continue with Hiroshi's discussion of wormholes and time travel."

That was 100% pure bullshit. Brett had no intention of putting Charlie back on nationally syndicated radio. For the next two hours, Hiroshi entertained another dozen callers. A couple of those callers were certified nuts, but other callers were quite informed, asking some probing questions. At 4 a.m. Eastern, Brett Hoffman wrapped another wildly successful *Sea-to-Sea* broadcast.

Brett continued his conversation with Hiroshi off air, "Hiroshi, thank you for calling in tonight. I owe you big time!"

"No problem. I thoroughly enjoy my appearances on your show. Now, I have a question for you."

"Certainly, ask away!"

"Why did you cut off Charlie from Idaho?"

"There's something funny going on, my friend. Something to do with that Kecksburg UFO incident. Without going into detail, two men are already dead. An attempt was made on another man's life. I really don't want you involved. Just watch yourself. Keep your doors locked and let me know if you suspect you are being followed or observed."

"Are you serious?"

"Never been more serious in my life. Serious enough that I'm packin' heat."

Minutes after his off-air warning to Hiroshi, Brett called Charlie, "Charlie, can we talk?"

"Brett, why in the hell didn't you let me finish my story?"

"Please Charlie, tell me that you really saw that UFO?"

"Hell yes! I saw them both!"

"Both of them?"

"If you would just give an old prospector the courtesy of completing his story, before pulling the plug, you might get a more accurate account of what actually happened."

Brett was completely confused, "OK Charlie. I apologize. What happened?"

"As I was saying, before I was so rudely interrupted, a guy in a black uniform came out of that thing. He was just as human as you or I. He walked around listening to a radio but couldn't get good reception out there in the middle of Bumfuck Egypt. He went back into that thing and came back out dressed in civilian clothing, decidedly European, and somewhat old fashion."

"You said you have photos."

"Hell yes! Fly on out here and you can have a set for your very own. Just give me a little taste if any money is involved."

"Charlie, any pictures are your property. The tabloids pay for good UFO evidence, so you may indeed profit. I'll even help you. But first, I must warn you. There's something strange going on."

"You ain't just a shitting, I followed that dude."

"What dude?"

"The guy who got out of that contraption."

"You followed him?"

"Yeah. He hiked over to the highway and caught a ride into town."

"Town?"

"Yeah. He hitchhiked into Plains, the town of Plains, Montana."

"You followed him?"

"Yeah. I tailed him at a discrete distance. He went straight to the Public Library. He seemed to know his way around town. Maybe he had already been in town a couple of times before I found his machine. Anyway, he hung out in the Library for several hours. While he was in there, I bought a fifth of Jack to steady my nerves. It sure helped me on the return trip."

"So, he hitchhiked back to the UFO?"

"Sure as hell did. I gave him a ride back."

"You what?"

"I drove him back. He gave me an ounce of pure gold. $300 was a nice day's work back in '85!"

"That's outrageous! Charlie please don't take offense, you weren't drunk, were you?"

"It takes a whole lot more than a couple of swigs of Old No. 7 to inebriate this old prospector. I was stone cold sobor for the entire 20-minute drive back to the UFO."

"So, you spoke with him?"

"Yeah, Heinz, I spoke to Heinz. He seemed OK. Said he was from Luxembourg, visiting out West on holidays. Of course, that was all pure horse hockey.

"He spoke perfect English with a slight Kraut accent. Heinz asked a million questions."

"What kind of questions?"

"Definitely not your tourist type questions. He asked about President Reagan and the Russians, excepting he called them Bolsheviks. Heinz was very curious about Israel. All his questions dealt with politics and current events."

"Could you tell if he was armed?"

"You know, I didn't really think about that at the time. Heinz was really a nice guy.

"Anyway, I dropped him off at Hugo Creek. He said he was camping up the creek. After dropping him off, I continued eastward for about a mile, pulled the Winnebago off the road under some cover, then made my way back to the landing site on foot. That's when things got real interesting."

Brett was incredulous, "You're telling me that giving a hitchhiking UFO pilot a ride wasn't interesting enough?"

"Damn it, Hoffman! Quit interrupting and maybe you'll agree. Now, where was I?

"Oh yeah, I snuck back through the trees and watched as Heinz climbed back into that machine and buttoned up. About a half hour later, that black bell started whining, then it started glowing. I'd guess, less than a minute later, it up and disappeared. Although it was gone, the area where it had sat continued crackling with static electricity and bluish plasma was dancing all around.

"I took some pictures of that, but none came out. The guy down at the drug store said those frames were way over exposed.

"I wasn't about to go anywhere near that electrical maelstrom. After a couple of hours watching and waiting, the air was still hissing and glowing, so I just hiked on back to my Winnebago. The sun was setting. So, I built a fire, unfolded my chaise lounge, and cooked some beans & franks.

"There I lay with my belly full of hot dogs & beans, about to doze off to sleep. Then all hell broke loose. Something came streaking in from the northeast. Something like Heinz' UFO, only larger.

"Wouldn't you know, a second UFO landed over at Hugo Creek, right next to Heinz' UFO. Yeah, Heinz' ship had rematerialized, and the second UFO landed right next to it."

"Tell me you got pictures…"

"Nope. Too dark. After the fact, I sketched the second UFO in proportion to the first UFO. Those sketches are stashed away along with the photos.

"The second UFO was at least 3 times the size of the first one. It was more flattened. Looked more a typical flying saucer, albeit a fat one."

"Did anyone get out of the larger craft?"

"I don't know."

"What do you mean, you don't know?"

"He got the drop on me. One moment I was observing the two UFOs and the next moment pistol rounds were whizzing past my head.

"I still recall those chilling words, 'Hände hoch!' For a moment, I thought I was a goner. I ran like a bat out of hell!

"I raced headlong through the darkness, jumped back into my Winnebago, and floored it all the way into the Plains Police Department. I had just polished off that fifth of Jack when the second UFO arrived. The Plains patrolman on duty smelled the booze on my breath and wouldn't listen to my story. He figured I was just out on a Saturday night drunk. He took my keys and locked my ass up for the night. They kept me locked up all day the next day. It was a Sunday."

"They finally let me out come Monday morning. The Chief agreed to follow me up to Hugo Creek. By the time we got up there, both machines were long gone. This time, I don't think they flew away, or disappeared. Some heavy equipment came in there and hauled those machines away. The Chief believed I saw something and agreed that some heavy equipment had been up in the canyon, but, as far as he could tell, no crime had been committed. He politely sent me on my way and rather bluntly suggested that I not return."

Vocational Training

The Austin School was a modern facility, having been built in 2020, just six years prior to the Peoples' Revolution. Austin, and its environs, were sparsely populated. It made sense to build a single school complex serving grades K through 12. The School lay on the northern outskirts of town, about a mile and a half north of the National Café. Not far from the School, the Pony Express Trail crossed Nevada Highway 305. Even in 2041, that narrow, rutted, historic dirt path was clearly visible.

Tony covered his bald head before stepping out into the late December early morning chill. He borrowed one of Vince's horses and took a leisurely morning horseback ride to his training session. The week between Christmas and New Year's was the perfect time for Lin to earn his degree in Custodial Sciences.

An oval running track encircled the football field. The track was surrounded by a 6-foot chain-link fence. Since the Revolution, many teachers, pupils, and staff rode horses and ponies to school. During the school day, their mounts grazed on the football field. There were no bleachers, merely two water troughs on either end of the 50-yard line.

Tony carried his saddle with him as he walked a couple of hundred feet from the ballfield to the school's delivery dock. A short, thin, old, Black gentleman with snow-white hair was standing out on the dock. Tony climbed the four steps up onto the dock and dropped his saddle.

"Boy, we got cages, over there by the horse troughs. That's where you should store your saddle."

"Can I just leave it here for now?'

The old gentleman scratched his head, then replied, "I guess it'll be OK. We're the onliest ones here today and I'm not expecting any deliveries. You must be Tony."

Tony extended his gloved right hand, "You must be Gilbert."

Gilbert chuckled as he shook Tony's hand, "Yeah, I'm Gilbert Goins. Folks around here called me GG. I see you're ready for work."

Tony was confused, "Ready for work?"

"Yessiree Bob! I see you got your gloves on. That's good 'cause we're gonna start with the toilets."

That entire week, between the holidays, GG taught Tony Lin the intricacies of school sanitation. That included stripping, waxing, and buffing floors, sanitizing rest rooms, cleaning windows, and a myriad of other routine tasks. By week's end, Tony graduated janitorial school with flying colors.

Hitler's Favorite Commando

"Skorzeny, if only all my officers were as dependable as you."

Lieutenant Colonel Otto Skorzeny was the Führer's favorite commando. Otto had unfettered access to his Führer and Hitler relished Skorzeny's visits. Perhaps Skorzeny's most famous raid was Operation Oak, the rescue of Italian strongman Benito Mussolini from a mountaintop Italian prison in September 1943.

Another of Skorzeny's projects, Operation Griffin, has been immortalized both in literature and on the silver screen. During the December 1944 Battle of the Bulge, English speaking Germans, dressed as American GIs, wreaked havoc as they infiltrated Allied positions in the Ardennes. General Omar Bradley was even stopped and questioned by American MPs. When asked, "What's the capital of Illinois?" Bradley responded, "Springfield." That answer was correct, but the MP mistakenly thought Chicago was the capital and detained Bradley for a short time.

Skorzeny saluted his Führer, then the two men embraced as comrades.

"What news of Werewolf and Die Spinne?"

With the collapse of the Ardennes Offensive, Skorzeny, aka: Scarface, relocated to Bavaria and was busy organizing two covert post-war operations. Operation Werewolf was a planned Nazi guerilla resistance against the occupying Allied powers. This resistance would be based in the mountains of Southern Germany, Austria, and Czechoslovakia's Sudetenland. The other operation was codenamed Die Spinne (the Spider). The Spider was a world-wide covert network of Nazi operatives, industrialists, scientists, and financiers who would lay the groundwork for a reincarnated Reich at some future place & time.

"Mein Führer, both projects are progressing satisfactorily."

"I take it that Kammler has been of assistance?"

Per the Führer's orders, Scarface was now assisted by SS-Obergruppenführer Hans Kammler. Kammler had acted as a liaison between Reichsminister Speer and Himmler's SS. Kammler organized slave labor from Himmler's camps to work on Speer's wunderwaffen. During early 1945, Kammler was kept busy either moving or destroying wunderwaffen, preventing them from falling into Allied hands. Those wonder weapons included the V-1 flying bomb, V-2 ballistic missile, and Me 262 jet fighter.

Skorzeny enthusiastically replied, "Jawohl, Speer and Himmler are not exactly kameraden!"

Hitler nodded in agreement with a grin, "Jawohl, Skorzeny, Jawohl!

"Have you contacted Generalissimo Franco? He is indebted to me."

"Jawohl!"

"Are your contacts in the Middle East still viable?"

"Jawohl! Our allies in Iran, the Qashqai People, hate both the Russians and the British. Although Operation Francois achieved only minimal success, the Qashqai people are still friends of the Reich."

"Zehr gut Skorzeny! Have you been following events in Argentina?"

"Nein mein Führer."

"Of course not. You are far too busy. Two years ago, the impotent democratic Argentine government was toppled by a military junta. Fortuitously, last January, a devastating earthquake struck Argentina taking over 10,000 lives. A minor player in the junta has captured the imagination of his people and is organizing relief efforts. Juan Peron is a man to watch."

"I am confused. Hasn't Argentina severed diplomatic relations with the Reich?"

"Ja, Ja. That is all just window dressing. This man, Peron, is building his own brand of National Socialism in Argentina. I have opened back-channel negotiations with this man. Peron will help us. He is a man of destiny.

"You must fashion a spider's web of loyal National Socialists throughout the world. This secret network of bankers, industrialists, scientists, politicians, and journalists will pave the way for a resurrected Reich. But I warn you, the Jews will attempt to destroy die Spinne. You must do whatever is necessary to outwit and even co-opt the Jews.

"I have learned, Otto. Yes, even your Führer must constantly learn and adapt. Next time, I will be sly. I will play the filthy Jews against themselves. You must do likewise."

Skorzeny appeared confused, "Next time?"

The Führer smiled as he gave his henchman more specific instructions, top secret instructions.

Back To Ruidoso

While Tony began his janitorial training at the Austin School, a well-maintained Land Rover with a full tank of diesel headed westward on US 70 toward Ruidoso, New Mexico. Tom Jackson was driving, with Lame Wolf snoozing in the rear seat.

No one at the hotel, not even spooky Jones, had the slightest idea what happened to Colonel Cooper. Cooper hadn't checked out. He hadn't boarded a flight back to West Virginia. He simply disappeared without a trace.

As the Land Rover neared the western edge of town, Tom pulled into a convenience store. He woke the old Navajo snoring in the back seat and the two amigos headed for the restroom. When they finished doing their business, the duo got back into the Land Rover. Tom passed a hot coffee to the man in the Cattleman hat and thermal coveralls, now occupying the front passenger seat.

Lame Wolf introduced himself by busting the Colonel's balls, "Mister Bluecoat, aren't you out of uniform in that black Stetson?"

Tom grimaced, then attempted to laugh off Lame Wolf's unique brand of humor, "Colonel, Sir, around these parts, that sort of bilge passes for comedy."

The Colonel took an immediate liking to the old Navajo, "Mister Wolf, aren't you out of uniform in that top hat? A hat with only two eagle feathers?"

Lame Wolf lamented his lack of plumage, "When I was young and strong, I wore many eagle feathers. Now I am old and lame, without family, wealth, or deeds. If I should wear more than these two eagle feathers, The People would only ridicule me. I get no respect."

Lone Wolf's Rodney Dangerfield act somewhat amused Colonel Cooper.

"Has The Collective dulled The People's senses? Can they no longer recognize a Navajo brave? I have heard Jackson's account of the firefight at the big dish. Only a Navajo brave would battle armed men with nothing but a handful of rocks."

Lame Wolf replied with droll self-deprecation, "You are right, The Collective must have dulled my senses. No Navajo or Apache brave would face down pistoleros with mere rocks. That was a damned fool thing to do."

Cooper nodded, "Perhaps foolish, but brave. You can fight on my team anytime, Mister Wolf."

Upon hearing those words of respect, Lame Wolf's face beamed with pride, "Jackson, you chose your friends well.

"Colonel Cooper, Jackson will take us to meet Great Chief Cloud. We will parlay and carefully lay our plans. Together, we will drive these Chinese from our lands. We will purge our ranks of those who put greed above honor."

Cooper silently nodded his agreement.

An hour and a half after leaving Roswell, the Land Rover pulled into the former Walmart Supercenter on Billy the Kid Drive in Ruidoso, New Mexico. Tom had his travel pass in hand, but it wasn't needed.

"Sergeant Jackson, Captain Cloud is expecting you and your comrades." The sentry escorted the trio through the cavernous Walmart.

Cloud's Adjutant immediately ushered the three men into the Captain's corner office. The Captain was standing at the head of a small conference table. When Colonel Cooper removed his Cattleman hat, Captain Cloud immediately stood to and saluted.

Cooper returned the salute, then walked over and gave William a warm handshake.

"Captain Cloud, we were all wondering what in the hell happened to you."

"Colonel, Sir, I've been occupied in the service of my people."

Cloud motioned for everyone to sit down, "Have a seat and I'll try my best to answer all your questions."

Captain Cloud briefly rehashed how the Dark Cloud legend got started and the facts on the ground in New Mexico. Colonel Cooper was not so concerned with the actions of the Cartel and The Collective along the Rio Grande. He was most concerned with the unlawful and aggressive actions of Texas mercenaries west of the Pecos.

"Captain Cloud, before we can rectify the situation west of the Pecos, we must get the initial shipment of rare earth concentrate down to Houston and sort out all this science fiction mumbo jumbo over at the Array. That will open a corridor for future shipments of rare earths to Houston and shipments of refined diesel and gasoline from Texas back to Arizona. Once that route is established, we'll root out these West Texas gangsters and return law and order to the lands west of the Pecos."

The Pathfinder

Leutnant Heinz Schuster had his orders. By 1 March 1945, the southern pincer of the Soviet advance had reached the Owl Mountains of southwestern Poland. All diagrams and specifications for die Glocke and die Größe Glocke were loaded onboard the remaining prototype, along with one metric ton of 1 troy oz gold bars. The cavern with the first prototype protruding from its wall had already been imploded.

Without warning, as Leutnant Schuster closed die Glocke's hatch, all doors into the Ksiaz Castle tunnel complex were sealed. As die Glocke began glowing, pellets of Zyklon B and boiling hot water were poured down multiple vent pipes leading into the tunnel complex. As die Glocke vanished, the underground complex filled with hydrogen cyanide gas. Cyanide is an equal opportunity executioner. It killed everyone in the tunnels, Poles, Jews, Gypsies, Russian prisoners of war, German scientists, and even SS guards. Then, a series of powerful demolition charges collapsed the entire underground complex.

In the blink of an eye, die Glocke was reentering Earth's atmosphere.

Heinz was relieved, "Von Braun and his wunderkind certainly have this heat shield technology down pat."

At 20,000 feet, Heinz activated the antigravity field. Die Glocke gradually slowed, hitting the ground with a soft thud. The craft's exterior was glowing red hot. Although the chronometer technology was somewhat primitive and unproven, the display read December 1965. After 15 minutes, the exterior of die Glocke cooled to 100 C. Heinz cracked the hatch. A cold breeze smacked the fighter ace in the face. A few snowflakes sizzled as they hit the exterior of die Glocke. The sun had set, but it was not quite dark. Heinz carefully exited the craft, taking care not to touch its boiling hot exterior.

Die Glocke had landed in a small clearing, surrounded by forest. The countryside was hilly, but not mountainous. The forest was a mixture of leafless deciduous hardwood and softwood species. This was definitely not an Alpine Forest. The clearing was covered with grass. A rooster crowed as darkness fell. Then, a cow mooed somewhere off in the darkness. This was farm country.

The cold north wind chilled Heinz to the bone. He turned up the collar of his SS uniform to cover his exposed neck. Unseen, a small white flower fell from his lapel. The Pathfinder dared not wander too far from die Glocke. He reached back into the craft and retrieved his radio receiver. The AM band was quite active.

"Football, Amerikanisher football!" A radio program was previewing the upcoming Pittsburgh Steelers football game.

Heinz quickly pointed his flashlight into a nearby tree. He thought he heard some movement.

When Heinz couldn't find anything amiss in the tree, he merely shrugged his shoulders, "Probably just a squirrel, or bird."

Heinz continued scanning up and down the AM band. Three distinctive tones issued from the radio. Two NBC commentators, Huntley & Brinkley, were discussing a Southeast Asian conflict in a place called Vietnam.

"Communists! They are talking about Bolsheviks!"

Heinz briefly listened to some music, "What are these Beatles? Ach so, Englander! I should have known."

From out of nowhere, Heinz saw car headlights headed in his direction. He quickly climbed back into die Glocke and buttoned up.

Heinz pondered his situation, "The liquid rare earth metal must cool for several hours before die Glocke can jump once again. I am currently somewhere near Pittsburgh, Pennsylvania. The next temporal jump must span a minimum of 20 years to allow sufficient spatial displacement."

Heinz just sat there in die Glocke for the next few hours. Then he felt movement. The entire craft was being lifted. Then, all was quiet again for several minutes. Heinz thought about peeking outside, but once again felt movement, bumpy movement. He sensed motion.

"Die Glocke is being hauled away!"

It took a further two hours for the liquid heavy metal to cool to zero state. As soon as die Glocke was ready, Heinz energized the liquid rare earth metal dynamo and made another jump.

Heading West

The Xanax began kicking in as the Boeing 777 Dreamliner levelled off at 35,000 feet on its flight from Pittsburgh to Salt Lake City. Brett Hoffman was not afraid of ghosts, aliens, demons, or Sasquatch, but his fear of heights and his claustrophobia were major issues for a paranormal investigator and multimedia celebrity. Hoffman's analyst blamed "control issues" as the root cause of Brett's assorted phobias. Whenever Brett fastened his seatbelt and the cabin door closed, his subconscious mind realized he had lost all control. His heart began racing and his face flushed as that "fight or flight" reflex kicked in.

Brett usually flew first-class and always sat in an aisle seat. There was absolutely no way he could sit all smushed, in a middle seat, somewhere back in coach, for four long hours. Although a semi-celebrity, Hoffman was not a rich man, but he recognized that first-class airfare was a small price to pay for maintaining his sanity. Besides, the business-related airfare was tax deductible.

Marian had no problem flying coach. The Simon Wiesenthal Foundation helped support Marian's extracurricular Nazi hunting activities, since her Mossad handlers most certainly would not. She had noticed that her Israeli mentors had grown increasingly hostile and became quite agitated whenever she mentioned certain Nazis, particularly Skorzeny and Kammler. For reasons unknown, those two names were verboten in the Mossad lexicon.

Once the seat belt sign was off, Brett made a quick pass through the coach cabin, merely as a precaution. He didn't know exactly what he was looking for, but Marian's blonde wig served its purpose. Brett felt somewhat helpless with his Luger packed away in his checked baggage, but the Xanax helped calm his fears. Surprisingly, Hoffman managed to catch a few winks on the relatively smooth flight out to Salt Lake.

Brett hated connecting flights, but there weren't any direct flights from Pittsburgh to Spokane, so he connected with a puddle jumper in Salt Lake for the final leg. The Salt Lake terminal was a zoo. Earlier that day, radical environmentalists had penetrated security and wreaked havoc. After several hour's delay, Brett boarded his connecting flight.

The small commuter jet had a single row of seats along the port side and a double row along the starboard side. Brett sat in seat 1A. A blonde Marian stumbled and almost fell in the aisle as she entered the aircraft.

"Excuse me, I'm such a klutz!" The young woman apologized as she grabbed Brett's shoulder to steady herself.

Brett smiled and nodded, thinking nothing of the incident, but recalled seeing that same young lady sitting back in coach on his earlier Pittsburg flight. She was quite a looker.

The commuter jet touched down in Spokane in just under two hours. Brett was first off the plane and headed directly to the rental car lot, not knowing he had been tagged. Marian made a quick stop in the ladies' room and changed into a flannel shirt and jeans. From the chill in the air, she figured she would need her fleece lined denim jacket. The final touch was ditching the blonde wig in exchange for a Stetson. Brett took no notice as cowgirl Marian adjusted her sunglasses and fell into the long queue behind him at the rental car counter.

Brett drove eastward on I-90 for 150 miles. Charlie suggested that Brett book a River Cabin at Quinn's Hot Springs Resort in Paradise, Montana.

Charlie was patiently waiting for Brett at the resort's Hardwood House Restaurant.

Unknown to either Charlie or Brett, cowgirl Marian was following Herr Hoffman at a discrete distance, thanks to the patch she had placed behind his right shoulder. This wasn't Marian's first rodeo. She noticed that Brett rented a Jeep Grand Cherokee Trailhawk 4x4 and she rented the same, figuring she should be prepared to go off-road.

When Brett arrived at Quinn's, despite having never met the man, he instantly spotted Charlie. Think back upon every old, cantankerous, scraggly prospector you ever saw on TV, or in the movies. That's Charlie in a nutshell, with the only difference being Charlie had a Winnebago named Nellie instead of a mule, or Jeep.

"Brett Hoffman, I presume?"

"Nice meeting you Charlie. This is quite a place. Great recommendation. Have you been followed?"

"Good Lord in heaven! I thought I was paranoid!"

Brett was unfazed by Charlie's comment, "Let's park our vehicles somewhere out of sight, then get inside."

Brett requested a corner table in the restaurant.

"Let me see them! Show me those photos."

Charlie handed Hoffman a large manilla envelope, "OK, here they are! My goodness, you are direct!"

Brett was sitting with his back to the corner of the dining room. He could see every table and booth and everyone who entered or left the dining room. He nervously scanned the room as he placed the envelope in his lap, out of sight.

"In just the past few days, this affair has resulted in the deaths of two men. Who knows how many more have died? You almost bit the dust 37 years ago."

"Yeah, that was a close one. I've got a sneaking suspicion that Heinz was not from Luxembourg. I've got a good headshot in there of my boy Heinz in uniform. Yeah, that's the one."

Brett silently stared at the photo. His face lost all expression.

Charlie addressed the spaceman's photo, "Look on his right lapel. See the double lightning bolts? Now look on his cap. See the Death's Head? I've got a picture in there torn from a photo history of Himmler's SS. It's a spot-on match. Heinz was a Lieutenant in Liebstandarte Adolf Hitler, Hitler's Bodyguard."

"Who developed these photos?"

"At ease, Hoffman. I had those developed at a drug store in downtown Helena 40 years ago. I told the clerk they were photos from a movie set out in Hollywood.

"Do you see my sketches in there? Go ahead and pull those out next."

Brett pulled out a half dozen colored pencil sketches of both die Glocke and die Größe Glocke.

"Look down in the lower right-hand corner of all my sketches. See? I had them notarized."

"You what?"

"Damn it, Hoffman, you don't listen worth a shit. I said I had my sketches notarized!"

"Charlie, whatever possessed you to have your sketches notarized?"

"Look at my face. I've spent my entire life out in the sun. I've prospected all over the West. In my younger days, I was twice swindled out of some damned lucrative mining claims by devious bastards with slick lawyers. I finally learned my lesson. Now I cover all my bases.

"Now, tell me the truth. If these here sketches weren't notarized, you would doubt whether they were 'contemporaneous'. Isn't that the word you investigator boys like to toss around?"

Hoffman chuckled as he finally realized that Charlie was no bumpkin, "I see you graduated summa cum laude from the School of Hard Knocks."

"Yep, got a Ph.D. in getting my ass kicked."

"Well, Herr Doktor Charlie, these photos and your 'contemporaneous' sketches are definitely worth a small fortune to the tabloids. Why have you sat on them for 40 years?"

"Cause, I've been chicken shit for 40 years. I figured if these pictures ever got out, Herr Heinz, and maybe his associates in the bigger UFO, might come gunning for me. My Pappy fought those bastards over there at Anzio. Strange how he hated those sons of bitches, but always bought a VW. He said those Pricks were as methodical as machines. He respected them.

"Guess what Herr Hoffman?"

Hoffman shrugged his shoulders.

"I think we both should respect them."

"Jawohl, Charlie. We better watch our asses. You mentioned Heinz' associates in the second UFO. I thought you didn't see anyone get out of the second UFO."

"I didn't. That second UFO appeared to be at least 3 times the size of Heinz' craft. I figure at least 3 or 4 of Heinz' kameraden were in that larger UFO. That's just a guess.

"Thinking back, I don't recall you ever talking about Nazis on *Sea-to-Sea,* but the regular host, Vince, has hosted several episodes dealing with secret Nazi organizations."

"You're talking about Odessa?"

"Yeah, that's what they called it in the movies."

Marian was carefully taking notes. She had parked her blue Grand Cherokee in the restaurant parking lot and focused her laser listening device on the window next to Brett and Charlie's table. Just as the conversation was getting interesting, a third voice interrupted.

"Excuse me. The restaurant will be closing to the general public in an hour. We're expecting a packed house later this evening. The Senator will be speaking and, rumor has it, his son will be with him. What a dynamic duo."

Along The Rio Grande

January 2042 was even colder than December 2041. An early January arctic blast brought freezing rain and heavy snow to the upper Rio Grande Valley. The terrible weather grounded all air reconnaissance assets. While everyone else was cursing the windy, wet, cold weather, it was an answer to Captain William Cloud's most fervent prayers.

Under cover of horrendous weather, two strike forces gathered in the high desert badlands known as the White Sands Missile Range. The Great Chief split the Mescalero forces into a northern force and a southern force.

North Force would take out the meagre Collective forces in San Antonio, then establish a line, just south of Socorro, blocking enemy reinforcements from Albuquerque & Santa Fe. Cloud was counting on North Force's assault to draw Chinese & Collective forces away from the Very Large Array. Once North Force had established a blocking position, south of Socorro, a detachment would speed westward toward Magdalena, then onward to the Very Large Array.

South Force would cross the Rio Grande at Truth or Consequences. South Force would establish a line on the northside of T or C, blocking enemy reinforcements from Las Cruces & El Paso.

In the aftermath of the Peoples' Revolution, Bill Cloud brought peace to central New Mexico. He did not disarm, nor disband the opposing parties. On the contrary, he recruited both sides into his Mescalero Legion. The Apache taught the Palefaces the bow, the horse, and the Apache knife. The White Man schooled the Apache on the instruments of modern war. The Mescalero

Legion resembled a desert thunderstorm, appearing from nowhere, striking like lightning, then disappearing into the desert from whence they came.

On the night of January 8, 2042, in the midst of a historic blizzard, all was quiet along the Rio Grande. In fact, it was too quiet. The Peoples' Militia outpost at Elephant Butte, just to the east of T or C, had gone silent, as had the outpost at Fite Ranch, just to the east of San Antonio, New Mexico. The Collective chalked it all up to the horrendous weather.

The Seelow Heights

Shortly before dawn on 16 April 1945, 9,000 Soviet guns opened fire targeting the 100,000 men of the German 9th Army entrenched upon the Seelow Heights. Next, a 1,000,000-man strong Red Army stormed across the Oder River, the Nazi's last line of defense to the east of Berlin. Soviet pincers were now closing to the north and south around the beleaguered German capital. American, British, Canadian, and Free French forces were rapidly approaching Berlin from the west.

"Das ist das ende!" Adolf Hitler knew the jig was up.

Speer was making his final visit to the Führerbunker. His later best-selling account of Hitler's Germany, *Inside the Third Reich,* would, one day, make Speer a wealthy man. Most of that account was factual. The very best liars present fact, skewed by omission, and misdirected by hyperbole. They always feed their audience what they hunger to hear. Herr Speer had learned this fine art from perhaps the greatest liar of the age.

"Speer, you will make your escape north to Flensburg. Dönitz will be in charge. The Allies will demand unconditional surrender. Make the best deal possible for yourself. Remember what I have taught you. Skorzeny and Kammler are activating die Spinne."

"What of yourself, mein Führer?"

"It would be ironic if Doktor Goebbels were directing the final act of this charade. Under his direction, I could probably win one of those filthy Jewish Oscars. But alas, my meagre acting talents must suffice. I will remain here, playing the part of a defeated suicidal psychopath. Yes, that's the perfect picture. Remember that Speer. The Allies will lap up as much of that as you can dish out."

Hitler then held out a seemingly normal left arm.

"I will now admit something, but only to you, my Architect, one of the few men I truly admire. This war has taken a terrible toll on me. Don't deny it! You have observed the tremors, here in my left arm and hand. But look at that arm today!

"That arm was trembling in fear. Not out of fear for my own life, but fear for the Fatherland. Fear of how the Bolsheviks would replace National Socialism with their Jew infected communism. That fear is now gone. Once again, I have survived a great test. As Nietzsche said, *'That which does not kill us makes us stronger.'*

"Is die Größe Glocke ready?"

Speer confidently replied, "Jawohl! Die Größe Glocke has been assembled in one of Templehof's underground hangars. Our best intelligence indicates that the Soviet 8th Guards Army, led by General Chuikov, has been ordered to capture Templehof as quickly as possible to prevent your escape. The Reds recently broke through our Seelow Heights defenses, but at great cost. They are now advancing toward the southern outskirts of Berlin."

"So, those Red bastards intend to parade me in shackles through Red Square!"

"Mein Führer, that will never happen. The main entrance to the underground hangar has been imploded. A temporal jump is the only way die Größe Glocke will ever leave that hangar. The only way to enter that hangar is via a small utility tunnel. That tunnel may only be accessed through a grate in the sidewalk along Platz der Luftbrücke. Leutnant Schneider has repeatedly traversed this route. He could walk it in his sleep.

"All the airport 88mm flak guns are well supplied with high explosive and armor piercing rounds. Elements of a panzer division and several SS units are also well positioned around Templehof.

"The prototype Glocke has already departed Ksiaz Castle. All traces of its existence are buried under untold tons of rock."

"What of the workers and technicians?"

"Everyone involved has been liquidated."

"What of Herr Doktor Heisenberg?"

"Mein Führer, we could not eliminate a Nobel Laureate. That would raise too many questions. Heisenberg believes both Glockes have been sent far into the future to prevent them from falling into Soviet hands. He has been sworn to secrecy under penalty of death.

"The two body doubles are standing by. They have been led to believe that they will be instrumental in an elaborate escape plan."

Totally out of character, the Führer embraced Speer, "My generals say it is now only a matter of days. We have called out the Volkssturm and Hitler Jugend. The Bolsheviks will pay dearly for every meter of sacred German soil, but Berlin will soon fall, along with the rest of Germany. My brilliant Architect, it is time for you to go. You have already accomplished much, but you have much more work to do over the coming years. Do not forget Skorzeny and Kammler. They will be laying the foundation for the new Reich. This is not goodbye, my dear Speer. This is merely auf wiedersehen."

Bedtime Buddies

"Brett, you ain't half as big an asshole as I first thought!"

"Well, thank you Charlie. That's the best compliment I've received all day."

"No, I'm serious. It was damned nice of you to book a two-bedroom cabin. Once in a blue moon, it's nice to get out of my Winnebago and sleep in a real bed."

"Charlie, do you have a weapon?"

"You mean a gun?"

"Yeah, a gun."

"This ain't fucking Pittsburgh! This is the West! With all these far-left loons stirring up all this shit, of course I've got a gun. I've got a shotgun, rifle, and a handgun. Which one do you want?"

"All of them."

"Jumping Jehoshaphat, Brett. What are you going to do with three guns?"

"Just go get them. I've got my Luger here with me. Please, go ahead and bring your weapons inside."

A couple of minutes later, Charlie returned to the cabin carrying a large, soft side gun case.

"Man, that restaurant parking lot has sure filled up. I'll never understand politics. People will drive for hours just to hear a clueless politician bloviate. Then, they'll shell out thousands so that same politician can ride around in a limo and fly about in a private jet." Charlie was shaking his head in a combination of disbelief and disgust.

Cowgirl Marian was nodding her head in agreement as she listened to Charlie. She had followed Brett and Charlie through her binoculars as they left the restaurant, moved their vehicles, and parked beside the Riverside Deluxe Cabin. There was limited parking space down by the river, so Marian parked her rental Jeep just off the driveway, behind a couple of Ponderosa Pines. From that vantage point, she could focus her laser listening device on the cabin's front window.

Charlie continued his rant, "Damn politicians! There's so damned many yahoos parked up at the restaurant, they're even parking down here along the driveway. That blue Jeep out there is identical to yours, except for the color."

Brett walked over to the window and glanced out at the driveway.

"Charlie, why would anyone park all the way down here? They could have parked much closer to the restaurant."

"Maybe they just need the exercise."

"You got a scope in your bag?"

"Sure do! Hang on a minute."

Just as Brett zoomed in on Marian's blue Jeep, she bugged out, trailing a cloud of dust.

"Charlie, someone was in that Jeep. They bugged out as I zoomed in with your scope."

"That's some damned coincidence."

"Perhaps. Maybe they saw me, or maybe they were listening."

"Holy shit! You think this cabin is bugged?"

"Don't think so. That would be difficult to arrange. You know, laser listening devices can be focused through windows or focused on a glass windowpane. The beam is invisible to the naked eye. Someone may have been listening to us. Next time we talk business, let's go out to the Winnebago and keep the motor running."

"Brett, is that a digital recorder I see in your bag?"

"Yeah."

"I've got an idea…"

Insertion

In early January 2042, the Resistance mole planted inside the Human Resources Department at Lawrence Livermore National Laboratories took advantage of a golden opportunity. There was an unexpected opening in the janitorial staff. One of the janitors had been denounced as a closet Christian. He was gone.

Member Kayla West steadied her nerves, then knocked on her Coordinator's office door.

"Come in!"

Kayla cracked opened the door, "Member Coordinator Rice, may I have a word?"

"Make it quick Member West." The HR Coordinator motioned for Kayla to enter. The Coordinator was overdue for a Department Coordinator luncheon at a posh local restaurant.

"I was approached yesterday by a Chinese man who just escaped from the Mormon fanatics in Deseret. He is a skilled custodian and is looking for work. He wishes to assume his rightful place in The Collective."

Member Coordinator Rita Rice smiled as she considered the advantages of bringing a new racially Chinese Member into The Collective, "This could indeed be a good fit. Has he given you any details of his life in bondage?"

Kayla forced out a few tears, "It was horrible. Those White Mormon fanatics forced him to adhere to their patriarchal, racist lifestyle."

Coordinator Rice continued gaming things out in her mind, "His story might be compelling material for a Peoples' News Network special. He's not chipped?"

"No, Coordinator Rice. He is not yet a Member."

"Eager as we are to bring a new productive Member into The Collective, we must follow all security protocols. What's his name?"

"Tony, Tony Lin."

The Boss

"Chuikov, this is Khrushchev. The Boss demands that you immediately capture Templehof."

General Chuikov's stammering and apprehensive voice crackled back over the radio, but Khrushchev cut him off midsentence. Khrushchev had little time for excuses.

"The Boss wants to see that Bohemian Corporal paraded in chains through the Big Hall of the State Kremlin Palace."

It was April 1945. The Soviet Union's murderous despot, Joseph Stalin, had sent his ace troubleshooter to light a fire under his generals' asses. Nikita Sergeyevich Khrushchev had once before crossed paths with General Chuikov. In late 1942, Chuikov was in command of the crumbling defense of Stalingrad. The Boss sent Khrushchev to Stalingrad to shake things up. The German 6th Army was poised to personally embarrass Stalin by capturing his namesake metropolis on the banks of the River Volga. Hitler and Stalin had transformed the Battle of Stalingrad into a dictatorial deathmatch.

"Comrade Khrushchev, I can personally guarantee Comrade Stalin that not a single Fascist aircraft will take off from Templehof."

"Like you guaranteed me you would hold Stalingrad? You should kiss Zhukov's hairy ass for saving your worthless hide at Stalingrad. I am not willing to once again stake my neck upon your guarantees!"

Khrushchev wasn't joking. The price of failure in Stalin's Red Army was typically death. Of course, all too often, the reward for victory was also death. Stalin routinely purged his military. There could only be one Boss!

"The Boss wants him taken alive. There will be hell to pay if the Americans, or the bloody British, get to him first."

Stalin constantly played his generals against one another. The Boss trusted no one, let alone his generals.

After the Russian victory at Stalingrad, Stalin placed Khrushchev in charge of the Ukraine, Russia's breadbasket. As the Nazis were slowly, but surely, pushed back out of Ukraine, it was Khrushchev's responsibility to first eliminate collaborators and other counterrevolutionaries, then get both Ukrainian industry and agriculture back online. His ruthlessness earned him the nickname, "Butcher of the Ukraine".

Khrushchev's mission to the front was top secret. The Boss put out the cover story that he had granted Khrushchev a one-week vacation at a luxury Georgian Black Sea dacha as a reward for his work in Ukraine. In reality, Khrushchev had been given one week's accommodations in Chuikov's forward command post on the Seelow Heights. It was now 26 April 1945 and Khrushchev's "life clock" was ticking down, second by second. If Hitler was not captured within the week, Nikita Khrushchev would be toast.

General Chuikov was not gaslighting Khrushchev. Soviet forces were now advancing through the southern outskirts of Berlin with lead elements camped amongst the rubble on the southern edge of Templehof Airport. Soviet fighter aircraft freely roamed the skies over Berlin. Templehof's runways and taxiways resembled the cratered surface of the moon. There was no way anyone could fly into, or out of Templehof. The Soviets were convinced that Adolf Hitler could not escape.

Charlie's Trap

Brett and Charlie's impromptu recording session was interrupted by Brett's cellphone's spooky ring tone.

"Hey Brett, it's Mike. Got some info on the dead man."

"Let me guess. He's a Kraut!"

"Nope, not even close."

Brett was now totally confused, "Then who in the hell was he?"

"Israeli national, name and all other personal information withheld per Tel Aviv's request.

"My contact, down at the morgue, confirms that he definitely could be Jewish, if you know what I mean."

"Mike, I'm smelling Mossad."

"Me too, ol' buddy. I'm here to tell you; this police investigation was quashed from the very top."

"Why would any Israeli, particularly Mossad, try to coverup a Nazi wunderwaffen?"

"That's a question for you to answer. You're the paranormal investigator. I'll keep you posted."

Brett was noticeably distracted as he and Charlie continued their recording session. As Brett's long silence filled the riverside cabin, a disgusted Charlie reached over and shut off the recorder.

"Damn it, Hoffman! What are you doing? Thinking about Christmas?"

Brett snapped out of his trance, "Sorry about that. I guess you overheard some of my conversation?"

Charlie sarcastically replied, "Only the inconsequential reference to Mossad covering for Nazis. That's all."

"Seriously Charlie, what in the hell is going on?"

"I don't know, my friend, but whatever is going on, we're already ass deep into it."

Brett was still operating on Pittsburgh time, so he was up with the sun. Charlie always operated on prospector time, so he was up before Brett. Jerry Patel was actually in Pittsburgh, so he was already in his office, calling Brett, before Brett had finished dressing.

"Good morning, Brett. I've finished that IT work you requested."

"Fantastic. Did you find anything of interest?"

"Nope. Didn't examine any data. Just downloaded information. That's all."

"I gotcha. I'm out of town. I'll give you a call when I get back."

Brett knew exactly what Jerry was doing. Jerry was pursuing a policy of plausible deniability. Sure, he hacked into the two devices for a friend, a noted celebrity, but he had absolutely no idea what was on those devices. He had no idea those devices were potential evidence in a criminal investigation. That was Jerry's story, and he was sticking to it.

Charlie's stomach growled like a Montana grizzly, "Come on Hoffman, let's grab a bite to eat, your treat."

Then Charlie whispered, "Don't forget to switch it on."

As the digital recorder began replaying the duo's fake conversation, they snuck out the cabin's backdoor and kept mostly to the trees on their quarter mile hike to the restaurant. The mountain air was cold and clear with the pleasant aroma of woodsmoke thrown in for good measure. Brett enjoyed the walk.

Two young lads were at their post, just inside the lodge's front door, handing out flyers. Another pre-teen was armed with mop and broom, cleaning up any snow, mud, or water tracked in by the patrons.

Charlie pointed at the boys, "You don't see young people like that anymore!"

The boys all wore long sleeve, white, pinpoint oxford cloth shirts with navy blue slacks and a red "power necktie". An American flag tie clip kept that necktie anchored neatly in place. They were immaculately groomed with regular haircuts and spit shined Corfam shoes.

"Sir, there's some mud on your shoes. May I wipe them for you?"

Brett was totally unprepared for this, "No, no thank you." Brett now felt totally self-conscious and frantically wiped his shoes on the large doormat.

"Sir, would you like a copy of the Senator's plan for America?"

Charlie took one of the flyers just out of respect, with no intention of ever reading it.

A folding table was set up next to the restaurant doorway. Two young ladies were selling brownies, cookies, and cupcakes. The blonde haired and blue eyed pre-adolescent girls were drop dead gorgeous, dressed in navy blue skirts, white, oxford cloth blouses, and red scarves tied around their necks. They both wore American flag themed jewelry. A large goldfish bowl was sitting on the table and Brett noticed several $20 bills and at least one C-note stuff in the glass bowl amongst all the fives and tens.

The restaurant hostess was a retired lady, supplementing her Social Security. She was smooth as silk, a real pro.

Hoffman figured she would be in the know, "What's going on around here? I didn't know the Mormons started evangelizing at such a young age."

The hostess giggled like a schoolgirl, "Aren't they precious? We have a large LDS community here in the valley, but those children are not all Mormon. They are all volunteers."

"Excuse me, I'm from back East. For what have they volunteered?"

"Oh, back East? That explains it. Let me guess…"

The hostess paused for a split second, in deep thought, then replied, "Pittsburgh! Did I get it right?"

"That's amazing! You got me pegged. You were explaining the kids…"

"They're supporting the Senator's son. He's running in the special election for Montana's open US Senate seat. Can you imagine father and son Senators?"

Hoffman followed the paranormal, not politics, "Oh, that's pretty cool. Please seat us away from any windows."

Prepping the Bitch

Captain Delvin Smith waited in anticipation as the snow accumulated on Main Street in Springerville, Arizona. It was only a matter of time until his rare earth convoy made its run across the Rio Grande. Slick was more than a little thankful that he brought along a snowplow. Our man hadn't yet worked out all the details, but he had the sequence down pat, more or less. When all hell broke loose in Socorro and Truth or Consequences, his team would grab a couple of eggheads from the Very Large Array, neutralize any security protecting that asset, then Lieutenant Josephine Parker and Badass Bitch would lay waste to the entire complex. After the smoke cleared, the rare earth convoy would haul ass straight through to Roswell.

Big Sid and his Daddy, Bobby Lee Skipper, were snug inside a hangar at the Springerville Municipal Airport. Badass Bitch remained perched upon her lowboy trailer as the Skippers gave the warbird a thorough once over. Ever the perfectionist, Lieutenant Josephine Parker rolled up her sleeves and worked alongside the Skipper boys. Jo scrutinized the Huey Cobra from bow to stern. Her life depended on it.

"Boys, once we finish the preflight checks, we'll load the ordnance. Skip the armor piercing munitions. Concentrate on high explosives and incendiaries."

Big Sid pointed at a crate full of 70 mm rockets.

Jo shot Sid a thumbs up, "That's right, Big Man. The yellow ones are HE and the light red ones are incendiaries."

Halfway through the ordnance loading process, a gust of cold air wafted through the hangar as the man door burst open. Former Army Ranger, John Nicolescu, was standing in the doorway, barely recognizable, all bundled up like an Eskimo.

"Hey, Big Man, we got a mission."

Caught

Unknown to Marian, Brett & Charlie were just finishing their breakfast. While Brett was paying the check, Marian plopped her rather shapely ass down on a tree stump amid several Ponderosa Pines and pointed her laser at Brett's Riverside Cabin's window. Brett's Jeep was there, as was Charlie's Winnebago.

"Yep, looks like they're still in there." Over her laser listening device, Marian could hear the two chit-chatting.

Meanwhile Brett & Charlie were skulking through the woods, heading back to their cabin.

"Charlie, you have your Smith & Wesson?"

Charlie chuckled, "Never leave the Winnebago without it! How about you?"

"Yeah, I'm packing."

About halfway back to the cabin, Charlie pulled out his binoculars.

"Let's stick to the trees while I scope things out.

"Don't see that blue Grand Cherokee…

"Hold it! Hold it. There's a little gal in a Stetson down there amongst those Ponderosa Pines."

Brett reached for the field glasses, "Let me take a look…

"Holy shit!"

"What's wrong Hoffman? One of your exes finally track you down? That little filly is quite a looker."

"That 'little filly' has followed me from Pittsburgh all the way out here. She's somehow in on this whole thing."

Charlie replied, "I guess it's time we make our introductions. You go right, I'll go left."

Both Brett and Charlie pulled their sidearms and quietly, but swiftly, moved towards their quarry.

"Drop the laser and reach for the sky!" Brett had his Luger pointed right between Marian's pretty brown eyes.

"The three of us, Smith, Wesson, and me, suggest you do as Mr. Hoffman says." Charlie levelled his .44 Magnum on the Squirrel Hill cowgirl.

Brett sternly shouted, "Put your hands on your head with fingers intertwined. OK, now take a knee!"

This was a real life and death situation, not some cheap novel, or cheesy TV show. Marian did exactly as Brett instructed.

"Charlie, check her pockets."

Charlie pulled an iPhone and a Beretta from Marian's pockets and tossed them to Brett.

"I think she's clean."

"Not so fast. Check her shoes."

"Come on Brett, you think she's got a razor in her Adidas?"

Brett shot Charlie a rebuking stare.

Charlie reluctantly checked out Marian's feet, "Like I said, she's clean."

Brett shouted again, "Let's get her ass inside the cabin."

Brett held his gun on Marian's back while Charlie kept his S&W pointed right between her eyes. Then, they all three marched over to the cabin, with Brett locking the door behind them as they entered.

Brett shut off the digital recorder and got down to business, "OK, Annie Oakley, start talking."

"My name is Marian. I live in Squirrel Hill. I was at Chatham for your Halloween lecture."

Charlie interrupted, "So Hoffman, she really is a groupie."

"Don't think so. She was at the lecture asking questions about the Kecksburg incident. Afterwards, she followed me to a diner in Squirrel Hill. She's been tailing me off and on ever since."

Brett noticed Marian's beautiful brown eyes and softly curled raven hair, "OK, Marian, you don't look like a fucking Nazi. Sind Sie Juden?"

Brett caught a glimpse of a fine gold chain necklace beneath Marian's flannel shirt. He reached out and grabbed the necklace, breaking its clasp in the process. There it was. A small 22 karat gold Star of David hung from Marian's necklace.

Brett turned to Charlie, necklace in hand, and pointed at Marian, "Juden."

"Yes, I'm Jewish, you German son of a bitch!"

"Your friend in the black leather trench coat is dead."

"I don't know what you're talking about."

Hoffman didn't believe her, "Why are your Israeli kameraden covering for those Nazi bastards?"

Marian was totally confused, "Listen, we're on the same side, I've heard enough to know that you're tracking those bastards too."

"Yes, we're tracking some bastards, but just who are they?"

"Here, call this number." Marian scribbled a phone number on a hotel notepad.

"306 area code is Los Angeles. Why should I call LA?"

"Just call it, you obstinate Kraut!"

"Charlie, dial that 306 number on the room telephone."

Charlie dialed the number.

A recorded voice answered, "*Simon Wiesenthal Center…*"

Marian snarled at Brett, "OK, Hoffman follow the prompts, my extension is 101."

Brett took the phone from Charlie and followed the prompts.

"*You've reached the voicemail of Marian Metzner. I'm out of the office on assignment. You can leave a message at the tone, or call my cellphone…*"

That was definitely Marian's voice on the recorded message.

Marian sarcastically prompted Brett, "OK Hoffman, dial the damned cell number!"

Hoffman hung up the room phone, then dialed the cellphone number. Marian's iPhone rang.

"Now, are you satisfied?"

Brett curtly replied, "I'm satisfied that you are associated with Wiesenthal, but you could be a mole."

Marian was exasperated, "Let me get this straight. A female Jew, associated with Wiesenthal, working for the Nazis?"

Brett quickly replied, "Or a female Jew, associated with Wiesenthal, actually a Mossad agent, covering for the Nazis!

"I'm going to count to three. You're going to tell me about the guy in the black trench coat."

Charlie was now holding the barrel of his .44 Magnum up against Marian's left temple.

"One, two, three!"

Charlie pulled the trigger.

Marian flinched as the Smith & Wesson's hammer slammed down on an empty chamber with a loud click.

Brett spun the pistol's cylinder randomly, "Are you ready for the bonus round? Quite a game those Ruskies invented.

"Now, before Charlie tries again, who was the guy tailing you the other night after you left the Drive-n-Dine?"

Marian suspected Brett was bluffing, "I'm telling you the truth. I don't know."

Brett shook his head negatively, "Auf wiedersehen Marian!"

Marian decided not to take the chance, "You two amateurs are going to get yourselves killed and probably get me killed in the process! I don't know that guy. He began tailing me immediately after I left your lecture on Halloween."

"Why would anyone tail you? From what I know of the Wiesenthal Center, they don't conduct field operations. They leave the dirty work up to Mossad." Bret carefully focused on Marian's body language as he mentioned Israeli Intelligence.

"Yes, you're right. I'm just an analyst!"

"Bullshit! That's a state-of-the-art laser eavesdropping device. I bet your Grand Cherokee is loaded with a bunch of other toys. Since when do analysts pack heat?"

"My pistol is for self-defense. It's a .22, a lady's pistol."

"Once again, I call bullshit! I know my handguns. That's a Beretta Model 70. Marian, please fill Charlie in on the details."

"What details?"

"Tell Charlie all about your damned pistol."

"Well, the Model 70 is a very dependable handgun."

"Please continue…"

"It fires a .22 caliber Long Rifle round. The magazine holds 8 rounds."

"Yes, but who carries the Model 70?"

Marian hesitated, then scowled at Brett, "You insipid bastard, you know damned well that's a Mossad handgun."

Brett smiled, ignoring Marian's aggravation, "The Model 70 was replaced years ago by a 9 mm, but many Mossad operatives still carry the Beretta. It's a good close quarters weapon. Just powerful enough to kill without a lot of collateral damage. Great for assassination."

Brett walked over to Marian, put the Beretta to her head, and reprised the role of *Sonny Corleone*, *"You gotta get up close like this and bada bing!"*

Das Ende

BADA BING! A single muffled shot emanated from Hitler's private quarters and echoed throughout the Führerbunker.

It was 30 April 1945. The Soviets were making their final assault upon the Reich Chancellery. Meanwhile, the situation at Templehof Airport was chaotic. Diehard SS units were firing 20 mm flak guns from point blank range into advancing Soviet forces. Brainwashed 12-year-old Hitler Youth crawled through the rubble, firing handheld Panzerfaust anti-tank weapons at Russian armored vehicles from ranges measured in mere feet. Most of the old men in the Volkssturm either melted away, or just gave up, although the few remaining Gestapo did not hesitate shooting anyone attempting to surrender.

Leutnant Wolfgang Schneider, Otto Günsche (Hitler's personal adjutant), and two unidentified Wehrmacht grenadiers carried the bodies of Adolf Hitler and Ava Braun, now Frau Hitler, up to the Reich Chancellery garden. The Führer's barely recognizable face was contorted and bloody, courtesy of a self-inflicted gunshot to the head. Frau Hitler's body smelled of bitter almonds. Her contorted face was yet further evidence of cyanide poisoning.

Günsche laid both bodies atop a small pile of petrol-soaked wood, then, for good measure, doused the bodies themselves with diesel. The few bystanders in the garden stood to attention as Günsche ignited a flare and tossed it upon the makeshift funeral pyre. Moments later, a weeping Günsche turned to seek condolences from Leutnant Schneider. To his dismay, Schneider and his two Wehrmacht helpers had vanished.

Wolf whimpered as he poked his head out from under one of the grenadier's greatcoat. Both grenadiers had their coat collars turned up for warmth. As was customary on the frigid Eastern Front, the grenadiers wore balaclavas, covering their faces for warmth.

Wolf was crying for his mother. Blondi's body, along with the bodies of the other four of her five pups, was now burning in the Reich Chancellery garden. Mother and pups had been given cyanide. Wolf was the only canine survivor from the bunker.

Moments later, Schneider and his kameraden were running through the pitch-black escape tunnel. It was now that Schneider's relentless rehearsals paid off. Russian shelling had interrupted electrical power. Constant shelling shook the tunnel, filling it with dust. Small chunks of concrete fell from the ceiling at several points during the 3-kilometer underground exodus, but the tunnel did not collapse.

40 minutes after departing the Führerbunker, Schneider poked his head out into the Luftbrücke Underground Station, with MP 40 machine pistol in hand. As his two companions exited the tunnel, Schneider fired a short burst over the heads of the four enslaved Polish stonemasons posted at the tunnel entrance.

"Seal the opening and cover the brick with plaster. I will return in two hours. I expect the job to be completed to my satisfaction!"

The trio pushed and shoved their way through masses of humanity. Berlin's underground was now packed like sardines in a can, with residents fleeing the shear carnage unfolding on the streets above. Schneider led the way, not stopping until they reached the surface.

He pointed to the southeast, "We must traverse 200 meters of open ground. Follow me, stay close, and keep low."

Three new targets popped out of the Luftbrücke Station and began running erratically to the southeast. The two-man crew of a Dushka heavy machinegun spotted the movement and engaged the three targets with 12.7 mm rounds. Schneider shoved both his companions down into a shell crater. He returned fire with his MP 40, but his fire was ineffective due to range limitations. Wolfgang lobbed a couple of smoke grenades in the general direction of the Soviet machinegun nest.

"To your feet, follow me!"

The smoke from the two grenades merged with the dust and haze inherent to the battlefield, obstructing the Russians' view. Leutnant Schneider used that brief opening to make their escape. In mere moments, all three fugitives were lying prone behind a burning Sturmgeschütz III tank destroyer. Three nearby Soviet T-34s were engulfed in flame, having been killed by the lone StuG III.

Schneider pulled a pry bar from his backpack and lifted a cast iron grate set into the sidewalk.

"We must go back underground." Schneider helped lower his two companions down into the dark, dank, utility tunnel, then followed them, closing the grate behind him.

As they traversed the utility tunnel, Schneider reassured them, "This tunnel is short, only about 50 meters to go."

Leutnant Schneider ignited a couple of flares and tossed them into the underground hangar. Before abandoning their posts and fleeing the utility tunnel, the Gestapo guards had murdered the handful of concentration camp laborers servicing die Größe Glocke. Their emaciated, bullet riddled, bloody bodies were scattered all about. It is hard to imagine that this was the Führer's first glimpse of Himmler's handiwork. Hitler was characteristically unmoved.

Schneider was pissed, "Damned Gestapo! The device should be energized and ready to jump!"

Nothing ever goes according to plan in a military operation. Now was time for Schneider's Aryan mind to once again improvise.

Adolf Hitler removed his helmet and his balaclava, "Leutnant, how long until we jump?"

"30 minutes mein Führer!"

By now, Frau Hitler had also removed her headgear. She was standing by the utility tunnel entrance, sickened by the ghastly scene on display in the hangar.

She whispered to Hitler, "Adi, someone is following us. I hear someone back in the tunnel."

Schneider stuck his head back into the tunnel, "Frau Hitler is right. There is movement down the tunnel. Mein Führer, over there are some demolition charges, in case circumstances force the destruction of die Größe Glocke. They have a short time delay fuse."

"Very good. Leutnant Schneider, take Frau Hitler onboard the craft and begin energization. I will place a charge a short distance back in the tunnel, then join you in the machine. The blast will seal the tunnel and we will jump shortly thereafter."

Eva Hitler cradled Wolf in her arms as she boarded die Größe Glocke, "Adi, do be careful!"

Adolph Hitler's mind flashed back to his daring exploits during the Great War. With satchel charge in-hand, he kicked an emaciated, bullet-riddled Jewish corpse out of his way and ran back into the utility tunnel.

A disgusted Hitler exclaimed, "Bolsheviks!"

The Führer of the German Reich could now clearly discern Russian voices in the tunnel.

This was merely another critical mission for Corporal Hitler. He recalled many such missions, running through No Man's Land, carrying urgent dispatches, thousands of lives dependent upon him. Now, the stakes were much higher. The very future of civilization depended upon him. Only he could defeat the untermenschen and their twisted, Jew inspired, communist ideology. Hitler pulled the cord on the satchel charge and began to toss it further up the tunnel. Yes, he was certain that Providence would once again smile upon Adolf Hitler.

Before the charge left the Führer's hand, it prematurely detonated, blowing him to bits and burying what little remained under tons of dirt, concrete, rock, and steel, never again to see the light of day.

Speer Faces Defeat

After his final visit to the Führerbunker, Albert Speer flew to Hamburg, then made his way by motorcar northward to Flensburg, on the Danish border. There, Hitler's successor, Admiral Karl Dönitz, was assembling a provisional government. The Admiral hoped, in some way, to salvage something for the German people. Speer assumed the role of Minister of Industry and Production for the Flensburg Government. By that time, Germany had little industry and virtually no production.

The day after Hitler met his end, Doktor Joseph Goebbels and his wife refused to abandon their quarters in the Vorbunker. The Goebbels poisoned their 6 children, then committed suicide. Most accounts state that they took cyanide and were subsequently shot for good measure.

One week after the Führer's demise, Dönitz ordered his Chief of Staff, Alfred Jodl, to unconditionally surrender to General Eisenhower in Rheims, France. A couple of weeks later, the Flensburg government was dissolved as British forces arrested Dönitz, Speer, and the rest of the Flensburg leadership.

Germany was now partitioned. The Russians controlled the East, with the West divided into French, British, and American occupied zones.

Speer cooperated with the Allies from the start. The Allies, particularly the Americans, were amazed that German war production had not collapsed under the intense strategic bombing campaign. The urbane, dignified, literate, and articulate Speer held his interrogators spellbound as he succinctly and calmly described his bureaucratic function within the Third Reich. From the time of his arrest, Speer meticulously cultivated the "Good Nazi" myth.

Speer was placed on trial in Nuremburg along with 23 other major war criminals. Fatso Hermann Göring was the de facto leader of the defendants. He was arrogant and unapologetic. It was only natural that Göring and Speer would clash. Ultimately, Göring was convicted and sentenced to death. He cheated the hangman by taking cyanide the night before his scheduled execution.

Hitler's enigmatic #2, Rudolf Hess, was sentenced to life in prison. Hess had suffered a breakdown, of sorts, back in May 1941. At that time, Hess flew a plane to Scotland and was immediately arrested. Ostensibly, Hess was distraught with his loss of Hitler's favor and was against the impending invasion of the Soviet Union. He hoped to negotiate a deal with Churchill. Hess was mad as a hatter. He committed suicide in Spandau Prison in 1987.

A few days before Hitler's apparent suicide, the BBC broadcast a Reuter's news report claiming that Himmler was seeking a separate peace deal with the Western Allies. Hitler subsequently stripped Himmler of his powers and ordered his arrest. Himmler went into hiding, disguised as a common soldier. Three weeks after Hitler's suicide, Himmler was detained at a Russian checkpoint and, shortly thereafter, committed suicide using a concealed cyanide capsule.

The daring Admiral Dönitz did not apologize for his ruthless use of unrestricted submarine warfare. He took no active part in the Holocaust. When the Allies attempted to convict Dönitz of war crimes, based upon his use of unrestricted submarine warfare, Dönitz' defense countered by describing the Allies' unrestricted use of submarines. Dönitz was basically convicted of fighting on the losing side. He served 10 years in prison, then lived out the remainder of his life in relative obscurity. He died of a heart attack on Christmas Eve 1989 at age 89.

While Speer did accept responsibility for his role in Nazi arms production, he categorically denied any knowledge of Himmler's Final Solution of the Jewish Question. Three of the eight judges weren't buying what Speer was peddling and advocated the death penalty. Speer remembered his Führer's advice. He claimed to be apolitical, merely a technocrat thrust into an impossible situation. Speer's use of slave labor nearly sent him to the gallows, but after two days of heated deliberations, the 8-judge tribunal compromised and sentenced Speer to 20 years in Spandau prison.

Outwardly, Speer was cool, calm, and collected as his 20-year sentence was announced.

Deep in his Nazi heart, Speer sighed with relief, "Wherever and whenever you are, mein Führer, vielen dank und auf wiedersehen."

The Vet & Sid Show

20 minutes after leaving the hangar, Big Sid & Vet were seated in the cafeteria at the Arizona Ranger outpost on Main Street in downtown Springerville. Before the shit hit the fan, the outpost had been a fairly successful motor lodge. The attached lounge & restaurant now served as a cafeteria and a briefing room for the Springerville Ranger detachment.

John & Sid rose in unison as Captain Smith entered the room. After exchanging salutes, Slick got down to business.

"Sergeant Nicolescu, before this convoy can proceed eastward, we must take out a large facility known as the Very Large Array. The Array sits directly in our path, astride US 60, between Datil and Magdalena. You may be somewhat familiar with the Array. Back in the real world, the Array was a favorite subject of science fiction movies and pulp fiction. There is a large security detachment protecting the Array, both Peoples' Militia and Red Chinese Falcon Commandos."

John (aka: Vet) interrupted Slick, "Captain Smith, Sir, Lieutenant Parker is at the airport prepping her Cobra. Can't Badass Bitch take out the Array?"

Delvin nodded in agreement, "Yes, she can and yes, she will, but that task may not be so easy. The Falcon Commandos are most probably equipped with the latest upgrade of the HN-6 man portable surface-to-air missile. Our Mescalero ground intel assets report that a mechanized Chinese convoy recently passed through Magdalena, heading west. Four 6x6 armored vehicles led that convoy, followed by several straight trucks. Our SIGINT analysts suspect that a Chinese HQ-7B SAM battery has taken up residence at the Array. If so, one of the battery's armored vehicles carries a sophisticated acquisition radar. That asset is most probably stationed near the center of the Array. An armored launch vehicle is probably assigned to each of the Array's three spokes. Each launch vehicle carries four missiles and its own fire control radar.

"Vet, our girl Josephine can take those bastards out if she gets the drop on them, but that damned acquisition radar has a detection range of 25 klicks. Those SAMs are ineffective at ranges under 700 meters. If you and the Big Man can sneak in there and take out that acquisition radar, then maybe our girl Jo can slip inside those missiles' effective range and take them out.

"While you're at the center of the Array, you'll be near the Operations Center. That's where you'll grab a couple of technicians. Better still, grab a couple of their scientists. We gotta know what those bastards are doing out there."

"Captain, I know Josephine can fly that Cobra on the razor's edge, but, once we blow that acquisition radar, its gonna get hairy real fast. Those Chinese HN-6 shoulder fired missiles are very capable. I've heard that they're hard to jam, or decoy."

"John, you'll be wearing your CZ suit with Big Sid covering your six. I'm expecting you to suppress their air defense and I'm counting on Josephine to work her magic and come up with some innovative tactics."

Marian's Mea Culpa

"Get the fucking guns out of my face!" Marian had enough of Brett & Charlie's asinine theatrics.

Brett lowered the Beretta, "So, you're ready to talk?"

"No, but I am ready to have a conversation."

Brett paused momentarily, unloaded the Beretta, then handed it to Marian, "You are Mossad?"

"That's my regular gig, but I moonlight hunting fucking Nazis."

Brett flippantly replied, "Well Maid Marian, me thinks you need a new business model. The Nazi herd is gradually thinning out, year-by-year."

"That doesn't seem to be discouraging you, Herr Hoffman. Looks like you've recently taken up the same sideline."

"Not voluntarily. Seems certain subjects featured on *Sea-to-Sea AM* are taboo, verboten!

"One of your homies capped a hundred-year-old Army Air Force veteran, then got himself wasted when he attempted to murder another Glocke eyewitness. This Glocke mystery seems to be cloaked in murder. Charlie almost got himself shot back in 1985 when he witnessed the appearance of not just one, but two Glocke. I can't blame Mossad for Charlie's close call. His brush with death was courtesy of Leutnant Heinz of Liebstandarte Adolf Hitler."

Marian flashed Brett the side eye, "Since when is Mossad in the business of assassinating veterans, particularly those who bombed the hell out of those Nazi bastards?"

"Perhaps not, but Pee Wee's assassin was Jewish, I'll know more when I get back to Pittsburgh."

"Back home to all your *Sea-to-Sea* groupies at Carnegie Mellon?" Marian would never admit it, but she too was a *Sea-to-Sea* groupie and more than a little jealous of Brett's Carnegie Mellon fan club.

Sea-to-Sea's regular emcee, Vince Vittito, occasionally hosted Nazi themed episodes. Most of those episodes were pure crap, but Marian carefully listened, hoping to garner every shred of useful information.

While Marian never missed a *Sea-to-Sea AM* episode, she lived for the next Brett Hoffman radio or TV appearance. Marian would never admit it, but she was Brett's most devoted groupie. She recorded every Hoffman TV appearance and replayed them ad nauseum. In her most erotic dreams, Hoffman would appear as a Gestapo officer and Marian would be the alluring Jewess who seduced him.

Marian's mother had no clue that her daughter was Mossad.

She constantly harangued her daughter, "Marian, you're a beautiful, smart young lady. When are you going to settle down with a nice Jewish boy and give me some grandchildren? My friends tell me all about their sons, or nephews, or neighbors, who are looking for a wife. CPAs, doctors, lawyers, even a rabbi, all looking for a proper Jewish wife."

Bad girl Marian tuned all that out. She knew what she wanted. She wanted to taste the forbidden fruit. Her Mom could keep the fumbling CPAs with their dorky pocket protectors. Even now, as Hoffman confronted her and interrogated her, Marian found herself staring at him and unconsciously brushing back her hair. Before speaking, Marian would softly bite her lip. Marian had a bad case of the hots for Brett.

Marian quickly snapped out of her momentary erotic fantasy, "And what in the hell were the SS doing in Idaho back in 1985?"

TW POWELL © 2023

Everything suddenly fell into place in Charlie's mind, "Heinz was gathering information. He was the pathfinder. Then he called in the cavalry."

Hoffman and Marian looked at Charlie, then looked at one another.

"Marian, something very big is going down."

"You're right, Hoffman. My superiors in Tel Aviv have practically ordered me to stand down on my Nazi hunt. I'm even taking some flak from the Foundation. They're talking about scaling back their support for my field operations, citing fundraising shortfalls. Most troubling is the uptick in die Spinne activities."

The Jump

Frau Hitler was crying hysterically, "Leutnant Schneider, we cannot leave. Adi is back there in the tunnel."

Schneider was busy, preparing to jump, "Die Größe Glocke is nearing 100% energization. I fear our Führer is dead."

Wolfgang tightly strapped Eva into her seat. She was clutching whimpering Wolf in her arms. Die Größe Glocke was whining and glowing. A bluish aura filled the underground hangar. St. Elmo's Fire now danced along all the metallic surfaces throughout the hangar.

"Frau Hitler, Eva, I am only following my Führer's orders."

Eva was now quite ill, "I think I'm going to be sick. My Adi is gone."

"Leutnant, what is happening?"

Die Größe Glocke was buffeted about as it streaked down through the clear Montana sky.

"Leutnant, it is getting uncomfortably hot in here. I am getting nauseous."

Schneider had prepared for all foreseeable eventualities. He handed Frau Hitler a motion sickness bag.

At 20,000 feet, Wolfgang activated the antigravity drive, praying that it worked.

"Have we departed?"

"Jawohl, Frau Hitler! We are even now approaching our destination."

Die Größe Glocke gradually slowed its descent and landed with a thud only a few meters from the prototype.

"Leutnant, where are we?"

"Frau Hitler, we have arrived. According to the chronometer, it is 1985 and we are somewhere in the American West. We must stay seated for about 30 minutes and allow the exterior to cool."

Five loud bangs reverberated throughout die Größe Glocke.

"That's Heinz! That's our comrade! That's the signal!"

Heinz was banging on the red-hot exterior of die Größe Glocke with a trenching shovel.

30 minutes later, Leutnant Schneider cracked the exterior hatch.

A covey of California quail suddenly flushed. Heinz turned toward some movement in the nearby tree line.

"Crack! Crack! Crack! Crack!"

"Stay inside Frau Hitler, that's pistol fire. That's Heinz' Luger."

Heinz pursued Charlie for a short distance. He saw no blood trail. His quarry had eluded him. Heinz quickly returned to the two Glockes.

By now, both Schneider and Eva had emerged from die Größe Glocke. Wolf was romping through the tall, spring grass. Evening was approaching and the June mountain air was crisp and clean.

Eva inhaled the clean Montana air, "Wunderbar, just like the Berghof! My Adi planned this so perfectly."

Schneider took Eva by the hand, "Our Führer died for us and for all Aryans. He died fighting the untermenschen and their Jew inspired Bolshevik ideology. We must never forget."

Heinz chimed in, "We must never forget."

Eva made it a trio, "We must never forget. Adi, I will never forget."

Heinz saluted Schneider and gave him a brief report, "We should sleep in die Größe Glocke tonight. We can keep the device in standby mode, ready to jump on short notice. Tomorrow, I will hitchhike into the town of Plains, Montana. I have already contacted an excavation company and paid them a deposit. We must move both devices to a secure location."

Schneider was surprised by the urgency in Heinz' voice, "Leutnant Schuster, please explain your cause for concern. We seem to be quite safe in this remote location."

"Herr Leutnant, my initial jump took me to Pennsylvania in 1965. Within hours, the prototype was surrounded by US military police, loaded onto a truck, and was being hauled away. I made the second jump, here, to this place and time, to escape captivity.

"Just now, I fired my pistol at someone watching from the woods. I fear they have escaped.

"I've had somewhat limited opportunity to research this society. There is much suspicion. They are locked in a life and death struggle with the Bolsheviks. They call it a 'Cold War'. The technology at their disposal is unbelievable, although much of that technology was conceived by Reich scientists. They now have uranium devices and hydrogen augmented uranium devices that can vaporize entire cities with a single blast. Jet aircraft now fly several times the speed of sound. Their missiles make the V-2 look like a toy. In 1969, the Americans landed men on the Moon and safely returned them to Earth."

Eva looked up into the sky and pointed, "They have visited the Moon. Mein Gott!"

Heinz also stared into the sky as he continued, "There is another mania, or fascination, gripping this culture. They are obsessed with all things science fiction. They are fixated upon unidentified flying objects. This fixation began shortly after the war as reports of 'flying saucers' poured in. Upon reflection, this phenomenon may have its roots in the wunderwaffen. American aviators reported our wunderwaffen as Foo Fighters. We must relocate die Glocke to a hidden secure location. I fear that one, or both, Glocke may have been spotted during their descent, either visually, or on radar."

Wolfgang replied, "Once more, time has vindicated our Führer. He knew the Americans would be the dominant power, but he feared they lacked the mettle down deep in their souls to defeat the Bolsheviks. He idolized the American pioneers but was disgusted by the dilution of America's racial purity. Jews, Negroes, and untermenschen have polluted America. They should have heeded Frau Sanger's advice."

In the short time they shared together in the Führerbunker, Adolf Hitler had bared his dark soul to Leutnant Schneider.

Heinz verified the Führer's suspicion, "Jawohl, that has already occurred in Indochina. In late Summer 1945, after the Americans vaporized two Japanese cities with uranium devices, the Japanese Emperor surrendered. The nation of Korea was then partitioned with the Bolsheviks occupying the northern half and the Allies supporting the democratic southern half. In 1950, the Bolsheviks invaded the South and almost conquered all Korea. The Americans finally pushed the Bolsheviks out of the South but lacked the will to use their uranium devices to decisively defeat the Chinese Bolsheviks. In the 1960s and 70s the same thing happened in Vietnam. The American military defeated the Bolsheviks, but their bourgeois civilian leadership lacked the political will to secure a political victory."

Schneider was lost in thought, "Heinz, can you imagine what we could do with those missiles, jet aeroplanes, and uranium devices?

"Heinz, what of the Fatherland?"

"Since the end of the war, Germany has been divided into two countries. East Germany is controlled by Bolsheviks while West Germany is democratic, under the protection of the allies. Berlin is a divided city and a potential flash point for a nuclear war."

"I have some very disturbing news. In 1948, a Jewish state was established in Palestine. Israel has ruthlessly hunted National Socialists around the globe. We must be careful. The Jews know very little of die Spinne, but they do know bits and pieces."

"Israel must go! Heinz, that must be our top priority!

"What of our benefactor, Reichsminister Speer?"

"After the German surrender, a war crimes tribunal sentenced Herr Speer to 20 years in Spandau prison. He served out his sentence and was released in 1966. Many prominent National Socialists were sentenced to death, while others were imprisoned or committed suicide. I do not know all the details, but Herr Speer only recently died of natural causes."

"Heinz, we owe Herr Speer a debt almost equal to the debt we owe our Führer. It was Speer's final solution that brought us to this time and place. The Führer sacrificed himself that we may succeed. This is no accident. Providence has selected us to save the Aryan race and exterminate the Jews and their Bolshevik puppets."

Eva now clutched her stomach with both hands, "Leutnant Schneider, I am again feeling nauseous."

"Frau Hitler, henceforth, I request that you call me Wolfgang. I shall call you by your Christian name, Eva. To avoid confusion, we will refer to Blondi's pup as Wolfy. You will only speak German, no English. We are husband and wife. Is that clear?"

"But I am Frau Hitler!"

"Eva, how long would the despicable Israelis allow Frau Hitler to live?"

Eva paused to consider all aspects of her current situation, "Yes, I understand the circumstances. Thank you, Wolfgang, my loving husband."

"Heinz, you are my cousin."

"Jawohl."

"We have escaped from, from…" Wolfgang was searching for just the right words.

Heinz completed Wolfgang's thought in the language of the contemporary news broadcasts, "We have escaped from behind the Iron Curtain. We fled East Germany. We lost our dear uncle along the way, murdered by the Stasi, the East German Secret Police."

Then Heinz continued, "So, Wolfgang, dear cousin, you do not plan on hiding. You plan to reveal our existence under these new personae?"

"Der Führer counselled Herr Speer to concoct a similar fabrication. We will give the Americans a story they long to hear. If die Spinne is still out there, we will make contact. We will blend into this society, learn its ways, and prosper. But we will never forget! We will grow strong. We will grow powerful!"

In the Hangar with Josephine

John Nicolescu was right. Delvin trusted Vet & Sid to wreak havoc amongst the VLA's defenders, but once the shooting started, Badass Bitch would be targeted by every shooter defending the Array. Slick typically didn't micromanage his Marines, but this mission was different. Delvin needed to know that Josephine understood the risks involved and, more importantly, he needed to know that Jo had a plan.

When Slick entered the hangar, Jo was sitting flat on her ass upon the cold concrete floor. She had drawn a big red "Y" on the floor using a chunk of crumbling brick. Nine beer bottle caps were positioned along each arm of the "Y". Parker emptied a 50 pound bag of floor sweep and was using it to model the terrain surrounding the Array.

"At ease Josephine, I see you're planning your assault."

Jo glanced up into Badass Bitch's empty cockpit, "Slick, I'm not knocking Rascal. He's a good front seater, but I want Dead Eye up front on this mission."

"Do you think the Jackson boy is ready?"

"Captain, that kid has ice water in his veins. He's the best gunner I've ever seen. That boy is a natural born aviator."

"Aye Jo, Private Jackson is one hell of a Marine. Just remember, that's Cowboy Tom's baby boy. We'll have hell to pay if anything happens to him."

"Slick, you're a much better con man than I am. Can you dream up some kind of bullshit story to tell Rascal?"

"Yeah, I'll think of something."

Jo pointed down at her makeshift sand table, "Any new intel you care to share?"

"The intel's not good Lieutenant. The VLA is protected by a couple of hundred Peoples' Militia with a smaller number of Falcon Commandos. Hopefully, some of those forces will be drawn off by coordinated attacks upon Socorro & Truth or Consequences."

Jo busted out laughing, "Who in the fuck names a town after a game show?"

Delvin shrugged, "I don't know, but it's a good sized town, so is Socorro. Both should be defended by sizable garrisons.

"The garrison at the Array will almost certainly be equipped with the latest ChiCom man portable SAMs. I don't know how effective the Bitch's countermeasures will be."

"Gee, thanks Slick. Any more good news?"

Delvin retrieved four scrap Cessna spark plugs from a trash barrel. He placed one in the center of the "Y" and one along each of the three arms.

"Assume the Chinese have a SAM battery defending the Array. A few days ago, HUMINT spotted a convoy heading for the Array with four 6x6 armored vehicles leading the way. SIGINT has since identified intermittent target acquisition radar emissions that are a spot on match for an HQ-7B SAM battery."

"Holy shit! They'll spot the Bitch at 15 miles out. Those Red bastards have upgraded their acquisition radars."

"Chill girlfriend. What if we take out that acquisition radar before it can paint the Bitch?"

"Slick, my man! If you can take out that search radar, I'll slip the Bitch inside the SAM's minimum engagement envelope."

Jo's overconfidence didn't convince Delvin, "What about the shoulder fired threats? We can't expect Vet & Big Sid to take them all out."

Josephine snatched up a bottlecap from her makeshift sand table, "Captain, I need the exact dimensions of those big dishes and a diagram of their current configuration."

Delvin came prepared, pulling a diagram of the VLA from his coat pocket, "They've added several new dishes but haven't completed the rail line extensions. They've got a bunch of those new dishes parked all along the southwestern arm of the Array, the arm that runs alongside the Antenna Assembly Building."

Josephine looked at the diagram and smiled, "Guess we better load the Bitch with a few armor piercing rockets."

Die Spinne

Postwar, Otto Skorzeny and Hans Kammler occupied prominent positions on the Allies Most Wanted Nazis List.

The Allies could never draw a clear bead on SS-Obergruppenführer Kammler. One second-hand account tells how Kammler, along with 21 SS men, defended a bunker near Prague to the bitter end against 500 Czech partisans. Other reports indicate that Kammler took cyanide, telling his companions that the Americans would never take him alive. The most intriguing account suggests that the American OSS spirited Kammler out of Europe and into the United States. On 9 July 1945, Frau Kammler petitioned the German courts to declare her husband dead as of 9 May 1945. The Court so ruled on 7 September 1948.

It took some time for word of that ruling to reach Hans down in southern Iran, where he was being hosted by Skorzeny's friends, the nomadic Qashqai People.

Skorzeny was arrested and interned for two years prior to his trial as a war criminal in 1947. At the Dachau US Military Tribunal, Skorzeny and nine of his comrades were accused of the improper use of US military uniforms and insignia during the Battle of the Bulge. Skorzeny was acquitted when, under intense cross examination, British special forces were forced to admit that their troops had worn German uniforms during special operations.

On 27 July 1948, Skorzeny escaped from a Darmstadt internment camp. Rumor has it, several Americans aided Skorzeny in his escape. After his escape, the daring Skorzeny hid out at a Bavarian farm for 18 months, under the loving care of Countess Ilse Lüthje, whom he later married. During that time, Skorzeny was in contact with numerous former Nazi officials.

In early 1950, Hitler's favorite commando was photographed at a café on the Champs Elysees in Paris. The very next day, those photos were splashed all over the French press, necessitating Otto's quick departure to Salzburg. By April 1950, with the blessing of Franco's government, Skorzeny relocated to sunny Madrid. There he established a small engineering firm.

In 1952, the Egyptian government was overthrown in a military coup led by General Mohammed Naguib. The next year, Skorzeny surfaced in Egypt as Naguib's military advisor. Skorzeny recruited several of his SS kameraden who, in turn, trained Egypt's armed forces. Skorzeny enlisted the aid of Hans Kammler to recruit Nazi rocket scientists for Egypt's missile program.

During the early 1950s, Skorzeny made regular visits to Argentina as a military advisor to Juan Peron. Until her death in 1952, Skorzeny occasionally acted as a bodyguard for Peron's glamorous wife, Evita.

The most twisted chapter in Skorzeny's twisted career may have occurred in the early 1960s. Various sources allege that Skorzeny worked for Mossad providing intelligence on Israel's Arab neighbors. He may have assassinated Egyptian rocket scientists and maybe assassinated a German rocket scientist. In return for his cooperation, Skorzeny was removed from Mossad's hit list. Kammler may have been removed from Mossad's hit list as part of Skorzeny's deal.

In the 1960s & 1970s, Skorzeny created the Paladin Group, a band of elite mercenaries. These mercenaries trained guerilla fighters and conducted covert operation for various nation states including Spain. During the later years of his life, Skorzeny resided in Madrid. He remained a dedicated Nazi until his death from lung cancer in 1975.

While Skorzeny died in 1975, die Spinne did not die with him. A new generation of National Socialists replaced the old, watching and waiting for the return of their Messiah. As they watched and waited, they grew rich and powerful.

Assimilation

A bespectacled, bald, and chubby Tony Lin stumbled into the Badge Office at the Westgate Entrance to Lawrence Livermore Laboratories. Tony gave an Oscar worthy performance as he aimlessly walked, hither and yon, before finally asking a security guard for directions.

"Sir, I'm here for a job interview."

The very tall Peoples' Militia Security Officer peered down his nose at the chubby, bald, Chinese geek who just interrupted his morning cup of cappuccino, "Extend your right hand."

"Sir, I'm not a Member."

A Falcon Commando decked out in full tactical gear was overseeing operations at the Badge Office. When he overheard Tony's response, the Chinese lieutenant levelled his Norinco QBZ-95 assault rifle on his seemingly clueless countryman.

The well trained Falcon Commando confronted Tony in Mandarin, "Comrade, where are your papers?"

This was just Jimmy Wu's luck. His Mandarin sucked. James knew his Mandarin sucked. During his tenure with Chinese State Security, James had been repeatedly told that his Mandarin sucked. Inspector Wu repeatedly promised his superiors that he would work on his Mandarin. Regardless of all that, Jimmy's Mandarin still sucked.

Tony replied in broken, stammering, and barely comprehensible Mandarin, "A thousand apologies Sir. My Mandarin dishonors me. I had the great misfortune of being born in Utah. I have lived my entire life as a coolie, a slave to those White Mormon fanatics. I am neither a Member, nor a Comrade. I am less than nothing."

The Falcon Commando switched to English. His English was infinitely better than Tony's Mandarin, "You must go through Security Screening & Assimilation. What is your name?"

"Tony, Tony Lin."

The Commando lowered his weapon and shook his head in disgust, "Fall into that queue. Tony, stick to English, your Mandarin sucks."

Tony stood in line at Security Screening & Assimilation for the better part of an hour. Human Resources had given SS&A a heads up that Tony would be checking in that morning. First off, they fingerprinted Tony and ran his prints through The Collective's fingerprint recognition software. Tony's prints were clean. Next, they took DNA samples which confirmed Tony's ancestry was 100% Chinese, without a trace of Japanese blood. Tony stood motionless as a 3D scanner snapped multiple pictures and measured Tony's biometrics. Tony was then required to take a loyalty oath to The Collective. The final step was the insertion of an RFID chip into the webbing between Tony's right index finger and thumb. Tony heaved a sigh of relief as he was proclaimed the newest Member of The Collective.

Asylum

Exactly one week after the Sherriff escorted Charlie out of Plains, Montana, three German refugees and a German Shepherd puppy appeared at the Sanders County Courthouse in Thompson Falls, Montana.

"Madame, may we please speak to the Sheriff?"

"Why do you fine folks need to see the Sheriff?"

Wolfgang Schneider glanced to his left, then to his right, took a half step forward, then whispered to the receptionist, "Mam, this is my cousin Heinz, my wife Eva, and I am Wolfgang. My companions and I are illegally in the United States. One month ago, we escaped from East Germany. Our lives are in danger. We have information that would greatly embarrass the East German communist regime. We seek asylum and protection. We are placing our very lives in your hands."

The receptionist picked up the telephone, "Eddy, I need to see you out front right away."

"Sherriff Johnson, please pardon my wife. She does not speak English, but Eva loves everything American."

"Wolfgang, your story is truly remarkable. America was built by immigrants, and may I say that your English is impeccable. You sound like you're from Minnesota."

Wolfgang Schneider gregariously replied. "How perceptive of you Sherriff. You must be a formidable investigator."

Sherriff Eddy Johnson's face beamed as he leaned forward, savoring the bullshit Wolfgang was dishing out.

"Sherriff, you have an amazing ear for accents. My mother's family moved to Idaho from Minnesota. Although I was born in Idaho, I have no papers to show you."

"Then you are not here illegally, we must merely locate your birth certificate. My goodness Wolfgang, if you are a native born American, then you are a citizen." Sherriff Johnson paused for a moment, then mused, "One day, you could even be President!"

As the trio left the Sanders County Courthouse, Wolfgang and Eva were holding hands, with Heinz cradling little Wolfy in his arms.

"Have the documents been altered?"

"Jawohl, Leutnant Schneider!" Heinz reached into his pocket and retrieved a folded document. "This technology is amazing. I am holding what they call a Xerox copy of Wolfgang Schneider's Birth Certificate. I bribed a local bureaucrat for a mere 10 ounces of gold."

Eva responded auf Deutsch, "What does it say?"

"Wolfgang Americus Snyder, born July 4, 1958, in Coeur d'Alene, Idaho."

"Zehr gut! The original 1918 birth year was a big problem and your idea to change the day to July 4 was a nice touch. Since I am an American citizen, my wife will be assigned resident alien status. Heinz, you too will almost certainly be granted political asylum. We will probably be interviewed by the immigration authorities, but that should be perfunctory. I suspect we may be questioned by the FBI and perhaps American intelligence. Heinz, what again do they call it?"

"CIA, the Central Intelligence Agency."

"Yes, the FBI and CIA. I'm counting on them.

"By the way, you kept the name and address of the bureaucrat who altered my record of birth?"

"Jawohl, Leutnant Schneider!"

"Give it a couple of weeks, then liquidate him!"

"Leutnant Schneider, the bureaucrat is a single mother of two."

"Das macht nichts."

As they walked the sidewalks of the small town of Thompson Falls, Wolfgang's nose twitched, "Heinz, what is that heavenly aroma?"

"That, my dear Wolfgang, is something uniquely American. They call it barbeque."

Eva turned up her nose, "That smell is making me nauseous."

Heinz couldn't believe Eva's reaction, "First they marinade, or apply a spice mixture, to the meat. Next, they grill the beef, pork, chicken, sausages, and even salmon over a smoldering, smoky charcoal fire. Here in the West, the charcoal is made from a desert tree called Mesquite. There are a variety of sauces one can apply, mostly based on tomato and molasses. I am quite partial to the baby back pork ribs."

Eva put her hand over her mouth as she gagged, "I'm about to vomit. Get me away from that burnt meat smell."

Heinz ran a couple of blocks and retrieved their VW Jetta. Wolf and Eva piled into the backseat.

Eva was no longer nauseous, "I would really like some chocolate. Real Swiss chocolate, not that imitation Amerikanisher stuff."

Heinz couldn't believe Eva was hungry, "I thought you were nauseous. Now you want chocolate?"

"Jawohl, either chocolate or ice cream. Better still, chocolate ice cream!"

Wolfgang was putting two and two together, while Heinz remained clueless.

Schneider leaned over and whispered to Eva, "Frau Hitler, I am uncomfortable discussing such matters, but I promised the Führer that I would look after you. Please do not take offense. When was your last cycle?"

Eva turned beet red, "Wolfgang! Really? You dare ask me such questions?"

Wolfgang took Eva's hand and firmly replied, "Yes, and you will answer me. You will answer truthfully!"

Eva heard the strength of her Adi in Leutnant Schneider's voice.

She hung her head and answered in a trembling whisper, "I have now missed two cycles."

Eva was no fool. Weeks earlier, she suspected something was amiss, but feared revealing her condition prior to her marriage.

Wolfgang placed his hand on Eva's tummy, "Hold your head high, Frau Hitler. Providence has blessed you above all women. Our Führer is with us. He is invincible. The untermenschen could not kill him. He will rise again and lead us to victory."

Eva then placed her hand in Wolfgang's hand, "Danke, Wolfgang. I am indeed blessed to have you as my husband."

Teamwork

The atmosphere in the cabin was growing a bit more relaxed. Brett, Marian, and Charlie were sitting in the living room, comparing notes.

Brett was still a rookie Nazi hunter, "Although I am an investigator, I'm no Nazi hunter. Just what is die Spinne?"

Marian couldn't believe Brett's ignorance, "Hoffman, don't you ever listen to *Sea-to-Sea AM?* About a year ago, Vince hosted an entire episode dedicated to die Spinne."

Charlie fessed up, "I missed that one too. Must have been camped up in a box canyon, or somewhere else with piss-poor reception."

"You're excused Charlie, but Herr Hoffman should listen to his own damned show." Marian gave Brett another side eye before filling him in on Nazi post-war projects, "Die Spinne translates to 'The Spider'. The global elites would have us believe that die Spinne is a tin foil hat conspiracy theory. Pop culture has depicted die Spinne as an organization called Odessa."

Charlie piped up, "Oh yeah, back in my younger days, I watched a movie called *The Odessa File.* Then there was another flick called *The Boys from Brazil* that referred to Odessa. I remember that one because Gregory Peck played the bad guy. What was his name?"

"Mengele, the Angel of Death, SS-Hauptsturmführer Doktor Josef Mengele. He was the biggest bastard of the whole damned bunch." As she repeated that name, Brett could see the hatred burning in Marian's eyes.

"Not only did that bastard escape, Mengele lived openly in South America until 1979. He moved back and forth between Paraguay, Brazil, and Argentina. Mossad was hot on his tail until 1962, that's when Mossad called off their manhunt. That's when Skorzeny must have made his deal with Mossad."

Brett was trying to sort through all these names in his mind, "OK, I've heard of Doktor Mengele. He held doctorates in both anthropology as well as medicine. Mengele did all sorts of crazy and horrendous experiments at Auschwitz. I've heard that he actually enjoyed the selection process. He volunteered to work extra shifts, making the selections as Jews entered the camp. Most were sent to the showers, the showers with no water. A few would be kept alive and worked to death. Mengele singled out twins for his experiments. One twin would be the test subject, the other twin would be the control.

"But who was this Skorzeny character?"

"He was no character. He was Hitler's personal commando!"

Marian then gave both Brett and Charlie a short synopsis of Skorzeny's colorful career through 1962, then her demeanor abruptly changed.

"In the early '60s, Mossad decided they needed to do something with Skorzeny. Skorzeny had recruited a gang of his former SS buddies to train Egypt's military. He was also training Palestinian terrorists. Yasser Arafat was one of his prized pupils.

"Mossad originally planned to assassinate that Nazi pig, then they came up with the bright idea of recruiting Skorzeny.

"Apparently, Mossad and Skorzeny reached some sort of deal. I don't know exactly what that deal was, but I do know when Mossad stopped hunting Skorzeny, Egyptian rocket scientists started turning up dead."

Hoffman began laughing.

"What's so funny?"

"Do you really believe Mossad would make a deal with Skorzeny? I mean, Jews dealing with Nazis? We're not talking about *Jake & Elwood's* Illinois Nazis. We're talking about Sieg Hiel, Iron Cross, Jew killin' Nazis of the German persuasion."

Now it was Marian's turn to laugh.

Brett was dismayed, "What's so funny?"

"Skorzeny had a buddy, SS-Obergruppenführer Hans Kammler. Kammler provided the 'Good Nazi', Albert Speer, with slave labor from the camps. Kammler was also in charge of the wunderwaffen. Nobody knows exactly what happened to Hans, but rumor has it that Hans made a deal with his CIA friends and helped Herr Doktor von Braun develop America's ballistic missiles. The rockets that propelled Americans to the moon were developed by those bloody bastards."

Marian paused, then continued, "Why aren't you laughing now, Herr Hoffman?"

"Marian, please do not refer to me in that tone as 'Herr Hoffman'. I have German ancestry, but I'm no Nazi."

Marian's harsh demeanor was a defense mechanism. She was trying her best to remain aloof and keep Brett at arm's length. She did not respond. She just continued talking.

"Back in '62, Mossad even pressured Wiesenthal, trying to get him to lay off Skorzeny."

Brett could only shake his head in disgust, "And I've always thought that I live in a spooky world. Marian, you don't really know who's your friend and who's your enemy, present company excluded." Brett smiled and gave Marian a wink.

Marian smiled and winked back, then gave Brett one of those puppy dog stares, not often associated with Mossad operatives.

As Marian gazed into Hoffman's steel blue eyes, she faced reality, "My God, I'm in big trouble."

Brett wasted no time, "Charlie, how far is it over to Plains?"

"15 or 20 minutes."

"How far to ground zero?"

"From here, about the same, 15 or 20 minutes."

Brett headed out the cabin door, "OK, let's get this investigation rolling. Charlie, you drive Marian's Jeep."

"OK Marian, what sort of *007* gadgets do you have in here? Give us a peek on our way over to the landing site."

Charlie was growing tired of the never-ending stream of complaints, "Yeah, I know the road is winding, but most all the roads up here in the high country run alongside rivers, creeks, or dry washes.

"Yeah, I know it's a gravel road, but it's well graded. Keep the damn windows rolled up and we'll be fine.

"I'll pull off the road under these trees, then it's a short hike up Hugo Creek. This time of year, the creek is all froze up. We can walk right up the creek bed. As I recall, the landing site is just a shade over a mile up Hugo Creek."

Charlie led the way up the icy, gravelly creek bed, with metal detector in hand, closely followed by Brett, with Marian bringing up the rear.

"You know it's been 40 years. Probably aren't any traces remaining up there."

Charlie pointed at a clearing, "The smaller craft was sitting right here in this little saddle. Nothing here now but a few saplings."

Marian pulled out a magnetic compass and it functioned normally, no magnetic anomalies.

"The larger craft was sitting right over here." Then, Charlie pointed up into the tree line, "That's where I was hiding when Heinz spotted me and started shooting."

Brett surveyed the mostly barren, snow-covered ground, "Where exactly was Leutnant Heinz standing?"

"Come this way. about five paces. OK, OK, that's about right."

"How many shots Charlie?" Hoffman was gazing down at the dusting of snow. brushing it aside with the heel of his boot.

"I think four shots, maybe five."

Charlie swept the metal detector across the spot Brett had just cleared. The detector made a screeching sound.

"Brett, stop! Hold on for a minute. I think Charlie's found something." Marian pulled out a big assed knife and began probing the spot of ground that just set off Charlie's metal detector.

"Look at this!" Marian held up a weathered 9mm brass cartridge casing between her fingers.

Brett reached into his pocket and pulled out a 9mm round, then held it side-by-side with Marian's cartridge.

"Charlie, it looks like we found one of Heinz' spent 9mm cartridges.

"We should really scan this entire area, but I've got to get back home day after tomorrow. I've got a book tour scheduled."

"Yeah, the Center has cut back my funding. I can't stay out here forever either. Quinn's Lodge ain't cheap. Looks like I'll being spending two more wonderful nights in the Grand Cherokee."

Charlie was a true gentleman, "The hell you say. I'll stay out in my Winnebago. You can sleep in the cabin. There's two bedrooms."

Brett agreed, "Charlie's right. It'll be safer that way and a hell of a lot more comfortable. We still don't know exactly what we're dealing with. Let's go into Plains, grab some lunch, and maybe snoop around town just a bit."

It was a short drive northwest on Montana State Road 200 to the small town of Plains. There were no billboards along the highway to spoil the beautiful scenery, but there were red, white, and blue yard signs everywhere. There were yard signs stuck in front lawns. Large banners adorned business facades. Signs were hanging from the trees.

"Americus for America." Brett had no idea what the signs meant. All they said was, "Americus for America."

"Tuesday is the special election to fill Montana's open Senate seat. I don't get all wrapped up in politics, but I always vote." Charlie kept one hand on the wheel as he pointed out all the yard signs with the other, "That guy's got my vote."

Brett was inquisitive by nature, "Charlie, I don't mean to be political, but what's his party affiliation, Democrat or Republican?"

Charlie chuckled, "Neither! That's what I like about him. That's what everyone likes about him. He's a chip off the old block. Well, appearances can be deceiving."

"What in the hell are you talking about?"

"Hoffman, once again you're talking when you should be listening! I'm talking about Americus. His Dad, Wolfgang, is Montana's Senior Senator and Americus is running for the other seat, the open seat. Wolfgang is the founder of the American People's Party."

"What did you mean when you said that appearances can be deceiving?"

"Americus don't look nothing like his Dad. His Dad looks like, like…"

"Like whom?"

"Like you, Hoffman. His Dad looks like a Kraut."

Marian had been sitting in the back seat, content to be amused by Brett and Charlie's banter, but now her interest was piqued, "What does Americus look like?"

"He's not tall, maybe 5 foot 9.

"He's got black hair, black straight hair, no curl.

"He's slightly built, maybe 150 lbs. soaking wet."

"Eye color, what color are his eyes?"

"Damn it, Marian! You're as bad as Hoffman. His eyes are a very light blue. There's something about those eyes.

Something almost hypnotic.

Brett raised an eyebrow, "Please don't tell me the APP is far right."

"I won't, cause it's not. It's sorta a common-sense party. That Collective bunch says the APP are far right, but you gotta consider the source."

"Give me some examples of the APP platform."

"Take defense for example. Wolfgang strongly supports the military, but he is against foreign intervention unless a strong case can be made based upon national interest. 'America First' is Wolfgang's policy."

Marian asked the $64,000 question, "What's Wolfgang's views on racial minorities?"

"Let me guess. You're interested in what he thinks of Jews?"

"That's right. Is he an anti-Semite?"

"His campaign manager is a Black woman. His campaign treasurer is Jewish. Schneider strongly supports Israel."

Brett shrugged, "So much for that conspiracy theory, let's grab some lunch."

Insertion

Captain Delvin Smith had invited Sergeant Nicolescu & Big Sid to the big show at the Very Large Array, but they were having trouble catching a ride. The lousy weather ruled out an air assault. Just before Christmas, Tom Jackson, Lame Wolf, and Dr. Leroy shot it out with the Peoples' Militia guarding the Array. As a result of that altercation, the Array's security forces were on high alert. All the roads into the Plains of San Augustin were under surveillance. To make matters worse, wind driven snow rendered those roads impassable.

Timing was critical. The Mescalero Legion would get the show rolling, launching simultaneous assaults upon Socorro & Truth or Consequences. The Very Large Array lay 100 miles east of Springerville. Vet & Sid had to be there, in place, ready to smash that Red Chinese air search radar, just as the weather cleared. Lieutenant Josephine Parker would then swoop in with Badass Bitch's guns a blazing. Jo would first take out the SAMs, then take out the Array. In the final act, Sergeant John Nicolescu would capture Chinese technicians for interrogation. The encore would feature Delvin's rare earth convoy as it rumbled eastward, along US 60, with horns blaring.

The terrain between Springerville and the VLA was unsuitable for snowmobiles. Although the historic blizzard of January 2042 had dumped over a foot of snow across the high deserts of Arizona & New Mexico, the swirling winds cleared some areas, while sculpting mountainous drifts in others.

While lesser men might have been deterred by such arctic conditions, Sergeant John Nicolescu felt right at home. John's Romanian parents were native to the rugged Transylvanian Alps. After they escaped the murderous Ceausescu regime, the Nicolescus followed a circuitous path, finally settling in Northern Nevada. Vet was born and raised in Nevada's Big Smoky Valley. He had grown up hiking, hunting, skiing, and spelunking in the rugged Toiyabe Range. John was just the man for this mission.

Immigration

In 1985 America, immigration was taken very seriously.

"Good morning, Mr. & Mrs. Schneider. Thank you for taking time out of your busy schedule to meet with us here in Missoula."

Wolfgang & Eva Schneider were seated in a small conference room in the Federal Building in downtown Missoula, Montana.

"I'm Agent Brenner, Federal Bureau of Investigation. The young lady seated to my left is Case Officer Upton and the gentleman to my right is Immigration Officer Compton. Do we have your approval to record this session?"

Wolfgang nodded, "Yes, certainly."

Eva nodded, "Ja, Ich verstehe."

"Agent Brenner, please excuse my wife, she speaks little English. She agrees and understands."

"Thank you, Mr. Schneider. That is no problem. I am fluent in German as is Case Officer Upton."

Wolfgang slightly fidgeted in his seat.

Agent Brenner noticed Wolfgang's uneasy body language, "This is not a criminal proceeding, but you may have counsel present, if you so desire."

Wolfgang shook his head negatively, "That will not be necessary. We have placed our very lives in your hands."

"This is a somewhat unusual meeting. It is rare that the Bureau, Intelligence, and Immigration sit down together to interview refugees. Your case has come to President Reagan's attention. The President's goal is to topple the Berlin Wall and reunite Germany. He passes along his congratulations for your daring escape and conveys his deepest sympathies for the loss of your uncle. We are here to expedite your assimilation into American society and to assure your continued safety and anonymity.

"Mr. Schneider, we have retrieved your birth certificate. You are an American citizen by birth. Per our request, the State of Montana has issued you a driver's license. The Social Security Administration has issued you a Social Security Number. After we're done here, we'll snap some passport photos and get you set up with a passport, but we suggest you remain in the country for the foreseeable future."

Case Officer Upton took over, "Wolfgang, whatever you do, stay away from Europe. We expect the East German Ministry for State Security, Stasi, will work overtime to eliminate you, your wife, and your cousin. To the best of our knowledge, for the moment, they're doing nothing. Either they don't know you escaped, don't care, or else, they're cooking up a big surprise."

"Miss Upton, you are CIA?"

"Wolfgang, let's just say that I represent the Intelligence Community."

"Mr. Brenner, please pass along our deepest thanks and kindest regards to The Gipper." Wolfgang then passed a sealed manila envelope to Upton.

"What's this?"

"Miss Upton, may we speak privately for just a few minutes?"

"Brenner, Compton, please excuse me while I speak to Mr. & Mrs. Schneider in private."

Wolfgang, Eva and Upton stepped out into the empty hallway.

"Miss Upton, when the Nazi's swept across Europe, they looted art from museums, galleries, churches, public buildings, and even private homes. They stole paintings, sculptures, rare books, jewels, even stained-glass windows."

"I am aware of all that. How does that impact the current situation?"

"My late uncle was part of a small, secretive group who knew where much of that Nazi plunder was hidden. Some has been recovered and returned to its rightful owners. The Russian Bolsheviks recovered some and now secretly hold it for themselves, as do the East German Bolsheviks. The Bolsheviks feared my uncle would expose their thievery."

"Bolsheviks? My, my Mr. Schneider, I haven't heard that term used in some time."

"Pardon me, force of habit. My uncle used the term Bolshevik as a pejorative.

"The East German Communists were tracking down members of my uncle's underground cell. That gave us little choice. We fled East Germany on very short notice."

"Tell me, how exactly did your uncle die?"

"We were escaping through a long-forgotten Nazi tunnel. Uncle Wolf was bringing up the rear when an explosion collapsed the tunnel." As his Führer had instructed him, Wolf skillfully weaved his tale, blending truth with lies.

Eva understood the gist of the conversation and burst into tears.

"Now, we are the voice of my uncle's group here in the United States. That envelope contains the exact location of a small Nazi treasure trove of stolen art hidden in southern West Germany, in Bavaria."

"Mr. Schneider, if your information is accurate and we recover even a small fraction of the missing treasures, you will be an international hero."

"No, no. This must all be kept secret. My uncle's group continues his life's work. Do not mention our names, or even hint at the existence of my uncle's group. If the rightful owners wish to show their appreciation, we will gladly accept any honorarium they may deem appropriate. Who knows what other treasures our friends may uncover?"

The Junkyard

"How did the meeting go?"

"Fantastic, Heinz. We now have the complete sympathy and cooperation of the United States government."

"Shall we head home, or shall we grab a bite to eat?"

"Let's stop at Dairy Queen. We can grab a hot dog, or hamburger and Eva can get a banana split with hot fudge and peanuts on top."

Eva didn't need to speak fluent English to make out the words "Dairy Queen".

She enthusiastically clapped her hands and squealed, "Wunderbar!"

"Wolfgang, these Americans are an inventive sort." Heinz was enjoying a footlong chili cheese dog smothered with chopped red onions.

"How so?" Wolfgang was savoring a double-deck bacon cheeseburger with all the trimmings.

"We Germans practically invented the sausage. We have endless varieties of sausages. These American hotdogs are actually frankfurters."

"So, what's your point?"

"It took the Americans to grill the frankfurter, slap it on a toasted bun, and smother it with chili, melted cheese, and diced red onion. They do this with everything. Even the potatoes we're eating are French Fries!"

"Yes. Our dear uncle correctly identified that American trait. They seem to extract the best from all the immigrants, then like magic, they reassemble the various disparate pieces into something new and much greater than the sum of its parts.

Then, Wolfgang leaned forward and continued in a whisper, "The danger lies in the untermenschen, the Jews, Negroes, American Indians, and other undesirables. They have polluted America's Aryan blood. They will ultimately destroy America. It is up to us to save America and the Aryan race. Only then can we save the Fatherland."

Eva had just finished her banana split and grabbed a bite of Heinz' chili cheese dog, "Wunderbar, but it could use more onions!"

Wolfgang quickly polished off his fries and was ready to roll, "On our way back home, let's swing by the junkyard."

Heinz drove through Plains and headed due north a couple of miles to Clark Fork Auto Salvage.

"Good afternoon, Heinz."

"Good day, Mr. Hansen. We're just here to check on our movie props."

"Those Hollywood guys still haven't given you any idea when shooting will begin?"

"Regrettably, no. We are indeed fortunate to have such a secure location in which to store our props. A science fiction movie cannot succeed without quality props. I trust that both you and your daughters will be available as extras once we commence filming?"

After a few minutes of small talk with the owner, Heinz proceeded to drive on through the junkyard. At the north end of the yard, Heinz parked the VW Jetta at a gated area enclosed by an 8 ft chain link fence topped with razor wire. Heinz got out and unlocked the gate. The fenced area was roughly 100 ft by 80 ft. Several junk cars were stacked along the front fence, obscuring the yard's contents from the curious.

After driving through the gate, Heinz closed and locked the gate behind him. The trio then walked to the rear of the yard. To their left was a large mound of scrap metal, to their right was a much smaller mound. Mufflers, tail pipes, bumpers, 55-gallon steel drums, scrap of all sorts were stacked in those piles. Only from the rear of those piles could one see beneath the junk.

At the core of each junkpile was a Glocke, Größe Glocke in the larger pile, prototype Glocke in the smaller. Heinz squeezed between the junk and, in a prescribed sequence, touched three runes etched into the exterior of the prototype Glocke. A hatchway swung open. Heinz stuck his head inside.

"Alles in ordnung!"

Then he checked out die Größe Glocke.

"Everything's OK over here, too."

"Heinz, let's take about a hundred ounces back with us."

"OK, I brought an empty briefcase with me."

Wolfgang, Eva, and Heinz then drove back to their Plains apartment carrying 100 ounces of 24 karat gold stuffed inside the briefcase, confident that the remaining 3 metric tons of gold were secure inside the Glockes.

Lunch

Charlie parked Marian's Grand Cherokee out front of The Butcher Block, a popular restaurant in Downtown Plains, Montana.

"This place is great. It's like a deli, fast food joint, and bakery all rolled into one. I stop in here every chance I get."

Marian and Brett had their doubts but went along with Charlie's recommendation and placed their orders.

Minutes later, Brett was devouring a bratwurst, "Charlie, this food is great, the prices are reasonable, and the mood is casual. Great choice!"

"This Reuben would give any Squirrel Hill deli a run for its money." Marian also liked the joint.

As the three fearless Nazi hunters enjoyed their lunch, a recurring scene unfolded in the restaurant's parking lot. Two young men, probably around 15 or 16, were handing out flyers. One lad was Black, the other appeared to be of Asian descent. Both were attired in the uniform du jour, navy blue Dockers, white pinpoint oxford shirt, and red tie. It was cold outside, so they wore black leather bomber jackets and leather jackboots. The boys were immaculately groomed, articulate, and appeared sincere.

Brett noticed them first, "Our local Boy Scout Troop seems to be active again today."

Charlie rose from his seat, "You two go ahead and eat, I'll step outside and see what's up. I think I know these boys."

Charlie stepped out into the lot and was immediately approached by the lads. Apparently, they knew Charlie. They shook hands, exchanged a few words, then handed Charlie a flyer. Meanwhile, a Sherriff's Deputy pulled into the lot and parked his patrol car. When the two young men saw the Deputy, they immediately stood to and saluted.

"Marian, what do you make of that?"

"I don't know what to make of that. While police are being spit on and murdered across the country by mobs of young radicals, here in Plains, we have this scene. A White police officer is saluted by two minority youths. Not that I'm complaining. I'm fascinated."

Brett started asking questions before Charlie even had a chance to sit back down, "What is going on here?"

"My young friends out there are members of the 'Rainbow Corps'. I know those two kids, but not very well. We're really just acquaintances."

"What's that flyer all about?"

"Big Schneider rally tonight in Helena. Both Wolfgang and Americus will be speaking."

"What's the venue? An auditorium?"

"Oh no, these affairs are always held outdoors, like in a stadium. The night rallies are something to behold."

"What's so awe inspiring about a political camp meeting?" Hoffman continued watching the two young men out in the parking lot.

Charlie shook his head, "Oh no, these rallies are pure political theater, but you are partially right, they are also part camp meeting.

Charlie showed his flair for the theatric as he set the scene for his two new friends, "Just imagine, the lights are low, the crowd is seated in silence, then the bugles sound and the drums beat. That's when the procession begins."

Marian was mesmerized by Charlie's description, "What procession?"

"The torchlight procession! Don't you guys keep up with current events?

"The Rainbow Corps leads the procession, with torches and American flags in hand. Then it begins. At first, it is only a murmur, but the volume steadily grows until it is deafening. Wolfgang! Wolfgang! Wolfgang!

"I know it's a little over the top, but Wolfgang motivates people. He galvanizes the crowd as he pushes back against the Bolsheviks."

Marian was caught off guard, "Bolsheviks?"

"You know, the Commies, that Collective bunch."

Marian began peppering Charlie with more questions, "Is there violence?"

"No."

"Is there hate speech?"

Charlie laughed, "Heavens no! At first, it's like a Tony Robbins motivational seminar on steroids, except, as a finale, Wolfgang has an altar call, of sorts. It reminds me of a Billy Graham Crusade."

"How about the Jews? The Blacks? The Indians?"

"They're all in 'The Rainbow' and that includes both kinds of Indians. All the convenience stores in town shut down for a Schneider rally."

Marian was stumped, "Somebody must be portrayed as the enemy."

Charlie thought for a moment, "The Bolsheviks! Just think about it. They are the root of all our problems. They hate the police. They turn racial groups against one another. They hate freedom. They hate capitalism. Yeah, the Bolsheviks are the enemy. They're tearing America apart!"

Marian quickly responded, "Ah ha! Do they really use the term Bolsheviks?"

Hoffman continued watching the two lads in the parking lot, "Ah ha my ass! Most Americans aren't fond of communism, even more so out here in the West. This is a land of rugged individuals. Many are deeply religious and patriotic with strong family ties.

"I've been watching Charlie's two young friends out in the parking lot. So far, they've saluted a Sherriff's Deputy, helped an elderly lady into a vehicle, and given directions to some lost tourists. I'm not heading back to Pittsburgh until day after tomorrow. Why don't we drive on down to Helena and catch tonight's Americus rally?"

"Charlie, that was an excellent choice for lunch. Let's snoop around town a bit this afternoon before we head down to Helena."

As Charlie pulled Marian's Grand Cherokee out of the parking lot, a scraggly middle-aged vagrant walked up to Charlie's two young friends, looking for a handout and some information.

"Yes sir! We can help. We see you are a veteran."

"Thank you, but I wasn't in the Army. I wear this flag bandana and all the camo in protest."

The Asian American youth seemed sincerely interested, "Please, tell us more."

"I was down in Berkeley on 9/11. That's when my eyes were opened. America really sucks. Those people in those buildings and on those planes got just what they deserved."

"That is an interesting point of view. Did you say you need a warm place to sleep?"

"Yeah, do you guys know a place?"

"Certainly, follow us. We're glad to help."

The two youths led the America hater behind the adjacent convenience store, with the Black kid in front and the Asian boy bringing up the rear. As they passed a dumpster, the Asian American youth retrieved a broken 2x4 and smacked the vagrant across the back of his head. Their victim wasn't dead, but he hit the pavement hard. The two Rainbow Corpsmen finished him off with the heels of their jackboots.

Death & Rebirth

After his meeting with the government officials in Missoula's Federal Building, Wolfgang was eager to tie up any loose ends.

"Heinz, have you taken care of that matter down in Boise?"

"You mean the paperwork registering our engineering company in Idaho?"

"Nein! Heinz, this is the third time I have asked about this.

"Wolfgang, I cannot bring myself to kill a woman in cold blood."

"Don't be ridiculous! She is not a woman; she is a Negro."

"Wolf, she is a mother!"

"All the better! Eliminate her and both her children!"

"I cannot."

"Leutnant Schuster, are you refusing to follow a direct order?"

"I object to this order on moral grounds."

"Very well. I am deeply disappointed in you. You stay here with Eva. I will take care of this tonight."

"Wolfgang, you will kill the woman?"

"Nein Schuster, I will kill all three!"

"Leutnant Schneider, I have reconsidered. Give me a week to work out the details. This must be done carefully and thoughtfully."

Wolfgang smiled, "I thought you might change your mind."

The Grab 'n Go convenience store was located just a couple of blocks from the Alpine Woods Apartments in Boise, Idaho. Michelle Smith normally did not leave her boys home alone, but her oldest son, Jamal, was now twelve and she was sure he could hold down the fort for a half hour.

Michelle had run out of milk and needed a loaf of bread. As she walked along the deserted side street to the convenience store, a familiar black VW Jetta pulled up beside her.

"Mr. Heinz, what are you doing here? I thought our business was satisfactorily completed."

By the time Michelle saw the gun, it was too late. Heinz scrambled her brains with two 9 mm rounds.

It was early morning by the time Heinz made it back home. Wolfgang & Eva were not home. A note was lying on the kitchen table.

"Have taken Eva to Valley Hospital – Wolfgang."

Heinz made a beeline to the Emergency Room.

"Wolfgang, how is she?"

"I don't know. Is everything OK in Boise?"

"Yes, that is handled."

Wolfgang paced the floor like any expectant father. Heinz was equally apprehensive, but he remained seated, anxiously tapping his toes on the floor.

After what seemed like an eternity, a nurse came out into the waiting room, "Mr. Schneider, you have a son. He has a full head of black hair and the voice of a carnival barker!"

The television in the Emergency Waiting Room was tuned to the early morning local news.

"Early this morning, a young mother of two was murdered outside a Boise apartment complex. Police report that she appears to have been killed execution style with two pistol shots to the head. There were no signs robbery or sexual assault. If you have any information regarding this crime, please call CRIME STOPPERS '85."

Wolfgang nodded his head in approval, "Zehr gut, Heinz!"

Heinz replied, "I told you I would handle it!"

TW POWELL © 2023

Spec Ops

You may recall, during the summer of 2041, the Red Chinese unleashed a squad of Super Soldiers (Chaoji zhanshi) upon Resistance forces in Nevada's Big Smoky Valley.

The first encounter with the Super Soldiers occurred at the Jackson family's Stonewall Ranch. John Nicolescu, Big Sid, Grandpa John Jackson, and Bobby Ray Skipper faced off against the Super Soldier prototype, CZ-101. After an epic battle, Big Sid decapitated CZ-101 with the razor sharp edge of his depleted uranium shield. Big Sid's Daddy, Bobby Lee Skipper, handcrafted that shield from the wreckage of an M1A1 Abrams main battle tank.

The remaining Super Soldiers subsequently attacked Resistance forces in Austin, Nevada. After a fierce, bloody action, the Mormon Cavalry defeated the Super Soldier squad with the help of Teflon coated, armor penetrating, .50 caliber discarding sabot rounds. That ammunition, affectionately called Sugar SLAPS, were also Bobby Lee Skipper's handiwork.

Several Super Soldier suits were salvaged from the Austin battlefield. All but one of the salvaged CZ suits were spirited away to Japan for reverse engineering. Captain Smith retained one suit and John Nicolescu became the designated Super Soldier. Besides rendering him bulletproof, the CZ suit provided Vet complete environmental protection. Once in his CZ suit, Vet could hike through subzero blizzard conditions snug as a bug in a rug. The CZ helmet featured enhanced audio and optics. CZ Nicolescu could hike through a blinding snowstorm with no visual impairment. The helmet's full spectrum vision enabled John to see across the visual, infrared, and ultraviolet wavelengths.

Sid & Vet were in the mess hall, prepping for their mission. Big Sid was from Macon, Georgia. The Big Man hated the cold. The Chinese CZ suit would not fit the man mountain, so the Arizona Rangers scrounged up a pair of jumbo sized heated thermal coveralls. For good measure, Sid put on a pair of long johns beneath the coveralls.

John handed his compadre a pair of socks, "Big Man, each battery pack will last about 10 hours. With your body mass, you'll only need to turn on the heat at night. You've got four fully charged batteries. Slide these socks on over your long johns. Plug them into your coveralls. Yeah, the socks are heated too."

Sid's thermal coveralls were adorned with a winter camo pattern, a dirty white background, mottled with streaks of gray and olive drab. Sid pulled a light gray woolen baclava down over his face, then pulled his hood up over the baclava. The piece de resistance was Sid's googles.

Vet took one look at his huge protégé and laughed till he cried, "Damn Big Man! All I need to do is give you a fucking chainsaw and you could star in one of them Hollywood slasher flicks."

While Vet was still doubled over in laughter, Darius "RAMBRO" Johnson entered the room carrying what appeared to be two violin cases.

"If you two boys are gonna make a movie, how about making a gangster shoot 'em up?"

Neither Sid, nor John, had the foggiest idea what Junior was talking about.

Darius continued, "Which one of you will play Cagney and which one will play Bogie?"

Vet & Sid pointed at one another in confusion, still totally clueless. Darius laid the violin cases on a folding table and opened them. Each case contained a vintage M1928A1 Thompson submachine gun with a 50-round drum magazine, the infamous Tommy Gun.

The Thompson fired Josephine's favorite ammo, the ACP .45 caliber pistol round. The Tommy Gun was designed during the Great War as a "trench broom". Its intended purpose was to clear enemy trenches. Originally christened "Annihilator 1", the Thompson featured neither range, nor accuracy. It was just as heavy as a rifle and even heavier when equipped with a 50-round drum magazine. Its .45 caliber round was relatively low velocity and lacked penetrating power.

Despite its apparent shortcomings, the Thompson did what it was designed to do. Packing a Tommy Gun, a single man could lay down a massive volume of fire, while on the move. Those heavy, low velocity rounds packaged tremendous kinetic energy, inflicting horrendous carnage at close range. During the interwar period (1918 to 1939), the Thompson was used with great effect in various brush wars around the globe. But it took Prohibition to cement the Thompson's place in America's pop culture.

America's Depression-era gangsters, the likes of John Dillinger, Baby Face Nelson, Pretty Boy Floyd, and the Barker gang, all packed Tommy Guns. In response, law enforcement, including the FBI, adopted the Thompson. Iconic images of the Thompson, both in print and on the silver screen, depicted the Tommy Gun fitted with a drum magazine. Herr Doktor Joseph Goebbels appropriated a photo of Winston Churchill, chomping down on a cigar, with Tommy Gun in hand, while inspecting British troops. The photo was used to depict Churchill as a gangster and war criminal in Nazi propaganda.

"Captain Smith saw these in the Springerville Ranger armory. They are practically cherry. The Rangers had a bunch of drum magazines. The Captain says these Thompsons are just the weapon for this mission."

Junior led fully armed and dressed CZ Nicolescu & Big Sid out into the motor lodge's parking lot. There, in the midst of a blizzard, stood a fully loaded pack mule.

"She may not be Miss Daisy, but the Quartermaster tells me she's one strong, dependable, mare mule."

An extra-long, woolen, cargo pad was thrown over Henrietta's back, keeping her warm while cushioning her load.

Junior slipped Henrietta a carrot, "The Quartermaster tossed a grass sack full of high protein hay cubes in with the load. He said she can lick the snow for water and find enough forage beneath the snow to keep herself going. Just toss her a few protein cubes daily to give the old girl a boost."

The Quartermaster had also packed backpacks for Sid & Vet, carefully checking off each item on Delvin's list.

"Big Man, your Daddy said you'll probably need this." Junior handed Sid his *Captain America* shield.

Bobby Lee had coated Sid's dark gray shield with a flat, off-white paint to blend in with the snowy terrain.

Sid smiled, "That's everything. I guess we'll leave at dawn."

The sun was already setting on another short January day.

Vet shouldered his backpack and slung his weapon, "Dawn hell! Let's go now!"

Big Sid replied, "Hell yes!"

Junior peered through the blinding snow as Sid tied a nylon lifeline tied to Henrietta's bridle and led her onto the horse trailer hitched behind a Dodge Ram 4x4. CZ John joined Sid and Henrietta up in the trailer and secured the tailgate ramp behind them.

Although he couldn't see a thing, Junior heard the snowplow's Komatsu diesel struggle to life in the arctic cold. Henrietta whinnied, then whimpered, as the trailer lurched forward. In less than 10 seconds, the snowplow, Dodge 4x4, and attached horse trailer vanished from sight.

A solemn Junior glanced upward into the blinding blizzard and whispered a fervent prayer for his friends.

The Rally

Charlie wasted no time, "The rally starts at 8 p.m. We should get an early start because the traffic will be crazy around Kindrick Field. Good thing we've got good weather. Let's catch the 5 o'clock news as we pass through Missoula. They'll probably broadcast pre-rally traffic reports."

"It's 5 o'clock at Missoula's newstalk leader, KVGO. This just in from Plains. An attempted sexual assault targeting two Rainbow Corps youth volunteers was foiled this afternoon when one of the youths managed to fend off his assailant with a scrap of lumber. Witnesses report that the two youths were performing community service in the parking lot of a popular Plains restaurant. They were approached by an anti-American, leftwing activist, who attempted to sexually assault one of the boys. The other young man had the presence of mind to fend off the attacker with a mere scrap of wood. Unfortunately, the sexual predator died from injuries incurred during the assault. The Plains Sheriff Office is withholding the names of the two minors, who were released without being charged.

"The Americus for America '25 campaign has issued a brief statement, *'All Americans should be shaken by the continued violence perpetrated by far-left anti-American terrorists against the Rainbow Youth Corps. These young people epitomize the American people and American values. They will not be intimidated. God bless America.'*

"We will be following this story closely ahead of tonight's Helena rally."

No one in the Jeep spoke a word. It took a few moments for the news report to sink in.

Charlie finally broke the silence, "Holy shit! We were just there and must have just missed all that."

Brett was still in disbelief, "You're right Charlie. Can you believe anyone would assault those two boys?"

Marian was a spy by trade and never took things at face value, "If it is so unbelievable, perhaps we should not believe the news reports offhand."

Hoffman couldn't figure out where Marian was going with her comment, "Marian, are you suggesting the news media fabricated the incident?"

"No, not fabricated, but perhaps tailored the incident to fit a narrative. The media have been known to do that sort of thing, from time to time."

Charlie shook his head affirmatively, "Now that's the Gospel truth, young lady. The best liar always tells his version of the truth."

"Charlie, after Marian and I return to Pittsburgh, can you check out this sexual assault incident and scan Hugo Creek with your metal detector?"

Overcome with excitement, Charlie slapped both hands on the steering wheel, "Man, oh man, I can't believe this. I'm actually working on a Brett Hoffman investigation. I wouldn't miss this for all the tea in China."

"Aren't you guys glad we left a little early this afternoon? I told you the traffic would be crazy. I wouldn't be a bit surprised if Wolfgang and Americus pack in at least 50,000 tonight. That might not be a big deal in Pittsburgh, but Montana's population is only a shade over a million. That's one million people spread out over a huge, mountainous state. This is a big deal."

As they entered Helena, Charlie gave Brett and Marian the lay of the land.

"There's overflow parking at the High School.

"Hey Hoffman, dig out a five to tip the kids.

"After we park, we'll take one of the free shuttles over to the stadium."

"I don't want to hear any bellyaching. The best seats are down on the field. Let's stand out in centerfield, just beyond second base. Don't want to stand on either baseline."

The trio followed Charlie's lead and huddled together in the frigid November night air. Brett was stamping his feet to keep warm.

Charlie pointed at his wristwatch, "Here it comes, Mickey's little hand is pointing directly at 8!"

The stadium lights dimmed. An eerie silence fell over the baseball field. The bleachers were packed, prompting the Fire Marshal to close further admission to the playing field. The vast overflow crowd was directed to nearby Memorial Park, where the Schneider Campaign had set up two Jumbotrons.

"Charlie, this is amazing!"

"Shut your trap, Hoffman. Embrace the silence!"

The silence was abruptly broken as the drum & bugle corps sounded ruffles and flourishes. Next, the drummers beat a martial cadence as 2,000 members of the Rainbow Corps marched into the stadium. 1,000 boys marched in from right field along the first baseline. 1,000 girls marched in along the third baseline. The Fire Marshal objected to flaming torches, so, in their right hand, the Rainbow Corps carried those orange marshalling wands used at the airport. The girls cradled bouquets of red roses in their left arm, while each boy carried a tool of some sort in his left hand. Some carried picks, or shovels, or hammers, others carried wrenches, and the more tech savvy carried laptops, or tablets. They formed several ranks along the first and third baselines. When the cadence stopped, in unison, the Rainbow Corps dropped their wands, placed their right hand over their heart, and turned to face the flagpole, out beyond the centerfield fence.

"I pledge allegiance to the flag of the United States of America,
and to the Republic for which it stands,

one nation, under God, indivisible, with liberty and justice for all."

The drum and bugle corps sounded ruffles and flourishes once more. Then a lone bugler pierced the cold night air with a stirring rendition of the *Star-Spangled Banner.*

While all this was going on, teams of youth were out in the parking lots cleaning windshields and rear-view mirrors and sliding "Americus for America" bumper stickers under the front windshield wipers along with self-addressed, postage paid, Schneider Campaign contribution envelopes.

2025 Helena was home to a small Jewish community numbering perhaps 1,000. During the late 19th Century Gold Rush, Helena hosted one of the West's largest and most vibrant Jewish communities. Most of those Jews had immigrated from Germany, seeking a better life in the new promised land, America.

At Wolfgang's request, local Rabbi, David Levi, gave the benediction. Senator Schneider was perhaps Israel's best friend in the US Senate. His Rainbow Corps featured a special "Star of David Brigade". All Jewish Corpsmen were required to wear a special Star of David lapel pin.

Without further ado, the bugles sounded once more as Senator Schneider made his way to the dais. Wolfgang's remarks were short and sweet, hitting his major themes of inclusion, tolerance, patriotism, industry, law & order, and peace through strength. Then he introduced his son.

While Wolfgang was dressed in typical business attire, fortyish Americus was dressed as a member of the Rainbow Corps. His Distinguished Service Cross and Purple Heart, earned in Iraq & Afghanistan, were pinned to his chest. Once he took the dais, Americus stood there like a statue, surveying the crowd. He didn't flinch a muscle. As he stood there in motionless silence, his hypnotic eyes darted from face to face in the crowd, always making eye contact.

Brett could sense the tension building amid the absolute silence. The crowd was ready to explode without Americus having spoken a single word.

Then, Americus lifted his right hand and pointed out toward the flag. As he pointed, the entire crowd, numbering over 55,000, turned in unison toward that flag. It had now been two minutes since Americus came on stage, two minutes of absolute silence.

Slowly and softly Americus began speaking. The crowd hung on his every word. He spoke of duty, honor, unity, work, and community. As Americus spoke, his voice transported Hoffman back to his disc jockey days, reminding Brett of Neil Diamond's golden oldie, *Brother Love*. Americus started soft and slow, but when he let go, half Helena Valley shook. Americus' voiced reached a fever pitched crescendo as he identified America's true enemy.

After speaking 15 minutes, Americus once again stood alone, at the dais, in total silence. It started as a murmur, then spread throughout the crowd, growing ever louder. Americus, Americus, Americus! Americus began nodding his head in approval, making more eye contact throughout the crowd. He began pointing out random members of the crowd, who would, in turn, point back with their outstretched right hand.

Brett noticed that, like an automaton, Charlie was chanting along with the crowd. Marian's eye scanned the crowd. This was no longer a political rally. It had morphed into a quasi-religious experience.

Americus left the stage to the tune of *God Bless America*. Schneider's campaign manager, a Black woman, asked the audience for a commitment. All they had to do was step forward and publicly make a commitment to Americus and America. A stampede of humanity surged into the infield, Latinos, Blacks, Asians, Native Americans, and Whites. This was Americus' Rainbow Coalition.

As they returned to the Grand Cherokee, Brett could see that Marian was visibly shaken, but said nothing.

After they were seated in the car, with the doors closed, Marian felt it safe to speak, "My God, we just spent a couple of hours in 1934 Nuremberg!"

Prosperity

Upon his arrival in 1985 America, everything Wolfgang touched turned to gold. Heinz was kept busy running their fledging engineering firm. Their competitors could not understand how a small upstart firm, such as Adler Engineering, could be awarded multimillion-dollar contracts from around the world. Adler's first international office was in downtown Buenos Aires. The Madrid office opened next, soon followed by the Cairo office. Each location was managed by a team of competent German & Austrian engineers.

The Middle East was fertile ground for Adler Engineering. Lucrative contracts poured in from the Emirates, Bahrain, Jordan, Saddam Hussein's Iraq, and even the Islamic Republic of Iran. Business with Saddam and Iran was conducted via an intricately spun web of front companies. Soon, Wolfgang and the Crown Prince were on a first name basis and Schneider was gifted an oceanfront villa near Aqaba. Wolfgang was always welcome in the Kingdom and, by Allah, did the oil money ever roll in. Wolfgang carefully walked a tightrope bridging two worlds. He was as welcome in Tel Aviv and Jerusalem as he was in Riyadh. He held great influence throughout Israel and was Mossad's "very special friend".

Schneider secretly loathed the Jews. He longed for that day of reckoning when he could reveal his hatred to the world. He did not know exactly how he would eliminate this Jewish infestation known as the State of Israel, but it must be done. Chemical weapons? Uranium devices? Biological warfare? Maybe all the above.

Over the last 40 years, Die Spinne had spun its web around the world, ensnaring politicians, financiers, clergy, and even some in the Vatican and Tel Aviv. Murder, blackmail, sex, drug addiction, media smear campaigns, Schneider used every trick & tool at his disposal.

Every few years, Wolfgang would share further information with his political insiders in Washington, supposedly obtained from the remnants of Uncle Wolf's organization. Every time another treasure trove of art was rescued, Wolfgang would receive huge honorariums and make friends in ever higher positions of power. Once the Iron Curtain was lifted and the Berlin Wall came crashing down, Wolfgang's good deeds were publicized by the easily manipulated mainstream media. He was even honored at the Kennedy Center.

In the 1990s, Adler Engineering gorged itself on contracts for the rebuilding of Kuwait. After 9/11 and Operation Iraqi Freedom, Adler Engineering took its rightful place at the bottomless feeding trough of US foreign aid dollars pouring into Afghanistan and Iraq. Wolfgang was now one of the richest men in the world. But he was much richer than *Fortune* magazine could ever imagine. Through die Spinne, Wolfgang commanded vast resources and held secret hordes of gold, art, and strategic minerals, but information and influence were Schneider's most valuable treasures.

Surprisingly, Wolfgang found friends in Moscow. The Russians were obviously untermenschen, but no longer Bolsheviks. Schneider hated Bolsheviks but was more than comfortable dealing with Russian gangsters. Although the Bolsheviks were no longer in power in Russia, there was no shortage of their ilk in other parts of the world.

China! How Wolfgang despised the Red Chinese! Obviously, all Asians were untermenschen, but those damned Chinese were Bolshevik untermenschen! At least the Japanese were a warrior race.

Schneider admired the Japanese code of Bushido. He admired the discipline of the Japanese people. He clearly understood why the Führer allied himself with the Japanese. Wolfgang could work with the Japanese, and he did! He learned to speak Japanese and spent much time in Japan. The more time he spent in Japan, the clearer it became. The Japanese people had been "stabbed in the back" just like the Germans. Those two Jews, Oppenheimer and Einstein, and their puppet, the Jew loving Roosevelt, had murdered tens of thousands of innocent Japanese civilians with those uranium and plutonium devices. Wolfgang hungered for the day when he had those devices at his disposal.

Schneider mixed business with terror and murder. Wolfgang took the vestiges of Skorzeny's Gruppe Paladin underground in the 1990s. Paladin morphed into Wolfgang's private Gestapo, protecting die Spinne and eliminating Wolfgang's enemies.

Eva was a devoted mother. "Eric" was her pride and joy. The child was intelligent and learned quickly. Wolfgang spared no expense on Eric's education. Wolfgang's major concern was Eric's physical growth. Americus was a frail child, slightly built and shorter than average. Wolf hired a nutritionist and personal trainer, with a pediatrician on call 24/7. By the time Eric was 18, he was only slightly below average height and in excellent shape.

Americus was not movie star handsome, but projected a striking visage, jet black hair and pale, steel blue eyes. He spoke fluent German, with a Bavarian twist, and spoke Mexican Spanish like a homie. His native tongue was pure Midwestern American English. Courtesy of his voice coaches, Americus sounded just like the man on the 6 o'clock news.

In summer 2004, Wolfgang scheduled a week-long mano a mano camping trip for Eric's 18th birthday. While they hiked and fished in the Kootenai

National Forest, Wolfgang revealed to Americus what the history books had missed.

"Eric, your mother and I strived to prepare you for this moment since your birth. Now you know the whole truth. You are my beloved son, but you are also mein Führer."

Afghanistan

During the winter of 2005, Corporal Americus "Kraut" Schneider was freezing his ass off in the mountainous terrain southeast of Kabul, along the Pakistani border. Since the fall of the Taliban, CIA analysts speculated that Osama Bin Laden was hiding in the Tora Bora cave complex. Elements of the elite 75th Ranger Regiment were sent in to support the Green Berets and Navy Seals, who followed up on every lead.

Wolfgang agreed with his stepson's decision to join the Army, as an enlisted man, not an officer. Wolfgang advised Eric to aspire to elite status and always seek a combat posting.

"Remember my son, only in the crucible of combat can a true leader be forged!"

Kraut learned quickly in the caves of Tora Bora, just as his stepfather, Wolfgang, had learned in the turret of his Tiger tank at Pokrovka. As Army Ranger Schneider fought the Islamic untermenschen, he learned to give no quarter. As the commendations stacked up, Kraut's reputation spread throughout the 75th Ranger Regiment, then throughout the entire Spec Ops community. He was fearless, ruthless, and relentless.

After his tour in Afghanistan, Sergeant Schneider spent his second tour in Iraq, operating out of bases recently constructed by Adler Engineering. One close shave followed another. Just when it seemed that Providence favored Sergeant Schneider, his luck ran out.

Schneider's squad was clearing insurgents, mostly veterans of Saddam's Republican Guard, out of a warehouse complex near Tikrit. CIA informants claimed to have spotted some chemical artillery shells stashed away in an outbuilding. The information was a setup. As the Rangers cleared the empty warehouses, several mustard gas shells were detonated. As always, Kraut was leading the way and bore the brunt of the gas attack.

Mustard gas is a blistering agent, not nearly as deadly as nerve agents such as Tabun or Sarin. Kraut almost instantly realized that chemical agents had been released. He withdrew his squad and immediately initiated decontamination protocols. Sergeant Schneider saved his squad but paid a price. He was rushed to the US Military Hospital in Balad, Iraq.

When Wolfgang's Pentagon insider friends contacted him with the grave news, his response was pure Nietzsche.

"He who has a why to live can bear almost any how."

While Americus was deployed to Iraq, Eva was diagnosed with breast cancer. A mastectomy was not indicated, as the cancer had already metastasized. Wolfgang & Eva decided they would not tell Americus about the cancer diagnosis until he returned home. Wolfgang spared no time, nor expense, as he sought to find a cure for Eva's cancer. They tried radiation, nutrition, and chemotherapy, but nothing worked. Eva died while Americus was being gassed in Iraq.

Eva's last request was that Wolfgang complete his mission. Americus must become the Führer. That was her son's birthright.

"Father, is that you?" Sergeant Schneider could not see. He had been blinded by the mustard gas.

The Army ophthalmologist whispered in Wolfgang's ear, "Mr. Schneider, he cannot see. We don't know how long the blindness will persist. Both corneas were damaged by the gas, but the optic nerve is unaffected. He has a good chance of a full recovery."

"Yes, Eric, I'm here. The doctor says you should make a complete recovery."

"Hajii can't win a standup fight." Sergeant Schneider then whispered, "That's the way it is with all untermenschen, right Pops?"

Wolfgang broke up laughing, "I see you have become a regular GI! That is good. I understand that your entire squad was saved by your quick action."

"Just doing my job. When can I leave this sandbox?"

Wolfgang sat down next to Americus and whispered "I'm pulling some strings. Should have you home in a couple of weeks."

"It will be great to see Mom. What am I saying? I can't see anything!"

Wolfgang took his stepson by the hand, "Eric, your mother is dead."

A tearful Americus replied, "Dead? What happened?"

"She has been sick for some time with breast cancer. We decided it would be best if you concentrated on your mission."

For a moment, Americus laid there in silence before answering, "I understand. She understood. Our mission is bigger than any one of us. Dad, you were right. This has not been fun, but now I know what it means to command men; what it means to confront the enemy; to do what one must to obtain victory."

The Forced March

The snowplow came to an abrupt stop about 5 miles east of the New Mexico state line, 5 miles west of the Red Hill "toll gate".

Through the whiteout, Slick ran back to the horse trailer and dropped the tail gate, "That's 20 miles down, only 80 miles to go."

Sergeant Nicolescu raised his CZ helmet's visor as he exited the trailer, "Aye, aye, Captain. We'll push it all night and should be in Quemado come early morning. We'll hole up somewhere in Quemado for a few hours, then push on to Pie Town. We'll rest and recoup a bit in Lame Wolf's hogan, then make the final push to the Array. We should be in place in about 48 hours."

Delvin shivered, then replied, "I hope so. The meteorologist says this storm will taper off in about 24 hours and clear out 24 hours thereafter. You must be prepared to attack upon arrival."

As the snowplow and Dodge 4x4 headed back to Springerville, John Nicolescu gave Sid his marching orders, "Big Man, we're gonna veer slightly to the south. In his report, Cowboy Tom warned us to steer clear of Red Hill. We need to put 30 miles behind us. Once we reach Quemado, we'll find a spot to hunker down until mid-morning."

CZ Nicolescu set a relentless pace as he led the way eastward through the howling blizzard. Sid couldn't see a thing. He just kept marching, mile after grueling mile, connected to Henrietta and Vet with that safety yellow nylon lifeline,.

After skirting Red Hill to the south, John once again followed US 60 east, retracing Cowboy Tom's trail. The highway was treacherous. The fierce winds had cleared the snow from short stretches of pavement, while sculpting huge drifts in other spots. Hour after grueling hour they marched.

7 hours and 20 miles into the night march, John paused and raised his visor, "Sid, are you OK?"

Sid replied into the pitch black night, "Yes Sergeant. I switched on my coveralls about a half hour ago."

The two men stepped back to check on Henrietta. CZ Nicolescu switched on his CZ helmet's spotlight. The mare mule was gulping down mouthfuls of snow. John had packed a curry comb and quickly brushed a thick layer of ice and snow off Henrietta while Sid fed the mule a double handful of protein cubes.

Once Henrietta was de-iced, John shouted, "Let's double-time it for the next two hours. That should put us in Quemado before dawn."

Two hours later, a dog-tired Sergeant Nicolescu kicked open the door of a long abandoned propane distributorship on the western outskirts of Quemado. Sid led Henrietta into the abandoned building. The shop's only means of heating was a propane furnace. There was no propane in the Peoples' United States. Although it was freezing inside, the structure was relatively intact, keeping it weathertight. The entire team was exhausted. They unpacked an exhausted Miss Henrietta, and she promptly laid down.

"Sergeant John, I thought mules always sleep standing up."

Vet stroked Henrietta's withers as he laid down beside her, "Sometimes, if they feel safe and at ease, a mule will lay down to sleep."

Big Sid laid down on Henrietta's other side. Within minutes, all three were sound asleep.

Late the following morning, the team was ready to move out.

Big Sid peered out a boarded up window, "The blizzard is letting up. The wind has died down a mite."

Vet nodded, "We've gotta move our asses. No pun intended Henrietta."

The mare mule snorted.

"With the weather improving, we dare not go through town. Cowboy's scouting report mentioned a small Peoples' Militia outpost in the old Post Office."

"Mr. John, let's take out those bastards."

Vet furiously replied, "Damn it, Sid! Haven't I taught you a thing? It'll be another day before we reach the Array. If we waste those bastards at the Post Office, that won't go unnoticed. Every Member in New Mexico will go on high alert. Get your head out of your ass and concentrate on our mission."

Vet bypassed Quemado and headed straight over US 60 toward Pie Town. That afternoon, they made better time than the night before, but it was no cake walk. Cowboy Tom's scouting report included GPS coordinates of all major waypoints along his route. CZ John verbally input the coordinates of Lame Wolf's hogan into his helmet's navigational computer. The CZ helm's visor featured a heads-up display, much like that on a modern fighter jet. After another 7 hour forced march, the team arrived at Lame Wolf's hogan.

Lame Wolf's lodge was just as he left it a few weeks earlier. A stack of well-seasoned firewood sat along the south interior wall. While Big Sid unpacked Henrietta, John got a fire going in the barrel stove.

"I hope Mr. Tom's Navajo friend won't mind me using his cast iron skillet."

"Sid, what are you gonna cook in a skillet? We only packed MREs."

Sid laughed as he held up a roll of pork sausage and a half dozen eggs.

"Aren't those eggs frozen?"

Sid snickered as he pointed at an ancient *Captain America* lunchbox, half filled with packing popcorn, "I packed this here lunchbox under Henrietta's cargo pad. Them eggs are cold, but they didn't freeze."

Minutes later, John & Sid were scarfing down sausage & eggs, while Henrietta munched on protein cubes. After dinner, the two soldiers stripped down to their skivvies and spread their bedrolls next to the barrel stove. Once again, Henrietta laid down, this time up close to the stove.

The team hit the trail by dawn. Vet planned on arriving at the Array shortly after sunset. All day long, the weather improved.

"We gotta move it. If those clouds lift and the sun pops out, we'll be spotted by aerial recon."

Vet was taking no chances. As US 60 wound through the Crosby Mountains, the team stuck to the trees alongside the road. As the sun set, the team bypassed the small town of Datil and came down onto the Plains of San Augustin.

"Big Man, it's about 13 miles to the Array." Vet pointed upward, "See those stars? We've run out of time."

Late Night

"Charlie, where does a man your age get all that energy?"

"Don't tell me it's past your bedtime Hoffman. It's only 1 a.m. back in Pittsburgh."

"Hey Marian, does this rental car have satellite radio?"

Marian was nodding off in the backseat, "Radio? Satellite? Yes, I think it does."

Brett started playing with the radio, "Charlie, you keep your eyes on the road. I think *Sea-to-Sea* is on Channel 666."

Charlie cackled like a hyena, "I guess you picked that channel number?"

"No, but I wish I had. That's the new *Paranormal & Conspiracies Channel*. Here we go."

The *Sea-to-Sea AM* bumper music was just fading out. Vince Vittito was back to full strength and introduced his guests, a team of ghost hunters from down New Orleans way.

While listening, Charlie pondered his current situation out loud, "I can't imagine why it had to be Nazis. That damn spaceship should have been piloted by those little grey guys with the big heads and black eyes. What did I get? Leutnant Heinz!"

Brett popped Charlie's balloon, "You know, I'm not so sure you saw a spaceship."

Charlie quickly clarified, "Two spaceships."

"OK, OK! Two spaceships! But I don't think those craft fly between worlds."

"Brett, I saw them both streak down, like space capsules reentering the atmosphere."

"Think about it. Why would Nazis be traveling to Earth in 1985? There's only one answer. They were fleeing Germany, probably Berlin, and I bet they departed sometime in April or May 1945. That's what Pee Wee saw back in '45. That's why he was assassinated. God rest his soul."

Charlie wasn't buying it, "Really? Methinks you've been hanging around your Japanese physicist friend just a wee bit too much."

Marian opened her eyes and joined in from the backseat, "No. I think Brett's got a point. Like I said, we just spent two hours in 1934 Nuremberg. The torchlight parade, the drums & bugles, the Hitler Youth, and that Americus guy. My God, can't you see it?"

Brett was slowly and negatively shaking his head, "It doesn't add up. Nazi's do not have Black female campaign managers. Nazi's do not ask rabbis to give invocations. Some of the trappings of tonight's rally may harken back to the days of the Third Reich, but maybe Wolfgang uses those memes because they are so effective.

"Tomorrow morning, I'll call my buddy at the Carnegie Mellon Institute for Politics & Strategy."

Marian sighed, "Another one of your academic groupies?"

"Look, we don't know anything about Wolfgang, or Americus. It's time we got educated."

A couple of hours later, they arrived back at Quinn's Resort. Marian was sound asleep in the backseat.

Brett opened the rear passenger door. A blast of cold Montana air jolted the Squirrel Hill cowgirl awake.

"Are we back already?"

Brett smiled, "Yes sweet cheeks, we're back at the cabin."

As Brett turned to unlock the cabin, Marian checked out his sweet cheeks.

Charlie opened a small door on the side of his motorhome, uncoiled a heavy-duty power cord, then plugged into an exterior power outlet.

"I'll be snug as a bug tonight. You two children best get to bed."

Although Brett went straight to bed, he couldn't go straight to sleep. The day's events repeatedly looped through his mind. There was a story here, he could feel it in his bones. As he began to finally doze off to sleep, there was a knock at his door. He jumped out of bed, wearing nothing but his skivvies.

"Doggone it, Charlie. I was just about to doze off."

Hoffman opened the door, ranting at Charlie all the while.

There stood Marian, wearing nothing but her Stetson and a wry smile.

Activism

Americus was back home in Montana and discharged from the Army within two weeks of Wolfgang's visit to Iraq. His vision gradually returned. With Eva gone, Wolfgang took a few months to reassess the trajectory of his life and his solemn mission. In the 23 years since the jump, Wolfgang had become the wealthiest, most influential private citizen on the planet. Once again, Wolfgang scheduled a week-long mano a mano camping trip with his son.

"Eric, I think it is time."

"You are concerned with the direction of the country?"

"Yes, but that doesn't really matter. One way, or the other, we must take control. You must save the Aryan race."

"What are your plans?"

"The question should be, what are our plans? The answer is not simple, but we have time on our side."

Both men laughed at Wolfgang's double entendre.

"Whatever we do, we must remember what our Führer, your father, realized too late. We must keep our National Socialist principles close to our vest and manipulate the masses. Once you are in power, we can reveal those principles to the world. Woe be unto the Bolsheviks, Jews, and all untermenschen on that glorious day!"

"Once you are in power, Israel must be obliterated. Next, we must crush the Red Chinese. We may possibly enlist the aid of the Japanese and Taiwanese in that effort. The developing situation in Hong Kong and Taiwan may allow us to defeat the Chinese Bolsheviks without the use of uranium devices."

"Father, what of the Slavs, the Russians?"

"They are no longer Bolsheviks, but they are still untermenschen. This new man, Putin, is nothing more than a gangster. We can do business with such a man and bide our time.

"This great country must be purged of all untermenschen. The Negroes, Jews, American Indians, and Asians must be exterminated. Perhaps the Hispanics can be relegated to a lower servant caste, like the Negro slaves in the Confederacy. We will sorely miss not having learned men, like Herr Doktor Mengele, around to sort out such racial issues."

"How will we take power?"

"Just as your father took power. The people will vote you into power!"

"What role will Uncle Heinz play in our efforts?"

"Schuster will be our Borman. He will manage all business activities. Adler Group has interests around the world. He cannot be involved with our political activities. I fear Heinz does not have the Wagnerian essence to do what must be done."

The Morning After

"Herr Hoffman…" Marian was whispering in Brett's ear. "Herr Hoffman, this is your 6 a.m. wake up call."

"I thought, after last night, we were past all that Herr Hoffman crap."

"Nein, Herr Oberst. What would you have me do?"

Brett was surprised by Marian's playful side, "Charlie will be knocking at the door any second now. If you're a good girl, perhaps we can pick up a length of rope somewhere today."

"Jawohl, Herr Hoffman, Jawohl!"

As Brett started to get out of bed, Marian was having none of it. It wasn't difficult for her to coax him into changing his mind. It is safe to say, by 6:30 a.m., Brett had been ridden hard and put up wet.

The cabin phone rang, and Marian answered, "Marian, I'm waiting for you two guys outside the restaurant. Bang on Hoffman's door and make sure his sorry ass is up and at 'em."

"OK, I'll see if I can get his lazy ass out of bed."

Brett was looking Marian straight in the face while she spoke. He indignantly wagged his finger in her direction as she hung up the phone.

Marian was standing there, by the bed, in her birthday suit, pointing toward the bathroom, "To the showers Hoffman!"

Marian was beaming as she walked to the restaurant hand-in-hand with Brett. Hoffman was still in a daze. Marian was very attractive. She was smart and definitely one tough cookie. Brett loved her humor. As that thought crossed his mind, he squeezed Marian's hand. Marian stopped, pulled Brett close, and gave him a long, passionate kiss.

As Brett caught his breathe, another thought crossed his mind, "My God, I'm in big trouble!"

After ordering breakfast, Brett and Charlie rehashed the previous day's events. Marian was quiet. She was lost in thought. Brett could not imagine the depth of his troubles.

"How am I going to introduce Hoffman to Mother? I didn't see any gold or silver crosses, but I know he's not Jewish. Obviously not! He's tall, with blonde hair and blue eyes. Maybe, he's not Catholic. Maybe, he's a Protestant, a Lutheran. Maybe he's an atheist! My God, I don't know anything about this man, but I do know one thing, I've got him!"

"Earth to Marian, come in Marian." Charlie was slowly waving his hand at a seemingly catatonic Marian.

"Oh, excuse me, I was just reliving last night's events in my mind." Marian smiled at Charlie and gave Brett a quick side eye wink.

Brett saw the wink, but chose to ignore it, "Charlie, will we have cell service all the way into Plains?"

"Pretty much."

"Good! On our way into town, I'll call Adam Goldberg at CMU's Institute for Politics and Strategy. He's a Postdoc Fellow and rubs elbows with all the Washington insiders. He specializes in Mideast policy, focusing on Israel. Adam has a passion for all things Holocaust related.

Marian moaned a somewhat jealous moan, "Don't tell me, another Brett Hoffman groupie?"

Brett whimsically replied, "Jawohl!"

"Adam, it's Brett. I need your expertise."

"Good morning, Brett. Are you negotiating a treaty with Andromeda?"

"Not yet, but who knows? Right now, I'm interested in some background on Senator Wolfgang Schneider from the great state of Montana."

"Americus too?"

"Yeah. I was at their rally in Helena last night."

"Pretty impressive, huh?"

"Adam, are they for real?"

"As far as I know, yes. One, or both, are likely future Presidents."

"I'll be back home in a couple of days. Dig up everything you can on the Schneiders."

"OK, what's in it for me?"

"You just gave me a great idea. How about appearing with Hiroshi on an upcoming *Sea-to-Sea* and you two discuss interplanetary politics?"

"But there isn't any interplanetary politics."

"Not yet, as far as we know. Start gathering your thoughts and I'll bounce some ideas off Hiroshi. You know, things like first contact, inter-species communications, alien belief systems and social mores. How would you like to be the first ambassador to Andromeda?"

When Brett got off the phone, Charlie sarcastically murmured, "What a fucking con artist."

Mini-Marathon

A year earlier, Big Sid couldn't have made the forced march to the Array. Over the past few months Sergeant Nicolescu had molded Sid into the quintessential Army Ranger. The Big Man had stamina. He was nimble as a cat. Most of all, he had heart, a heart as big as the State of Georgia. That heart would be sorely tested that star spangled night.

"Big Sid, slip on your night vision."

Sid did as Vet directed. The sky was clearing. Enough starlight and moonlight filtered through the scattered clouds for Sid's night vision to be effective.

As Sid put on his night vision, CZ John broadcast an encrypted radio burst. The clock was now running.

Back in Springerville, Captain Delvin Smith shot Lieutenant Josephine Parker a thumbs up. Amidst a swirling cyclone of snow, Badass Bitch lifted off from the Springerville Airport. Jo was in the rear seat, piloting the Bitch, while Dead Eye Adam Jackson was up front in the co-pilot/gunner's seat. Once Badass Bitch was airborne, Jo switched off her navigation lights and headed eastward, following a NOE flight profile. The Bitch was going to war.

There was little cover out on the San Augustin Plain. Vet made the best use possible of the small arroyos running roughly parallel to US 60. As John ran from bush to bush and from one stunted tree to another, like the chameleon, the coloration of his CZ suit constantly adapted to match his surroundings. Big Sid & Henrietta were not so invisible. John instinctively increased the spacing between him and Sid. The wily old Sergeant wanted to spot the enemy before they spotted the Big Man, or his four legged girlfriend.

Nicolescu was not quite running. He was scampering, zigging then zagging. Every so often, Vet would pause, look, and listen. In addition to full spectrum vision, the CZ helmet provided its wearer with superhuman hearing across a wide range of sonic frequencies. CZ Vet's enhanced hearing caught a rumble to his front.

Vet motioned for Sid to freeze and drop, then he slowly crept forward.

"This isn't on Cowboy Tom's scouting report." John checked his heads up display.

Vet was a couple of miles south of US 60 and a little over 3 miles west of the Array's Operations Center. The team was hanging a little south of Tom Jackson's route. During his recon, Tom had not spotted this large ranch house and assorted outbuildings.

CZ John glanced again at his heads up display and began pawing the snow covered ground beneath his feet, "What the hell? Is that asphalt?"

"I must be standing on the remnants of Old US 60." John was right. The crumbling, snow packed highway beneath his feet was indeed the old highway.

John spotted a 4x4 diesel pickup truck chugging away from the ranch house, heading eastward, toward the Array. Then, he spotted smoke emanating from two of the ranch house's chimneys. He actually didn't see smoke; he saw IR signatures rising from both chimneys. One of the nearby metal outbuildings was also glowing red in the IR spectrum.

"Holy shit!" John's Super Soldier suit suddenly detected high intensity microwaves, S band radiation, smacking him in the face. His CZ suit's onboard computer was familiar with the radar's signature and immediately identified the source as Red Chinese JY-9F air search radar. Moments thereafter, complete schematics of the JY-9F system flashed up on John's visor. Too bad Sergeant Nicolescu couldn't read Chinese hanzi. Although Vet couldn't read, nor speak Chinese, it was apparent from the schematic that the radar system consisted of three modules, parabolic antennae, diesel generator, and control room.

Nicolescu had no clue that the JY-9F radar specialized in detecting low altitude threats such as drones, cruise missiles, and helicopters. The JY-9F was difficult to jam and could distinguish an incoming threat from surrounding ground clutter.

This JY-9F radar was an unexpected wrinkle. While John pondered the JY-9F radar's schematic, his CZ suit sounded another alarm. Another S band radar had just gone active. This new signature was an Active Electronically Scanned Array (AESA). The CZ suit immediately identified that radar as the acquisition radar for a Red Chinese HQ-7B SAM battery. John was expecting this radar. He checked the time. The SAM's radar went active at precisely 2200 hours. That radar emitted for exactly 60 seconds, then went dark.

John squatted down to rest and sort things out in his head. If he took out the search radar at the ranch house, the Array would go on high alert. The SAM battery's search radar wasn't emitting because it was hiding from anti-radiation missiles and similar radar homing ordnance. John suspected that the SAM's search radar had briefly gone active for a systems check.

One thing was certain, that search radar ensconced in the ranch house was a wild card. It had to be taken out. If not, it would paint Badass Bitch as she swooped down, out of the mountains, onto the San Augustin Plain. How could they take out that radar without raising an alarm?

Nicolescu jogged back 50 yards to find Sid and the mare mule hunkered down amongst some snow covered desert scrub.

John raised his CZ visor, "Sid, if I ordered you to take out a search radar in an undetectable manner, how would you do it?"

The Big Man cocked his head as he went into Bobby Lee Skipper mode, "Mister John, those radars require a lot of power, don't they?"

"They sure do. There's a radar straight ahead of us powered by a couple of diesel generators. The generators are located in a metal pole barn next to a ranch house."

"Are you sure?"

"Yeah, I saw both diesels' IR signature. That pole barn is hot as a firecracker."

"Are they vented? Scratch that silly question. Carbon monoxide won't bother you in your Super Soldier suit."

"Yeah, those diesels are exhausted through the roof, but I'm not going inside that pole barn, you are. Who better than a mechanic to fuck up an engine? How will you do it?"

Sid reached down, brushed away the snow, and picked up a handful of coarse desert sand, "I'm gonna sneak down there into that shed, pop loose those air filters, pour a little sand into those engines, then replace the filters. You and the mule will be waiting for me on the far side of the ranch house. I'll put just enough sand in one diesel so it will run for a few minutes before it seizes. I'll put a little less sand in the other. Hopefully, it'll run just a little longer. I don't want them crashing simultaneously."

Vet was not a mechanic, "Won't they suspect sabotage?"

"If'n I was runnin' that radar and both generators suddenly stopped, I'd first check the oil. Next, I'd check the diesel fuel. Then, I would probably check the air filters. The air filters will be clean. They may suspect foul play, but they will need to tear down those engines to prove it."

Minutes later, after bypassing the ranch house, John & Henrietta were hunkered down in a small gravel pit. CZ John's heads up display indicated the pit was just under a half mile to the east northeast of the ranch house.

Meanwhile, Big Sid, with Thompson in hand, approached his objective from the west, crawling through the sparse high desert brush and snow. The Big Man dared not stand. The lone sentry leaning against the warm metal

TW POWELL © 2023

outbuilding would surely spot him. Sid couldn't see much detail, but the red star on the sentry's Ushanka winter hat identified him as PLAN.

"Damn, I think he's wearing night vision."

The Big Man was right. The Falcon Commando pointed his Norinco QBZ-95 assault rifle in Sid's direction.

"Yank, you come out with hands up!"

Sid didn't move a muscle. He was about 100 feet from the Commando. The ChiCom was looking in Sid's general direction, but didn't seem to be focused directly on the Big Man.

Sid played it cool, "Maybe the ChiCom heard the snap, crackle, pop of the frozen brush. Maybe he saw movement. I don't think he can see me lying here amid all this snow and scrub."

The sentry switched on a powerful flashlight and began advancing toward the Big Man, "I hear you, Joe. You come out and you live. You don't, you die!"

"Damn! I could cut him to pieces with this here Tommy Gun, but the gunfire would give us away. If I rush him, he'll cut me down before I even get close."

It was catch-22 for Big Sid. The entire mission was on the line. The Falcon Commando was slowly and methodically approaching, now only 25 yards away. It was now or never. Sid reached around and unsnapped the 18 inch depleted uranium shield slung across his back and silently waited for his opportunity.

An angry Burrowing Owl popped his head out from an abandoned badger's sett, announcing his displeasure with his unique call. The startled Falcon Commando glanced toward the terrifying sound. Although the Chinese soldier was unacquainted with Nuevo Mexico's nocturnal raptors, his site specific training included rattlesnake recognition. The Burrowing Owl is known for its rather unique defense mechanism. The subterranean raptor can expertly mimic a rattlesnake's hiss. The Commando froze in place, uneager to get snake bit.

With the agility of a Danseur Noble, Big Sid sprang to his feet, tossing his *Captain America* shield as if it were a super-sized frisbee. The last thing the ChiCom sentry saw was an off-white UFO, hurtling his way, with his name on it. The razor sharp edge of the depleted uranium disc decapitated the Falcon Commando before he could even begin to react.

Before the sentry's severed head hit the ground, Sid was running toward the warm outbuilding. Sid whizzed past the Commando's still upright, staggering, headless body and retrieved his bloody shield without breaking stride.

"Now I've screwed the pooch. When those Red bastards realize their comrade is missing, they'll sound the alarm."

Big Trouble in Steel City

Jack had his good days and bad days, but the good days were now few and far between. Before winter set in, Jack had to finish raking the leaves inundating his front yard, probably for one last time. He didn't know how much longer he could live alone in his suburban Monroeville home, but as long as he lived there, the place would look presentable.

Jack's wife, JoAnn, had passed a couple of years earlier. Jack was preparing to follow. That's why he had to tell someone about his Kecksburg experience and Brett Hoffman seemed to be the logical person to tell.

On Halloween night, Brett called Jack warning him that a man in a black leather trench coat tailed him out of the Drive-n-Dine. Brett called Jack again after the shootout at Stan's place. Jack was happy that Brett had located Stan the Man, as Stan could verify most of Jack's unbelievable story. Jack was elated when Brett shared Stan's contact information. The old Airman contacted Stan and scheduled a reunion lunch. Perhaps Jack could go to his grave knowing that someone was seriously looking into the Kecksburg event.

It was beautiful leaf raking weather, temperature in the low 60s, bright sunshine, and no wind. Jack decided this would be a good day to work outside for a while before Stan picked him up. As he raked, Jack savored the fragrance of the fallen leaves. Knowing that his days were numbered, Jack relished every moment, every sensation. He was living in the moment.

Everyone in the neighborhood seemed to be outside either enjoying themselves, or busy preparing for another hard Pittsburgh winter. In the past,

Jack would have burned those leaves, but those days were long gone. Gangs of self-appointed climate police roamed the suburbs, violently enforcing their climate religion. Jack filled plastic bag after bag with leaves and sat them out by the curb to be picked up by the city.

The old Airman zip tied the final leaf bag as a black BMW slowly inched its way up Harvard Road. Jack did a double take as he recalled seeing that same car a couple of times earlier that morning. As the BMW passed for the third time, Jack fell to the ground. With all the noise in the neighborhood, leaf blowers, children playing, and dogs barking, nobody heard the muffled sound of the suppressed .22 caliber Beretta as it fired 5 shots in rapid succession from close range.

A few minutes later, a couple of neighborhood kids noticed Jack lying motionless on the sidewalk, amid a puddle of blood. They ran home to their parents, who immediately called the police. The police took a couple of hours to arrive, due to recent defunding measures.

Stan the Man was not familiar with Monroeville and had a little bit of trouble finding Jack's place. Let's face it, to a country boy Stan's age, GPS was an alien technology. The cops and EMS arrived mere minutes before Stan. Seeing the commotion ahead, Stan stopped a few houses up the road and quizzed a neighbor.

"What happened? Somebody have a heart attack?"

Jack's middle-aged neighbor replied, "I can't believe it. Some asshole shot Jack!"

Stan didn't need any further police complications, "This Jack guy, was he involved with drugs, or the mob?"

"Hell no! Jack lived here most all his life. He was an old man. The poor guy had pancreatic cancer. Why would anyone want to kill him?"

No sooner had Brett got off the phone with Adam, his cell phone rang again.

Marian covered both ears with her hands, "Gee Hoffman, can't you change that ring tone? It gives me the willies."

Brett ignored Marian's complaint and answered.

"Hoffman, we got another dead body."

"Stan, calm down. Who's dead?"

"They got Jack."

Stan's earlier close call at home got his attention, but Jack's assassination was traumatic. This was for real. Stan was no longer a kid up a tree. His ass was in deep trouble. He couldn't go back to the police. They wouldn't believe his story. Hoffman was his only hope, his only friend."

"OK Stan, listen to me. You and Blue Dog pack up and stay at a hotel tonight. Don't book it online. Don't call out on your cellphone. Don't make a reservation. Use cash. Go find a room a couple of hours from home. Don't tell anyone where you're staying. I'll be home late tomorrow afternoon. Then you can bunk with me until we figure things out. I'll call you tomorrow."

"That was Stan the Man on the phone. You know, the kid in the tree back in '65. Someone just assassinated Jack, the Airman who was there with Stan in Kecksburg.

"Charlie, we have to assume they, whoever 'they' are, heard you on *Sea-to-Sea* the other night. After Marian and I leave tomorrow, you should stock up your Winnebago and drop off the grid. No internet and turn off your cell phone. Withdraw plenty of cash today and don't use your credit cards."

"I thought you wanted me to snoop around and gather intel on that alleged sexual assault yesterday at the Butcher Block."

"That can wait. We must assume you are being hunted. Get the hell out of town.

"Marian, does that cover it?"

"You got it Hoffman."

Then Marian added her two cents, "Charlie, once you start moving, the only way they can track you is electronically. Credit cards, internet, and cell phone use must be avoided. Avoid the police. They may be compromised, but most likely just sloppy."

Brett began naming the list of suspects, "Could be Heinz, or his kameraden."

Marian added another suspect, "Could be Paladin Gruppe."

"I think Marian would agree that it could be Mossad."

Marian reluctantly nodded her head in agreement then added, "It could be a US Agency. You know, The Company."

Detective Work

As the intrepid trio drove into Plains, Brett picked Charlie's brain, "Charlie, you said that it was obvious that heavy equipment was used to haul away the two Glocke,"

Charlie replied in his typically crotchety manner, "You two walked up that creek bed yesterday. You saw the terrain. Ain't no way a regular flatbed could get up that canyon. If we are to believe the tale Jack told you, may he rest in peace, it would require a substantial crane to lift those two puppies, especially the big one. So, 40 years ago, back in 1985, where around here would my old Luxembourg buddy, Heinz, rent some heavy equipment, on short notice?"

"Charlie, you're spot on target. Plains was a different place back in '85, there wasn't all this home construction."

Marian agreed with Brett, "Yeah, we're looking for someplace close by that operated heavy equipment back in '85."

The three fearless Nazi hunters spent the entire day in Plains. They stopped into the water & sewer district, called the local electric co-op, visited several realtors, and talked to a couple of building contractors. Everyone gave them the same answer. Back in 1985, if you needed a foundation dug, or a road graded, or heavy equipment hauled, you talked to Kurt Hansen.

Kurt Hansen owned both Clark Fork Auto Salvage and Hansen Excavating & Hauling. Kurt passed away in 1999. Upon his death, Hansen's two heirs sold off both businesses. Neither of Hansen's daughters were involved with the day-to-day operation of those businesses.

Charlie was dejected, "Well, we just ran into a brick wall. There's no way we're gonna find out if Hansen hauled those machines out of Hugo Creek."

Brett was grasping at straws, "I can't find Clark Fork Auto Salvage on the GPS. Pull over and I'll ask this State Trooper for directions."

Charlie pulled over beside a Montana State Police SUV and Brett cranked down his window, "Officer, we're trying to find Clark Fork Auto Salvage."

The middle-aged cop chuckled, "I haven't heard anyone mention the old junkyard in years. It ain't there anymore."

"So, that's why I couldn't pull it up on my GPS."

"Yep! Since Y2K, that large tract north of town belongs to Schneider. He's cleaned it all up and made it a showplace. If you want to check it out, just head due north of town and take Clark Creek Loop. Please, do me a favor, look all you want, but don't bother the Senator."

"Thank you, officer. We won't be any trouble." Brett rolled up the window, "Step on it, Charlie."

Everyone was quiet on the short drive up to the Schneider family compound until Marian finally broke the ice, "Isn't this interesting? Schneider now owns the site of Hansen's junkyard and excavation company."

Brett cautioned her, "Marian, Wolfgang owns a whole bunch of stuff. Don't jump to conclusions."

The Schneider estate was indeed a showplace.

"My goodness, this is beautiful country!" Marian couldn't believe the scenery unfolding before her eyes. "Look over in that meadow, is that buffalo?"

Charlie quipped back, "Betcha you don't see that in frigging Pittsburgh!"

An 8-foot-high security fence lined the western side of the road.

"That fence started 2 miles back. A fence like that ain't cheap. Just look at the forest, mountains, lakes, and meadows. This is a fucking Nordic wet dream!" Always the investigator, Brett was taking stock of every detail.

"Slow down, Charlie! There's an entry road." Brett was pointing to his left, "Turn in here."

A gatehouse was sited 100 yards up the blacktop entry road, flanking a black, wrought iron, security gate. Charlie slowly pulled up to the gate and lowered his window.

A uniformed Rainbow Corps volunteer stepped out and greeted him, "Good day, sir. How may I help you?

"We're tourists, just passing through. We've been told the Schneider compound is worth seeing."

The young man smiled in agreement, "It sure is beautiful. I'm sorry, it's not open to the public. You should contact either Senator Wolfgang, Americus, or Mr. Schuster for admittance."

"Mr. Schuster? I'm not familiar with that name."

"That's understandable. Mr. Heinz Schuster is Chief Operating Officer of Adler Industries. He maintains a low profile.

"You can make a U-turn here."

"Thank you. Tell the Schneiders they have a nice spread out here."

As Charlie rolled up his window and turned the Jeep around, Brett exclaimed, "Charlie, we may have just identified your long-lost friend from Luxembourg."

On the Warpath

John Nicolescu's encrypted radio burst set a complex military operation in motion. After Badass Bitch took off from the Springerville Airport, Captain Delvin Smith climbed into the snowplow's passenger's seat and lead the rare earth convoy eastward, along US 60, toward the Very Large Array.

Vet & Sid now had a mere 60 minutes to destroy the radars protecting the Array, then neutralize any man portable air defenses. In one hour, Badass Bitch would swoop down and take out the Very Large Array before the meddling Chinese physicists could screw up our one and only metastable universe.

6 minutes after Vet broadcast the radio burst, the leading elements of the Mescalero North Force s crossed the Rio Grande in silent EV passenger vehicles, dressed as Peoples' Militia. The small San Antonio Peoples' Militia contingent was billeted in a cluster of tourist cabins at the corner of New Mexico Highway 1 & 2nd Street. That cold winter's evening, most all the Militia were across the street, raising hell, at the Hoot Owl Bar & Grill.

A frigid breeze swept through the smoke-filled Hoot Owl as a dozen strangers sauntered in the front door. The strangers silently smiled and nodded as they deliberately dispersed themselves throughout the bar and adjoining café. The group's apparent ringleader bellied up to the bar.

"What will it be, Pilgrim?" The old barkeep didn't recognize a single one of these strangers.

The ringleader didn't reply. He turned his back to the bar and surveyed the tavern through the billowing clouds of reefer smoke. His compadres were now dispersed and looked to him for direction.

The ringleader's .45 caliber UZI machine pistol fired the same round as Vet & Sid's Thompsons. The Uzi packed knockdown power out the ying-yang. The ringleader loudly whistled, then pulled his weapon from beneath his long coat. .45 caliber rounds crisscrossed the barroom as the dozen UZI toting strangers wasted everyone. I mean everyone. That night, inside the Hoot Owl, the old barkeeper, three waitresses, two short order cooks, and 10 Peoples' Militia all met their maker. The civilians died along with the combatants. As terrible as that sounds, such is the nature of war.

Moments later, scores of Humvees and pickup trucks rumbled along San Antonio's 2nd Street. Half the vehicles turned north on NM 1. The rest of the vehicles continued westward another kilometer and merged onto Interstate 25 Northbound.

A feverish Member, lying flat on her back, down with the flu, was awakened by the crackling gunfire at the bar across the road. The local Militia leader had quarantined the young woman in a cold, dark, windowless shed behind one of the tourist cabins. The bed-ridden young woman staggered to her feet and peeked out the door. Her head was spinning as she lost count of the military vehicles speeding through town. Although she was completely disoriented, she was certain that a massive Mescalero force was heading northward, toward Socorro.

Meanwhile, the Southern Mescalero force crossed the Rio Grande at Truth or Consequences. There they faced an entirely different scenario. Unlike San Antonio, T or C is a substantial town with several thousand inhabitants. Many of those inhabitants were dedicated Members of The Collective. Others were dedicated members of the New Juarez Cartel. An unholy alliance had evolved between The Collective and the Cartel. The Collective allowed the Cartel to freely operate along the Rio Grande. In return, the Cartel helped maintain order and help defend The Collective from Resistance & Mescalero forces.

Offhand, one would expect Cartel gunmen to be vicious, but highly undisciplined soldiers. That would be an accurate expectation, if the Cartel used its gunmen as soldiers. The Cartel's gunmen stuck to routine business. The Cartel defended its territory with a highly professional, mercenary force. Some of those mercenaries were Cuban communists, who fled the island after their decisive defeat in the 2027 Battle of Havana. Others were Chechen, Ukrainian, and Russian deserters, who had no problem working for flaming assholes, if the price was right. The Nuevo Juarez Brigada was a well-equipped, fearsome, disciplined, fighting force, in some ways reminiscent of the French Foreign Legion.

Mescalero Intelligence estimated that at least 1,000 NJB mercenaries defended T or C, along with an unknown number of Peoples' Militia. If push came to shove, the Cartel gunmen could lend their support. Taking T or C would be a long, grueling, urban campaign. The Great Chief was a wiser commander than Wolfgang's former boss. Captain Cloud would not allow T or C to become his Stalingrad.

Captain Cloud directed his forces to cross over the Elephant Butte Dam and streak northwestward along Lakeshore Road and capture the T or C Airport, on the northern outskirts of town. After a brief, close quarters, firefight at the dam and another, shorter shootout at the Airport, South Force blocked all the roads leading northward from T or C.

Meanwhile, 10 minutes after blowing through San Antonio, North Force captured the Socorro Municipal Airport without firing a shot. Socorro's population was somewhat larger than T or C, but the town was only defended by Peoples' Milita. The Airport lay on the southside of Socorro. From that operating base, North Force blocked all roads leading southward out of Socorro. The Rio Grande bridge at San Antonio now laid wide open for

Delvin's rare earth convoy. The only obstacles in Delvin's path were the hostiles at the Array and those in Magdalena. Captain Cloud sent a detachment of North Force westward along US 60 to take out hostile forces in Magdalena, then advance upon the Array.

The Robbery

Marian's cellphone rang as they returned to town, "Marian, Maury here. Something terrible has happened."

The mere fact that Maury Dreyfus was calling Marian, while she was away on business, was quite unusual.

"It's Ben! Someone robbed the Computer Shop this afternoon while I was out on a locksmith call."

"Maury, is Ben OK?"

Marian could hear Maury sobbing between his words, "No, he's not. I'm up here in the Emergency Room at UPMC Shadyside. The thieves shot Ben. They must have thought he was dead, but he wasn't. He's in really bad shape. The doctors say it's touch and go."

"How's the shop?"

"The police say it was a typical robbery. They stole cash and new electronics, didn't bother with reconditioned merchandise, or customer goods in for repairs." Then Maury hesitated before continuing. "There's more. I haven't been by the shop. I came directly to the hospital. The police tell me, when they searched the building, they found the doors to my flat and Ben's flat locked, but the door to your apartment had been smashed and your place was ransacked."

Marian comforted Ben, "Don't you worry about me and my apartment, you just take care of brother Ben. I'll be home tomorrow."

Once off the phone, Marian shared the details of Ben's condition and the robbery with her two friends.

Brett asked the obvious question, "Why didn't the thieves break into Maury's or Ben's apartment?"

Marian somberly replied, "They were after me and my stuff and Ben got in their way. The robbery is just a cover story." Marian then thought a little more, "Whoever shot Ben knows who I am and what I do."

Brett went down the list. "Mossad, Wiesenthal Center, FBI, CIA?"

Marian narrowed the list, "Think you can rule out CIA and FBI. Shooting a citizen on American soil? Don't think so.

"You can probably rule out Wiesenthal too. They aren't in the muscle end of the business."

Another suspect popped into Brett's brain, "What did you call that other group? Gruppe, gruppe…"

Marian filled in the blank, "Gruppe Paladin."

Brett continued his line of deduction, "If the guy who tried to kill Stan the Man was indeed Israeli, then we gotta move Mossad to the top of the list.

"Marian, your own people may be trying to kill you!"

Vagabonds

Later that afternoon, after an early dinner, Charlie climbed into his Winnebago and got the hell out of Dodge.

As the Winnebago pulled out of the parking lot, Marian turned to Brett, "Hoffman, do you think the old geezer will be OK?"

"Yeah, he mostly lives off the grid. He's smart. He'll go dark for a few days. He'll move around. He'll keep his powder dry. Yeah, he'll be OK!

"The question is, will we be OK?"

Brett & Marian had an early wakeup call the next morning. They had to drive back to Spokane, drop their rentals, and still make a 9 a.m. flight back to Salt Lake. Marian was eager to get it on that evening. Brett had a tiger by the tail and was enjoying every minute of it, but he decided, for now, it was better to let the head on his shoulders do his thinking.

"Hang on cowgirl. Let's not get sloppy. We both used credit cards to pay for our rooms."

"Yeah, but my credit card matches my fake ID, Casey Wright."

"Well Miss Casey, radio & TV personalities don't usually carry fake IDs."

"Hoffman, do you really think we're in any danger way out here?"

"Yes, I do. We may be out in the wilds of Montana, but we're only a 25-minute drive from the Wolf's lair, to turn a phrase. Pull your Jeep around back and I'll pull mine right up next to the front porch. We'll sleep with our pieces at hand and wedge chairs under the front and back doorknobs."

With those security precautions in place, Marian shoved a fully clothed Brett into bed and got down to the business at hand.

While Marian & Brett were otherwise indisposed, Charlie was well on his way north to Kalispell. He pulled his Winnebago off the road, under some trees, in Lone Pine State Park. He avoided the campgrounds, parking in a secluded spot off High Road. Charlie built a small campfire and fried some bologna and melted some cheese on top. He slapped his culinary masterpiece between two slices of sourdough bread and chowed down.

Charlie got comfortable in his sleeping bag, atop his chaise lounge, and gazed up at the stars. His belly was full of bologna and cheese. His Smith & Wesson .44 Magnum was discretely hidden inside the sleeping bag. Within minutes, he was sound asleep.

The town of Breezewood, PA is known among tourists and truckers as the "Town of Motels". Breezewood lies about 90 miles east of Kecksburg and is one of the few spots where the interstate highway system is discontinuous. In order to enter, or exit, the Pennsylvania Turnpike from I-70, one has to travel a short distance along US 30 through the town of Breezewood. Every inch of the route through town is lined with restaurants, gas stations, and motels. At dusk, Stan the Man pulled his Ford F-150 pickup into the pet friendly Keystone Motor Lodge. Stan and Blue Dog had previously stayed at the Keystone on several occasions. Blue began barking out his approval as they pulled into the parking lot.

"Now settle down Blue. I gotta go inside and get us a room."

When Stan stepped out of his truck, there was no need to lockup. Blue Dog was on guard in the front seat. Stan was in and out of the office in a matter of minutes, paying cash for his room. Stan wasn't taking any chances, on his way out of the lobby, he handed the young desk clerk a twenty and told him to keep his trap shut. After Blue took a potty break, Stan strategically placed Blue's doggy bed right next to the door, wedged a chairback under the doorknob, and leaned his double barreled 12 gauge up against the nightstand. Both Blue and Stan were asleep in minutes.

Meanwhile, Maury Dreyfus was trying to grab a little shut eye while camped out in Shadyside's ICU waiting room. Along about 11 p.m., a young Black guy in a blue & gold Pitt hoodie entered the waiting room. He sat down across the room from Maury. Before sitting down, the young man slightly adjusted his chair, waking Maury from a shallow snooze.

"My bad, didn't mean to wake you up."

Maury drowsily mumbled, "Wasn't really asleep. This waiting isn't much fun."

"Man, these chairs aren't very comfortable. How long you been waiting?"

"I've been up here since mid-morning. My brother was shot."

"How in the hell did that happen? I mean, you don't look like no gangsta."

"It was an armed robbery. He was working in his computer shop and some thieves robbed the shop.

"How about you? What brings you here tonight?"

"It's my Nana. She's old and has a bunch of health problems." Then the young man glanced down at his watch, "Nice talking to you, but I've got to go. Working night shift."

45 minutes after the young man departed, a nurse came out to update Maury, "Mr. Dreyfus, your brother has regained consciousness and is stable. The doctors think it would be best if he had no visitors until tomorrow. Why don't you go home and get some rest?"

"Yes, I'm not doing anybody any good sitting around here." As Maury got up to leave, he turned back to the nurse, "By the way, how's the old Black lady doing? I just met her grandson out here in the waiting room."

"Black lady? We don't have any ladies in ICU tonight, Black or White. Maybe the young man was mistaken…"

Sometime during the middle of the night, Brett violently jolted up in bed. The commotion woke Marian.

"Hoffman, what's wrong? Are you OK?"

"Yeah, I'm OK. What if Wolfgang and Heinz are Nazis fleeing 1945 Germany? How could we prove it? As far as the law is concerned, what crimes have they committed? This stuff Charlie gave me is good evidence for a *Sea-to-Sea AM* broadcast, but it wouldn't hold up in a court of law. Hell, we'd be laughed out of court, maybe tossed in the loony bin."

A now wide-awake Marian replied, "Yeah. Senator Schneider, is one of the richest and most powerful men in the world."

Senator Wolfgang

The 2012 Presidential election infuriated Wolfgang Schneider more than the 2008 election. He was more infuriated by the Republican loss than the Democrat victory. By then, Americus had recovered from his exposure to mustard gas and had immersed himself in the Rainbow Corps and Adler Industries.

Heinz was the consummate manager. Under Heinz' leadership, Adler Industries became an international juggernaut. Wolfgang maintained the high-level contacts with international power brokers, but Heinz managed the day to day business. Heinz took Americus under his wing and mentored the young man.

Wolfgang decided it was once again time to make a move. He was contemptuous of both American political parties. In February 2013, at a gala press event in Helena, Wolfgang announced that he was entering the 2014 Montana Senate race. When the media inquired as to Wolf's party affiliation he replied, "American People's Party".

The APP got off to a rousing start. Wolfgang had unlimited funds and a virtually unlimited pool of volunteers. Within a matter of weeks, the newly formed Rainbow Corps had collected enough signatures to get Wolfgang on the 2014 ballot. Wolfgang was not satisfied. He recruited a well-respected German American Montana businessman and philanthropist to run for Montana's single House seat. The APP also began recruiting candidates for statewide offices in the 2016 election.

Schneider had many bona fide friends in the media and had bought off many more media shills. A flurry of pseudo-documentaries hit the airways chronicling the rise of the Schneiders, from their harrowing escape from East Germany to the pinnacle of wealth and fame. Some of the propaganda pieces featured Adler Industries, some heralded Wolfgang as the savior of European culture, others featured the Rainbow Corps, but Americus was the media's darling, a true American hero.

Within minutes of the polls closing on Tuesday, November 4, 2014, the Associated Press declared Wolfgang Schneider Senator-elect from Montana. The APP Congressional candidate had a somewhat closer race, but, within an hour, the major networks declared that the APP had also captured Montana's sole Congressional seat. APP candidates also swept most of the down ballot races during that off-year election.

Wolfgang was a shrewd politician. Once in the Senate, he sat in the middle aisle and would not caucus with either party. The Senate was closely divided. Schneider's vote was always in demand. To the public, Schneider was his own man, unbeholden to the Swamp. Wolfgang would not endorse either Presidential candidate in either the tumultuous 2016 or 2020 elections, but easily won re-election to the Senate in 2020. By then, the APP controlled the Montana Governor's Mansion, Montana's sole seat in Congress, and both chambers of Montana's legislature. Montana's other Senate seat would not be up for grabs until 2026. By then, Americus would be 40 years old, old enough to be a Senator, old enough to be President. Fortuitously for the Schneiders, Montana's other Senator unexpectedly died in 2025, at the height of the Great Pacific War.

Back to Pittsburgh

Brett redeemed a frequent flyer award and upgraded Marian to First Class. Then he used his charm on the ticketing agent to get adjacent seating. During the flight back, Marian skillfully conducted her interrogation.

"So, Hoffman, what's your story? I know the smooth voice on the radio and the handsome face on TV, but who are you?"

Brett replied, "Around the same time that Heinz emerged from that UFO out in Montana, yours truly entered this world kicking and screaming."

"You were born in Pittsburgh?"

"East Allegheny, you know, Deutschstown."

"Holy shit Hoffman, you really are a Kraut."

"You don't know the half of it. My grandpa immigrated to America after the war."

Marian hesitantly followed up, "Was he, you know, a soldier?"

Brett flippantly replied, "Jawohl! Ein deutscher Soldat. He fought on the Eastern Front. Grandfather Hoffman was an infantryman. He fought those Russian bastards, down in the trenches, many times hand-to-hand."

Marian was mesmerized, "Was he a..." Marian hesitated.

"Nazi?" Brett said what Marian couldn't say, "He fought for his Fatherland, for his family, and for his kameraden. He fought against those godless, communist bastards."

"He wasn't SS? Was he?" Marian didn't know if she wanted to hear Brett's answer.

"No! He wasn't a Nazi. He was Wehrmacht. When the end was near, his unit surrendered to the Americans.

"He got to know a couple of GIs while he was being held in a POW camp. One GI's father was a Federal judge in the Pittsburgh area. He sponsored Grandpa's immigration."

"What happened after he immigrated?"

"Grandpa was a watchmaker's apprentice before the war and continued that trade after immigrating. When television gained popularity, Grandpa learned TV & radio repair. Eventually, he opened a storefront shop in East Allegheny."

"That sounds just like my landlords, the Dreyfus brothers."

"Yeah. The world isn't black or white, it's usually various shades of gray, full of uncertainty. Grandpa was a German soldier, but he was no monster. He wanted to live the American dream and gradually expanded his shop. He began selling new and refurbished TVs and appliances. He continued repairing watches and began selling high-end watches. My father grew up helping Grandpa. When my Dad turned 18, he went to the local recruiting office and joined the army. They shipped his ass off to Vietnam."

"What did your grandfather think about that? Was he upset?"

"Hell no! He told my Dad to join up. Grandpa came to America to be an American. He was proud of his son!"

"Dad served two tours in 'Nam. When he came home, Grandpa threw a party. While other soldiers were being spit on and called 'baby killer', my Dad received a hero's welcome in the old neighborhood.

"Dad went to Carnegie Mellon on the GI Bill and got in on the ground floor of computer science. He was a natural. Dad already knew electronics, was mechanically inclined, and had a logical mind. His younger brother, my uncle, still runs the family business. Since he retired from his real job, Pop works there part time, at least he says it's part time."

"How about your Mom?"

"She's in good health. Mom & Dad still live in the same row house on Middle Street, only a block from church and a couple of blocks from the shop. We'll all get together sometime."

Marian quickly thought to herself, "Is he Catholic, or Lutheran?'"

"OK, Hoffman! That's your family. What about you?"

"I was born in that row house, baptized in that Lutheran Church, and grew up in Grandpa's shop around radios, TVs, and computers. Over the years, we got to know some people in the Pittsburgh broadcasting community. I could operate the equipment and read and speak reasonably well, so I picked up some DJ gigs on holidays and weekends.

"Now, what's your story, secret agent woman?"

"Knock it off Hoffman. You're more of a secret agent than I am."

"Like hell I am. You're a Mossad agent."

"Only on TV and in the movies is it glamorous. It's a lot of legwork, reading, listening, and countless hours on the computer. I have never fired my piece in anger. Just like you, I deal in information."

"So, you live in a fourth floor flat above a computer shop and send information back to your handlers in Tel Aviv?"

"That's about it. The work I do for the Wiesenthal Center is only a hobby."

Brett whispered in Marian's ear, "You haven't told me anything about you. I would like to get to know the woman who has practically raped me the last couple of nights." Brett was smirking and Marian was blushing.

"I grew up in Squirrel Hill, a proper Jewish girl. My mother can vouch for me. According to her I'm as pure as your Virgin Mary."

Brett was sipping a bloody Mary when Marian dropped that comment. He frantically covered his mouth as a geyser of that tomato and vodka concoction spewed from his lips.

Marian laughed a naughty laugh, then whispered in Brett's ear as she kissed his cheek, "I'm a bad little girl."

The Boeing 757 was making its final approach into Pittsburgh.

As the pilot illuminated the fasten seatbelt light, Brett whispered to Marian, "I think it best if you stay at my place for a while."

There was no way Marian was going to pass up that opportunity, "Let's swing by my place, survey the damage, check on Maury, and I'll grab some clothes."

Custodial Work

Tony had to watch himself. He knew the layout of Livermore Labs from his past life as Inspector James Wu. He reminded himself to constantly ask directions and, periodically, appear lost. Today, Tony was assigned to the National Ignition Facility. Member Lin was up on a ladder, dusting light fixtures, and changing light bulbs.

Before the Peoples' Revolution, the NIF was occasionally in the news. The NIF was a nuclear fusion laboratory. The goal of the NIF was to develop an inertial confinement fusion (ICF) reactor. Whereas nuclear fission is a messy business, relying upon radioactive uranium fuel and producing radioactive waste, nuclear fusion is the Eldorado of nuclear power. Nuclear fusion powers the stars, including our sun. Fusion reactors use abundant, non-radioactive hydrogen isotopes as fuel and produce harmless helium as waste.

The ICF approach to initiating nuclear fusion employed multiple high energy lasers to uniformly heat the surface of a small sphere of hydrogen isotopes (a mixture of deuterium & tritium). The resulting temperatures approach those found in the sun's interior. When the surface of the sphere implodes, the hydrogen fuel is almost instantaneously compressed to 100 times the density of lead. The incredible heat & pressure fuses pairs of hydrogen atoms, forming one helium atom, and releasing a tremendous amount of energy as a by-product.

The NIF became operational in mid-2009. From 2009 to December 2022, the nuclear gurus at Livermore gradually increased the strength of their lasers and incrementally refined the ICF technology. Finally, on 5 December 2022, the NIF achieved 'scientific breakeven'. For the first time in history, an ICF device produced more energy than it consumed.

On April Fool's Day 2026, The Collective was enthusiastically welcomed throughout the Bay Area. They immediately shut down the NIF. Very few of the woke Members could grasp the importance of the research being conducted at the NIF, but when they heard the word "nuclear", they reflexively shut it all down.

In the late 2030s, Chinese scientists reactivated the NIF, but not for fusion research. The NIF's multiple high energy lasers were combined with various types of concentrated electromagnetic energy. All that concentrated energy was focused on a single point. Utilizing heretofore unknown physics, the Chinese began tweaking their 魔术穴 (Magic Tunnel) device. During subsequent trials, on numerous occasions, the attendant technicians fled the NIF in terror, fearing unforeseen, catastrophic results. One of those technicians was arrested and executed by firing squad after discussing his terrifying experience with the media.

As the Chinese researchers rewrote the physics textbooks, they stumbled onto some interesting phenomena involving exotic mixtures of rare earth elements. When I say "stumbled", I mean "stumbled". In early 2041, during a high energy Magic Tunnel trial, a junior technician tripped and fell. The resulting chain reaction of careening carts, toppling work lights, and falling tools resembled that classic children's boardgame, *Mousetrap.* A novel, prototype, rare earth magnet accidently fell into the Magic Tunnel energy stream with astounding results. The room suddenly filled with a bluish aura. All electronic equipment abruptly shut down. The magnet vanished in a flash of light, only to rematerialize, a split second later, on the far side of the room. In vain, the Chinese physicists feverishly sought to recreate, control, and understand the results of that freak accident. It had something to do with the exotic mixture of rare earth elements in the magnet.

Before the shit hit the fan, Professor Cathy Chung and her Purdue University team developed a method of extracting rare earth elements from all sorts of common industrial wastes. For the last 15 years, Cathy and her team had been held prisoner on the Peoples' Midwest Polytechnic campus (formerly Purdue University) and forced to work on projects involving rare earth elements. It is safe to say that Professor Chung was the World's foremost rare earth expert. Double XX recognized Cathy's expertise. The sadistic Red Chinese butcher always recruited the very best talent, whether they liked it, or not.

After Lieutenant Josephine Parker's partially successful summertime rescue of Cathy's teammates from Peoples' Midwest Polytechnic, XX the Executioner shanghaied Professor Cathy Chung and her two remaining research associates out to California. After Double X's demise, Cathy and her associates were transferred to Livermore to work on the Magic Tunnel project. Since her arrival at Livermore, Professor Cathy was routinely beaten for her lack of cooperation. Chung was Taiwanese and hated the Red Chinese with a purple passion.

Cathy hated Double X's replacement even more than Double X himself. Baihu, the White Tiger, deserved his mythological nickname. Hailing from China's far western Hotan Prefecture, Baihu specialized in securing China's strategic metals resources around the globe.

White Tiger "made his bones" as a young officer in the People's Liberation Army. While he secured the vast gold, silver, copper, uranium, and rare earth resources of far western China, Baihu systematically eliminated thousands of indigenous Muslim Uyghurs. The Tiger was racially Han Chinese, as were 92% of China's population. Despite all the Red Chinese propaganda concerning diversity, equality, and equity, racism was alive and well in the People's Republic.

James Wu's physical transformation into Tony Lin was only part of his preparation for his undercover mission. The Stanford educated engineer immersed himself in rare earth chemistry, radio astronomy, and laser technology. He also memorized every detail of Dr. Cathy's face.

As Tony unscrewed a flickering lightbulb, in a busy corridor at the NIF, he did a double take. Tony recognized Professor Cathy shuffling toward him amongst the crowd. Cathy's face was battered. An apparent leg injury necessitated Cathy's use of a cane. Tony bit his lower lip, trying his best to conceal his rage. The distinguished Professor had obviously been beaten, perhaps tortured.

Montana's Junior Senator

On special election night 2025, moments after the polls closed, the major networks declared Americus Schneider Montana's new junior Senator-elect.

Americus threw a gala victory celebration in Helena's Civic Center's Ballroom. Father & Son Schneider made their way on stage with hands clasped together, raised high overhead. Americus was not dressed as a Rainbow Corpsman, although the Rainbow Corps were everywhere. Both father & son were decked out in Brooks Brothers suits. The media was out in force and the talking heads on the cable news channels were debating whether Wolfgang, or Americus, would run for President in 2028. One brave soul suggested that perhaps they would run together, an all-Schneider ticket.

Across the country, the APP now held 5 Senate seats and 16 House seats. That small minority placed Wolfgang in the catbird's seat. Both major political parties were kissing his Bavarian ass. Although the APP held only a small fraction of seats in Congress, without Wolfgang's support, neither major party could do diddly-squat.

That night, while the Schneiders celebrated in Montana, back in the nation's capital, the D.C. Swamp had its 'come to Jesus moment'. While the blithering pundits in the media discussed policy, demographics, and legislative agendas, the bosses of both major parties met to discuss one agenda item, power. How could they maintain power? Only a portion of these 'bosses' were politicians. Some were tech billionaires. Others were media moguls. Wall Street was well represented, as was the defense industry. The most terrifying attendees were the unelected civil servants of America's

Alphabet Agencies, FBI, CIA, and NSA. While the politicians labelled themselves "Progressives" or "Conservatives" and claimed to represent various segments of American political thought, these cynical, career apparatchiks represented themselves. Unelected and unknown to the public, these swamp creatures held few core beliefs. They lived to perpetuate their own wealth & power.

The meeting assumed the guise of a black-tie gala, unrelated to the Montana Special Election. The D.C. swamp creatures were not the naïve, feckless Weimar bureaucrats who faced Wolfgang's paper hanging mentor in the early 1930s. There were no agenda items, speeches, or power point presentations. The Washington power brokers whispered amongst themselves in nuanced terms over champagne cocktails. They kept their hands clean behind a wall of plausible deniability while their aides carried out the dirty work.

A clear consensus emerged. Eliminate Wolfgang and the APP would shrivel up and die on the vine. Americus was a political newcomer. His heroism in the War on Terror and his leadership of the Rainbow Corps led intelligence analysts to brand him an idealist. The power elite considered Americus a naïve do-gooder. Americus posed no threat.

Over the years, Wolfgang cultivated many special friends in the arts community as he revealed the locations of long-lost Nazi plunder. A few of those special friends were privy to the inner workings of the shadow government. Within hours of the black-tie event, Gruppe Paladin was aware that the Swamp had targeted Wolfgang and, to a lesser extent, Americus. Gruppe Paladin didn't know all the details, but they knew the deep state and its minions were out to kill, discredit, or imprison both German American Senators.

Watchdog

Stan the Man paid politics no mind. He called it an early evening, not bothering to watch the evening news. This would be his last night in Breezewood. The next morning, Stan & Blue were heading up to Pittsburgh to shack up with Brett. Stan was unaware that he would also be sharing Brett's condo with Marian.

It was a cold early November night. Blue Dog was curled up in his doggy bed and Stan was snuggled up under the blankets. Around 1 a.m., Blue Dog rose from his bed, turned toward the door, and growled that low territorial growl. Stan reached over, grabbed his shotgun, and listened. Blue Dog was now up on his tippy toes, ready to pounce.

Blue just stood there growling for a couple of minutes, then laid back down to sleep. Stan sat there in bed, with shotgun in hand, for a couple more minutes. Finally, Stan got up and peered out the door's peep hole. Nothing, Stan saw nothing. He rechecked the security of the door lock and wedged the chairback even tighter under the door handle. Once Stan felt secure, he crawled back into bed.

The following morning, Stan was up before sunrise. He packed his suitcase and took Blue Dog for a walk. Stan stopped by the motel's front desk on his way out.

"Mister, are you his son?"

"Whose son?"

"Why Stan Musial, of course. A whole bunch of Musials live south of Pittsburgh. Your last name is Musial, ain't it?"

Stan laughed, "Yeah, I'm probably some sorta distant relative. My Dad was a baseball fan and named me after Stan the Man. You know, the real Stan the Man was from Donora, PA, just a half hour west of Kecksburg."

"Did your friend catch up with you last night?"

"What friend?"

"Your friend wearing the St. Louis Cardinals baseball cap. He said he was looking for Stan the Man."

"Son, you didn't tell him anything, did you?"

"Hell no! I did just what you told me to do. I told him that motel privacy rules didn't allow me to give out any information, but I hadn't seen anybody named Stan."

Stan looked to his left, then his right, then handed the young man another $20 bill, "You done good young feller. Now take this money and if anybody asks you anything about Stan the Man, you continue playing dumb. Got it?"

"Yes sir! Thanks!"

As Stan left the office, the young night clerk yelled out, "Are you sure you're not his illegitimate son, or second cousin, or something?"

Two hours later, Stan lucked out and found a parking spot on Dithridge Street. Although Brett owned his condo, the condo association had its rules. Brett advised the association that a friend would be visiting for a few days along with his housebroke Australian Blue Heeler and the association approved.

When Stan rang the buzzer downstairs, Marian answered over the intercom, "Is this Stan My Man?"

Stan chuckled as Marian bastardized his moniker, "Why yes, it is. With whom am I speaking?"

"Hi Stan! I'm Marian. Come on up. Did you bring along your Blue Dog?"

"Yes, I did."

Marian buzzed Stan in, "Well, bring him up too!"

Marian was waiting out in the hallway as Stan & Blue emerged from the stairwell.

"My goodness, he really is a blue dog!" Marian had never seen an Australian Cattle Dog.

Blue Dog let out a single yap, then ran over, jumped up, and gave Marian a big sloppy lick.

"Well young Lady, I don't know who you are, but Blue has already given you his seal of approval. I'm Stan the Man."

Brett heard Blue's yap and joined his friends out in the hallway. Brett gave Blue a pet on his muzzle, then shook Stan's hand.

"Let's get inside."

Stan quickly glanced around the condo, "Hoffman, you got a nice place here. Don't worry about Blue. He's housebroke. He'll let us know if he needs to go outside. Blue doesn't like it, but I brought along his leash.

"Now, please introduce me to this lovely young lady."

"Stan, this is Marian. Marian is in the investigation business, too. She's also a local, from Squirrel Hill.

"Marian, this is the one and only Stan the Man. He saw our friend Heinz way back in 1965."

A flummoxed look came over Stan's face, "Heinz???"

"We'll cover that later."

Brett smiled as he glanced over at Marian, "I see that you and Blue Dog are already acquainted." Blue was sitting beside Marian, licking her hand.

Brett's condo was a 2-2, "Stan, you can camp out in the guest bedroom. There's a common bathroom out here in the hallway. Marian and I will use the master bath."

Stan smiled and gave Brett a wink, "You and Marian? If you don't mind, I'll put Blue's doggy bed right beside the front door."

Brett nodded in agreement, "Good idea. I know Blue is a great watchdog."

Monkeywrench in the Works

Big Sid had no time to waste. He hustled over to the pole barn housing the two diesel generators. The man door was unlocked, requiring no forced entry. Sid was unfamiliar with the two Chinese diesel generators, but the Big Man was a capable diesel mechanic. He instantly spotted and removed the air filters. Sid poured a fraction of a handful of coarse desert sand into both air intakes, then quickly replaced the filters. Sid was just guessing how much sand should go into each engine. Sid guessed wrong. One of the diesel engines seized immediately.

"Holy shit!" the Big Man rushed out of the barn and sprinted to the northeast. He heard the second diesel engine lock up as he entered an empty corral, close by the ranch house. Sid ducked down behind a large, galvanized stock tank and gazed back at the pole barn. Through his night vision, the Big Man could see a couple of figures rushing from the ranch house out to the pole barn. Simultaneously, from his position over at the gravel pit, John no long detected any radar emissions emanating from the ranch house.

Sid wasn't happy with the recent turn of events, "I wonder how long it will take them to figure things out?"

Sid wasn't about to hang around to find out. After the two figures entered the pole barn, Sid resumed running to the northeast. A couple of minutes later and 600 meters further, Sid rejoined Super Soldier John & Henrietta, hunkered down in the gravel pit.

John raised his visor, "Sid, it's about four and a half klicks to the Antennae Assembly Building. We gotta hustle."

Nicolescu didn't know the half of it. As the team climbed up out of the shallow pit, a conversation was heating up inside the pole barn, a conversation in Mandarin.

The young Chinese mechanic was flummoxed, "There are no visual contaminants in either the oil or fuel."

His boss needed an answer, "Both those engines didn't malfunction nearly simultaneously! Look at the air filters!"

"The air filters are both clean!"

As the young mechanic nervously replaced the second filter, he accidently dropped it upon the floor. That's when he saw the tracks.

"Comrade Chief Mechanic, look at the floor!"

There were three sets of tracks leading into the pole barn. The mechanics' two sets of snowy tracks led over to the engines and stopped. A third set of tracks led into the building, over to the diesels, then back outside. Those tracks were made by someone with big feet and a long stride. Most of the snow associated with those tracks had melted, but not all.

The Chief Mechanic turned white as a Klansman's sheet, "We have an intruder!"

The Chief Mechanic motioned toward the exit with his right index finger, "Quickly! Report this to the Lieutenant!" There was no way the Chief was going to be the first man out that door.

John Nicolescu didn't need enhanced audio to hear the sirens blaring throughout the Very Large Array. Every huge dish and every major building sported at least one siren and several floodlights.

John hollered back to Sid, "So much for the element of surprise."

Although the Big Man had been in a couple of firefights and was no coward, the lights and sirens unnerved him, "Sergeant John, what are we gonna do? Do we abort?"

"Abort hell!"

Just then, John's CZ suit was once again blasted by S band radiation emitted by the HQ-7B SAM battery's acquisition radar.

"We took out that radar at the ranch house. Now, they've lit up the SAM's air search radar. In a few minutes, Josephine is gonna be popping out of those Crosby Mountains. If we don't take out that search radar they'll paint Badass Bitch before Jo can fire a shot."

"What are we gonna do?"

"Let's find a good spot to tie ol' Henrietta, then we'll fight our way into the Operations Center. Just like down at the pier in Long Beach. Are you wearing your body armor?"

"Yes Sergeant."

"How about those ceramic inserts?"

"Those inserts are heavy."

"You'll be a lot heavier if those Chinese riddle you full of lead. Slide those damned inserts into your body armor!"

Sid unzipped his coveralls and began sliding small ceramic inserts into the small pockets on his ballistic vest. The combination of the vest's Kevlar fibers and the ceramic strike plates could stop high caliber rifle rounds dead in their tracks.

"Slap on your helmet too!"

"Come on Sarge, you know I hate the helmet."

"Private, put on your helmet. Things are about to get hairy real fast."

Conundrum

Wolfgang Schneider had been protected by the Three Letter Agencies ever since that meeting at the Missoula Federal Courthouse back in 1985. Since the demise of the Soviet Union and its East Bloc puppet states, that protection was largely unnecessary. Wolfgang remained a darling of the Washington elites until the appearance of the Rainbow Corps. After that, Wolfgang could sense that his friends in powerful places were slowly distancing themselves.

Once Wolfgang became Senator Schneider, there was a rapprochement, for a time, as both major parties curried his favor. The Montana special election of 2025 changed all that. Media coverage of Americus' Senate victory and the rise of the APP was reminiscent of Presidential election year coverage. Wolfgang was no longer a passing anomaly, someone to be managed and co-opted. He was now a threat.

Meanwhile, while Brett, Stan, and Marian hunkered down at Brett's condo, the country convulsed with civil unrest. Armed bands of left-wing thugs took control of major cities as feckless liberal politicians kissed their woke asses. In the Mountain West, amongst the small towns and cities of Idaho, Montana, Wyoming, Eastern Oregon, and Eastern Washington State, the Rainbow Corps fought pitched street battles against The Collective.

As the situation deteriorated, Montana's two Senators, father & son Schneider, were required to spend more of their time in Washington, D.C. Wolfgang hoped to consolidate power before the mob could take control. The Nation's Capital had long been a crime-ridden hellhole. Violent crime was endemic. Now, politically motivated mob violence was thrown into that noxious mix. Add to that the various threats posed by the denizens of the D.C. Swamp, and it became readily apparent, the Schneiders were no longer safe in the District.

Adler Engineering's international business office was strategically located on Washington's K Street. Nearby Newport News, Virginia hosted a large Adler Engineering yard. Lucrative US Navy contracts kept the Newport News yard abuzz. Boilers, gas turbines, large pumps, and other bulky hardware were coming and going on a regular basis. The yard handled the heaviest and largest freight with ease. Located just west of Interstate 64, with several sidings along the Bay Coast Railway, the yard's location was ideal. Wolfgang paid several visits to that yard during Q4 2025.

During those closing months of 2025, Wolfgang began gathering information on the myriad of tunnels running beneath Washington, focusing on the secret tunnel running from the Capitol to the White House. The tunnel running to the Capitol from the Russell Senate Office Building was no secret. It was in constant use, featuring its own tram system. Both Wolfgang and Americus used that tunnel most every day, as they travelled from their Russell Building offices to the Senate Chamber in the north wing of the United States Capitol. They memorized all the minutia of that tunnel's operation.

While the White House H Street Exit was not secret, it was relatively obscure and seldom used. Two tunnels and a covered alleyway ran about 1,000 feet, from beneath the East Wing of the White House to the nondescript H Street Exit. It was rumored that Marilyn Monroe used that exit to visit JFK whenever Jackie Kennedy left her husband "alone" in the White House.

The President courted good relations with the Schneiders as she vainly sought the American People's Party support in the closely divided House and Senate. Under the guise of writing a history of "Underground Washington", both Americus & Wolfgang obtained Presidential passes granting them unfettered access to most of underground D.C. The Schneiders cultivated a first name relationship with the Capitol Police & Secret Service securing those tunnels. Complimentary NFL, NBA, and MLB tickets bought the Schneiders a measure of goodwill. Wolfgang was once again plotting a subterranean escape route, while praying he would never need it.

When the armed robbers ransacked Marian's apartment, they found steel file cabinets secured by case-hardened steel bars running down the front and secured by padlocks. The padlocks, just as tough as the aforementioned steel bars, were locksmith Maury's handiwork. The burglars couldn't afford to hang around the apartment very long. After all, this was a computer shop. They assumed some sort of alarm had already been tripped and feared they were guest stars on CCTV.

The only electronic device visible to the thieves was a wireless keyboard sitting on Marian's desk. That keyboard was connected via wireless modem to Marian's computer, hidden behind the flag, inside the back wall of Marian's closet. Marian retrieved the system box when she surveyed the damage at her apartment.

After helping Stan and Blue get settled in, Marian read her encrypted email from her Tel Aviv handlers.

"Guys, this is quite interesting. I've been directed to gather intelligence on Wolfgang & Americus Schneider."

Brett had already read the morning headlines, "I imagine so. Americus won his Senate race. It was a blowout. The APP now controls 5 Senate and 16 House seats. I suggest you play along, but only send your handlers the information we want them to see."

Marian sighed in exasperation, "This is all we need, Mossad has just issued an advisory for all Jews in the United States."

Hoffman replied, "Does Mossad's warning mention the Schneiders?"

A puzzled Marian replied, "No, not at all. The advisory is focused on this new far left group called 'The Collective'. That's the mob responsible for all the rioting, looting, and wanton murder we're seeing on TV."

Brett & Marian sat down with Stan and brought him up to speed on the entire investigation and Stan brought them up to date on Jack's assassination.

"So, my Nazi spaceman's name is Heinz?"

Brett continued, "Yeah, and we suspect his buddy, Wolfgang, piloted the larger UFO."

Stan scratched his head, "I can't believe there's a bigger one of those contraptions. Wolfgang Schneider, I've heard that name somewhere, sometime…"

Brett clued Stan in, "I should think you have. He's one of the richest men in the world and he's the senior Senator from Montana. Last night, his son, Americus, won Montana's open Senate seat.

"Stan, could you and Blue hold down the fort while Marian and I go see a man about a digital camera and a cellphone?"

"Yeah, it's about time I found those items. I've heard that they're evidence in a police investigation." Stan started out snickering, but then turned serious, "You two best watch your asses. Whoever shot Jack is still out there. Before you go, I gotta tell you. Last night someone was snooping around my hotel in Breezewood."

"Stan, how in the hell could anyone track you down to Breezewood? Did you use your cellphone?"

"No!"

"How about your credit card?"

"Hoffman, I ain't no idiot. I covered all my bases. I say we gotta assume that we're all being surveilled."

Data Retrieval

Brett & Marian decided to hoof it over to Jerry Patel's office in Carnegie Mellon's Gates Center for Computer Science. The two Nazi hunting lovebirds took Hampton Hall's rear exit, made their way through the adjoining parking lot, then leisurely strolled, hand-in-hand, southward on Craig Street. Their free hands were stuffed in their coat pockets, grasping their sidearms.

Six blocks down Craig, the pair hung a left onto ever busy Forbes Avenue. The Carnegie Mellon campus was only a couple of blocks further east on Forbes. Although it was early morning, violent demonstrators were already out in force.

Brett turned to Marian, "This is exactly why we walked. They're barricading the streets. Let's pick up our pace. Things could get ugly fast."

The Gates Center was located on the northwestern corner of the CMU campus, now only a couple of buildings away. Brett & Marian broke into a near jog as riot police formed a skirmish line to their rear. Marian couldn't believe her eyes as she saw the graffiti. Vile, antisemitic graffiti was spray painted everywhere. Pseudo intellectual CMU students, proud of their so-called progressive ideology, were plastering the CMU campus with the same sort of vulgar slogans that Herr Doktor Joseph Goebbels had popularized in 1930s Nazi Germany.

"I was here on campus only a couple of days ago and everything was normal. Things are going downhill fast."

This was Brett's moment of clarity. For the first time, he realized that he no longer needed to go hunting Nazis. He was surrounded by them. Like most Americans, Hoffman had not recognized the evil staring him in the face. All the signs were there, the focus on race, the manipulation of language, the thought police, and the political violence, but very few Americans took heed. "Nothing like that could ever happen here!"

As the duo entered the Gates Center, Brett steered Marian toward an isolated corner, "Marian, we've got big trouble brewing right here in Steel City."

Marian silently nodded in agreement.

The pair quickly ascended the flight of stairs to Jerry Patel's office. The door was locked. Brett banged on the door.

"Go away, I'm busy." Brett recognized Jerry's voice.

"Jerry, it's me, Brett Hoffman!"

Jerry cracked open the door and peeked out, "Brett, thank God! Quick, come in my friend."

Brett & Marian ducked into Patel's office and Jerry quickly locked the door behind them.

"Hoffman, who's your lady friend?"

"Jerry, this is Marian. Marian, this is Jerry Patel, computer hacker extraordinaire.

"Marian is a fellow investigator."

The introductions were cut short by a great commotion in the office next to Jerry's. It sounded like the place was being ransacked, and it was.

Brett whispered to Jerry, "What in the hell is going on?"

An obviously terrified Jerry replied, "That's Dr. Rosenbaum's office. I hope they don't kill him."

Brett pulled his Luger from his pocket and Marian pulled her Beretta. They turned back toward the door.

Jerry slid between them and the doorway, frantically waving his hands, "Stop! Put those away. CMU is a gun free zone."

Brett pushed Jerry aside, "Gun free my ass! An innocent man is being beaten in the next office."

Jerry pleaded, "Please, just leave it alone. If we leave them alone, we'll be OK. Rosenbaum should have kept his opinions to himself."

Brett paid Jerry no mind as he stepped out into the hallway. A gang of a half dozen Members had dragged the outspoken Jewish computer scientist from his office and were pummeling him in the hallway. Brett fired a warning shot into the ceiling. He got the woke mob's attention.

"I swear I'll kill the next person who lays a finger on that man."

The Member closest to Hoffman, brandishing a tire iron in his right hand, made a careless move. Another gunshot rang out. The tire iron fell to the floor as a .22 caliber long rifle round from Marian's Beretta ripped through the villain's hand.

Marian shouted, "I'll place my next round right between your eyes." Katsa Metzner was not a woman to be fucked with.

Dr. Rosenbaum slowly picked himself up off the floor. Although the 62-year-old was badly beaten, he could walk.

"Professor, stick with me like glue." Marian had the mob covered. They knew she wasn't afraid to shoot.

Brett stepped back into Patel's office, "Give me the data and the devices."

Jerry handed Brett a plastic bag containing two thumb drives, a cellphone, and a digital camera.

"Thank you. Jerry, this is for your own good." Brett spun around and cold cocked the hacker with his Luger.

Hoffman shouted at the mob, "I just knocked the hell out of your friend, that Pakistani piece of shit Patel."

The trio quickly made their way out of the Gates Center.

Marian was not familiar with the CMU campus, "What now Hoffman?"

"I'll lead the way. Rosenbaum, you follow me. Marian, cover our rear."

It was pure chaos out on Forbes Avenue. Oily, acrid smoke from burning tires and torched storefronts mixed with police tear gas to form a noxious mixture.

"We've gotta get off Forbes Avenue."

Brett broke into a run. He crossed Forbes and headed northward on Neville Street. He continued running for four blocks, finally stopping to catch his breath at the corner of Fifth Avenue. It took Marian and Rosenbaum a few seconds to catch up.

Brett finally felt safe enough to pause for introductions, "Dr. Rosenbaum, I'm Brett Hoffman and the little lady packing the pistol is Marian."

Rosenbaum squinted as he stared at Brett, "I know you. You're that guy on TV, the flying saucer guy."

"Yes, yes, I host paranormal radio and TV shows, but, for the moment, we have more pressing problems. I think you better hole up at my place for a bit. You'll be safe there. We've got one bad assed dog and a bunch of guns."

Brett turned left onto Fifth Avenue. The street was empty. He jogged a couple of blocks westward on Fifth Avenue, then hung a right onto Craig Street. Once on Craig, Brett slowed to a brisk walk. Three blocks later, Brett cut through the adjoining parking lot and ducked into Hampton Hall's rear entrance. Hoffman held the rear exit open with his left hand, while clutching his Luger and the plastic bag in his right.

"Rosenbaum, get your ass moving!"

Marian & Brett led Rosenbaum up the rear stairwell with pistols drawn.

Brett rapped five times on his condo's door. Stan the Man cracked open the door without removing the security chain. Blue Dog peered out through the barely open door, snarling and ready to pounce.

Stan heaved a sigh of relief as he removed the chain and opened the door, "Holy shit Hoffman, am I ever glad to see you."

Stan had the TV tuned to a major news network, "All hell is breaking loose."

Brett replied, "Where?"

"Everywhere, I think."

Stan noticed the drawn pistols, "Sweet Jesus, Marian, what's with the guns?"

Marian made the introductions without answering Stan, "Dr. Rosenbaum, this is Stan the Man. Stan, this is Dr. Rosenbaum."

Brett pointed across the living room, "Rosenbaum, take a seat over there in that easy chair."

"Marian, I'm guessing you are well versed in basic first aid?"

Marian winked and smiled, "Jawohl, Herr Hoffman!"

Seeing Marian smile calmed Brett a wee bit, "See what you can do for the Professor. I've got some first aid supplies stashed in the master bathroom pantry."

"Stan, you and Blue Dog guard the door. Nothing gets through. Is that clear?"

Stan already had his Remington in hand, "Jawohl, Herr Oberst!"

Stan's attempt at humor was not so well received. Brett flashed Stan a stern stare.

Hoffman glanced at the television. Video was coming in from major cities across the country. Coordinated acts of sabotage, riots, and targeted killings were spreading like wildfire.

Brett spoke as he watched, "We saw some of that over by CMU. Forbes Avenue is an active war zone."

Stan lowered his voice to a near whisper, just loud enough for Brett to hear, and pointed at Rosenbaum, "What's his story?"

"Rosenbaum is CMU Faculty. A half dozen, or so, of his enlightened students dragged him out of his office and were beating him to death. That's when we pulled our pistols."

Stan briefly pondered the broader situation, "You don't reckon all this turmoil has any connection with our friend Heinz, do you?"

Brett unsurely shook his head, "I don't think so. There may be some common elements, but this terror appears to have its roots in the opposite end of the political spectrum."

Reparations & Preparations

Washington D.C. was the focal point of the turmoil sweeping America in late 2025. As Wolfgang watched the mayhem unfold in America's streets, his mind flashed back to his early childhood days in Munich. In June 1919, the Treaty of Versailles ended World War I. That treaty, dictated by the United Kingdom, France, and the United States, imposed crushing reparations upon war ravaged Germany. Those reparations would not be paid in full until 2010, 90 years later.

In the years following the abdication of the German Kaiser, the fledgling German Weimar Republic borrowed from America and printed money as it struggled to pay those reparations. Regardless of what politicians would have you believe; reckless borrowing and irresponsible monetary policy always results in inflation. In 1914, 4.2 German Marks equaled 1 US Dollar. 9 short years later, 4.2 **Trillion** Marks equaled 1 US Dollar. Then came the Great Depression.

Wolfgang recalled the turmoil of the late 1920s and early 1930s. Across Germany, street battles raged between the Bolsheviks and the National Socialists. Schneider recalled how his once prosperous father became an unemployed pauper. He blamed his father's misfortune on a "stab in the back" by Jewish moneychangers. Panic, despair, hunger, and violence swept throughout the Fatherland. Wolfgang recalled how one man with a vision brought order, clarity, and purpose to the German people.

Adolf Hitler barnstormed across Germany by airplane, visiting several towns per day. In his 'Hitler over Germany' campaign, he carefully honed his message and his image. Herr Hitler clearly identified what he considered the root causes of all Germany's problems, Jews & Bolsheviks. Hitler identified Jewish bankers and financiers as the architects of Germany's financial collapse. If the Jew inspired Bolsheviks ever came to power, the German people would be reduced to serfdom, forever under the thumb of the Bolshevik untermenschen in the Kremlin.

Hitler clearly identified the causes of Germany's problems, as he saw them, but dared not reveal his solutions. He made no mention of his intention to commit murder on an industrial scale, 6 million Jews and 5 million Poles, Slavs, Gypsies, and other undesirables. Neither did he mention his plans to go to war with Britain, France, the Soviet Union, and ultimately, the United States of America.

Hitler's National Socialist Party came to power through free and fair elections. Schneider's American People's Party was following that same blueprint. From its stronghold in the Mountain West, the APP was metastasizing, but not fast enough. Wolfgang clenched both fists in a fit of rage. The effete, Bolshevik loving, sexually deviant, American media was the problem. They spoon fed the masses a daily stream of far-left propaganda disguised as news. Schneider saw the handwriting on the wall. America was not yet ready for National Socialism to take root. Perhaps Schneider could insulate his Mountain West stronghold from the Bolshevik terror yet to come, but he had to be prepared for any eventuality. Americus must survive! Americus must fulfill his destiny!

The railroad flatcar arrived at the Newport News warehouse around midnight. A select team of Adler employees set about unloading it, utilizing the yard's heavy lift cranes. This particular cargo, whatever it was, was quite heavy for its size. The mystery machine was covered in a thick, yellowish, expanding shipping foam. Its acorn shape was reminiscent of some type of dynamo, or generator. Once unloaded, the foam encased device was stored in a small, secure Newport News warehouse, ready if ever needed.

Meanwhile, back in Montana, Heinz Shuster carefully monitored the developing political situation. Adler Industries rapidly converted all its US Dollar holdings into physical gold. That gold was held in vaults in Zürich, Tokyo, and Dubai. Heinz kept several tons of gold & silver on hand at the Schneider's Montana compound. A small portion of that gold was stashed inside die Größe Glocke. Heinz also stashed weapons, rations, and medical supplies inside that machine, leaving just enough room for a pilot and two passengers. Die Größe Glocke was secreted away, inside an obscure natural cavern, located on the sprawling Schneider estate. The entrance to the cavern was rigged for demolition, just like the underground hangar at Tempelhof Airport back in 1945.

In response to the civil unrest, the governors of Wyoming, Idaho, and Montana, all members of the APP, called up their state's National Guard. They deputized the Rainbow Corps in mass torchlight ceremonies. Heinz coordinated all those activities. Some of the recent California, Oregon, and Washington State transplants to the Boise area took issue with those emergency measures. The Rainbow Corps quickly identified and silenced any troublemakers.

Because he was filling an empty seat, Americus was sworn into office immediately upon certification of his election. Americus won with over 70% of the vote. With the country in turmoil, neither major party dared object to Americus Schneider being seated as Montana's Junior Senator.

Americus's office was located across the hall from Wolfgang's office in the Russell Senate Office Building. Immediately after moving Americus into his office, Wolfgang took his stepson on a tour of the tunnels beneath the nation's capital.

Wolfgang was very familiar with the tunnel leading from the Russell Office Building to the Capitol. Wolfgang knew all the Capitol Police along that route by their given names and many by their nicknames.

Wolfgang whispered in his stepson's ear, "This big Irishman, Ian, is one of the few Capitol Policemen who takes his job seriously. He will not accept even the most innocent gifts. He's not a bad sort but will ask to see our IDs before we board the tram.

"Good morning, Ian. May I introduce my son, Americus?"

"Good morning, Senator Schneider. Nice meeting you Senator Schneider."

Wolfgang whispered to Eric, "Watch what happens next."

The two Montana Senators walked past Ian without showing their IDs.

"Excuse me Senators, may I see your IDs?"

Both Schneiders flashed their IDs and Officer Ian waved them onto the tram.

"Make a mental note of that Eric. The Irish are an Aryan people. If you are ever in trouble, you can count on Ian to do his job. Conversely, if you need to con the Capitol Police, don't pick Ian as your mark."

Upon arrival at the Capitol, Father & Son Schneider did not follow the crowd exiting the tram. Wolfgang led Americus in the other direction, to a nondescript door, in a deserted corner, guarded by a uniformed Secret Service Officer.

"Good morning, Manny. How's the wife and kids?"

"They're doing great Senator Schneider. Are you working on your book today?"

Americus extended his hand, hoping to make a new friend, "Manny, it's a pleasure meeting you. Yes, Dad thought it would be a good use of our time to research his new book as he gives me a tour of the D.C. tunnels."

As Manny shook Americus' hand, he clarified the situation, "The pleasure is all mine Senator Schneider, but I do need to clarify one point. Officially, this tunnel doesn't exist. The tunnel from your office to the Capitol is fair game, as is the White House H Street Entrance, but this tunnel, from the Capitol to the White House, does not exist!"

Having issued that advisory, Manny buzzed the Schneiders through a small, steel door.

Americus slid his right index finger and thumb across his lips in a zipping motion. He replied, "Gotcha Manny!", then entered the non-existent tunnel.

The secret narrow passageway ran under Pennsylvania Avenue for 1.5 miles, all the way from the Capitol to the White House. The tunnel was much like the Body Chute at Waverly Hills, but with a gentler slope.

Once in the White House basement, beneath the East Wing, the Schneiders approached another nondescript doorway guarded by another uniformed Secret Service Agent. The H Street White House Exit, also known as the Alley Exit, was a two-block long escape route traversing two subterranean tunnels and an enclosed alleyway, linking the White House basement with an innocuous exit at 1510 H Street NW. Wolfgang's pass, issued by the Secret Service Director at the behest of the President, allowed him to access the H Street Exit.

Wolfgang's Escape Plan A utilized a white Dodge panel van stashed in valet parking at the Hilton Garden Inn Downtown, two blocks east of the Alley Exit. Plan B substituted an identical van stashed at the Marriott Crystal Gateway, across the Potomac River, in Crystal City, Virginia. Crystal City Station was the next to last stop on D.C. Metro's Blue Line and a short walk from the Marriott Crystal Gateway. The Blue Line could be accessed at the McPherson Square Metro Station, a short 3 block walk from the White House Alley Exit.

Wolfgang was taking no chances. He had powerful political enemies in the Washington Swamp. The Schneiders were prime targets of the radical Bolshevik mob, known as The Collective. The Schneiders repeatedly traversed their subterranean escape route, planning for any eventuality.

"Eric, we must be capable of traversing these tunnels in total darkness."

They also rehearsed their escape from D.C. ad nauseum, using both Plans A & B.

"Once we enter the first H Street Exit tunnel, we must change into these coveralls. We will pose as plumbers heading to the Hilton Downtown. If there is any problem at the Hilton, we will divert to McPherson Station and take the Blue Line to the Marriott in Crystal City, Virginia.

"Father, why not simply escape by air?"

"Eric, Washington air space is highly restricted, more so around the Capitol and White House. In times of national emergency, this airspace will be closed. Likewise, the Potomac River is patrolled by the Coast Guard. Neither can we escape via the river.

"Once in our work van, we will head directly to the Adler Yard in Newport News. Weapons are hidden amongst the plumber's tools in both vans, as are copious amounts of silver & gold.

"The temporal controls of die Glocke have been preset for 20 years. The spatial controls are preset for our compound in Plains, Montana."

"Father, what of the temporal and spatial uncertainties? We could wind up on Alpha Centauri."

"If we must jump, we will send Heinz the code word. Heinz must acknowledge before we jump."

"Father, what is the code word?"

"Blut und Ehre, Blood & Honor!"

"But, what of the uncertainties?"

"20 years from now, in 2045, Heinz will place die Größe Glocke in standby mode, forming a depression in spacetime. The Glocke should 'fall' into that 'dimple' with a high degree of certainty. It will be tight, but we can both squeeze into the prototype."

"Father, 20 years from now, Heinz will be in his 80s. What if he should die, or be incapacitated?"

Wolfgang patted Americus on the back, "Good thinking, my boy. Our Führer would be proud. We have covered that eventuality. Heinz is grooming several protégés, selected from amongst the ranks of the Rainbow Corps. They are being trained on a simulator. They have no idea of die Größe Glocke's purpose, or how it operates. We have thought of everything. If we are forced to jump, we will land 20 years in the future, on our estate in Montana, with or without our dear Heinz waiting there to greet us. We have eliminated all uncertainty! Herr Heisenberg must be turning in his grave!"

The Assault on the Radars

Sid tied Henrietta to a utility pole about a half mile west of the Antennae Assembly Building. Sid emptied the burlap sack of protein cubes at the mule's feet, not knowing when, or if, he would ever return.

John didn't need his CZ suit's advanced optics to see the Array's huge, ice covered, dish antennae, with their floodlights all aglow.

John handed Sid a pair of binoculars.

"Holy shit, Mister John, I mean, Sergeant John, that looks like something outta *Star Wars.*"

"Count 'em, Big Man."

"You can probably see 'em better than I can, but there's more than a dozen of 'em to our front."

"I count maybe 18 on this arm of the Array. Usually, there are only 9 dishes per arm. See that huge building up ahead? The one with all the floodlights, inside and out?"

"Yeah, I see it."

"That's The Barn. That's where they assemble and maintain the big dishes. They must be building the dishes in there, then stockpiling them along this southwestern arm. See how those new dishes are lined up along that arm?"

John transmitted another encrypted radio burst, then unpacked an M32A1 Multi-shot Grenade Launcher.

Sid snickered, "That's one hellacious weapon you've got there Sarge."

The M32A1 was a handheld grenade launcher with a revolving cylinder holding a half dozen 40 mm grenades. John loaded his launcher with HEAT rounds (High Explosive Anti-Tank) intent upon taking out the HQ-7B SAM battery's four armored vehicles, a vehicle mounted air search radar and three launch vehicles. Vet slung two bandoliers around his neck, each containing another dozen grenades. John handed Sid two ammo belts. Each belt held a half dozen blocks of C-4 plastic explosive kitted out with timers and detonators.

"Private Sid, when I say "GO", you're gonna run to the southeast and place a charge on the first dish you come to. Place the charge on the undercarriage, right beneath the dish. Once you immobilize that dish, they won't be able to move those other dishes stockpiled behind it. Set your first charge on a 30 second delay, then, in succession, take out the next couple of dishes as you head inward along the southwestern arm. Save the rest of the C4 for The Barn. Take out anything alive in The Barn with your Thompson, then blow it all to Mars with the plastique. While you're blowing The Barn, I'll take out the search radar and the first two launchers. We'll rendezvous at the vertex, then go after the third launcher, somewhere along the southeastern arm.

"Remember, we're under strict EMCON. Stay off your radio. If you emit, they'll find you."

"Sergeant John, no mission ever goes exactly as planned. How will I know what to do if things go south?"

"I hate to say it Big Man, but take those Jarhead's advice, "Improvise, Adapt, Overcome."

Sergeant, how will I find you in the dark, amongst the smoke, with you wearing your chameleon suit?"

"It won't be difficult to find me. Run toward the explosions and machinegun fire."

"Are you ready?"
Sid nodded.

"Let's go!"

Sid sprinted to the southeast, while CZ John cautiously hopscotched his way to the east-northeast. The virtually invisible Romanian super soldier traversed the desert terrain with all the skill & agility of a young *Kwai Chang Caine* walking the rice paper.

Three minutes later, Sid approached his first target. Without warning, an intense bluish beam streaked skyward from the humongous dish. Identical beams shot skyward from the other 26 operational dishes. As the 27 beams cut through the desert night, an ear piercing thundercrack shook the San Augustin Plain. Sid's eyes followed the beam skyward. Somewhere, up beyond the sky, the beams converged. Sid didn't know if he was catching a glimpse of heaven, or hell.

Sid was just a good ol' boy from Georgia. Theoretical physics was way above his pay grade.

"I gotta concentrate on my mission!"

The dish's motion sensing CCTV security camera pivoted in Sid's direction. Without hesitation, Sid tossed his depleted uranium frisbee, smashing the security camera before it could alert the enemy to his presence.

The air around the Big Man was now sizzling and crackling. Sid ignored all that and slapped a block of C-4 explosive putty on the gigantic dish antennae's undercarriage. He glanced at his wristwatch. Sid's watch had stopped. As he reached out to set the demolition charge's timer, his wrist was yanked toward the dish's steel undercarriage. Sid was stuck like a fly on flypaper. Sid pulled with all his might but couldn't free his wrist.

Sid had to think on his feet, "I've been here before. When me & Daddy was working on that magnetic separator at the kaolin plant, some fool cut Daddy's lock off the control panel and energized the cryogenic electromagnet. That damned magnet grabbed me by my wristwatch and wouldn't let go!"

Sid stopped trying to pull his arm away from the undercarriage and slowly slid his wrist out of his *Twist-O-Flex* watchband. Now free, Sid set the timer, then began running to the northeast, along the Array's tandem rail lines.

Ka-boom! The blast destroyed both the undercarriage and the underlying tracks. Sid kept running, without looking back. A few seconds later, Sid heard metal bending and scraping. Only then did the Big Man glance back over his shoulder. Sid smiled as the gigantic dish antennae slowly collapsed down upon its burning undercarriage.

When Sid's target dish collapsed, the computers controlling the Array detected a fault. The Magic Tunnel test automatically aborted.

A squad of Falcon Commandos, on alert at The Barn, ran outside and focused on the explosion, about a half mile down the tandem railroad tracks. The Chinese Lieutenant in charge suspicioned that a dish had just been taken out by a kamikaze drone or cruise missile.

He radioed Operations, "Are we under aerial attack?"

"No Comrade Lieutenant. The search radar is clear."

The Lieutenant ordered two of his men to guard The Barn. Then he and the other 8 commandos piled into two Dongfeng EQ2050 Humvee knockoffs and headed southwest, down the dirt access road leading to the demolished dish.

Sid swiftly advanced another thousand feet, to his next target. When he heard two vehicles approaching, Sid instinctively crouched behind the undercarriage of the next dish. The Big Man yanked back the bolt on his Tommy Gun and stuffed a chaw of Red Man in his mouth.

CZ John had not heard the distinctive RAT-A-TAT-TAT of Sid's Tommy Gun, so he correctly surmised that Sid had not yet engaged the enemy. John was now about a half mile due west of the center of the Array. He must now traverse three 300 foot square shallow pits. Those pits supplied fill dirt for all the new construction around the Array.

Vet's CZ helmet was still tracking those radar emissions. In fact, the emissions were growing ever stronger as John advanced toward the vertex. CZ John remained undetected as his Chaoji zhanshi suit's adaptive camouflage mimicked his surroundings. Upon entering the third pit, Vet acquired his target. The armored vehicle carrying the HQ-7B's search radar was dug in, surrounded by earthen berms, in the center of that pit.

John slowly advanced, searching for a good firing position. Vet readied his grenade launcher, intent upon destroying the search radar with a couple of HEAT rounds. He was rudely interrupted when the Array's 27 dishes simultaneously shot their dazzling blue beams into the heavens.

The most amazing feature of John's CZ suit was its magnetorheological liquid armor. The suit was compose of two layers of Kevlar cloth separated by a thin layer of silicone fluid. The silicone fluid was filled with nanoscopic magnetic particles. An intricate network of electromagnets permeated the silicone fluid. Whenever the CZ suit detected an impact, those electromagnets instantaneously induced a magnetic field at the point of contact. The engineered nanoparticles oriented themselves along magnetic field lines to form a bulletproof barrier. John's CZ suit could stop virtually any bullet.

The Red Chinese super soldier suit had few weaknesses, but one of those weaknesses was intense magnetic fields. A strong magnetic field could disrupt the magnetorheological armor. The disrupted liquid armor could either lose its integrity, rendering it vulnerable to gunfire, or harden in place, rendering the super soldier immobile. When the Chinese test fired the upgraded Array, the swirling electromagnetic maelstrom unexpectedly disrupted John's CZ suit.

"What the shit?"

John couldn't move any body part covered by his suit. He couldn't even pull the trigger on his grenade launcher. To make matters worse, the search radar's microwave radiation combined with the high energy emissions streaming from the Array's dishes. That high energy cocktail interacted with the phosphors embedded in John's suit. The CZ suit's adaptive camouflage suddenly morphed into a glowing neon blue "Kick Me" sign.

The Falcon Commando sentry protecting the search radar rubbed his eyes in disbelief. On the rim of the pit, less than 50 yards away, stood a motionless, glowing, blue, humanoid figure.

The terrified Commando had heard all the rumors. He raised his weapon and shouted a warning at the unearthly invader, first in Mandarin, then in broken English, "Hands up or I shoot!"

Nicolescu couldn't raise his pinky, much less his hands.

The Sentry didn't hesitate. He fired a short burst from his assault rifle. At that close range, against an immobile and illuminated target, he couldn't miss. Every round hit its mark, only to ricocheted off.

As the last 7.62 mm round bounced off CZ John's left knee, a loud explosion, a mile or so to the southwest, distracted the Falcon Commando. Moments later, the Commando was further spooked by the sound of a massive dish antennae crashing to the ground. Then, the Magic Tunnel emissions abruptly terminated.

Once the Array went dark, John's suit instantaneously regained its flexibility and adaptive camouflage.

"Pop, pop!" Two 40 mm HEAT grenades arced toward the entrenched search radar.

"Boom-Ka-Boom!! Both anti-tank rounds hit the exposed thinly armored top of the vehicle.

The armored vehicle erupted in smoke & flame. All air search radar emissions ceased.

The Falcon Commando sentry saw the incoming grenades and dropped down behind the berm surrounding the armored vehicle. He survived the grenade blasts and alerted the Operations Center. The Chinese Commander didn't believe the Commando's talk of neon blue aliens, but it was obvious that all hell was breaking loose at the Very Large Array.

Stern's Escape

Brett, Marian, Stan the Man, Dr. Julius Rosenbaum, and Blue Dog remained holed up at Brett's condo for the next several days. Stan made a day trip back home to Kecksburg and brought back all the canned and dry food he had squirrelled away. He stopped at several small country markets along the way, stocking up on other necessities, including Blue Dog's favorite kibble. Stan loaded much of the food in two 55-gallon plastic drums. Upon returning to Brett's condo and emptying the drums, he rolled them into Brett's kitchen and filled them both with water, just in case.

During a spate of miserable weather, Brett & Marian visited their banks and made substantial withdrawals. With cash in hand, they made a beeline for a Squirrel Hill gold & silver dealer, a longtime friend of the brothers Dreyfus. They returned to Hampton Hall carrying a small fortune in gold & silver coins.

Brett had been in the conspiracy business for several years. When he saw Stan's two blue plastic drums full of water sitting in the middle of his kitchen, Hoffman took it all in stride. That 100+ gallons of water could come in handy. Who knew how long this craziness might last?

Between bouts of miserable weather, the mayhem in the streets escalated. One week into Brett's self-imposed quarantine, someone knocked at Brett's door.

Brett opened the door with Luger in hand, "Stern, what in the hell happened to you?"

Brett's botanist friend, Dr. Isaac Stern, was teetering out in the hallway. He was badly beaten.

"I went into the office this morning, like any other day. I noticed a small crowd of students and faculty gathered out in the hallway. As I approached, the Department Chair, Dr. Crosby, raised her hand and ordered me to stop, turn around, and go home. She told me I was no longer welcome at CMU.

"When I asked her whatever in the world she was talking about, the crowd began chanting, 'Zionist Pig, Zionist Pig'. Dr. Crosby began chanting along with them.

"That's when someone whacked me from behind. I don't remember much after that, except being punched and kicked. Somehow, I broke free of that mob and stumbled my way out of the building.

"When I got to my car, it had been trashed. The tires were slashed, windows were broken, and the hood was caved in like somebody repeatedly smashed it with a sledgehammer.

"I started running with the mob chasing after me. After running several blocks, I glanced up, begging God for mercy. That's when I saw Hampton Hall and remembered that you live here. As I ran into the vestibule, I prayed that my friend Brett Hoffman would be home…"

Before Stern could finish his story, he collapsed in the hallway.

Brett's Luger followed his eyes as he made certain the hallway was clear.

"Marian, Stan, I need some help out here!"

Marian provided backup with her Beretta, while Stan led the way with his shotgun.

"We got a troublemaker out here?" Stan had both barrels trained on Stern, now lying prostrate in the corridor.

Brett replied, "Stan, help me get Dr. Stern inside. He's one of the good guys."

"Marian, cover us. A mob beat this man, then chased him into the building. They may follow him upstairs."

With Stern safely inside, Marian shut the door and locked it behind them, then whistled for Blue Dog to stand guard.

Brett and Stan carried Isaac to the guest bedroom, "Marian, I think Dr. Stern needs your first aid expertise."

As Marian evaluated Isaac's condition, she also evaluated the overall situation, "Hoffman, they're purging all Jewish faculty from the universities."

Isaac regained semi-consciousness and muttered, "The Collective, that's what they call themselves. They hate Jews. They hate Christians. They hate White people, but they also hate people of color with whom they disagree. Most of all, they hate America."

While recuperating from his earlier beating, Rosenbaum evaluated the data retrieved from Stan's would be assassin's cellphone and digital camera.

"Mister Hoffman, there wasn't much on either device. The photos all pertain to you, Marian, Mr. Stan, and two other older White gentlemen. All incoming phone calls were from restricted numbers. This device's owner made very few outgoing calls. None of those numbers are still in service."

Brett checked out the photos of the two old White guys, "That one is Pee Wee and the other guy is Jack.

"Stan, it looks like your assassin stalked both Pee Wee and Jack. He got Pee Wee, but you got 'em before he could whack Jack. That tells us he wasn't acting alone. One of his comrades must have fulfilled the contract on Jack."

As the brain trust of Brett, Marian, and Stan mulled the current situation, Brett blurted out, "My God, we haven't heard from Charlie. I know we told him to drop off the grid, but we should have heard from him by now."

Leaving Montana

For a few weeks following Brett & Marian's departure, Charlie kept moving from one campsite to another around Flathead Lake. The cagey old prospector cut himself off from the rest of the world amidst the mountain wilderness of Northern Montana.

Winter comes early and with a vengeance to the high country of Montana. After spending Thanksgiving snowed in, eating TV dinners and not hearing a peep from Brett, Charlie did some soul searching. The Schneiders ruled the roost in the Mountain West. The Rainbow Corps were everywhere. If the Schneiders were not involved in all this skullduggery, then some other Nazi or Jewish cloak & dagger outfit was out there, assassinating anyone who knew anything about that damn Kecksburg UFO incident. Charlie made an executive decision.

A brief early December thaw allowed Charlie to free Nellie from the snowdrifts and get the Winnebago back on the road. The National Weather Service was predicting a very cold and snowy December 2025 for the Northern Rockies. Charlie figured that he better get Nellie back to civilization before the next blizzard stranded her until spring.

Charlie's first stop was his bank in Kalispell, where he withdrew a sizeable amount of cash. He told his favorite teller that he planned on spending the Winter camped along nearby Flathead Lake.

Upon leaving the bank, Charlie pulled into his favorite convenience store and filled up thirsty Nellie, paying for the gas with his Mastercard. He told

Ricky, the owner's son, that he'd be stopping in more often since he would be spending the winter at a campground close to town.

Charlie dropped into his favorite diner and joined several of his old cronies for lunch. Charlie told everyone in the diner the same story. He would be spending the winter close to Kalispell. Charlie whipped out his Visa card, paid his check, and added a nice tip for waitress Mary Lou.

Using his Discover card, the old prospector paid Flathead Campground two months' rent in advance, then dropped by the post office and changed his mailing address to that campground.

Having run all his errands, Charlie cranked up Nellie and headed south on US 93. A little over two hours later, Charlie pulled into a Missoula, Montana truck stop to take a pee break and top off Nellie's tank. This time he paid for the gas with cash. Charlie was in no hurry. He drove another couple of hours east on I-95, then pulled into a truck stop outside of Butte. Charlie was a regular road warrior. The wind was getting up, so Charlie tucked Nellie in between two 18 wheelers. As the sun set and the north wind howled, Charlie took a nap, snug as a bug, inside his trusty Winnebago.

Charlie's alarm rang at 11 p.m. Mountain Time. He tuned his radio to KMMS Newstalk 1450, hoping to catch *Sea-to-Sea AM.* While on the run, up in the mountains, Charlie had poor radio reception and could rarely catch *Sea-to-Sea.* He was hoping against hope that his Nazi hunting friend, Brett Hoffman, would be on air that night. He needed to hear a friendly voice.

Aware that Pittsburgh was a river town, the Pittsburgh Collective devised a logical and systematic strategy to hopelessly snarl traffic. The Ohio, Monongahela, and Allegheny Rivers trisect Pittsburgh. The mob only needed to shut down a few key bridges to paralyze the Steel City.

Given the round the clock gridlock, neither Vince Vittito, nor Brett, could easily or safely make it to the KDKA studio. The COVID-19 pandemic had few upsides, but it forced the *Sea-to-Sea* broadcast team to focus on remote broadcasting. With a little finagling, Brett could broadcast from his small home office. Having an inhouse IT expert of Dr. Rosenbaum's caliber simplified remote broadcasting.

Hoffman was not one to sit idly by while innocent people were persecuted. The *Sea-to-Sea* talk show format allowed Brett to interview call-in guests with anonymity from the safety of their homes. Brett's topic that cold winter's evening was "Totalitarian Traits", highlighting the similarities of totalitarian movements across the political spectrum. Brett took no calls during his first hour. He had several guests, including leading historians and political scientists, discussing totalitarian cults from Hitler to Stalin to Mao to Saddam Hussein.

At the top of Brett's second hour, during the network news break, Mr. Call Screener shot Brett an urgent message, "Charlie from Montana on Line 3!"

"Charlie, where in the hell are you?"

"Hoffman, I'm OK. No problems so far. Don't want to say too much. This may be a party line."

With that, Charlie hung up.

Before dawn, Charlie was wide awake, heading east, and paying for everything in cash.

Rangers Lead the Way

The game clock was still running. Sergeant John Nicolescu and Private Sid Skipper had taken out both air search radars and temporarily shut down whatever God awful sci-fi project the Chinese were cobbling together. John figured he had maybe 30 minutes until Lieutenant Josephine Parker & Dead Eye Adam Jackson swooped in on Badass Bitch and laid waste to the entire Array complex. John hadn't heard another explosion to his south, nor heard Sid's Tommy Gun. He assumed the worst. Big Sid could be captured or KIA.

Although the HQ-7B air search radar was destroyed, the three launch vehicles still posed a threat. Once the Bitch closed within 10 miles of the launchers, their fire control radars could paint the Cobra and their SAMs could blow Josephine's shit away. John had to take them out. The entire complex was now awash in floodlights, spotlights, and the flickering glow from two roaring fires. With his enhanced optics, CZ John spotted an armored launch vehicle 1,000 feet to his southeast, just within range of his grenade launcher.

The Falcon Commando, crouching behind the berm, was firing blindly in John's direction. John's CZ suit's adaptive camouflage was now back online, rendering him virtually invisible.

John took aim with his grenade launcher, ignoring the lone Falcon Commando, "I can't waste time dealing with a single asshole. He's no threat."

John's first shot was long. His second shot was short. Third time was the charm. The grenade hit the launch vehicle, igniting the four SAM's solid fuel booster and fragmentation warheads. The armored launch vehicle erupted in a massive pyrotechnic display.

Rat-A-Tat-Tat. Big Sid opened up on the two Chinese Hummers as they approached his position. Private Skipper shredded the lead vehicle's engine block with a spray of .45 caliber rounds. Blinded by the spray of hot motor oil raining down upon his windshield, the trailing Hummer driver slammed on his brakes. 9 Falcon Commandos took up positions behind the Hummers and returned fire.

Big Sid sized up the situation. 9 well-trained, well-armed Falcon Commandos pitted against one jumbo sized, shade tree mechanic. Sid realized he didn't stand a chance. Our man had been well trained by Cowboy Tom, Junior, and his mentor, Sergeant John Nicolescu.

"Them Chinamen will establish a base of fire, pin me down, then flank me. Given their numbers, they may even try a double envelopment. Hell, I may be surrounded already. I'm a fucking dead man."

The anticipated hail of gunfire pinned down the Big Man. Sid lightened his load by discarding the two ammo belts with attached demolition blocks. He was preparing to make a last ditch bonsai charge. If he was gonna die, Sid was going out in a blaze of glory.

Private Skipper slapped a full drum magazine into his Thompson. With his *Captain America* shield in his left hand and his Tommy Gun in his right, Sid prepared to go "over the top". The Big Man was not a Bible thumper, but he was a God-fearing southern boy. He glanced upward. The skies had cleared. A million stars twinkled in the night. Sid made his peace with a mere nod.

As Private Skipper made his move, his feet got tangled up in the discarded ammo belts at his feet. Sid fell flat on his face, smashing a brick of C-4 all over his shield, and bloodying his nose in the process.

Each of Sid's M112 demolition blocks weighed 1.25 pounds. The 11 inch x 2 inch x 1.5 inch blocks were pliable, just like potter's clay. The user friendly blocks were packaged in plastic wrappers and backed with a self-adhesive strip. The force of Sid's fall split open a block's plastic wrapper and smushed its adhesive strip against Sid's shield. As the dazed Big Man shook the cobwebs from his head, he tugged at the block of C-4, trying to remove the pancaked plastic explosive from his shield. From out of nowhere, he had an epiphany.

With bullets whizzing past him, Sid slapped two additional demolition blocks onto his shield. The Macon mechanic "eyeballed it", as best as possible, trying to balance the weight on his shield, just like he was balancing a new set of tires. Sid set the detonator, then went over the top when it ticked down to "10".

Sid raced forward, zigzagging, leading with his shield. A couple of 7.62 mm rifle rounds splattered against his depleted uranium shield. His body armor's ceramic inserts stopped a 9 mm pistol round but left a nasty bruise on the Big Man's abdomen. Sid was 50 yards out when he opened up with his Thompson, aiming at nothing in particular, just spraying lead everywhere.

When the timer clicked down to "5", Sid flung his shield, then hit the deck. The depleted uranium disc sailed through the night with only a slight wobble. As Sid hit the dirt, he resumed firing. The explosive laden shield shattered the oil soaked windshield of the trailing Hummer, embedding itself in the rear seat. Two seconds later, 3.75 pounds of plastic explosive detonated inside the Hummer. Osama Bin Laden would have whole heartedly approved of Sid's improvised car bomb.

Sergeant Nicolescu made the Orthodox Sign of the Cross upon hearing Sid's Thompson firing off in the distance. When Sid's car bomb exploded, John whispered a short prayer. Despite John's affection for Sid, now was not the time to worry about his big friend. It sounded as if the Big Man was still very much in the fight.

CZ John advanced to his northeast. His next target was the armored launch vehicle presumedly stationed on the northern arm of the Array. Nicolescu reckoned that launcher should be about a half mile away.

The Array's Red Chinese Commander realized a lone saboteur could not be responsible for all this mayhem. The Array was under attack. An hour earlier, in response to a frantic report from a deathly ill San Antonio Peoples' Militiawoman, he sent half his force to Socorro and placed his off duty personnel in Magdalena on high alert. Despite being shorthanded, resistance at the Array was now stiffening.

With his enhanced vision, John could see vehicles moving along the service roads, paralleling the arms of the Array. Vet's CZ suit was once again detecting microwave radiation. The onboard computer immediately identified that radiation as HQ-7B fire control radar.

"We took out both their air search radars. They gotta light up their fire control radars, or they're blind as a bat."

The intensity of the radar increased with John's every step.

"Yeah, I'm getting closer. These guys are no rookies. Their third launcher, wherever it is, is not emitting."

Sid was lying face down, in the snow and muck. The smoke was clearing. All gunfire had subsided. The trailing Hummer had been blown to smithereens and the lead Hummer was afire, having been tossed several yards by the force of the blast. Sid picked himself up, grabbed the two explosive laden ammo belts, then slowly advanced. Blood soaked scraps of uniforms, burning tires, and shredded body parts littered the area. Big Sid was walking through a manmade hell. Through his night vision, Sid could see two figures fleeing toward The Barn. The Big Man squatted and surveyed the area, as if he were hunting wild boar in the Ocmulgee Swamp. A blood trail led back toward The Barn. One of the two surviving Falcon Commandos appeared to be bleeding out.

Sid began running toward The Barn. The Array's security forces were mobilizing. Sid didn't have time to backtrack and blow the dish immediately to his rear.

Sid recalled how Junior had schooled him on the Pearl Harbor attack. How the Japanese decimated Battleship Row but didn't take out Pearl's dry docks or fuel storage tank farm. Within a year, making use of that critical, undamaged, infrastructure, America's Pacific Fleet recovered and began pushing the Japanese back toward Tokyo.

"This won't be my Pearl Harbor! I gotta take out The Barn. That'll shut these bastards down for good."

"There it is! Behind those stacked 55 gallon drums!" CZ John spotted another armored launch vehicle 500 yards to his front.

"Holy shit! There's a mixed platoon, Militia & Commandos, out front of that vehicle. It's out of grenade range. I've gotta get closer. They'll surely spot me when I fire my grenade launcher."

John couldn't see the Type 87 towed antiaircraft gun behind the sand filled steel drums. The Type 87 was an "old school" weapon, a knockoff of an old Russian design. It wasn't self-propelled, nor radar targeted, but its optically targeted twin barrels could spit out 400 rounds per minute. John's CZ suit was not designed to stop 25 mm cannon fire.

Sergeant Nicolescu closed range to about 400 yards, then fired. As before, his first round was long, but, this time, his second round was on target. The launcher's four SAM missiles erupted, just like the missiles on the first launcher. Upon firing the grenades, John was immediately targeted by small arms fire. The enemy couldn't actually see CZ John, but they targeted the grenade launcher. A couple of 7.62 mm rounds hit Vet's CZ suit with no effect.

POP, POP, POP…. The Type 87's crew pushed over the top course of sand filled barrels and depressed the antiaircraft gun's elevation to engage the unidentified ground target. The gun's twin barrels began spitting out 7 rounds per second. 25 mm high explosive fragmentation shells were exploding all around the invisible Super Soldier.

"Shit! That's a damned 20 or 25 mm flak gun!"

John hit the dirt, "If those bastards have any armor piercing shells, I'm screwed!"

John was not exaggerating the threat. The Falcon Commando gun crew had a few discarding sabot tungsten penetrator rounds in their inventory. 25 mm armor piercing ordnance could easily shred CZ John's liquid armor.

Nicolescu reloaded his grenade launcher with high explosive fragmentation grenades.

"I can't pussy out now. That AA gun could give Badass Bitch a bad hair day. I gotta take it out."

The Barn was awash in floodlights. Sid could see the welcoming committee forming around its perimeter.

"Lord have mercy. There's a reinforced platoon out there."

A hail of 12.7 mm tracer rounds welcomed the Big Man.

"Damn! They've deployed a couple of heavy machineguns. They sure don't sound like Brownings. Must be some kinda ChiCom Ma Deuce knockoffs."

At that range, the Peoples' Militia hadn't yet drawn a good bead on Sid, but they were laying down disciplined suppressive fire.

"Shit! I'm all out of magic tricks. Ain't no way I can fight 30 or 40 men, armed with heavy weapons. I'm over a hundred yards out. They're all dug in. If I'm gonna make a run for it, I gotta go. I gotta go now."

Private Skipper ran like hell to the southeast. The Big Man wasn't suicidal. Since he couldn't take out The Barn, Sid decided to hit an alternate target, the third SAM launcher, presumedly on the Array's southeastern spoke.

Vet launched a 40 mm HE grenade at the entrenched 25 mm cannon. His shot fell short, exploding in front of the sand filled drums. John noticed the cannon fire abruptly changed. The 25 mm rounds were no longer exploding around him.

"Oh shit!"

CZ John felt like he had been hit by that proverbial Mack Truck. He was hurled backward a good four feet. The Romanian American Army Ranger was lying flat on his back with the breath knocked out of him. John winced in pain as he struggled to catch a breath.

"Man, I think I've got some busted ribs."

John ordered his CZ suit to enrich his oxygen feed. As he spoke, he coughed up a little blood. He instantly ordered his CZ suit to run a systems self-diagnostic, followed by a medical diagnostic on its occupant. Once again, John was at a slight disadvantage. The heads up display presented data in Chinese, but John could decipher most of the numerical and pictorial information.

Neither diagnosis was good. CZ John's mangnetorheolgical armor was inoperative. His CZ suit had been compromised. Exterior air was leaking into the suit. John glanced at his right side. A large gash had been ripped in his suit. A thick, milky, silver-grayish liquid was leaking from the gash. His suit's exterior layer of Kevlar had been slashed, but the interior layer seemed to be intact. John's body, beneath the Kevlar, was not intact. John screamed in pain as he reached around and probed the gash with his left index finger.

John's vital signs flashed up on the heads up display. His heart rate, blood pressure, and respiration were all elevated. Vet knew that shock was his worst enemy. He opened his visor and took a long drink of sports drink from his canteen and tried to relax. That's when he noticed his gray suit. Its adaptive camouflage was offline. Nicolescu realized that his worst fear had come to fruition. A 25 mm armor piercing round had just grazed his CZ suit.

Sid ran southeastward for a quarter mile, then turned due east. The Big Man heard vehicles to his rear. Searchlights were sweeping across the desert floor. As Sid continued running eastward, he could hear a 4-wheel drive vehicle closing in from behind. Sid suddenly found himself in another large shallow pit. Private Skipper assumed a prone position behind a small berm. The Big Man noticed the gravelly composition of the berm. He couldn't see exactly what type of vehicle was approaching, but it sounded like another one of those Chinese Hummers.

Once again, Sid's ingenuity took center stage. The Big Man ripped the plastic wrappers off a couple of blocks of C-4. He grabbed a big handful of sharp, angular gravel and kneaded it into a block of C-4. After rolling his improvised grenade into a ball, Sid reinserted the detonator and set the timer for 5 seconds. Sid completed the assembly of his second improvised grenade as a Chinese Hummer came to a skidding stop, a few meters short of the gravel pit. The Militiaman in the passenger seat swept the gravel pit with a spotlight.

Sid activated the timer, then leapt up and threw the ball. Luckily, in his younger days, Big Sid had been the star outfielder of the Macon Industrial Softball League. The oversized softball was right on target. The ball hit the hood of the Hummer but didn't bounce. It sorta smushed. For a second, the driver couldn't understand what hit the hood. That second was all he had.

To Sid's north, 25 mm HE rounds were once again bursting around the now not so super soldier. Vet's liquid armor was kaput, as was his adaptive camouflage. Dazed and injured, John was lucky to be alive. His suit's two Kevlar layers offered some protection from shrapnel, but the damaged CZ suit couldn't stop a full metal jacketed rifle round. Two spotlights intermittently illuminated the Sergeant as he scrambled about on all fours, writhing in pain, and searching for cover. There was none.

John heard another loud explosion, far to his south, followed by several unmistakable bursts from Sid's Thompson.

"The Big Man is still in the game!"

Through the searing pain, Vet focused on his target and launched three grenades in rapid succession. None of the grenades hit their intended target, but the three 40 mm bomblets bracketed the antiaircraft gun, filling the air with a blizzard of deadly shrapnel. The two man gun crew was shredded.

The Falcon Commando, who survived CZ John's earlier assault upon the HQ-7B search radar, was still in the game. The Red Chinese Commando had tracked John at a discreet distance. He now realized he was not tracking an extraterrestrial. He observed how CZ John's adaptive camouflage rendered him virtually invisible. He also observed how CZ John was seemingly invulnerable to gunfire. The dedicated Commando also observed the effect of a 25 mm AP round striking the Super Soldier.

Neutralizing the gun crew was little consolation for Sergeant Nicolescu. He was in bad shape, and he knew it. His CZ suit was in bad shape, and he knew it. Any thought of finding and destroying the third SAM launcher was pure folly, and he knew it. John loaded his only three smoke grenades into his launcher and laid down a smokescreen in front of the enemy positions.

"My only remaining advantages are my enhanced senses. My CZ helmet is undamaged."

Under cover of smoke, John staggered southward, toward the Array's Operations Center. Once there, he planned to lay low. Once Badass Bitch made her entrance, John would grab a scientist amidst all the confusion.

As John made his escape, a few 25 mm HE rounds emerged from the smoke, exploding all around him..

"They've got that 20 millimeter back in action."

Little did John know. The diligent Falcon Commando, the one who tracked him, the one he neglected to take out, was now manning the 25 mm canon. He targeted John with a few parting shots through the smoke screen.

As he ran toward Operations, John noted the time on his heads up display, "I've gotta find some cover. It's almost showtime."

Happy Holidays

The 2025 holiday season was anything but joyful. Reminiscent of the COVID lockdowns, most American cities were locked down tight in response to The Collective's growing terror campaign. Early one mid-December Sunday morning, Brett's cellphone rang. He did not recognize the number.

"Hello."

"Mr. Hoffman, I'm one of your biggest fans."

A half-asleep Brett immediately recognized Charlie's voice, "Thank you, it's always a pleasure chatting with my fans."

"I've got a few of your books and CDs. I've got your book about the 1947 Roswell crash. I've got your CD about the 1980 Rendlesham Forest close encounter. I'm on a cross country tour of UFO hotspots. I was wondering if you could meet me and sign some of my UFO paraphernalia. Maybe we can meet out back of Blue's house?"

Brett was laughing on the inside, "Charlie might be an old fart, but he was a wise old fart."

Brett replied, "Sure, what time?"

"Two hours. Can you make it?"

"Sure, I think so."

"Good! I'm already here. See you in a couple."

Charlie vividly recalled Brett's description of Stan the Man's foiled home invasion, down to the finest detail. Charlie suspected that Brett's condo was under surveillance. He didn't really want to risk taking Nellie into a strange, hostile, crowded city.

Charlie always wanted to visit Kecksburg. Once he finally got there, he asked around and got directions to Stan's place. He parked Nellie behind

Stan's house, next to Blue Dog's kennel. Charlie plugged Nellie into an exterior power outlet and screwed Stan's garden hose onto Nellie's water inlet. Charlie then set his alarm for two hours and took a little snooze with his old buddies, Smith & Wesson, close by his side.

Brett, Stan the Man, and Blue Dog piled into the cab of Stan's Ford F-150 4x4. Brett convinced Marian to stay at Hampton Hall and babysit the two professors. The previous evening, Stan had chained up his Ford pickup when the sleet and freezing rain started accumulating on Dithridge Street. Stan always kept a few cinder blocks in his truck bed for added weight and traction. Very few adventurous souls dared venture out onto the hazardous Pittsburgh roadways that icy morning. With his 4-wheel drive pickup, tire chains, and a lifetime of winter driving experience, Stan was undeterred.

"Stan, how can you drive on this ice?"

"Hoffman, are you telling me that you've lived here all your life and can't drive through a little snow and ice?"

Brett just closed his eyes as Stan slip slided his way along the surface streets, then took the William Penn Highway east.

Brett opened his eyes as Stan accelerated onto the ice-free interstate.

"See Hoffman, the main roads are clear. Just gotta watch out for that black ice. We'll be at the house in no time at all."

Stan paused out on the county road, checking things out before turning into the lane leading back to his house.

"What's that RV doing behind my house?"

"I think that's Nellie."

"Hoffman, who in the hell is Nellie?"

"That's Charlie's Winnebago. That son of a bitch drove all the way from Montana."

Brett grabbed Blue's leash as he leapt out of the Ford, "Stan, Blue & I will check it out. I'll sound Nellie's horn if it's OK."

Blue Dog practically dragged Brett down the lane. The Heeler was eager to get back home.

Brett tightly clutched his Luger in his coat pocket. He slightly relaxed about halfway down the lane. Hoffman recognized Nellie's slightly bent radio antennae.

Brett paused for a moment. He didn't see Charlie. So, he released Blue Dog.

Blue Dog streaked down the lane. When the Heeler spotted the Winnebago, he wasn't at all happy.

"What's this thing doing in my backyard?"

Blue Heelers are not overly vocal, but Blue Dog was pissed. He ran up to the Winnebago's side door and began raising Cain.

Blue's barking roused Charlie from his nap. The half-asleep prospector cracked open the side door, only to be greeted by a snarling Blue Heeler.

"You must be Stan the Man's Blue Dog. Hi Blue Dog! I'm Charlie."

Blue Dog wasn't in a friendly mood. No way was Charlie getting out of that Winnebago in one piece. Brett came running through the ice & snow to Charlie's rescue.

Hoffman grabbed Blue's leash, "It's OK Blue. Quiet Blue Dog!

"Charlie, honk Nellie's horn a bit."

Blue Dog calmed down a bit, but when Charlie honked the horn, Blue went totally bonkers.

Stan heard the honking horn and turned his pickup into the lane. As he pulled the F-150 up beside Nellie, Stan the Man rolled down his window and called off his snarling four-legged minion.

Charlie just stood there in Nellie's side doorway, afraid to come out until Stan secured the Heeler.

Once Stan locked Blue Dog in his kennel, Brett made the introductions. Once Blue saw Stan and Charlie shake hands, he calmed down.

"Charlie, am I ever glad to see you, but whatever possessed you to drive across country, through all this chaos?" Brett was completely perplexed.

"I brought Nellie down out of the high country before she got snowed in for the winter."

"Why didn't you just move down into the valley, closer to town?"

"That's exactly what I planned to do, but, when I got into town, the Rainbow Corps was everywhere. To make matters worse, the Corps is now backed up by the Montana National Guard. I couldn't risk hanging around Kalispell."

Charlie pointed at Blue Dog, "Seeing that the Rainbow Corps were hanging around town, thick as fleas on Stan's blue dog, I concocted a little misdirection campaign of my own."

Brett grinned a shit-eating grin, "What the hell did you do?"

"I ran all over Kalispell, using my credit cards, withdrawing money from the bank, and shooting off my mouth to all my old friends. I told everyone I was hanging close to town for the winter. I even paid two month's rent at a local campground."

"Charlie, you didn't call me on your cellphone, did you?"

"Nah, right after you and Marian bugged out, I dropped by Walmart and picked up a couple of those prepaid phones. Don't worry, that number is untraceable. Just to be safe, I stuck that cellphone under the bumper of a bus headed down to Tampa."

Stan unlocked his backdoor and the three amigos stepped into Stan's cold, dark kitchen.

"Have a seat. I'll turn up the furnace. Sorry, I can't offer you boys any coffee."

Charlie rushed out the backdoor and quickly returned with ground coffee, sugar, and creamer.

Minutes later, after Brett brought Charlie up to date on the Pittsburgh situation, the trio strategized over coffee.

"Boys, this Nazi hunting is fun, but I think we have more pressing matters at hand." Charlie had his Smith & Wesson lying within easy reach on Stan's kitchen table."

Stan nodded in agreement, "I agree! Me and Blue Dog bugged outta here because of all this assassination bullshit, but I'm beginning to think that moving from this here farm into Pittsburgh was like jumping from the frying pan into the fire."

Brett listened intently as he replayed recent events through his mind, "Come spring, the cities are gonna erupt. This so-called Collective is purposefully paralyzing transportation, sabotaging infrastructure, and terrorizing the public. When the pogrom begins in earnest, Marian and our two Jewish professors will be prime targets.

"You know, I've been watching The Collective's marches and rallies. Their racial hatred extends to more than just Jews. While they somewhat tolerate White women, they have little tolerance for White males."

Stan interrupted, "Hold it, Brett. I've had plenty of time on my hands while I've been couped up in your condo. I've seen a few White dudes at those demonstrations."

Brett replied, "Yes, but very few. Many of those few were Gay or Trans. Sexual preferences seem to trump Whiteness in The Collective's weird social ranking system. I'm telling you both, the three of us have no place in The Collective's vision for America."

"Brett, we need to get Marian and the professors the hell out of Pittsburgh. I've got a Buck stove in the living room and several cord of seasoned hardwood under tarps. I'm on city water, but if that gets cut off, my old hand pump well still works. We can hole up right here until we see how things shake out."

Charlie concurred, "Stan's right. We're much better off here in Kecksburg. If the shit hits the fan, we can bug out in Nellie and Stan's truck. We can high tail it down to West Virginia. Those politically correct assholes won't dare venture into those West Virginia hills. I've got family down there around Paw Paw. They've all got dogs and guns."

The Bitch is Back

Sergeant John Nicolescu was desperately searching for cover, preferably in proximity to Operations. His every step and every breath were excruciating. John's CZ suit featured autoinjectors capable of dispensing pain killers. The suit's self-diagnostic indicated that the autoinjectors were operational, but John would not issue the command. Painkillers would slow the Ranger's reaction time and dull his wits. Nicolescu sucked it up.

Peoples' Militia were everywhere, but they seemed to be concentrated around high value targets, such as the Operations Center. John was lucky. He managed to avoid roving patrols as he stumbled southward. But the Ranger wasn't kidding himself. Eventually, if he didn't find a place to hide, he would be killed or captured.

The CZ helmet was once more bombarded by microwaves.

"Damn! That third launcher's fire control radar just went hot."

Big Sid emerged from the gravel pit and headed to the northeast. He heard explosions and heavy weapons fire to his north. He assumed that John had taken out the search radar and the first two launch vehicles, but he hadn't heard anything to his east.

"There should be a launcher somewhere along that southeastern arm. I haven't heard any gunfire or explosions up north for a few minutes."

A lone tear ran down the Big Man's cheek, "I've gotta consider that Mr. John may be out of action. Now it's up to me."

Private Sid Skipper ran with a purpose. He was determined to take out that third launcher.

John was nearing the Operations Center.

"What's that on the tracks?"

Sergeant Nicolescu spotted a yellow railcar mover, hitched to two belly dump hopper cars, sitting on the left hand track. The railcar mover had both rail wheels and road wheels, capable of travelling on either. The mover was much smaller than a full-fledged locomotive but still capable of moving several loaded railcars at a time. The mover could also move the massive dish antennae.

Both hopper cars were full of track ballast, the crushed and sized rock that served as the tandem track's foundation. The Chinese were using the ballast to extend the Array's three arms. Longer arms with more dishes would dramatically increase the Array's capabilities, fulfilling the ChiCom's twisted purpose, whatever that may be.

The hopper cars were a godsend for Nicolescu. He climbed the ladder as rapidly as his broken ribs and punctured lung would allow. John peered down into the car before jumping in. He heaved a slight sigh of relief when he saw the ballast. The ballast would support his weight.

As Big Sid approached the southeastern arm of the Array, he acquired his target amongst a flurry of activity. While Sid watched, the HQ-7B launch vehicle turned westward and elevated its four launch tubes to 45 degrees. The vehicle's parabolic radar dish wasn't rotating through 360 degrees, it wasn't searching. The dish was scanning, from side to side, in a very narrow arc. The radar had locked onto a target.

Through his night vision the Big Man could see several two man teams deployed in a perimeter to the west of the launcher. Each team carried some sort of man portable missile launcher.

"What the fuck?" Sid was caught totally off-guard.

An HQ-7B missile roared out of its launch tube, trailing a noxious yellowish exhaust plume and lighting up the San Augustin Plain like the 4th of July.

"Miss Jo, we've been painted by radar." Adam's eagle eyes were searching for threats.

Lieutenant Josephine Parker's Huey Cobra gunship was ten miles west of the Array. The Bitch had been invisible as she weaved her way along the dry arroyos coming down out of the Crosby Mountains. Now, she was out on the open San Augustin Plain, with her ass hanging out.

Dead Eye Adam shouted, "SLAMEYE, 12 o'clock low!"

Josephine Parker did her thing. Most pilots would have immediately deployed flares. Josephine didn't. She pressed Badass Bitch to her limits.

Adam's eyes widened in sheer terror, as he felt the pull of 4 Gs, and momentarily found himself inverted. Our girl, Jo, had done the seemingly impossible, yet again. Most rotary winged aviators could not pull an inside loop. Most would probably tell you that a chopper cannot pull a loop. Most would be wrong.

Josephine was a perfectionist. She was well versed in SAM technology. Jo knew that modern heat seeking missiles utilize various strategies to defeat countermeasures. Advanced SAM seeker heads track the trajectory of decoy flares and ignore them if they simply float to the ground. Jo deployed her flares as the Bitch neared the apex of her loop. The flares were thrown upward and backward, thoroughly confusing the SAM. As the flares arced up and to the rear, the Bitch completed her inside loop. Now upright and back on course, Dead Eye watched the SAM streak by, high overhead.

Jo had remained silent during the entire close encounter, concentrating on evading the heat seeking threat.

"Yeehaw, Dead Eye! Was that ever hairy, or what?"

"Miss Jo, won't that missile come back after us?"

"Dead Eye, you been watching too many movies. Most SAMs burn up all their fuel in the first few seconds of flight. After that, they just coast. That's why aircraft frantically maneuver to escape a SAM. Missiles are fast, but with every maneuver, they lose momentum. By now, that there SAM has either self-destructed or crashed somewhere out in this God forsaken desert."

Josephine now had the Bitch back down on the deck, kicking up blizzard of snow and sand as she streaked toward the Array at 220 mph.

"Miss Jo, look out there. Is that our target?"

"Hell yes, they've got the place lit up like a ballpark."

Sergeant Nicolescu was hunkered down in that hopper car, trying to catch his breath, when the SAM streaked overhead.

"Damn it!" John deduced that the ChiComs were targeting Badass Bitch. Despite his injuries, John had to do something, but what?

The Sergeant climbed out of the hopper car and uncoupled it. Then he climbed into the railcar mover's cab and surveyed the controls.

"Thank God, it's not Chinese."

John fired up the diesel engine and engaged the mover's highway wheels. He removed his CZ helmet and slapped on a stripped, cotton, engineer's cap, hanging in the cab. Like a Romanian Casey Jones, Nicolescu drove the yellow beastie off the tracks and onto the adjacent access road. Amid all the confusion, none of the Array's defenders paid John any mind as he accelerated the railcar mover to its top speed of 14 mph and headed northeastward, toward the vertex.

"They gotta be shootin' at Badass Bitch!" The thought of the Red Chinese shooting at Miss Jo & Dead Eye riled Big Sid something awful.

Sid charged straight ahead at the two Falcon Commandos directly to his front. From a healthy distance, Sid clicked the timer, hesitated, then tossed his second gravel packed plastique softball.

"Pow-ka-Pow!" The exploding IED set off the man portable QW-18 SAM carried by the two man team.

Private Skipper's perfect strike drew the attention of the teams spaced about 100 yards to either side. Automatic rifle fire danced around the Big Man's feet as he ran straight through the gap, toward the launch vehicle. Sid didn't return fire. His adversaries were at the edge of his Thompson's effective range, they were not his priority. Sid was going for the gold. He was going for the last launch vehicle.

"Miss Jo, they've locked us up again!"

The Bitch was now approaching the dish packed southwestern arm of the Array.

"Dead Eye, blast those two dishes straight ahead with a couple of Hydras!"

Adam fired two 70 mm rockets, then yelled, "SLAMEYE 11 o'clock low!"

Two massive aluminum radio telescope dishes exploded in flames as the Bitch's 2.5 inch rockets struck home. A split second later, a HQ-7B SAM slammed into the northernmost burning dish.

Jo banked the Bitch to the northeast and followed the southwestern arm inward, toward the vertex. Josephine was weaving her way through the backlog of massive dishes parked along that arm.

"Dead Eye, shred those dishes with the 20 mike-mike, don't blow 'em up."

Once engineer John reach the vertex, he turned the railcar mover to the right and headed down the southeastern arm of the Array. A short distance to the southeast, he saw the double flash from Sid's exploding softball and the secondary explosion of the man portable SAM.

Sid was now a mere hundred yards out from the final launcher. Sid fired a burst from his Tommy Gun at the three Falcon Commandos blocking his path. The Chinese hit the dirt and returned fire, accurate fire.

Big Sid was a big target. Three 7.62 mm jacketed rounds simultaneously hit Sid, center mass. Sid dropped to the ground like he had been nailed by an Iron Mike Tyson three punch combination.

Dazed and confused, Big Sid was down, "Holy shit, what just hit me?"

Pain, Sid felt pain. He was lucky to be feeling anything. If Sergeant Nicolescu hadn't insisted that Sid slip those ceramic strike plates into his body armor, the Big Man would now be a dead man.

Before Sid could regain his senses, he was whacked upside the head by a Chinese rifle butt. Big Sid was down for the count.

Jo took her missions seriously, but savored every victory, "Kiss my ass and call me Sally, this here Array is more fun than one of your video games!" Jo was weaving around the dishes while Dead Eye cut them to shreds.

Dead Eye alerted Josephine as Badass Bitch approached The Barn, "That big Barn is at our twelve o'clock."

"Take it out with the grenade launcher."

Before Adam could target The Barn, his peripheral vision caught motion, but he had no time to react. A Falcon Commando targeted the Bitch from a range just over 100 yards. A man portable SAM streaked toward the Bitch.

Sometimes, it's better to be lucky than good. The Bitch was passing behind a dish parked along the southwestern arm and still warm from the Magic Tunnel test firing. The SAM impacted the dish instead of the Bitch.

"Holy shit, Dead Eye, where did that come from?"

"I don't know Miss Jo. There's hostiles scurrying about all over down there."

"Dead Eye, you see any signs of our two attack dogs?"

"No, but I can see one burning and collapsed dish along with a couple of mangled Hummers below us. To our north, there's three burning vehicles. Looks like all hell has broken loose down there.

"Take out The Barn."

Dead Eye fired four grenades into the open west side of the Antennae Assembly Building. The massive building, along with the flammable stores and partially assembled dish therein, went up in smoke & flames.

As the Bitch continued northward, toward the vertex, Dead Eye alerted Jo, "They've painted us again. Same radar as before."

"OK, those SAMs came from the east. Let's just hide behind that dish that's sitting right in the middle of the Array. I'll slowly rotate the Bitch while you take out everything within range. Everything, that is, except that big single story office building down there. That's Ops. We have unfinished business at Operations."

Squirrel Hill Rescue

Pittsburgh residents awoke on Christmas morning 2025 to suffocating clouds of acrid smoke. Every church and synagogue in the Steel City was afire. Despite the frigid temperatures, The Collective were out in the streets, blocking emergency vehicles, and pelting first responders with rocks and bottles. Brett & Company couldn't smell the smoke or hear the sirens. They had relocated to Stan's farmhouse in rural Kecksburg.

Since moving in with Stan & Blue Dog, the team felt much less threatened by either assassins or mobs. Stan kept his truck parked at the far end of the lane, blocking access to the house. Charlie kept Nellie parked by the backdoor, stocked up and ready to bug out at a moment's notice.

Over the years, Vince Vittito hosted innumerable shows dedicated to survivalism. No one was surprised when Vince bugged out, leaving Brett to host *Sea-to-Sea AM.* Hardheaded Brett Hoffman was not about to let The Collective, or any other fringe group, regardless of political persuasion, silence him. Every night, Brett remotely broadcast *Sea-to-Sea AM* from the safety of Stan the Man's parlor. Over the course of a few short weeks, Brett transitioned from the role of paranormal investigator to the roll of American patriot. In the fullness of time, Brett's outspoken coverage of The Collective would earn him the dubious title of "Peoples' Enemy #2", second only to Darius "RAMBRO" Johnson.

Brett's Boxing Day episode was entitled, "Terrors Throughout History". That early morning, he compared and contrasted various revolutions gone bad. Hoffman focused on the French Revolution, Russian Revolution, Hitler's rise to power, Chairman Mao's Cultural Revolution, and The Collective. Several of Brett's more courageous friends, historians, political scientists, even a couple of retired generals, called in from their secure locations. The switchboard was once again melting down as Americans voiced their opinions and asked questions. The Founding Fathers would have given Brett's show two thumbs up.

At the top of Brett's final hour, Marian nodded off to sleep while sitting in a chair next to her man. Wouldn't you know, Marian's cellphone rang. Maury Dreyfus was in trouble.

A sleepy Marian could barely hear her friend, "Maury, what's all that racket? I can barely hear you."

"They're breaking into the shop! They're torching every business on Murray Avenue."

"Where's brother Ben?"

"He's up in my apartment. He's OK. Hang on, they're coming in through the broken windows."

The scene out on Murray Avenue would have been quite familiar and acceptable to Leutnant Wolfgang Schneider.

Every shop's plate glass windows were shattered. Most of those shops were Jewish owned. It was another Kristallnacht, a night of broken glass.

Maury retreated up two flights of stairs to his apartment. The wise old Jew watched as the jeering mob crammed into the stairwell. After the recent armed robbery, mechanically inclined Maury had prepared a little surprise. As the intruders neared the top of the second flight, Maury leapt up and grabbed a hanging rope, pulling it with all his might. Several steel rods popped out of the iron staircase, collapsing it down upon the first flight. Maury grinned as the collapsing stairs took out at least a dozen Members and prevented the mob from reaching the third floor.

"Marian, I'm on the third floor. I've stopped them for now."

"Maury, stay on the phone. We'll be there within the hour."

Brett took an unscheduled commercial break when a frantic Marian shouted, "The mob is after the Dreyfus brothers."

Brett quickly signed off from that night's broadcast and issued an "all hands on deck". The entire Hoffman crew of Jews, Gentiles, and one blue canine stumbled half asleep out into the frigid Pennsylvania night. They piled into Stan's pickup and Brett's BMW.

Rosenbaum rode with Stan the Man, as did Charlie. Old man Julius was not quite 100% and had never fired a weapon. Stan decided to make use of him as best he could.

Stan tossed Rosenbaum the hickory axe handle concealed beneath the driver's seat, "When we get to Maury's shop, you and Blue Dog stick with the vehicles. Don't be skittish about bashing some heads!"

Marian and Stern tagged along with Brett.

Hoffman figured he could use more muscle, "Stern, can you handle a weapon?"

"What kind of weapon?"

"Charlie's shotgun."

"Yeah, I've shot some skeet."

Marian cut to the chase, "Have you ever shot a man?"

"No, have you?"

"Not until a few weeks ago. Stern, aim the shotgun center mass. Aim for the chest. It's better if you can catch 'em all bunched up. You clear the way. Hoffman and I will cover you."

Brett completed Stern's 30 second tactical training, "That's a 12-gauge Mossberg 500 pump action. One shell is in the chamber. You have 5 more in the magazine. Pump and fire!"

"Brett, you're talking about shooting people, really killing people."

"Yes Isaac. People just like that SS man in your glossy photo. The one wearing the edelweiss!"

Brett's BMW led the way onto the Pennsylvania Turnpike. The highway was deserted. The nation was paralyzed.

As Brett's posse passed New Stanton, Marian moaned, "Oh shit!"

Brett was caught off guard, "Now what's wrong?"

"Mother, my Mom lives at the corner of Maryland & Kentucky in Shadyside. We've got to get her out. Don't you think?"

"Holy shit! She's still in town?"

"I think so. If she's home, we gotta get her out!"

As Brett's BMW exited the I-376 Squirrel Hill Tunnel, an apocalyptic scene unfolded. Trash, broken glass, and burning vehicles littered the streets. During the best of times, the I-376 exit onto Murray Avenue is a convoluted, twisty-turny affair. You almost meet yourself coming and going. At the risk of plagiarizing Dickens, these were the worst of times. The mob was barricading the on/off ramps, bringing traffic to a standstill.

Brett had to think fast. It appeared that the mob had just begun barricading this exit ramp. The obstruction was not substantial, composed mainly of wooden pallets, empty 55-gallon steel drums, and shopping carts. Under his breathe, Hoffman apologized to his Bimmer as he put the hammer down.

"Everybody down! Cover your eyes!"

Stan the Man could barely see Brett's taillights through all the smoke.

When Stan saw the BMW crash through the barricade, he couldn't believe his eyes, "Holy shit!"

Brett's BMW plowed into the barricade at 73 mph. Tires, bodies, and shopping carts were sent flying.

Brett continued accelerating as his battered BMW fishtailed onto Murray Avenue. Marian opened her eyes, then wished she hadn't. She glanced over at the speedometer. Brett was doing 85 in a 25 zone.

"Damn it Hoffman! Hit the brakes!"

Brett slammed on his brakes, skidding to a stop a half block past Dreyfus Lock & Electronics. Stan began cursing Hoffman even before his pickup rear-ended Brett's BMW.

Stan sprang from his truck, raising holy hell, "Sweet Jesus Hoffman, you don't know shit about winter driving. Chains are great for driving through snow, but on clean pavement, they slide like skis. Now look at my front bumper."

Brett didn't answer. He was too busy staring at his trashed BMW. It looked like it had been through a demolition derby. Meanwhile, several boisterous Members approached the fender-bender, and you can bet they weren't Good Samaritans.

Marian whispered to a petrified Isaac Stern, cowering in the backseat, "Are you ready?"

Stern grimaced, then nodded, "Let's go!"

Stern and Marian piled out of the BMW and leveled their weapons upon the approaching rabble.

"Stan, Hoffman, get back on the clock!" Marian couldn't believe Hoffman's lack of situational awareness. Now was not the time, nor place, for petty bickering.

Charlie was standing tall, in the middle of Murray Avenue, brandishing his S&W .44 magnum, like a 21st Century *Dirty Harry*. Rosenbaum was in the truck bed, clutching the axe handle in his trembling hand, with a snarling Blue Dog close by his side.

The gathering mob rushed the accident scene. Boom! Boom! Boom! Stern began firing the Mossberg into the charging mob. Although he was scared shitless, Isaac Stern was one Jew who would not go quietly into the night.

Marian's scolding got Stan's attention. He reached back behind the seat of his pickup and retrieved his double-barreled Remington. Stan unleashed a lethal blizzard of double aught buckshot upon the angry Members. The

Remington and Mossberg 12-gauge shotguns were perfect weapons for riot control.

Brett hollered, "Marian, Charlie, follow me! Stern, Stan, you're with Rosenbaum & Blue. Guard the vehicles and keep that crowd out of the Dreyfus' shop."

Brett led the way into the ransacked computer shop. A dozen or more Members were inside, attempting to rescue the survivors of the staircase collapse.

"Get the hell out of this shop!" Brett's Luger was trained on a young Caucasian woman wielding a large pipe wrench.

Madame Goodwrench paid Hoffman no mind and continued her headlong advance. Brett fired once, hoping to knock the wrench from the woman's hand. She moved slightly to one side and Brett's aim was slightly off. The 9 mm round struck the women in the forehead, killing her instantly. After seeing their comrade cut down, the remaining ambulatory Members fled the scene.

A frantic Brett ran over to the wrench wielding woman, praying she was alive, but knowing she was dead. As Marian ran to her man's side, he turned and shook his head in hopelessness and remorse.

Marian squeezed Brett's hand, "What's done is done. Let's rescue the brothers and split."

Marian called up the collapsed stairwell, "Maury, are you and brother Ben OK?"

Maury unbolted his apartment's reinforced entry door and yelled out, "We're OK! I'm going to help Ben down the rear stairway to the garage. The door from the shop out to the garage is deadbolted and I can't find my keys."

"OK, we'll just pull around back and meet you in the concrete alley. We'll flash our headlights."

The pistol packing trio returned to Brett's BMW, parked out on Murray Avenue. Using their shotguns, Stan & Stern had cleared the immediate vicinity of hostiles. A dozen, or more, wounded Members littered the pavement, posing no real threat. Although both vehicles were all banged up, they were still drivable.

"Hang a right at the next cross street, then take an immediate right into the narrow concrete driveway." Marian and the brothers always referred to this long, private, rear access as "the concrete alley".

Brett yelled out to Stan the Man, "Follow me, but don't pull into the alley. Park your pickup out on the street and keep that alleyway open."

Brett followed Marian's directions. The driveway ended at the rear of the Dreyfus brother's shop. Marian reached over and flashed the BMW's one unbroken headlamp. In response, the rear garage door entrance to the Dreyfus shop rolled open. A barely mobile Ben leaned on brother Maury as they stumbled their way out to Brett's trashed BMW.

In the midst of the rescue, Marian finally got her mother on the phone.

Actually, Marian's mother called Marian's cellphone, "Marian, what's all that noise?"

"That's just my friend Isaac."

"Is he single?"

"I don't know, we're sort of busy right now."

"Where are you? Haven't you been watching the news?"

"I'm here in Squirrel Hill, picking up the Dreyfus brothers."

"You're on Murray Avenue? On my God!"

Just then, Stern began firing the Mossberg.

"Is that gunfire?" Marian's mother was hysterical.

"Mother, calm down. Throw some clothes in a suitcase. We're coming to get you. We'll be there in 10 minutes.

"Yes, you can bring Morris. Put him in his carrier."

Brett was clueless, "Who the hell is Morris?"

An exasperated Marian moaned, "That's Mom's cat."

10 minutes later, two battered vehicles came to a screeching halt at the corner of Kentucky & Maryland in Shadyside. Marian's mother, Norma, was standing on her front porch with an overnight bag in her right hand and a cat carrier in her left.

Marian rolled down the front passenger window and called out, "Mother, toss your bag and the cat in the pickup, then hop in the BMW's rear seat."

"Who are those two men with the guns?"

"The balding guy is Dr. Stern. The gentleman wearing the hooded parka is Charlie."

Norma shambled down the porch stairs and approached the BMW.

She whispered to Marian, "Are they single?"

Marian was beside herself, "Mother! There are seven eligible bachelors in these two vehicles."

Norma smiled and slid into the backseat without further comment.

By the time the crew arrived back at Stan's place, Norma surmised that Brett and Marian were a couple.

As Marian showed her mother up to her small attic bedroom, Norma whispered in her daughter's ear, "Brett is not Jewish."

Marian solemnly replied, "No, he isn't."

Norma smiled and winked, "He may not be Kosher, but he is quite a hunk. Now, where are my grandchildren?"

The Gathering Storm

Through the winter and early spring of 2026, Brett continued hosting *Sea-to-Sea AM* from the safety of Stan the Man's parlor. Hoffman was doing his best to warn of the impending apocalypse. The Collective was gaining the support of drug cartels, Mideast terrorist groups, and the Red Chinese. Most of the online and broadcast news outlets were staffed by leftists and opportunists beholden to Red Chinese money. They were more than happy to regurgitate The Collective's leftist mantra.

Many conservative states, mostly southern and midwestern states, began pushing back against the craziness. But it became readily apparent that the impending conflict would be more complicated than merely another "war between the states". Most major metropolitan areas were controlled by leftist mayors and woke city councils. Many of those metro governments, including Pittsburgh's, welcomed The Collective with open arms.

Stan the Man's farmhouse in Kecksburg was more secure than Brett's Oakland condo, but as the chaos intensified, roving bands of Members began fanning out into the Pennsylvania countryside. The cancerous Collective was metastasizing. Meanwhile, Marian received disturbing intelligence from her Tel Aviv handlers. In early March 2026, Mossad began warning Jews to evacuate major US metropolitan areas.

It started as a trickle. Stan the Man was out in his orchard, pruning and spraying his apple trees, tasks that must be completed in early spring, before budbreak. A Dodge minivan stopped out on the county road. Its driver got out and called out to Stan. Stan couldn't hear above the drone of his chain saw. The driver began frantically honking the horn.

Stan finally heard the blaring horn. He shut off his chainsaw, removed his ear protection, then walked over to the fence, waving his arms as he approached.

"You can lay off the horn!"

A young Hasidic Jew, standing beside the minivan, waved hello. At first sight, Stan thought the young man to be Amish or Mennonite, but the late model, well-appointed minivan belied that first impression. Upon closer inspection, Stan saw the young man's payos. He recalled seeing men wearing sidecurls on a childhood visit to Philly. Stan had spent his entire life in rural Pennsylvania. He was unfamiliar with Orthodox Jewish sects. Unbeknownst to Stan, the young man driving the minivan had spent his entire life in New York City. He was unfamiliar with 71 year old, White, Christian, farmers. Neither man knew what to expect from the other.

"Sir, do you have a bathroom we could use? I'm willing to pay."

Stan noticed the New York plates on the minivan, "Son, have you got kids in that car?"

"Yes Sir, my two sons, 4 and 6 years old."

"Did you drive all the way out here from the Big Apple?"

"From Brooklyn. We took the backroads. It's been a long trip."

"Are you folks hungry?"

"Like I said, I'm willing to pay." The young man had a handful of money.

"Once I move my pickup, you back up your jalopy, turn into my driveway, and park it behind my house." Stan pointed back toward his white, two story frame farmhouse.

Charlie & Stan had cooked for themselves for many years. By default, they became the Hoffman gang's short order cooks, but these visitors placed the two old geezers in a bit of a quandary. Bacon cheeseburgers would not quite cut it. In desperation, they turned to the only kosher cook on the premises.

Charlie whispered in Norma's ear, "Me & Stan don't know shit about kosher cooking. Rosenbaum, Stern, and Marian just pick and choose. The Dreyfus boys are a little pickier, but even they don't seem to take dietary restrictions too seriously. These here folks are Orthodox."

Norma smiled, "I'll handle it. We've got chicken, potatoes, and green beans, don't we?"

Charlie gave Norma a smile and a peck on the cheek. Norma giggled and blushed.

Three hours after their arrival, the two young Cohen boys were all washed up and scarfing down baked chicken, baked potatoes, and green beans. Stan brought each of the boys an ice cold bottle of soda pop and glanced over at their father. Seth Berg smiled and nodded his approval.

After supper, the men gathered in the living room while Norma, Marian, and Sarah Berg laid two of Charlie's sleeping bags down in the dining room floor and got the boys ready for bed.

Seth once again reached into his pocket and pulled out some cash.

"Damn it, Seth! Your money's no good around here!" Stan the Man was aggravated.

Seth feared he had offended Stan, "Mr. Musial, I'm not accustomed to such generosity."

"Damn it, Seth! Spit it out! You ain't accustomed to generosity from an old crotchety Gentile."

Seth was mesmerized. He didn't know what to say.

Isaac Stern began laughing, "Cohen, you better get used to plain spoken honesty around this bunch!"

Charlie pointed at Seth, "Let's see all that money again. Empty your pockets."

Seth didn't know what to do. Was he about to be robbed?

Charlie patted his Smith & Wesson, holstered on his hip, "I said empty your pockets."

The other men went silent. Seth emptied his pockets on the living room floor. Stan struck a match, picked up a C note, and lit the hundred dollar bill like it was Monopoly money.

Charlie dropped the burning bill onto his flagstone hearth, "All your paper money won't be worth diddly squat when the shit hits the fan."

Brett chimed in, "Mr. Cohen, my friend Charlie tends to be a bit dramatic, but he's right. That money is about to become worthless. Do you have any gold, silver, or jewels?"

"Nothing with me."

Brett continued, "Are you armed?"

Seth replied, "No, we live in the City. Possession of firearms is illegal."

Cohen couldn't believe his eyes as Charlie pulled his .44 Magnum and held it up close for inspection, "Seth, my boy, you better wrap your mind around this good and tight. You're here, amongst good company, but your only real friend is your gun."

Seth looked to his fellow Jews, the Dreyfus brothers, Rosenbaum, and Stern, for guidance. They all unabashedly nodded in agreement.

Brett continued, "Where in the hell did you think you were going?"

"I've got family in Chicago. We had to get out of Brooklyn. The Mob is looting and burning synagogues and shops. They've begun kidnapping Jews. Whole families have just gone missing."

Charlie holstered his pistol and gave Cohen another dose of bitter reality, "Unarmed, you'll never make it to Chicago. Even if you make it, Chicago ain't no better. The Loop is a war zone."

As Marian entered the living room, she caught the tail end of Charlie's warning. She issued a warning of her own.

"Tel Aviv advises that something big is coming down."

April Fool's Day

Wolfgang & Americus' Senate staffs could not understand why two ultra-rich senators were sleeping in their offices. Many congressmen, and a few less prosperous senators, sometimes lived out of their offices due to tight finances. A few more had recently adopted the practice due to the rampant violence and chaos unfolding in the District's streets. The Schneiders could afford the best accommodations D.C. had to offer. They had their own private security plus the Rainbow Corps at their disposal. Why were they holed up in their offices?

The new, improved, woke FBI issued several advisories downplaying the organized civil disobedience sweeping the nation. Like most of Washington, the Bureau's upper echelon had been infiltrated by The Collective. The Bureau issued statements discounting The Collective as simply concerned citizens voicing their displeasure with America's capitalistic, racist, sexist, and homophobic culture. The Bureau's rank & file was ordered to concentrate on right-wing domestic terrorist groups, such as Christian groups holding prayer vigils outside abortion clinics and parent groups protesting leftist school board policies. Those reactionary hayseeds were the real domestic threats.

Everyone inside the Beltway expected this turmoil would run its course and things would quickly return to normal, just like the Vietnam War protests in the '60s & '70s and the Black Lives Matter demonstrations in '20 & '21.

Throughout early 2026, Wolfgang was busy consolidating political power in Washington. He read the FBI advisories. He figured those reports were probably right but was not willing to stake the success of Americus' mission on questionable FBI assessments. At Wolfgang's direction, Gruppe Paladin agents staked out critical government sites throughout the District.

At 0200 EST on Sunday, 9 March 2026, the Paladin agent surveilling the National Archives nodded off to sleep. Minutes later, he was rudely awakened by slamming car doors. Several black SUVs blocked Constitution Avenue, cordoning off the National Archives. Secret Service agents, armed with Heckler & Koch MP5 submachineguns, took up positions behind the SUVs. Moments later, a Marine Super Huey helicopter landed smackdab in the middle of Constitution Avenue.

From his concealed location in the National Gallery Sculpture Garden, across Constitution Avenue from the Archives, the Gruppe Paladin operative had an unobstructed view. In the dead of night, Secret Service agents hurriedly removed three wooden crates from the Archives and loaded them onboard the Super Huey. The Nazi thug rubbed his eyes in disbelief. He couldn't be 100% certain, as the Huey's Marine pilot wore a loose fitting flight suit and helmet. But, as best he could tell, the Huey's pilot appeared to be a woman.

This intelligence was immediately forwarded to Wolfgang. Schneider surmised that, under the cover of darkness, something of great value had been removed from the Archives and transported to a more secure location. The senior citizen Nazi time traveler was puzzled. What location could be more secure than the National Archives? Why should a great treasure be spirited away at this time? Schneider could only come to one conclusion. The situation was more serious than the FBI realized or dared to admit.

As Washington's renowned cherry blossoms neared their peak, millions of Members descended upon the Nation's capital. They came by motorcar, bicycle, bus, plane, and Amtrak. Their number included radical environmentalists, social justice warriors, anarchists, communists, LGBTQ activists, and undocumented aliens, all funded by far-left billionaires and hostile foreign powers.

Many participants in the madness couldn't care less about politics, saving the earth, or social justice. They came to rape, murder, and loot. Several decades of corrupt liberal big city mayors and complicit city councils had transformed America's great cities into incubators of lawlessness. They had defunded and demonized the police. The justice system had become a revolving door, releasing criminals without bail and without consequences for their actions. While sanctuary cities welcomed the cartels, their fentanyl laced drugs killed untold thousands of young Americans.

After a tumultuous month of March, Wednesday, April 1, 2026, started out on a quiet note, but that quickly changed. By mid-morning, The Collective began gathering on the National Mall. The 5 million Member strong mob relieved themselves in the Reflecting Pool as they surged toward the Lincoln Memorial. Along the way, they thoroughly trashed the World War II Memorial, as well as the Korean War Veterans Memorial.

The Colorado Yule Marble exterior of the Parthenon inspired Lincoln Memorial was gleefully defaced with human excrement, spray paint, and sledgehammers. The mob's primary target was the magnificent statue of America's 16th President, seated inside the Memorial's central chamber. The social justice warriors laughed as they beheaded the statue of the man who freed America from the curse of slavery. As Honest Abe's head crashed to the floor, the enlightened Members began chiseling away at his Gettysburg Address inscribed upon the wall. The vast majority of those pseudo-intellectual hooligans had never read that short, but profound, message. They knew nothing of the homely lawyer, from the Illinois frontier, who preserved the Union and freed the slaves.

After cancelling Abraham Lincoln, the rabble made an about face and drifted eastward along the National Mall, toward the Washington Monument.

The most rabid Members in the crowd seethed with anger as they approached the 554-foot-tall marble, granite, and bluestone obelisk. They loathed the massive monument dedicated to the slave owning monster who founded the most despicable country on earth. As the mob reached Washington's Monument, half their number hung a left turn, targeting the White House. The other half continued on eastward, toward the Capitol Building.

Wolfgang switched on the television in his office, as Americus monitored the internet.

"Father, many of the social media sites are crashing."

Wolfgang pointed at the television, "Look at the size of that crowd. The Mall is packed with Bolsheviks and untermenschen. It looks like they're headed our way!" Wolfgang knew that both he and Americus were high value targets.

The chaos was not limited to D.C. Wolfgang scrolled through the news channels. Throughout the nation, transportation came to a standstill. Highways were snarled. Rail travel was sabotaged. Terrorist threats shut down all air travel.

The White House bound mob surged through the German American Friendship Garden as they entered The Ellipse, trampling a small bed of edelweiss beneath their feet. A network news camera zoomed in as the white, alpine blossoms were ground into the dust. A woke network reporterette explained to the nation how America must be torn down before it could be rebuilt.

Enough was enough, an enraged Wolfgang switched off the television, "Eric, text Heinz."

Americus texted Heinz, "Blut und Ehre".

Heinz texted back, "Jawohl, auf wiedersehen!"

Father & son Schneider each carried a large briefcase as they boarded the underground tram linking the Russell Senate Office Building with the Capitol Building.

"Senator Schneider, didn't you receive the advisory?"

Wolfgang smiled as he replied, "Yes Ian, we received the warning. Thank you for your concern."

The big Mick Capitol Policeman was dedicated, "Senator, Sir, there's a huge mob headed toward the Capitol."

The tram station was deserted. No one wanted to be anywhere near the Capitol Building.

Wolfgang reached out and shook the fair skinned Irishman's hand, "Ian, you are a good American. We must tend to some important business at the Capitol. May I offer you some advice?"

A confused Ian cocked his head and nodded.

"Change out of your uniform, go home, and get your family out of Washington."

An incredulous Ian replied, "Why Wolfgang? Why must I leave?"

Schneider held up both his hands, "See my hands? They're White. Your hands are White. To make matters worse, you are a policeman. Leave town Ian. Leave town and don't come back. Take along your sidearm."

Wolfgang grabbed the Irishman by the shoulders, gave him an affirmative nod, then motioned for him to split.

The D.C. Mayor placed an emergency conference call to the failed leftist President, requesting that she call out the National Guard. The woke duo were in way over their heads. They talked and talked, then talked some more. While the liberal brain trust dithered, The Collective continued their march on the White House and Capitol Hill. The President's National Security Advisory was a closet Member. After the President agreed to call out the Guard, her National Security Advisor suggested that she place the "politically reliable"

Major Gilbert Robinson in charge of the D.C. National Guard contingent. The Collective now controlled the Guard.

While Wolfgang & Americus were riding the tram to the Capitol, the mob surrounded the White House. By the time the Schneiders arrived at the Capitol Building, they found it deserted, except for a few Secret Service. The Capitol Police had long fled. The vanguard of the mob began breaking into the Capitol. At his underground post, Uniformed Secret Service Agent, Manny Perez, was unaware of the magnitude of the shitstorm unfolding around Capitol Hill.

"Senator Schneider, what are you doing here?"

"Manny, we're taking the tunnel to the White House."

Manny replied, "That's not such a good idea. The White House is under siege."

Americus clarified the situation, "Manny, there's millions of loons out on the Mall lynching anyone in uniform. You must get your ass out of here."

Wolfgang heard shots outside and smelled smoke, "Nein! It's too late for you to escape. Come with us, if you want to live!"

Self-preservation is a powerful motivator; Manny opened the tunnel door as Wolfgang requested. The trio disappeared down the tunnel. In his mind, Wolfgang replayed his desperate escape from the Führerbunker. He led the way, followed by Americus, with Manny bringing up the rear. Their pace gradually increased to a jog as they traversed the mile and a half secret tunnel to the White House.

"Senator, why are we headed to the Castle? It's surrounded, just like the Punch Bowl."

Eric was new to Washington, "Agent Manny, what in the hell are you talking about?"

Wolfgang answered, "Castle is Secret Service speak for the White House and Punch Bowl is their codename for the Capitol."

The three men spoke not another word as they jogged toward the Castle. As the tunnel neared the White House, it passed under 15th Street NW and continued on beneath Alexander Hamilton's statue, now being smashed to bits by the mob.

Wolfgang momentarily paused to speak, "Manny, are you familiar with the White House H Street Entrance?"

"Yes. I've only been assigned to that post a couple of times and only on a temporary basis, but I know the layout."

"Once we enter the East Wing basement, you will lead the way with your sidearm drawn."

Agent Manny slowly cracked opened the steel fire door leading to the East Wing Basement. The deafening sound of gunfire and shouting, upstairs in the executive mansion, reverberated down into the basement. The third generation Mexican American Secret Service agent scanned the seldom visited basement, searching for threats.

Manny proclaimed, "We're all clear!" then ran across the basement and unlocked another steel fire door.

Wolfgang shouted to be heard over the clamor, "Open it! Sofort!"

Manny opened the door to the H Street White House Entrance just as the power went out. He pointed his flashlight down the dark tunnel.

"We're clear."

Once inside the tunnel, Wolfgang & Eric shed their business suits and donned the coveralls and work boots they had stuffed inside their briefcases.

Wolfgang handed Americus' white shirt and suit trousers to Manny, "Lose the uniform and put these on, just the shirt, no jacket or necktie.

"Roll up your sleeves.

"Now, muss your hair!

"Zehr gut, Manny."

Manny peered out onto H Street, "Senator Schneider, I only see a few looters, no lynch mob!"

As the trio emerged onto H Street, Wolfgang continued barking out orders, "Head due east toward the Hilton Garden Inn. Shoot anyone who gets in our way!"

Manny led the way eastward along H Street. A spaced-out homeless man approached them, brandishing a baseball bat. Without hesitation, Manny fired his SIG Sauer P229 twice, at point blank range. The two .357 rounds hit home, instantly neutralizing the drug numbed assailant.

The two-block sprint to the Hilton Garden Inn took less than a minute. The Hilton's entire staff, including private security, had deserted their posts.

Wolfgang had rehearsed this escape ad nauseum, "Forget the elevator! We'll take those stairs down to the Valet level."

"Manny, waste those CCTV cameras!"

Manny blasted every parking garage security camera along their route.

When they reached the Valet level, Wolfgang pointed out their getaway vehicle, "There it is! That white panel van in the far corner."

"Manny, you cover me while I unlock the van."

Manny followed Wolfgang's direction, turning his back to the van.

Wolfgang opened the van's rear doors. He unscrewed the bottom on a fake can of Fix-a-Flat. A double handful of gold & silver coins poured out the bottom of the steel can.

Meanwhile, Americus opened a toolbox and removed a suppressed Luger.

Wolfgang casually strolled up behind Manny and patted him on the shoulder, "Zehr gut. Manny! So far, so good. You've done your country a great service. It's too bad there will be no place for untermenschen like you in our new America."

Before Manny could even begin to grasp Schneider's ill intent, Wolfgang gave his stepson the nod.

Americus' face showed no remorse as he double tapped the unsuspecting Hispanic agent from behind.

Three hours later, a white panel van arrived at the Adler Engineering Yard in Newport News, Virginia.

Fog of War

Badass Bitch slowly rotated, allowing Dead Eye to shoot up everything in proximity, giant dish antennae, huge electrical transformers, nondescript outbuildings, and vehicles. You name it, Dead Eye shot it.

Suddenly, the Bitch lurched to the right.

"Heads up kid! We've been hit!"

25 mm tracer rounds were streaking past the Cobra's cockpit. The Bitch was about to have a bad hair day.

That first round merely took out the Bitch's landing skis. Shrapnel from a subsequent round took out the Cobra's turbine.

Josephine autorotated the powerless Bitch to the ground. Minus her landing gear, the Bitch hit the desert floor with a metal crunching thump, then rolled over on her port side. The still spinning rotor blades disintegrated as they impacted the desert hardpan.

Joe pulled her trusty 1911 Colt as she threw open her canopy, "We gotta get out! I smell smoke!"

Adam was way ahead of her. He had already raised the plexiglass canopy and bailed, with MAC-10 machine pistol in hand.

The dedicated Falcon Commando, manning the 25 mm dual canon, smiled with satisfaction. He had taken out the Yankee gunship. Now, he would eliminate the crew. He poured a short burst of HE rounds into the downed chopper.

Both Dead Eye & Josephine were slammed face first, down on the ground, as Badass Bitch exploded.

As he began to stand, Josephine grabbed Adam by the pantleg and pulled him back down, "Stay down kid. All the Bitch's ordnance will soon cook off and there's a 20 mike-mike out there somewhere."

KABOOM! KABOOM!

"See what I mean. There goes the Bitch's grenades."

From the cab of the railcar mover, John saw Badass Bitch go down. With the Cobra out of action, the third SAM launcher became inconsequential. John turned the mover around and headed back to the crash site, intent upon helping his comrades.

"You got eyes on that gun?"

Dead Eye replied, "Yeah! I see his muzzle flashes real good! He's about a 500 yards to our northwest. He's got twin barrels."

"I reckon your MAC-10 doesn't have the reach."

"Not even close, neither does your pistol, they fire the same ammo. If I had my Barrett 50 sniper rifle, I'd plink him right between the eyes."

Another cluster of 25 mm HE rounds exploded all around the two downed Marine aviators. A small fragment bit Josephine in her right calf.

Jo & Dead Eye were in a world of hurt. Neither Marine was wearing body armor. Eventually, those fragmenting 25 mm rounds would hit something more vital than Jo's leg.

"Miss Jo, get ready. I'm gonna jump up and fire a short burst. I'm betting that Chinese dude out there will instinctively duck. After I fire, we'll both run like hell to that closest dish. Its undercarriage looks to be substantial."

Jo shot Adam a thumbs up!

RAT-A-TAT-TAT-TAT!

Adam fired a short burst, then they both ran like hell.

Twenty yards and 3 seconds later, the duo ducked behind the undercarriage of the nearest dish antennae.

A split second later, 25 mm HE rounds peppered the undercarriage.

Jo turned to her co-pilot, "Kid, I'm sorry I got you into this mess."

Adam gave Jo a hug, "Don't you worry Miss Jo. We'll get out of this. Remember the omen? Sempre Fi!"

From his seat in the cab of the railcar mover, Sergeant Nicolescu saw movement around the base of the dish antennae. John also saw the nearby, burning wreckage of Badass Bitch. Once John slipped on his CZ helmet, he saw large caliber high explosive rounds impacting all around that antenna's undercarriage.

"Dead Eye & Josephine are hunkered down behind that dish!"

Vet parked the railcar mover directly behind the dish.

Although it hurt like hell, John managed to shout in a raspy voice, "You two Jarheads need a lift?"

As she climbed into the cab of the railcar mover, Jo replied, "Nice ride Vet, where's the Big Man?"

Nicolescu solemnly replied, "He's gone Elvis."

Dead Eye wasn't that familiar with military slang. When he cocked his head in confusion and stared at Jo, she sadly shook her head.

An enraged Adam snarled, "Let's go get that gun!"

Jo thirsted for revenge, but the 25 mm wasn't a mission priority. She turned to Sergeant Nicolescu for guidance.

John concurred, "The kid is right. That 20 mm could shred Captain Smith's rare earth convoy. Seeing that the Bitch is toast, it's up to us to take out that gun."

Almost Heaven

The surprise arrival of the Cohen family spurred Brett & Marian to action. With the wholehearted cooperation of the entire Hoffman gang, they began organizing a modern day underground railway. The route led from New York City, through the New Jersey metroplex, southward to Philly, then made a beeline westward to Kecksburg. The refugees were screened at Stan's place prior to being routed to the freedom and safety of West Virginia's rugged mountain wilderness. Throughout the Mountaineer State, hundreds of evangelical churches banded together to shelter the Jewish refugees. Those churches were protected by men with guns, the very guns the woke politicians had sought to confiscate.

The events of April 1. 2026 forced the premature activation of the railway, as pogroms spontaneously erupted throughout the East Coast metropolitan areas. With the collaboration of the corrupt, woke, tech giants, all communications were shut down in order to prevent the spread of "disinformation". Luckily, a week earlier, at Brett's insistence, the Hoffman family had boarded up their shop in Deutschtown and bugged out to their vacation home near Bradford, deep in the northern Pennsylvania wilderness.

A steady stream of refugees now made its way to Stan's farm. Marian was in charge of security, carefully screening each new arrival, ensuring they weren't Collective informants. Stan cleaned out his large metal pole barn. The weather was warming, and the weather tight barn kept out the cold spring winds and rains. An old barrel stove provided just enough heat to keep the crowded barn comfortable.

Every few days, Charlie would lead a small caravan of vehicles southward along the southwestern Pennsylvania backroads, through Maryland's narrow panhandle, and across the Potomac River at Paw Paw, West Virginia. Stern, Stan the Man, and the Dreyfus brothers typically rode shotgun. Once safely in Paw Paw, the refugees were placed under the protection of various West Virginia Christian congregations.

With the disruption of most forms of telecommunication, Hoffman found it impossible to continue his *Sea-to-Sea AM* broadcasts. Brett now felt like a 5th wheel, totally without purpose. Stan the Man had no such problem. In addition to his stargazing, Stan was a gardener and orchardist extraordinaire. Like many rural Pennsylvanians, Stan was an avid hunter and fisherman. Stan was also an amateur radio enthusiast.

On the night of April 8, 2026, Stan was scanning through the shortwave band when he caught the inaugural *Voice of America* broadcast. Around midnight, Stan was pounding on Brett & Marian's bedroom door. Good thing they were decent.

Brett staggered as he opened the door, still half asleep, "Stan, what in the hell is wrong?"

"Hoffman, you've got to come downstairs and listen to this!"

Hoffman threw on his robe and followed Stan downstairs to the parlor.

Brett couldn't believe his ears, "Stan, there's a Resistance forming."

Stan gave Brett a high five, "You bet your sweet ass there's a Resistance!"

Fight to the Finish

John turned the railcar mover to the northwest and took it off road, heading directly for the Chinese 25 mm gun. The advancing mover drew no immediate response. After the big yellow diesel advanced about 100 yards, two warning shots whistled overhead.

John handed Dead Eye the grenade launcher, "You two hop out and follow behind this beast. Whatever remains of this suit should afford me some protection."

Nicolescu was right. Immediately after the Marines bailed, the mover was hit by no fewer than four 25 mm HE rounds. The large yellow beast lurched to an abrupt stop and burst into flames. The cab was instantly transformed into blazing inferno, but John's suit was still relatively impervious to fire. Before he was roasted alive, the Romanian Ranger leapt from the cab and joined his two friends huddled behind the burning mover.

"Dead Eye, what's the range to target?"

"Mister John, I make it to be about 375 yards, more or less."

John elevated his grenade launcher and fired a round.

Dead Eye called out, "Long and to the right."

John's shot was answered by another burst of 25 mm fire.

Nicolescu adjusted his launcher's elevation and fired again.

Dead Eye hesitated, "That looked like a hit."

Another burst of 25 mm shells proved Adam wrong.

"Mr. John, fire again, no adjustment."

Vet launched another grenade. This time, there was no doubt. The grenade hit several crates containing 25 mm canon rounds, initiating a chain reaction of secondary explosions.

The 25 mm canon, along with one diligent Falcon Commando, may have been destroyed, but the helo crash and subsequent exchange of heavy weapons fire attracted a crowd. Hostiles were converging on the vertex from every direction, except the north.

"Josephine, I realize we haven't completed our mission. We haven't snatched a scientist. But it's time to get while the getting's good." With his super senses, Nicolescu was already leading the way over to the northern arm of the Array.

Jo didn't put up a fuss, "It's time to go to the house."

The three fugitives scurried from dish to dish as they made their way along the northern arm of the Array. Several vehicles were in hot pursuit. Every so often, John would pause and launch a grenade at his pursuers. He didn't score any hits, but, with every shot, he slowed their pursuit.

As the trio approached Highway 60, near the terminus of the Array's northern arm, John fired his last grenade.

"We're gonna have to make our stand right here. This highway doesn't have much of a ditch, but it will have to do. I'll draw their fire. Their fire can't penetrate my CZ helmet. My CZ suit is no longer completely bulletproof, but it will give me some protection.

"I can see in the dark, so I'll call the shots.

"Josephine, hold your fire until they get close. That Colt just ain't accurate at long range.

"Dead Eye, if you see 'em, spray 'em with your MAC-10. Remember, that ain't no sniper rifle."

John once again made the Orthodox Sign of the Cross, "Here they come."

The approaching vehicles shook the ground beneath the three amigos, now lying prone in an icy ditch. Then, the dark desert night was illuminated by the muzzle flashes from over a thousand guns.

Captain Cloud's North Force had broken through Chinese & Collective forces in Magdalena and arrived at the Array en masse. Cowboy Tom & Lame Wolf were in the lead vehicle.

Scratching the Eight Ball

Wolfgang & Americus hurriedly removed the shipping foam covering the Glocke.

"Eric, concentrate on uncovering the runes encircling the device."

Once the runes were clear of foam, Wolfgang touched the prescribed sequence, opening the Glocke's hatchway.

"Eric, commence energization, just as we practiced on the simulator!"

Over the next half hour, the Glocke's liquid rare earth dynamo began extracting zero point energy from the surrounding environment. As Wolfgang stood watch, with his Luger in hand, the Glocke began whining and glowing. As the device neared the jump threshold, plasma began dancing along the warehouse's structural steel framework.

"Father, the device is fully energized!"

Wolfgang manned the Glocke's controls while Americus stood immediately behind him.

A momentary flash of light filled the Adler Newport News warehouse as the Glocke disappeared. The scant traffic on nearby I-64 came to an abrupt stop.

Americus clutched a couple of jury-rigged leather straps as the Glocke was buffeted about during reentry, "Father, have we successfully jumped?"

At 20,000 feet, Wolfgang engaged the antigravity drive, then responded, "Yes Eric, but I can't understand what has happened."

"Father, is there a problem?"

"We have successfully jumped, but the chronometer indicates the date is sometime in January 2042, not 2045 as planned. I cannot explain this temporal discrepancy."

The Glocke landed with a soft thud, briefly knocking Americus off his feet.

Wolfgang was perplexed, "Heinz should have energized the Größe Glocke in 2045 and we should now be back home in Montana. We seem to have arrived three years ahead of schedule. A half hour from now, once we open the hatch, we'll find out exactly where we have landed."

Newfound Purpose

On April Fool's Day 2026, while Wolfgang & Americus made their escape, both the President & Vice President were lynched by the very mob they helped empower. That Wednesday morning, the Speaker of the House, a Marine veteran, was not in Washington. He was at his home, in a gated suburb of Oklahoma City. He was preparing to visit a local hospital. His wife had scheduled an elective surgery for later that afternoon. Speaker Matthew Grimes was a conservative, a member of the opposition party, now holding the slimmest of majorities in the House. During the growing crisis, he had not been briefed, nor consulted, by either the President or D.C. Mayor. To make matters worse, Speaker Matt had been locked out of his social media accounts, as had all other members of his Conference, ostensibly to prevent the spread of "disinformation". He was reduced to getting his information from TV news, text messages, and email.

Shortly before noon Central Standard Time, two black sedans pulled into Matt's driveway. The Speaker had no idea exactly what had gone down in Washington. Matt answered his doorbell, clutching a loaded Colt Python in his right hand. The Speaker, although second in line to the Presidency, receives no Secret Service protection. To his surprise, a Federal District Judge, an Air Force Colonel, and two Secret Service Agents were standing on his front porch. Moments later, in his living room, President Grimes placed his hand upon his family's Bible while the Judge administered the oath of office. Matt was then spirited away to nearby Tinker Air Force Base.

An hour later, Air Force One landed at Tinker and was immediately refueled. The new President & First Lady scrambled up "Angel's" airstairs. An Air Force officer followed closely behind, carrying a modified Zero Halliburton aluminum briefcase, popularly known as the "nuclear football". Matthew was now Commander in Chief. Although many of his fellow countrymen were now in open revolt against the Constitution, Matt was responsible for defending all Americans against all threats, foreign and domestic. As Matthew fastened his seatbelt and Air Force One began its take off roll, the new President felt a great weight descend upon his shoulders, a burden not borne by any President since 1861.

Air Force One was initially escorted by two F-22 Raptors as she took the "great circle" route from Tinker AFB to Tokyo. Upon takeoff, the customized Boeing 747 made a beeline from Tinker to Colorado Springs. Angel then followed the Rockies northwestward into British Columbia. Over the Gulf of Alaska, Angel's F-22 escort was replaced by two F-35Cs operating off the recently reactivated USS Enterprise. South of Anchorage, Alaska, Air Force One slowly turned to the southwest, and followed the Aleutian Island chain. The F-35s were aerial refueled near Attu Island, at the far western end of the Aleutian archipelago.

Russian air defense radars on the Kamchatka Peninsula painted Air Force One, but they could not detect Angel's F-35 escort. Just to be safe, the 747 remained 200 miles off the Russian coastline as she continued on course to Tokyo.

At the end of World War II, Soviet forces occupied Sakhalin and the Kuril Islands. Those islands, to the south of Kamchatka, were historically claimed by the Japanese. For the subsequent 80 years, Russian military forces on Sakhalin and the Kurils threatened Japan's northernmost home island of Hokkaido. The Russians and Japanese never resolved the disputed status of those islands. Air Force One was flying through a potential flash point for a 21st Century Russo-Japanese War.

66 year old Emperor Naruhito ascended to Japan's Chrysanthemum Throne on 1 May 2019. Post-World War II, the Japanese Emperor became a figurehead, with no real political power. That's how the Emperor was written into the postwar Japanese constitution, but some of life's most important things go unwritten.

Most Western minds could not fathom the significance of the Emperor in Japanese culture. Prior to Japan's surrender in 1945, the Japanese people considered their Emperor a living god. 15 August 1945 was the first time the Japanese people ever heard their Emperor speak. In his "Jewel Voice" radio broadcast, Emperor Hirohito announced the Japanese surrender. Hirohito told his people they must "endure the unendurable and suffer what is not sufferable".

Naruhito had been on the throne a mere 6 years when China and North Korea thrust pacifist Japan smackdab into the middle of the Great Pacific War. Much as the crucible of combat on the Eastern Front forged young Leutnant Schneider, the aftermath of the Great Pacific War forged the elderly Emperor Naruhito.

As the Great Pacific War concluded, the Japanese Diet and Prime Minister followed America's policy of appeasing the Red Chinese and North Koreans. The Emperor remained silent as the Diet conducted disastrous, one-sided peace negotiations that threatened the Japanese people. Japan now faced hostile Red China and a unified, communist Korea to her west. To Japan's north, a belligerent, militaristic Russia continued increasing its forces on Sakhalin and the Kurils. To the south, Taiwan had been subjugated by the Chinese. Taiwan was a major Japanese trading partner and sat astride critical Japanese trade routes. The outrageous peace agreement required that Japan demilitarize its southern island province of Okinawa. Since the end of World

War II, Okinawa had been home to American naval and air forces key to Japan's defense.

Japan was one of the most technologically advanced countries on the planet, fully capable of producing nuclear weapons. The trauma inflicted upon the Japanese psyche by America's nuclear strikes on Hiroshima and Nagasaki was profound and lasting. As a result, Japan eschewed nuclear weapons development. For 80 years, Japan flourished beneath the safety of America's nuclear umbrella.

On 2 April 2026, Emperor Naruhito was awakened at 3 a.m. Japan Standard Time to take an urgent phone call. Breaking all protocols, the new President of the United States was calling from Air Force One. Due to his extensive experience abroad, the Oxford educated Emperor spoke fluent English. He spoke privately with President Grimes for over a half hour.

The Prime Minister and key members of the Diet had been awakened two hours earlier with the disturbing news out of Washington. This new American radical group, The Collective, was pro-Chinese. If America's nuclear arsenal fell into The Collective's hands, Japan would be defenseless, vulnerable to Chinese or Russian nuclear blackmail. The Japanese politicians, like their American counterparts, dithered and debated. If this so-called Collective now controlled America, the Prime Minister hoped to maintain good relations. When the new American President called the Japanese Prime Minister requesting an emergency meeting in Tokyo, the Prime Minister declined the President's request. The PM also withheld permission for Air Force One to land in Japan. The Prime Minister would not risk angering The Collective.

President Grimes did not know the Emperor personally, but he knew Emperor Naruhito to be a man of peace. If The Collective gained full control of America, there would be no peace for Japan.

After receiving the President's early morning phone call, Naruhito worked feverishly through the night. As Emperor, he was responsible for the lives of the Japanese people, moreover he was responsible for the life of Japan. He did not know this new exiled American President, but quickly determined Grime's geopolitical analysis was correct. The Emperor could be silent no longer. By 8 a.m. that morning, the entire Japanese government was notified that the Emperor would be making a joint address to both chambers of the National Diet at 5 p.m. local time.

A political tsunami swept Japan. In modern Japan, the Emperor opens each session of the Diet by reading a prepared speech, but that's a mere formality. This spur of the moment address was unprecedented. All day long, the Japanese media hyped the Emperor's upcoming speech as "Naruhito's Jewel Voice".

Naruhito's father, Emperor Akihito, was a pacifist. He repeatedly expressed regret for Japan's many 20th Century atrocities. Akihito worked tirelessly to improve relations with Japan's Asian neighbors. The pundits speculated that Naruhito would follow in his father's pacifist footsteps. Emperor Naruhito's continued silence during, and after, the Great Pacific War reinforced those speculations.

At 3 p.m. Tokyo time, a squad of armed, plainclothes, security police, members of Naruhito's Imperial Guard, entered the control tower at Tokyo's Narita International Airport. In typical Japanese fashion, an expressionless Captain Obi politely bowed and presented the chief air traffic controller a letter. The letter bore the Imperial Seal, a stylized wax chrysanthemum. The controller's face lost all color as he read the Imperial decree. Then, the controller deeply bowed and began barking out orders, in the service of his Imperial Majesty.

Narita Airport flight operations immediately shut down. Departing flights were held. Arriving flights were diverted to Haneda Airport. A black Toyota

Century Royal armored limousine appeared on the tarmac surrounded by a squad of uniformed Imperial Guards. The Guard's unmistakable dark blue uniforms with white gloves & helmets immediately garnered deep bows of respect and total obedience from the attendant ground crew.

The arrival of a Boeing 747 was not an unusual event at Narita, but this arrival was different. The blue & white four engined jumbo jet bore an American flag on its massive tail fin. As Angel touched down, her two escorting F-35s hit their afterburners and streaked back out to sea with a deafening roar.

Air Force One taxied up to Narita's Terminal 1 but did not park at a gate. Angel parked some distance away from the other aircraft and deployed both her front and rear airstairs. The Toyota limousine pulled up next to the front airstairs, along with several unmarked, black, Toyota Crown sedans. Most of the 747's seats were empty. The White House Press Pool missed this historic flight. They were too busy, back in DC, singing their praises of The Collective. President Grimes, the First Lady, and the Air Force officer, carrying the football, rapidly descended the front airstairs and ducked into the limousine. A small contingent of Oklahoma City based FBI and Secret Service agents piled into the accompanying sedans. Minutes later, without fanfare, the motorcade departed Narita, speeding southwestward toward Tokyo's Imperial Palace.

5 p.m. came, then went. The National Diet Building's Chamber of the House of Councillors was filled to overflowing. All 460 seats were taken. The seats in Public Gallery, normally reserved for members of the press and invited dignitaries, were also taken. It was standing room only in the aisles. The Emperor's throne, behind the dais, was empty. Anticipation filled the chamber as the minutes passed. No one knew what to expect. Japan is deeply rooted in its traditions. This event broke with all tradition.

At 5:29 the silence was broken as *Kimi Ga Yo*, one of the world's shortest national anthems, filled the Chamber. Immediately following the Japanese anthem, *The Star Spangled Banner* echoed throughout the massive hall. The Emperor entered the Chamber with the new American President at his side. From that moment on, Japan would no longer be the same. Japan's Emperor would no longer be the same. He would not be a living god, but neither would he be a mere figurehead.

The Bunker

The massive Bunker, beneath the Greenbriar Resort in southern West Virginia, was the perfect location for the American Resistance forward headquarters. Built during the Cold War to house the federal government in the event of a nuclear war, the subterranean fortress was self-contained and secure. The Bunker's communications center included radio and television studios. Most of the broadcast equipment predated the digital age, but the shortwave equipment was functional.

The Voice of America shortwave radio service was founded in the dark early days of World War II. Along with the BBC, VoA broadcast news to the brutalized millions in Nazi occupied Europe. VoA gave those millions hope and served an important intelligence function. After the Allied victory, the VoA broadcasts brought hope to enslaved millions behind Stalin's Iron Curtain. As the Cold War dragged on, VoA brought its message of hope to masses trapped behind Chairman Mao's "Bamboo Curtain" and others marooned upon Castro's imprisoned island. Critics claimed that the VoA was merely a state owned propaganda arm of the US Government. One man's truth is another man's propaganda.

VoA, as established, presented nonpartisan programming. Beginning in the 1960s, as America's universities began churning out indoctrinated communications majors, VoA began drifting to the left along with the rest of America's media.

A week after the April 1 Peoples' Revolution, a purged and refocused VoA relocated its broadcast studios to The Bunker. The reinvented VoA's target audience was the American people. Many of those people were new immigrants who knew nothing of America aside from Big Macs and the NBA. Most of America's youth had been taught a twisted, leftist, version of American history. They needed to hear the real story. Other Americans knew the real story. They needed hope. They needed to know they were not alone.

Those first VoA broadcasts from The Bunker delivered the news but were very dry and not very entertaining. The Resistance needed to capture the hearts and minds of the masses. The Resistance put out an all-points bulletin for disc jockeys, standup comedians, and newscasters.

On the evening of 15 April 2026, Marian was monitoring the VoA broadcast from the comfort of Stan's parlor. That's when she heard the appeal for radio personalities to join VoA.

Marian woke Brett, snoozing on the couch, "Hoffman, get a load of this!"

Brett listened intently to the announcement, then grabbed a road atlas from Charlie's Winnebago.

"Marian, it's about 250 miles from here down to White Sulphur Springs. Let's take a little road trip."

Sea to Shining Sea

While the Black Patriot's broadcasts adhered to no set schedule, you could set your watch by Brett Hoffman's *Sea to Shining Sea* broadcasts. Monday thru Friday, millions gathered around their shortwaves at 1 a.m. Eastern as Brett's spooky bumper music filled the airwaves.

Many of Brett's Carnegie Mellon groupies escaped The Collective's clutches. Professor Hiroshi Yasuda's ancestry was 100% Japanese. Hiroshi made his way down to Kecksburg shortly after the Peoples' Revolution. Hiroshi now resided in White Sulphur Springs and worked for the Resistance. In his spare time, Hiroshi sporadically appeared on Brett's broadcasts.

While many of Brett's broadcasts dealt with politics and the ongoing struggle against The Collective, Hoffman was a clever programmer. He mixed shows about Collective death camps and Chinese super weapons with shows documenting alien encounters and tales of the supernatural. Call Screener Teddy managed to escape the Pittsburgh Collective and found his way down to The Bunker, where he served as Brett's right hand man.

Marian joined Brett down in White Sulphur Springs and became a very effective Resistance liaison with the growing Jewish refugee population in the Mountaineer State. After the destruction of the Jewish State in 2030, Marian was instrumental in the formation of Gideon's 300, a small army of Mossad and IDF refugees bivouacked in Virginia's Blue Ridge Mountains.

Stan the Man, Blue Dog, Charlie, Stern, Rosenbaum, the Dreyfus brothers, and Norma continued their humanitarian work, spiriting enemies of The

Collective out of the Northeastern cities. In 2030, coincidently with the destruction of Israel, a Red Chinese genocide specialist, Double X, began rounding up the remaining Jews across the Peoples' United States. The Hoffman gang managed to escape Kecksburg by the hair of their chinny chin chins, mere minutes before Double X led a platoon of Peoples' Militia in an assault on Stan's farm. The gang relocated their humanitarian operations to Paw Paw and Marian sent them a platoon of Gideon's 300 for added security.

Over the next dozen years, one by one, the Hoffman gang passed on, all from natural causes. Neither Stan, nor Charlie ever brought up the Kecksburg incident, nor their suspicions regarding the Schneiders. They had pressing, real world, life & death problems to solve. By January 2042, Isaac Stern was the sole survivor of the original gang and carried on their work with bravado.

One cold, mid-January 2042 day, the day after the destruction of the Very Large Array, Brett was doing show prep, just as he had done for the last 15 years. His friend, Hiroshi Yasuda, had recently returned from classified Resistance business in New Mexico. Brett invited his physicist friend to join him in studio.

"Hiroshi, how about joining me tonight on *Sea to Shining Sea?*"

"That sounds great. What will we be discussing?"

Brett scratched his head in thought, "The older I get, the harder it gets to come up with good programming ideas.

"Hiroshi, what were you up to way out there in New Mexico?"

Hiroshi wagged his finger in his friend's face, "Brett, you know I can't discuss classified information."

Brett smiled a sheepish smile. An uneasy silence filled the studio.

Out of nowhere, a memory fleeted through Hiroshi's fertile mind, "Brett, remember that crazy night back in '25, when the guy from Idaho called your show? It was right after Halloween when he called. What was his name?"

"Hiroshi, you don't know the half of it." Brett then told Hiroshi the entire story of Jack, Stan the Man, Blue Dog, Charlie, Marian, and the Schneiders.

"Holy shit, Brett. You're telling me the Schneiders were time travelling Nazis?"

An exasperated Hoffman shook his head in disgust, "I don't know. Both Wolfgang and Americus disappeared on April Fool's Day '26. You know, they were at the top of The Collective's hit list. They both probably sleep with the fishes at the bottom of the Potomac."

Hiroshi replied, "Yeah, probably. Their Rainbow Corps duked it out with the Peoples' Militia out there in Montana, Idaho, and Wyoming. The Collective could never gain control out there. The Schneiders were certainly no friends of The Collective."

Hiroshi's comments piqued Brett's curiosity, "Who is in charge out there now? The Mormons?"

Hiroshi's work for the Resistance gave him some insight into the chaotic situation across the country, "The Collective is sure as hell not in charge. Neither are the Mormons. They guys in charge out there are resistance, but they are not part of the National Resistance. They're an outgrowth of the Schneider's American Peoples' Party. They call their territory 'The American Empire'. Sounds sorta hokey, huh?"

A stunned Hoffman replied, "Maybe it's not so hokey. 'The American Empire' translates into German as 'Das Amerikanisher Reich'.

"Hiroshi, we may have another problem on our hands, a problem of some magnitude."

Star Light, Star Bright

By noon, the following day, Captain Cloud's North Force was in firm control of what little remained of the Array. As the Chinese and their Collective flunkies retreated to the south, toward Las Cruces and El Paso, they burned all the files and destroyed all the remaining equipment at the Array.

After securing the Array, an intensive search was initiated. Drones and search teams scoured the San Augustin Plain and surrounding mountains. They found Henrietta, still tied to the utility pole, no worse for wear. They found Big Sid's depleted uranium shield amongst the car bomb debris, but the Big Man was nowhere to be found.

An hour after the arrival of the Mescalero North Force at the Array, Captain Smith's rare earth convoy barreled eastward on US 60, across the San Augustin Plain, headed toward Houston. They were running a little behind schedule due to a short stop at the Old Red Hill toll booth. Delvin used his "people skills" to charm the "Highway Commissioner". That and a troy ounce of gold bought the convoy unfettered passage across western New Mexico.

Colonel Cooper and Cowboy Tom debriefed Josephine, John, and Adam later that afternoon.

"Sergeant Nicolescu, did anything strange happen during your assault upon the Array?"

"Yes Sir. The ChiComs must have been conducting a test. Since we didn't capture any technical personnel, I don't know what they were doing. Right before I took out the HQ-7B air search radar, these crazy bluish beams of light, no not light, it was more like plasma. Crazy bluish streams of plasma shot skyward, one stream from each active dish.

"When those streams shot into the sky, my CZ suit malfunctioned."

"Please, explain how your CZ suit malfunctioned."

"The magnetorheological armor solidified. I couldn't move. To make matters worse, my adaptive camouflage also malfunctioned. The phosphors embedded in the suit glowed blue, like a neon light. Once Sid took out that dish, all the other dishes shut down. My CZ suit functioned normally thereafter. By 'thereafter', I mean until I got hit by that 25 mm armor piercing shell."

Josephine piped up, "As me and Dead Eye, I mean Private Jackson, commenced our run on the Array, we saw that bluish plasma shoot skyward. We didn't know what to make of it. Once the plasma streams shut off, we were sure everything was gonna be alright."

"Why is that Lieutenant? How could you be sure?"

"The shooting star."

Adam silently nodded in agreement.

Colonel Cooper dug a little deeper, "What shooting star?"

"When the blue beams shut off, this beautiful shooting star came in from the east. It was special."

Adam once again nodded in agreement.

Cooper was intrigued, "What was so special about that meteor?"

"It came in real shallow, the brightest shooting star I ever saw. Like I said, it was something special, a good omen. First time I ever saw a meteor slow down."

Printed in Great Britain
by Amazon

33319020R00205